THE VINE WEAVER

Sara Powter

Bible Quotes from King James Version

ISBN: 9780645441512
Paperback

Pacific Wanderland Publications
ABN 99 768 734 831

Kincumber NSW 2251

saragpowter@gmail.com
www.sarapowter.com.au

1st edition 2023 printed by Kindle, an Amazon Company;
available on Kindle Unlimited & KDP

Australian Historical Novels

A First Fleet Story (1788)

Gentle Annie Soames *(2024)*

The Hunter to Macquarie Trilogy (1795-1820)

When Upon Life's Billows *(2025)*
Saddler's Song *(2025)*
Tuppence to Pass *(2025)*

Unlikely Convict Ladies Trilogy (1792 - 1840s)

Dancing to her Own Tune
(co-authored by Sheila Hunter & Sara Powter)
Amelia's Tears
A Lady in Irons

The Lockleys of Parramatta (1800-1900)

Hands Upon the Anvil
Out Where the Brolgas Dance
Diamonds in the Dirt
The Earl's Shadow
Once a Jolly Swagman
Jonty's Journey

The Convict Stain Collection (1830s -1840s)

(All stand-alone books)
No More, My Love
The Vine Weaver
Scotch at The Rocks {*Sequel to The Vine Weaver*}
Waiting at the Sliprails
Convict Shadows of the Past
(The following are coming soon)
In Defence of Her Honour *(2024)*
I Can't Stop Tomorrow *(2024)*
Madeline's Boy *(2024)*
Jam or Marmalade for Tea *(2025)*

Shelia Hunter's
Australian Colonial Trilogy (1840s- 1850s)

Mattie
Ricky {*Jonty's Journey is a sequel*}
The Heather to the Hawkesbury

Authors note

This story is inspired by the stories told to me by my father,
who owned an orchard at Castlereagh on the Nepean section of the Hawkesbury/Nepean
River system. He used to purchase baskets from a lady who 'lived further along the river.' In
the 1920s, a destructive flood on the Hawkesbury River
washed away much of his orchard at Birdseye Corner in Castlereagh, and he lost many trees.
Thankfully there was no loss of life in that flood. It also uncovered some indigenous stone
axe heads that had been locally made.
In previous floods, many had died. As new people moved into the area, buildings encroached
on the floodplains. Disasters occurred because people would not learn from the past.
Amongst these brave pioneers are the women of the bush
who stood against adversity to continue to hack a life out of the scrub.
So many of our women were alone, rarely was it by choice in the early days; they had been
brought up in the British Isles and had not understood the rough conditions they later lived
in. Often their husbands had died, been imprisoned, or sometimes, they had all too often just
been abandoned by their men. To survive, they utilised their skills; cottage industries in the
early colony were a way of life. You made do with what you had and lived frugally by eating
what you grew. Occasionally new settlers tried to learn from the indigenous peoples in the
area. However, things didn't always go as planned. More often than not, the new settlers
didn't listen to the wisdom of the local people, like the tragedy in June 1852 when
a flood washed away the town of Gundagai.

As I write this story, the East Coast of Australia is in the middle of an unprecedented, once
in a thousand years, 'rain bomb' (2022).
The Hawkesbury River flooded three times in 2022, and the last time this occurred was in
1860 in April, July & November.
However, areas that have never flooded in known history
on the Northern Rivers were metres underwater.
I have seen the speed of a flash flood a few times and have heard horror stories of houses
swept away with people still inside.
Some of my ancestors died in the horrific Gundagai Floods of 1852.

Thanks

To Stephen, my wonderful husband, who is always so supportive.
Thank you from the bottom of my heart.

And thanks to Roby Aiken,
who patiently corrects all my punctuation errors.
To my Beta readers, Noreen Robertson and Linda Upcroft.
You are all wonderful!

Rebekah Robinson
from Beckon Creative for my new cover.
I love it.
Thank you all so much.

Table of Contents

The grammar and language in this book are
Australian English spelling

Chapter 1   A Carefree Life

Skipping along the riverbank, the little light-brown-haired girl occasionally stopped and picked dandelions, singing as she played. She had a hoop in one hand and a bunch of wilting flowers in the other. She ran up the hill to a lady reclining on the grassy embankment, thrusting the handful of bent and wilting yellow flowers towards the lady, "Mama, I wuv you." Molly abandoned the hoop and threw herself into the woman's open arms. The child's honey-brown eyes gazed lovingly at her mother.

The young mother watched her family spend the afternoon in the sunshine on the riverbank. Their timber homestead with an expansive covered verandah had just been freshly whitewashed. It was set some distance from the river, high on a broad grassy knoll and well out of flooding level. Around the homestead were various outbuildings, including a large stable and barn at the back of the house. It had an uninterrupted view of the Hawkesbury River for a long way in both directions. They could sit on the grassy bank because a small flood had passed through six months before and had left a muddy flat area that had now been grassed over. This area was reasonably new as a considerable flood a few years earlier had washed away the old farmhouse that had sat in this area. The previous owners had drowned when their house was carried down the river. Last year's flood had only been a minor one compared to that.

Joel and Hetty Walker had purchased the farm and the nearly completed new house only two years ago; if the building had been finished six months earlier, the previous owners would not have died. The farm had sat abandoned for nearly four years.

Before whitewashing the entire building, Joel and Hector had added a wide verandah to their new building. Their family had lived in the rooms above the stables until the house was completed. Hector had slept in the tack room on a small pallet bed; they had only one other staff member, a new girl named Charity, who did the cooking.

Hetty still missed Martha, the girl who had been her first rescue. She was woefully abused on the trip out and needed healing before her first Camden placement.

With Molly sitting comfortably in her arms, Hetty had abandoned her feeble attempt at weaving. Her baskets just fell apart, and she had no idea how to finish things off if she did manage to weave something that resembled a basket, but she was determined to keep trying. Now holding her daughter, Hetty relaxed and watched her young sons kick a homemade ball over the short river grasses. She had warned them to watch for snakes; they had only seen one so far. It had been a large black snake swimming away from them to the far side of the river.

Hetty kept her eyes open for more of the nasty slithery beasts. Her three children were all well away from the water and relatively safe. Her husband, Joel, was waist-deep in water gathering reeds for another basket-weaving idea she had. She loved him so much that she only mentioned that she had some hare-brained idea and Joel would do anything to please her. Even if that meant braving the snakes and leeches to do so.

Working beside her beloved husband was their Scottish houseman, Hector Macdougal. She had yet to hear him say a cross or angry word to anyone or anything. He was just a nice man. Everything about him was nice. He had nice manners, a lovely accent, and was nice to look at but not too handsome; he even smelled nice, masculine but not overpowering. She found it hard to believe that he was a life-sentence convict.

There was already a large pile of rushes on the riverbank, but they needed more. Hetty wished to make some natural hives that she knew were called bee skeps. She wasn't sure how to go about it, but she wanted to try. Hopefully, this new girl was as good as her word. They could do with another man on the property, but after Martha left, Joel and Hetty discussed turning the farm into a safe house for abused girls, so they held off asking for another pair of hands.

This had occurred after Hetty's first trip to the Parramatta Gaol, where she had found Charity.

The first girl Hetty had assisted was Martha Alexander. Her

temporary placement had finished, and she'd moved on to Camden. Martha had become a friend in the short time she had stayed; Hetty missed her. Sadly, she had only been with them for six months before being transferred. Even when she first arrived, they knew she would only be with them briefly. Martha had been abused so severely that Hetty brought her home to recuperate. After she left, Hetty decided to try to see if any other girls needed a safe house. Her visits to the female gaol showed her that the need was dire.

Hetty had found Charity. She was another young girl who had arrived a few weeks ago. She was distressed after being accosted by a guard in the courtyard at the gaol. Thankfully she had not been violated, but she was traumatised. Hetty had arrived only minutes after the attack and had Charity assigned to her immediately. Major Grace had seen that the paperwork was done without fuss. He was another really nice man, always helpful, and even the girls trusted him. Some of the soldiers were downright horrible.

If either Joel or Hetty needed anything, they always asked for Major Grace. Hetty found that he had even arranged for some of the badly abused girls to be placed with some of his friends in a safe room at an inn in town.

With thoughts of getting more girls and possibly one who could weave, Hetty had made a trip to Parramatta. She had returned with a very young lass who said she could weave. The poor girl was currently asleep in the house. Hetty was thrilled as she had seen some river rush baskets and knew they would be suitable for egg collection but had no knowledge of how to make them. Their farm produced many fresh things, and eggs were among the foods regularly sold. Hetty wanted baskets to fit a dozen eggs. They also had a few cows, a goat, half a dozen broodmares, and a single bee hive.

Franny Rea, their newest arrival, was a seventeen-year-old convict that had been savagely violated so frequently that she had lost her will to live. The sailors on the way out used her so often that she became a living shell. Worse still, she had arrived in the family way; sadly, even that didn't protect her. When the poor girl thought she was safe, locked in a gaol cell, some of Parramatta's guards took their fill of her there. Fran was virtually unresponsive when Hetty saw her carried out on a stretcher from the female gaol to go to the hospital. Hetty's compassion was stirred to such an extent that she asked Major Grace about the girl and had her assigned to her, as she had done with Charity and Martha.

Again, Major Grace hastened the paperwork for her. Thankfully he had been called to the gaol when he heard Fran had tried to kill herself. He had greeted Hetty with a nod and gone to see the matron.

Fran had been with them for three weeks and recovered slowly from both the stillbirth of her child and her appalling treatment. Fran was

3

initially somewhat wary of anyone prepared to help someone like her. She was raped repeatedly on the ship and became like a rag doll. Fran had become an unwilling plaything for the sailors on board. She had been degraded and passed from one to another so often that she had tried to jump overboard on more than one occasion. She had no idea who the child's father was, but she was thankful the poor mite had died at birth. For some months before the birth, Fran had been upstairs on the female floor in the men's gaol in horrific conditions. There was little privacy in this dreadful place. She could even hear the male prisoners calling for her from their rooms downstairs. She often lay with her hands over her ears.

Janey Brien knew but had no way of helping her. Janey was kind and cared.

Hetty had seen Martha in similar circumstances before taking her home over eight months ago. Martha had been curled in the foetal position on her pallet in the dormitory, having just been touched up by another warder. She had already been assigned to a farm in Camden but needed to be well first. Hetty asked if she could nurse her back to health.

Major Grace had compassion for the poor girl and let Hetty take her. Martha had bounced back under Hetty's love and care. Now Martha was gone.

In gaol, the one nice spot in Fran's day was Janey Brien, who brought her fresh milk. Janey also brought her clothes and some fabric, ensuring she had enough to eat and drink. Janey was a convict with a Ticket of Leave and living with a family in Parramatta. It was Janey who had called the doctor when Fran had her first few contractions. However, he would not come, and neither did the midwife. Janey didn't know what to do, and the child died. When the baby had been born dead, Franny wept with relief, but she had retreated into herself and refused assistance from anyone; she had just wanted to die. Three days after the birth, Janey found her after she had deep scratches on her face and had rubbed the skin from her wrists, hoping she would bleed to death. Fran was bleeding from her self-inflicted wounds, but not enough to be life-threatening; however, she was now virtually unresponsive. She was in an almost catatonic state, cringing at every sound or raised voice and shaking at every footstep that came near. Eventually, she collapsed. Only then did the matron send for help.

Hetty had arrived as they were taking her to the hospital. She had met Janey on previous visits and was concerned by her worried tears. They watched the wagon take the girl away before Hetty asked her what had occurred.

Janey met her question with concern etched on her brow. Janey told Hetty of Fran's trauma and added, "Matron told her that she would be assigned as soon as the child was born, and she was back on her feet. She just curled up in a ball and has hardly moved for three days; now, she wants to die. I almost don't blame her; she's had a rough time. I don't know what to do, Mrs Walker. It's just not fair for the pretty young lasses. I thought I could get her assigned to the baker as she weaves and can make baskets for him, but he doesn't want her." The hospital wagon was now out of sight, and they stood alone in the quadrangle, talking quietly.

Hetty had come in looking for a new maid or a dairy hand, but the knowledge she could weave stirred Hetty. "Janey, do you think she would want to come with me?" Fran could be the answer, and she would be safe.

The slow smile that spread across Janey's face was her answer. "I think so, Mrs Walker. I know you would see her well cared for and avoid that sort of man." Janey took Hetty's hand. "I hoped you would ask for her, ma'am."

Hetty had been horrified as Janey described what had happened to the girl. She smiled. "I am, and I will look after her. Janey, does this sort of thing happen often?"

Janey nodded. "All too often, I'm afraid. I wish I had somewhere I could send the worst of the abused and the really young girls." Janey looked mournfully out the gate. She could come and go at will; they couldn't.

Hetty thought of something and smiled. "Janey, I'll talk to my husband, but I think you have just found your safe haven."

Janey's face brightened, and she was thrilled. "Oh, ma'am, I could send you so many. The young ones are in the most need. The free men who claim them only take them because they are young. They are expected to warm their beds, usually without marriage banns. Only a couple will get good placements. Sadly, the young ones have minimal skills, so they are taken for wicked reasons. I've been in their position, ma'am, and I know how powerless they are."

Hetty knew she needed to see Major Grace before he left, and then she had to head to the hospital. "I'll be in contact, Janey, but keep a watch out for some girls for me. I'll take Franny home now but watch for more. Please send me the neediest. No more than six as I don't have room yet. However, we have nearly finished a room they can use."

Hetty visited the hospital soon after leaving the gaol. She walked into the building and asked to see Frances Rea. An orderly grunted and pointed her to a wooden pallet at their end of the room. There were both male and female patients in the overcrowded ward.

Franny lay on her side with her back to the rabble and was tucked as tightly into a ball as possible. She lay under a filthy, stained blanket.

Rats and cockroaches ran out of Hetty's pathway as she walked the length of the ward. Hetty could see no movement in the bed. She walked around to the far side of the girl and squatted near her head.

The girl's eyes were closed, and her hands were over her ears to shut out the world. "Franny dear, I'm Mrs Walker from a farm on the

Hawkesbury River. I've been talking to Janey Brien and wondered if you'd like to come and live with us. You would be safe, and I would look after and protect you. Will you come?"

Hetty wondered if she had heard when, slowly, a pair of beautiful cornflower blue eyes revealed themselves from the red and swollen eyelids, "Me?" was all she uttered.

"Yes, sweetheart, you! You will be safe if you come to us as a maid." Hetty didn't need to explain much more except to say, "I believe you can weave, and I need a teacher."

Franny nodded, weeping quietly. "Yes, please, take me away from here." Massive tears rolled down the young girl's face. "Even here, all the men want to touch me. The orderly won't even keep his hands off me." The poor woe-begotten girl wept again.

Hetty gave her forehead a caring caress and said she would sort out her assignment. "That won't happen at the farm." Hetty knew both Joel and Hector to be gentlemen. "You will be sleeping in a room with another lass, but the only male servant is out in the stables. And Fran, I trust he won't touch you either. He's a good man." Franny was gathered into Hetty's arms and began to sob with relief.

Sobbing and hiccoughing, Franny begged, "Take me away, please, missus."

~

Franny recuperated at Loganberry Farm on the Hawkesbury River for three weeks.

Hetty noticed Fran was awake and was sitting outside slightly above them on the hillside; she had plucked some long grass stems and began to weave them together.

As Hetty drew closer, she saw the intricately woven tiny basket and asked Fran if she would teach her how to make them. Franny's face lit up. She had woven baskets from when she was small and could make anything. It was the one thing she had learned in the orphanage that she actually liked doing. Taking off cut branches of a vine and making something useful felt good.

Over the past three weeks, Fran made some small sample baskets of many materials. She made one reed basket for the eggs.

As she walked up from the river, Hetty wanted a woven, thick liana laundry basket for Charity to use. The first rushes collected earlier that week had now dried enough and were ready to use. Fran quickly made them a fruit bowl to test if they were suitable for the project she had in mind. Hetty had mentioned they sold honey, and Charity had said something about bee skeps.

The children and even Joel were given instructions to prepare the materials. Soon the farm was humming with preparation for weaving.

With the dormitory now finished, Janey received a note from Hetty asking her to find at least five other girls who could weave or were interested in learning. They also needed any who had experience with beehives or dairying, as Joel had purchased three more dairy cows from a man in Richmond last week.

A small single-mast sailboat traversed the river daily but only stopped at their wharf on Fridays to collect the few items for the weekend markets. The skipper always waved as he passed but rarely had a reason to call in.

On a wet day, a month after Fran arrived, nine bedraggled but laughing women were assisted from the wobbling craft. Each was clutching a small bundle of clothing and a blanket. Following the new women was one tall, dark-haired man.

Hearing the laughter, Hetty had come hurrying out of the house and stood on the verandah watching the proceedings on the riverbank. "Fran, Janey has found some other girls."

Fran was still quiet but was beginning to relax a little. Hetty tried not to smother her with love and concern, but it was hard not to. "Mrs Walker, do I have to share with them?" Fran asked, knowing that the new dormitory had been completed. It had twelve new beds in it awaiting its occupants. Fran stood behind Hetty and watched the women walk towards them.

Hetty glanced over at her face. "No, dear; however, I was wondering if you would like the inside room to yourself? Charity may like to move into the new rooms with the other girls. I want to keep you close to me, Fran."

"Please, Mrs Walker, I'd like to stay inside," Franny's timid voice reached Hetty.

Hetty saw she still didn't want to be near people. "Then stay you shall. I promised to keep you safe, so you will stay near me." Hetty reached out for her hand and gave it a gentle press. "Will you come and help me get the new girls settled in?"

Fran nodded and followed her mistress around the other side of the verandah.

The girls were chattering all the way up the hill. Hetty even heard more laughter; at least they were relaxed. "Franny dear, I believe we may have some interesting characters arriving. Our little cottage industry project looks like it may well succeed," Hetty smiled to herself. "Let's go down and show them where to go." She walked off and expected Fran to follow her. She didn't hear the click of her shoes following. She turned and just said, "Fran?"

Franny was shaking her head. Her shaky voice hardly carried to Hetty. "There's a man behind them." She didn't wait; she fled inside. Hetty heard her bedroom door slam shut.

Hetty released a deep sigh and then went to meet the new arrivals. One by one, the girls stopped in front of her. Each gave a curtsy and then stood in line. Hetty was just about to greet them when Charity came flying out of the kitchen door and into two girls' arms. "Hope, Faith, what are you doing here?"

The two young girls met the maid with tears of joy and bouncing hugs. "Charity, we had no idea you were here too."

Charity turned to Hetty. "Mrs Walker, these are two of my little sisters, Faith and Hope." She saw Hetty's surprised look. "Please, don't laugh; Mama ran out of names for us; we were daughters twelve, thirteen and fourteen. We have four brothers, Matthew, Mark, Luke and John, and the two oldest ones are Adam and Abel. I won't go through the others, but there are over twenty children." Charity giggled and hugged her sisters again.

"Welcome, girls; now introduce me to everyone else." Hetty was thrilled. Charity would undoubtedly want to move into the girls' dormitory.

One by one, the girls bobbed a curtsy and said their names; Bess, Manda, Trixi, Agnes, Clara, Hannah, Dawn, Faith, and Hope.

The unexpected man had arrived with an enormous armload of the girls' luggage. He deposited it on the damp grass beside the girls. "Good afternoon, Desmond Bolton, at your service, ma'am." The tall, dark, handsome man swept an exaggerated, regal bow and gave her a big cheesy grin. "I believe you needed a vine gatherer or some such?" The man seemed a little too sure of himself for a convict. He was downright cocky.

Before she could reply, Joel arrived from the jetty. "Love, Des is here. Can you believe it? All the way from old Mother England!" Joel chuckled and gave the man a big one-armed hug.

Hetty still didn't know who the man was, but obviously, Joel knew him well. She replied, "It seems to be a day of reunions. Charity's sisters are two of the girls who have arrived today, Joel."

In a jovial voice, Joel said, "Well, that really will make us one big happy family doesn't it?" He saw a forced smile on Hetty's lips. "Love, this is Dessy, the boy from home I've spoken about, only we've grown up."

A micro frown crossed her brow. "Oh, that Dessy. I think of you as a small boy. Sorry Mr Bolton, welcome!" Her voice still had a slight chill to it.

"Des now, please, Mrs Walker." He bent and kissed her hand in a very debonaire way.

She slid her hand away from his. Something didn't sit entirely comfortably with his presence here. Was he a convict or free? Why didn't Joel say anything about his arrival? Dismissing him from her thoughts, she turned back to the girls and said, "Charity, show the girls where to go. Feel free to join your sisters if you wish. Fran will stay inside." With that, she led the way indoors. She didn't want this man around Fran. She didn't want him inside with her at all. "Joel, can you help me for a moment, please?" Hetty held their bedroom door open for him to pass her.

Joel gave her a quick peck on the lips as he entered. As he did, she closed the door behind him.

"Joel, darling, who is he really? Why didn't you tell me he was here?" She was quite angry with him and spoke somewhat angrily.

Her tall, fair-haired husband slid his hands around her trim waist. "I didn't know, sweetie, really; I had no idea he was here." Joel pleaded ignorance.

Hetty didn't want that new man even near her own room. Joel took her lovingly in his arms and was about to kiss her when she pulled back. "Are you even sure it's him? Is he a convict or free? I don't want him inside with Franny, Molly, or even me. Knowing another man is here, Franny has already shut herself in her room."

Joel shrugged but bent to give her a quick kiss. "Yes, I'm sure it's him, but I had no idea he was here either. I have no idea if he's free or not. I don't even know how he found me." Releasing her waist, he gently stroked her arms, sliding his hands caressingly up and down them. "Sweetie, I'll just tell him he'll have to share Hector's stable rooms. I don't want any man sharing a house with us anyway. I have not seen him for over twenty years, so I know little about him anymore."

"Are you sure?" she asked as she slid her arms around him. "Thank you, darling." She lifted her lips to him invitingly.

After a passionate kiss, he said, "As much as I don't wish to, we must see to our guest and new help." He gave her another brief peck on the lips and released her. "Later, my sweet!" With a big smile, he slid his hand to the curve of her derriere. With the promise of what would come later, they returned to their uninvited guest.

With Des settled in their old quarters above the stable with Hector, Fran emerged from her room. She returned to her duties as a kitchen hand.

Charity packed and moved her things from their shared room and settled in with her sisters and the other girls. Their happy giggles floated across the verandah while Fran peeled the vegetables.

Hetty decided to let Fran lock her bedroom door while Des was there. She usually did not allow staff to have keys for anything, but Fran was a special case. As she no longer had to share a room and was the only one who needed to enter it, Hetty handed her the large key and said, "Only lock it at night, Fran, but you will feel safe."

Fran was delighted; she could now lock herself in and could sleep without fear. Fran took the large key and then flung herself into Hetty's arms. "Thank you, Mrs Walker, thank you so much."

Hetty was worried; this poor girl had such a horrific time that she still needed much care. For such a gorgeous-looking girl, her stunning beauty was a curse. A riot of natural dark curls framed her beautiful heart-shaped face. She was lovely even in the filthy convict rags Hetty had first seen her wearing. Franny had been caught by Janey scratching at her face, trying to disfigure herself with her nails. Thankfully, Janey had been able to stop her and cut her fingernails very short. That had only been the day before Hetty had come, and she had brought her to Loganberry Farm. A month later, Hetty could still see faint traces of the scratch marks, but they would fade with time.

Fran emerged from her room the following day to find Des in the kitchen before her. Charity and Faith were already stoking the fire and saw her. Des had his back to her and had not heard her arrival; Fran backed out straight into Hetty's arms.

Hetty took her hand and led her into the sitting room. It was the furthest room away from the kitchen. "Franny, you have to meet him sometime. I'll take you in and introduce you, and later I will take him aside and lay down the rules." Hetty waited for her slight nod and, holding her hand tightly, took her back to the kitchen. "Des, I want to introduce you to Frances. She is my friend and my basket-weaving teacher. You said you were here to cut vines; Fran is here to teach us to weave various kinds of baskets." Hetty saw the startled look he gave the young girl; it was as though he had seen a ghost. Hetty was standing just behind Fran and caught Des's eye. She shook her head and saw that he understood. "Des, Joel wants to have a chat in the office now, please." Thus dismissed, Des bowed slightly and left the room.

Hetty heard Fran release her held breath. "See, all done; I'll ensure he stays away from you all. Mr Walker is laying down the rules now. We have yet to hear his story, as we didn't know he was coming." Hetty flicked Fran's cheek and tipped her lips to make her smile. "Sweet girl, we promised you would be safe. I shall keep that promise."

Charity embraced Franny. "Come and help get breakfast, Franny, and meet my sisters." The girls hugged and got on with the work.

Fran loved having new girls around her. All of them were the same age and size, and according to Faith, the new girls were all nice. Over the food preparation, Faith revealed that many of the girls had been abused. She also said that all had been hand-chosen by a lady known to Franny. Janey Brien had sent them all and said to say hello to Fran.

"Really, Faith? Yes, I know Janey; she also pointed me out to Mrs Walker. Have the others been abused too? So not just me?" Fran asked in her soft, timid voice.

Faith came over and slid her arm around the shoulders of the poor young girl. "Not all of us, dear, Hope was, but I wasn't. A few others got done too, but Janey singled us out as we were young and frightened. Mrs Walker asked for the youngest girls to be sent here for our safety. Hence, we were singing on the boat. Here we are all but free, and we are safe." Faith saw the hurt still on Franny's face.

"They are nice people, Faith, but it will take time for me to feel safe anywhere. I didn't have a good time before I came here." That was a vast understatement. It would take a miracle for her ever to feel safe again; the only men she didn't flee from were Mr Walker and Hector, the Scotsman. For some reason, she trusted him; she liked him because he kept his distance from her.

Meanwhile, in the office, Joel was sitting with his feet up on his desk and his hands behind his head. He was waiting for Des to arrive. Hetty and he had sat on their bed last night and discussed Des in depth. His arrival was both unwanted and problematic. First, Joel had to determine why he was here, as he had not requested any assigned males. Maybe he was here as a free settler, but surely he would have written first? Hopefully, Des would reveal all. Joel looked up when he heard the expected knock. "Enter."

Des sauntered in and sat in the plush armchair. "You hailed, Joely boy." He sat nonchalantly, checking his fingernails. "What can I do you for?"

Joel understood Hetty's concern. Something didn't sit quite right about Des. He took a deep breath and thought, I have to know. He asked, "Why are you here, Des? Are you a convict? Why did you come to the farm? And while you are at it, why didn't you tell us you were coming?"

Des didn't look too concerned about the interrogation. "Ah yes, well, they are good questions, aren't they?"

Joel frowned. "They are, but will you answer any of them?" Des's attitude was unchanged, but Joel was getting angry.

Des replied, "Hmm, well, some of them I may. But let me ask one first; who's the pretty wench, and why so protective?"

Joel sat back in his chair. "That's two questions, and I'm the one doing the asking, Des. You can catch the next boat back to Windsor if you don't answer them. All I will say is that we are a safe house for the young convict women who have been abused, just like your sister was. Franny is one of those. If you so much as look at her inappropriately, you will be asked to leave and wait on the jetty all day. The same goes for any of the new girls here. Hands off all of them, my family included. Understand?" He folded his arms defensively. "Now for my first questions; your answers, please."

"Fine, fine. I'll start with the last one. I didn't tell you I was coming because I didn't know I was going to. I only heard your name while standing on the Windsor wharf. I swapped places with the fellow supposed to get on board to collect your order." Des looked a little apologetic. "That sort of answers the first question too. And as to the second, well, um, yes, sort of." He glanced up at Joel.

"Escaped?" Joel asked.

"More like on a mini holiday. As I said, I was supposed to send someone else to collect a honey delivery from 'up the river.' I had no idea it was from you until the skipper mentioned your name. Yes, I'll have to head back on the next ship, but I was supposed to anyway. So, I was stretching the truth to say I'm staying, but I will arrange vines if required." Des now had the courtesy to look guilty. "I got done for embezzlement, Joely, if you would believe it. I was given fourteen blooming years for not investing money for the Croquet Club. Fourteen stupid years!" He gave a huff. "Yeah, okay, I invested it into my pocket, but I had all the good intentions to pay it back. I will one day. It was a measly £30."

This time Joel huffed. "I suspected as much. Something didn't sit right when you arrived. Hetty picked it in a breath. Des, you've always lived on the edge since…" he couldn't say it. "Since, well, you know when. But, this time, it sounds like it was a razor's edge." Joel blew out his cheeks in frustration. "I have the honey order ready. It was a good harvest this year. I would have had more barrels, but they are too expensive to buy. I need a cooper if you come across one. We are nearly an all-female farm, so if you find one, check them out first. Hector and I are the only males here. We sell the occasional foal, calf, dairy, eggs, honey and hopefully soon baskets as well. Fran is teaching us all to weave. She is the pretty one you saw earlier. She was severely abused almost daily, both on the ship and in gaol. On her way out to New South Wales, she fell with child to someone on board and lost a baby only a month ago. Poor girl had no idea who the father was as she was abused multiple times each night. She has recently tried to scour her wrists and scar her face to make herself less attractive. We have promised to protect her and her kind. While you are here, you are to avoid her at all costs. If you see her in a room, you do not enter. Do you understand? Stay away from her." Joel was now mad. Des had used his friendship for years at home, and now to presume on the acquaintance made him angry. He would supply this order and send him on his way. What they had experienced when young had eventually forced their lives down different paths. Des's journey was one of almost self-destruction. Joel did the opposite but still left his homeland to seek peace.

Des was stunned and sat upright. "Cor Joel, the poor kid. I had no idea, sorry. I promise I'll stay clear. Did she really have no say at all?" Des was gutted. He should have known; it should have occurred to him. He had never been refused by any of his light-skirt lady friends. He had never had to force any of them, and there had been many. "I promise I'll be a good boy; I'll collect the honey and run." Des's mind flashed back to his lovely older sister; his sister's dark curly hair and bluest of blue eyes reminded him of the gorgeous girl who was so fearful of him. Her similarity to Carly was astounding. However, this girl's fear of him made him think twice about Joel's words.

For the next fifteen minutes, they swapped notes on what they had been doing for the intervening years. Joel's anger had somewhat diminished, but he still was angry that Des had not come clean on arrival. He said, "Des, you may return, but no more lies." By the time Des left the office, Joel had found out where he was assigned and had just over ten years to go. He worked for a businessman downriver in Windsor. Richmond may be the closest town, but Joel had had a run-in with a few local men over his non-willingness to involve himself in the town affairs, which included killing the indigenous tribe members.

They left the office and went to eat breakfast with Hetty and the children. Fran was nowhere in sight.

Joel didn't explain anything other than saying that Des would be leaving on the next boat and taking the consignment of honey with him. Hetty's raised eyebrows at Joel's statement were met with a minute shake of his head.

Des left in the little sloop with Casey a few hours later and took the six small honey barrels. Once the craft was out of sight, Joel revealed Des's story to Hetty as they sat on the jetty.

"I knew it, Joel. Something just didn't sit right with me." Hetty looked a little concerned. "He's not coming back, is he?"

Joel slid his arm along her shoulder. "I'm sorry, sweetheart. I don't think so, but he knows he's not to approach any of the girls if he does. You should have seen his face when he heard what the poor girls had been through. I didn't pull my punches. Het, he went white. When I told him that we would become a refuge for these abused young girls, he asked if there was anything he could do. I said no, but I feel we have not seen the last of him. Het, I don't think he'll cause any problem now, but I'll watch him if he comes back." He turned her, and they strolled back up to the house. "Het, I told you what we had been made to watch as children. The girl attacked was Des's sister."

Hetty had known of the gruesome act of a girl being violated in front of two small boys. It was why she knew Joel would support her wish to start the haven.

He had revealed all that when they had collected the first abused girl. Martha had been welcomed and had poured out her story to Hetty. She, too, had a rough time on the way out, but there was something more about Martha that drew her. Martha had a strong faith, and although she rarely talked about it, she put it into practice. Martha and Hector had been observed sitting and praying together more than once. Her time with them was short, but she left a different girl, confident and at peace with her past.

Hetty and Martha had become friends in the short time they had together.

Hector had been sad at her departure, but they had not formed that bond. It had been merely friendship, but both seemed to share something, and Hetty couldn't put her finger on just what it was. But she had not been part of whatever it was, and neither had Joel.

Chapter 2 Egg Baskets and Hives

The reeds collected during the week were sitting ready to weave. Fran had started preparing the rushes for the morning lessons for everyone. At the end of the verandah was a pile of completed egg baskets. However, this morning Fran was to teach them something different. She sat weaving while she waited. Her hands were rarely idle.

Molly was sitting next to Fran, listening intently to her instructions. Fran had given Molly some long lengths of a wild vine and showed her how to twist them into circles. She had brought out a milk jug and measured the first loop around the top. Once she had the size, Fran showed Molly how to do two more wraps, twisting the vine as she wrapped. Fran had Molly make five of these loops before she tied the tops of all five together with twine.

Fran stripped off a length of the rush stem with deft fingers and started weaving. In and out, over and under, the odd-shaped, double-ended basket soon began to take shape. The first basket was complete when Hetty and Joel returned from the wharf. It was like a bent tube. These odd-shaped baskets Fran knew to be useful for children to collect eggs. However, this was just one design she had in mind. Soon Fran had a pile of different sorts of baskets sitting near her. She knew the other girls were in the dairy and had to milk the cows and goats and set the cream to rise. She had no knowledge of cows and was scared of them, but hand her a pile of vines and rushes, and she could make beautiful things. Thankfully each girl had their own skills, and Hetty encouraged each girl to bloom in their own way. Charity had taught Fran how to prepare vegetables and do some basic cooking, but she wasn't very good at it.

Molly watched Fran take a fat vine, make an oval shape, and use her arm to measure the length.

Fran wound the vine around her elbow and held the end. Again, she twisted more vines around the first until she had an oval-shaped loop. From this, she cut ten shorter lengths of the vine for ribs; she made them into curves, tucking each end in the blunt ends of the loop. Once all ten ribs were in situ, she started weaving through them with the cut and flattened rushes. With Molly making the large loops, Fran could make egg baskets in assorted styles. These baskets were quick to make and easily fit two dozen eggs. Next, she thought she would do a flat trivet like a mat. These could be placed on a table to protect it, and a pot hot from the stovetop would not burn into the wood. Fran chose twelve lengths of vine about twelve inches long. Again, she deftly wove the base with quick flicks of the fingers; the twelve twig-like lengths were woven into a flat star. Fran selected a few thin vines and alternately wove them in and out around the skeleton of the ribs. Again, in a very short space of time, she began twisting the rib ends in, poking them in as a decorative edge, and finishing the cane trivet.

The two boys came and joined them, and Fran knew that the others would soon follow. As the morning chores were completed, the piles of rushes picked two weeks ago were now dry and sat on the verandah, ready for use.

Two days before, Fran had asked Hector to make some strange-looking tools. She wanted a wooden mallet, a funnel with an inch-wide hole and a rough comb made from fencing wire off-cuts. Fran found a chicken bone and shaped it to a wedged point. She also needed a wooden needle.

Hector didn't question her but found a freshly dead gum twig and made a hole in one end, pointing the other end for a needle. Once the set of tools was complete, she asked that he make up more sets. With the first complete set of tools now laid out in front of her, she unwrapped another thing, and that was a ball of thin untangled vine that hung from some of the local trees. All was in readiness; she waited for everyone to arrive. She knew this project could make a lot of money for the family. She was going to get everyone making bee-skep hives for the family business. She had found Hector trying to make a wooden box hive for the farm. Fran knew how to create ones from rushes and vine, and if they could make a lot of these, they should be able to increase honey production tenfold. Once these were made, all they would need would be the bees.

Joel and Hector had decided to join the class as she was so mysterious about what they would make. Soon everyone was settled on the verandah while waiting for the last girls to arrive. Hector had one more thing to collect before he sat down. They watched Fran grip the rushes and feed a handful into a funnel. Knowing how the initial section was hard to do, Fran deftly twisted and sewed a spiral of rushes with a long tail of reeds sticking through the funnel. She told them to work in pairs and give themselves some room.

Hector finally arrived with a bucket and placed it beside him. Fran nodded her thanks but continued with the instruction about the strange item she was making. Fran didn't mind the boys near her or even Hector or Mr Walker. Des, however, made her shiver. It was something about the way he looked at her.

Fran, hopefully, would help pay the Walkers back by teaching them her skill. She started with her instruction, "We are going to be making beehives that are called skeps. These are what we use for hives at, um, home." She didn't want them all to know she grew up in an orphanage. "Once the first few spiral rounds have been done, you slowly move the coil down so it is no longer flat. At home, we used a frame, but it isn't essential. The bees are not fussy, as they normally use a hollow in the wild. This coil should slowly turn into a dome by changing the angle as you sew each row as you turn. Try to keep the sides as straight as possible, but it doesn't really matter. As I said, the bees don't really care if you can't. You will need to do about eighteen to twenty rows, and on the last one, you will have to give it to me as I then have to make a bee door. It must also be finished properly with a fatter roll for the final circuit." Fran had already started a couple for the group and pulled them out from under the pile of rushes beside her. "May I have the bucket, please, Hector?"

Hector passed it over; she dug into it and pulled out a strange-looking funnel. Carefully she threaded it over the protruding reeds. "This makes it easier to push in more reeds and keep it neat. Always poke them in the middle of the pile; you can twist the bunch as you sew it. That will make it stronger, as well as look better." Fran threaded some flattened thin vine through a wooden needle and passed it to the eager students. She set up three more skep spirals and handed them out.

Keen to assist, each thought it would be easy. Fran certainly made it look so.

Hetty had taken the first one and thought she was reasonably deft with her fingers until she tried this work. They worked diligently for about fifteen minutes before Hetty exclaimed, "Darn it, Franny, you made this look simple." "You have to do about six things at once."

Fran chuckled. "Get the children to stuff the reeds in the funnel while you twist and sew. That makes it easier. It's good if you can all work in groups as then you can either alternate or hold things in place for the other, one sorting the reeds, another sewing, and one stuffing, etcetera."

Soon, all the first rows were done, and she was going around each group, showing them how to turn down the sides. The first bee-skep was nearly complete; it was rough but would work. Fran had finished off the last bit. She was sure the bees would not care what it looked like.

Faith, Charity, and Hope had obviously done some weaving before and grasped the action of working together to stuff, twist and sew. As Fran finished off the first skep, two other girls brought out a tea tray and a large pile of tin mugs. They had given up and gone back to the kitchen.

The hot sweet tea was delicious and hit Fran's parched throat. She'd not talked so much for a long time. By lunchtime, twelve of these skep hives were woven. They were certainly not professional, but the bees typically weren't picky. All the skeps now needed were some smooth straight sticks poked through them as frames for the honeycomb they would make. At least six straight sticks were required for each hive in two vertical rows. The bees would build a free-form honeycomb onto these, and the sheer beauty of their design naturally circulated the air and kept the hive healthy. When the harvest of the hive occurred, the comb would be carefully taken out and honey removed. As so many rushes grew along the river, Fran thought she would make new skeps. She also realised that they could sell new skeps for the farm market.

Franny had only been able to source six of the required straight sticks, but she thought they could all do with some activity after lunch. Then she would show them how to make egg baskets during the afternoon.

Fran had yet to ask Hector to make an elevated covered shelf out the back of the stables but close to the existing hive. Hopefully, the bees would find these hives for themselves. Otherwise, they may need a helping hand. They would have to trick the bees into finding their new homes.

Hetty knew that the skep only needed a tiny entrance and something that smelled like their queen to attract bees. She thought she would try a lemony native bush leaf and hoped it would work. She preferred lemon grass but didn't have any. She mixed last season's beeswax, a little oil and a native lemon myrtle leaf.

Charity had made this mix earlier and had an old ceramic pot on the stove. The wax melted, and she added some olive oil and a few small fresh lemon myrtle leaves. Once it was melted, she carried it out to the weavers, and they daubed a square of the waxy substance on the inside back of the bee skeps. Now primed, they would be put on the shelf and wait until they found a bee swarm or better still, they hoped a free swarm would find the skeps. She made some beeswax wraps for the kitchen with the excess wax mixture. They were wonderful for keeping the flies off the food.

~

About a week later, Hector returned from wood and vine gathering and said he had seen a swarm on a shrub. He knew that getting one of the skeps close to the swarm might encourage it to make it their new home. Sure enough, the bees had taken residence within a couple of days. They knew they had to leave it in situ for six weeks before moving it to the house.

Over the next few weeks, more bees were seen swarming, and each was captured and returned to the new honey farm.

No more was seen of Des for some months. However, he sent a message to Joel via Casey.

"Dear Joel,

I have been searching for your Cooper and have found the perfect person. Your cooper should be on the boat tomorrow. Accept said person with my compliments. Janey Brien and Major Grace have sorted the paperwork for you.

Des.

P.S I am sorry to have upset you all. My ego still takes over. I am working on that!

DB"

Hetty was not too happy about a new man arriving uninvited. She wished she had been able to interview him first. Joel stood on the wharf waiting as the small sailboat came into view. He looked hard but could not make out the person on the seat. He had an order of baskets to load up, so he had to meet the boat anyway. Maybe the man decided not to come after all. Joel grabbed the rope and tied the little sloop as it released its sail. Then he hailed a greeting to the skipper.

Casey replied, "Hi Joel, I have a delivery from Des." Casey Stake was a be-whiskered, scruffy-looking sailor with a peg leg. His grey beard made his face look like a grey lion, but he was a delightful character and always good for a laugh. He tied off the rear rope and held his hand out to the passenger. "Joel, behold your delivery."

Jane Matthews was no delicately built frail lady. Her statuesque, buxom physique was a surprise to Joel. She was above his eye level as Joel was a shade under six feet.

Joel was stunned. "You are a cooper? Really?" he asked as he assisted her from the rocking deck.

Jane took his hand delicately. She had no wish to end up in the river. "Yes, sir, my father was a cooper and taught me his trade. I prefer to make small barrels, though, which I believe you want." As she stepped up onto the jetty, she explained the volume of her luggage. "I hope you don't mind, but I brought some supplies. Mr Bolton said there was no blacksmith here, so I also brought a case of pre-made hoop bands and other necessary items for my use." She was nervously clarifying the need for so many cases. She hoped he wasn't angry. "A Major Grace completed my paperwork in Parramatta and also supplied all this. He sends his greetings as he apparently knows you."

Joel's eyebrows raised; this explained much. He silently thanked both Des and Ned Grace. "I do indeed, lovely chap."

Casey had pushed a couple of significant-sized cases to the edge of the seat. "Four of these are for you, Joel; I need help getting them out."

Joel knew that Hetty was watching from the verandah; he turned, put his hand on the top of his head, and then made the riding action.

Hetty had seen this before. He wanted Hector and the horse and cart. She understood that, but where was the new cooper? Frowning, she sent the message to Hector and then returned to the rail and watched. She expected the tall woman to get back on board. However, the lady turned and gave a shy wave.

Hetty gasped. Was the cooper a woman? "Oh, perfect!" she voiced to herself, then said, "Franny, come here, sweetheart."

Fran came at her call but stood near the door, ready to flee again. She had been told about the new cooper. She knew they needed one, but she wasn't happy.

Hetty beckoned her. "Franny, come and stand beside me. What do you see?" Before Fran arrived beside Hetty, Joel had pointed to the visitor and signed a double thumbs up. Hetty was now sure the lady next to Joel was the new cooper.

Franny gazed at the small wharf. "I see the boat, Mr Joel, Captain Casey and a tall lady, ma'am. Where's the cooper that Mr Des was sending?"

Hetty's eyes danced with joy. "I believe we have a female cooper, Franny. It seems Des is quite apologetic." Hetty slid her arm around Fran's waist. "Happy, lass?"

Fran's face broke into a beaming smile. "Yes, Mrs Walker, I'm over the moon. Where would he have found a lady cooper?"

Hetty gave a chuckle. "I presume he found her at the gaol, but I'm unsure. However, I dare say we'll find out. Let's go and meet her."

Fran had become the companion for Hetty that she desperately wanted. The other girls were content to stay in the female dormitory, but Hetty and Fran spent most days working together.

The dormitory was built solidly but hot. Hector and the girls were in the process of weatherproofing and insulating the outside with the girls' help. He had added an extra layer of split logs, and the girls were busy stuffing the half-built external wall with soil and moss. As they filled behind the log, Hector added another row. Soon the entire building would have an earth-filled, four-inch-thick outer wall to insulate the building against both the cold and the heat. It would not be as good as a stone one but would undoubtedly be better than the breezy slabs it currently was. There were still some spare beds; if more girls came, they would move the table out and add bunks. With this woman's arrival, there would only be one bed spare in the dormitory. This new woman would have to share with the girls in the dormitory. They could always build a recreation room for them elsewhere.

As Hetty met the new lady, she called out for Charity. "We have a new lady arriving, Charity. Can you prepare a bed for the new girl, please?"

Charity was as bright and bubbly as ever, even more so since her sisters arrived. "Sure thing, Mrs Walker; I thought you said we were getting a cooper, though?" Charity had just set some bread to rise. Hope was helping with the insulation wall.

Hetty smiled. "I think that is who she is. I'm just going down to meet her. She may be another needy soul; either way, I'm guessing she'll be staying." Hetty walked out to greet them.

Hector loaded the cases onto the cart and brought them with Joel and the new lady.

Jane Matthews was as good as her boast to Des. The tools she brought were in one crate. Small barrel hoops, tools, and other pre-cut oak staves in the second and largest case, and rough-cut, dried oak lengths in the third box. She realised they would have little access to coopering timbers, but she also knew that she could use a variety of local wattle for her purposes. She was told it grew in this area.

Major Grace had arranged her new tools from Government Stores. The Government Store manager, Charles Lockley, had been with her while selecting the required items from the extensive range available. Some differed from what she had trained with, but she chose others that would suffice or have a dual purpose. There were the required planes, shaves, a jigger, an adze, a bung boner, a side axe, and a jointer. Des had told her they particularly wished to make honey barrels, so she had chosen all the smallest tools available. In the short time she had before she left, she asked the town cooper about local wood and found that the silver wattle would be suitable for the honey barrels. The black pine, gum tree wood, and other timbers like turpentine tainted the honey, but the silver wattle, once dry, worked well. It was considered stable and food safe. Many kinds of wood could be used for barrel making if it was not to be used for food, but the flavour of the honey had to remain pure and untainted. There were three main types of coopers, white; wet; and dry, and she could do them all. Like her father, Jane could cooper all sorts of things. She would need to wait until the one-inch wide roll of barrel hooping arrived from Mr Tindale in Parramatta to make different sizes. He had no stock when she left, but Major Grace assured her he would send some through. Once the coil came, Jane decided she would also make a larger half barrel to strain the honey and another full one to make honey vinegar. More items, like buckets, would follow.

Hector left the girls to finish insulating their dormitory and set to building Jane a coopering room. She needed a small fire source and a carpentry bench. He discovered that Jane could use a saw with the best men and split the timbers and chamfer the staves with minimal fuss. She had brought a tiny grinding wheel and could sharpen tools to razor-sharp. Hector was going to like having this skilled woman on the farm. Joel and Hector quickly erected a three-sided lean-to building that they would enclose and enlarge as they had time. There was enough room to add a drying room for freshly felled timber.

Jane was junoesque, dwarfing Hetty by some six inches, but as Hetty later found, she was quiet, gentle and exceptionally skilled. She discovered that Jane stood at six feet one inch. Jane had arrived only with two gowns that were now almost threadbare. The gowns Hetty supplied for the girls would not fit the tall Amazon. Some other girls set about making her some new dresses from Hetty's fabric stock. All the others had a selection of drill, serge, or other usable fabric for work clothes. Each also had a printed floral for a good dress. Jane would get the same.

The timber Jane had brought with her was already dried. She knew she needed to make a small kiln to dry freshly hewn timbers. If she couldn't, she would need to cut some fallen logs, seal the ends, and set them to dry. She'd need to find out the urgency of the requirement. Hopefully, she could buy in some dry timber; if not, find some standing dead trees. Thankfully, Charles Lockley had insisted on some tools that had no handles, as well as two bush saws. She could make the handles from recently dead saplings; she enjoyed doing that. There should be some in the vicinity as the wattles were a quick-grow, quick-die tree. Hector was able to show her where there was a stand of them. Some of the older trees had already died, and some had even recently fallen. She would start with these and set some larger trees to dry for later use.

Hetty's dream of a haven or sanctuary for the young women of the colony was growing faster than she had ever planned. She had only ever thought of one or two girls at a time. There were currently twelve. Hetty wondered what other cottage industries she could do to occupy the girls.

Hector was at their beck and call for everyone if they needed him to do any heavy lifting. He also made anything they needed. Hector had just surprised Hannah with some wooden rollers to squeeze the washing. She was delighted. By turning a crank handle, the rollers pressed out the water.

Bess and Manda were continuing the insulation of the sleeping quarters. Hector was called to add new rows of cladding as they filled them. As well as the laundry and cleaning for the family, Hannah, Dawn and Faith were busy making baskets of various sorts with Fran while Hope and Charity had the kitchen humming. All the girls had to first do milking chores and set the cream to rise before starting on other daily tasks. Basic plain cheese was also now made as Manda knew the technique, and she had teamed up with Bess. When the dairy work was done, they changed into their dirty work clothes and kept pounding the fill in the walls.

Hetty had discovered that Clara could read and write well and set her to school the children. She said she had been an under-governess before being accused of theft. She admitted she borrowed a book to read and forgot to put it back. It had been found under her bed; she was arrested and sentenced to four years. Hetty wondered; something about her story didn't quite make sense. Moreover, the story changed a little each time she told it. However, Clara loved it here and had asked if she had to leave when her term expired.

Hetty oversaw all the various activities. She used her spindle to make yarn but wished she had a spinning wheel. She wondered if when the first of the honey barrels were assembled, she could ask if Jane had the skill to make one. Hector had made Hetty the spindle, but it was slower than a wheel. She was using that to make her knitting yarn. Three fleeces were waiting to be spun. She sighed and persevered with the spindle even though it was so slow.

Joel overheard Hetty talking to Jane about a spinning wheel. He wondered if one was available in Parramatta or elsewhere in the colony. He decided to ask Casey the next time he passed by. He kept busy on the farm wishing Hector was not so occupied making things for the new girls. He liked working with him. Joel wondered why this man did not threaten the girls. Even Fran was comfortable with Hector. The Scotsman was youngish and quite attractive; Joel would have thought they would shrink from him, as Fran had with Des. As he sat waiting for the daily trip of the small sailboat, he thought about Hector. Something set him apart. Nothing was ever too much to ask from him. He would generally drop what he was doing and go to the assistance of the enquirer. Hector was an enigma. He had been assigned to them when they bought the farm. He had never volunteered any information about himself, but in the same thought, Joel admitted to himself that he had never asked about him. All he knew was that Hector was a lifer.

They had lived at Loganberry Farm for two years. Molly had been just walking when they arrived. Until Hetty decided to get some help in the house, Hector had been the only other person they had. Hetty had done all the cooking and cleaning; now, with twelve girls to help, she was at a loose end.

Joel's musing stopped as he saw the sail of the small boat come around the bend. He got to his feet and waited. Hector had met the boat yesterday as he was busy with a birthing cow. They now had a new heifer to help build up their herd. Joel lifted a hand in silent acknowledgement of Casey's arrival. He waited for the rope and tied up the craft.

Casey said, "Hector spoke to me yesterday, and I happened to see Des at the inn last night." Casey greeted him and said, "Des has sent you another delivery Joel. Something that Hector said the missus needed. It was for sale on the noticeboard for fifteen shillings, so I hope you don't mind, but he bought it for you on spec. He said you would pay him when you saw him." He drew back a sheet of old sail and revealed an upright spinning wheel.

Joel threw his head back and laughed. "I was sitting here with £5 in my pocket to ask you to see if you can find one for Hetty." Joel leaned into the boat and took delivery of the ingenious machine. It was made of dark-coloured timber and had a spike on top. "This is a lethal-looking weapon! I wonder what that's for?" Joel said aloud.

Casey was trying to regain his balance. "My missus has one similar, it is where you sit the rolag, and you spin the yarn from there. This one doesn't have any spare bobbins, though, but that Jane Matthews of yours should be able to whittle something similar. She can use the one on the wheel as a template." Casey watched as Joel put the wheel on the wharf.

Joel dug in his pocket and pulled out a sovereign coin. "Keep the change, Casey." The shiny gold coin spun through the air, flashing as it headed towards Casey's outstretched hand.

Casey deftly caught it and bit into the coin. "Just checking, Joel," he chuckled, "I haven't seen one of these for a long time."

Chapter 3 Hector

*J*oel carried the ungainly contraption carefully up to the house. It was still under the sheet. He sat it at the top of the stairs.

Rather than offer to assist, Hector stood watching Joel with an almost wicked grin. "He found one then, sir?"

Joel met his smile with his own grin. "Des did that, Hector, but how the heck did you know?" Joel placed the wheel down carefully on the edge of the verandah.

Joel observed Hector's gentle and loving attitude. "Your missus told Fran that she used to spin as a girl. With all the activity now being taken from her hands, I knew she would not wish to sit idle. My mama used to spin for pleasure, and it's also nice for the hands. I had no idea that Des would be able to obtain one so easily." Hector again folded his arms and watched Joel's face.

Joel noticed that he never asked for anything for himself; he just gave and gave and gave. However, this was the straw on the camel's back for Joel. "Hector, what gives? You are a felon for life, yet you never say a cruel or harsh word to anyone. And you bend over backwards to help anyone, never thinking of yourself. Hector, why?" Joel watched the smile go all the way to Hector's eyes.

Hector beamed as he replied, "Sir, my body is bound to this world for a short time, but my soul is free. I gave that away decades ago, for I follow my Master where He leads me. And He is no longer just of this world."

Joel looked puzzled.

Hector unfurled his arms and pointed upwards.

Joel's eyes widened, and his jaw dropped open. He was stunned.

"You mean you believe in God?"

Hector, being a man of few words, just nodded.

Joel asked, "But really? Is He not just a story our parents told us?"

Hector refolded his arms. He was leaning against the top pole of the staircase. He quietly said, "Far from that, sir, He, and I mean God, is real and far more than that. I know that I'm just biding my time here until I go to Him. For me, the best is yet to come." Hector had wanted to talk about his faith to Joel for some time, but something had occurred every time he attempted to bring it up. He realised he had to wait until the good Lord gave him the right opening. As Joel introduced the topic this time, Hector would not walk away. "Sir, why do you help these girls?"

Joel was surprised at Hector's question and wondered how he could associate the two; he said, somewhat puzzled, "Why? Because they need it. I have a farm, and they need protection."

Hector gave a single nod. He tipped his head to the side before saying, "That they do, sir, but why you? Why not leave it to someone else to do?"

Joel had often wondered why himself. He knew of the situation in his past, but surely it was more than just that. "Well, I suppose they come because we had somewhere safe. However, in a way, this is Hetty's project. If she's happy, then I'm happy." Joel had not given much time to reminiscing; those old memories hurt too much. He knew about what he saw when he was a young boy. He and Des had been together and never forgotten it, but he would not tell Hector about any of that yet. It had been the incident with Des's sister that had changed his attitude.

Hector spoke again, and Joel shook his head to make the memories flee.

"Sir, why do you think Mrs Walker wants to assist them?" Hector gently probed.

"Honestly, I can't pin it down to a single answer, Hector." He knew why, but he wasn't going to explain. Martha was the key to that. After her early years in the convict town, Hetty had seen far too much of the seedy side of life. Joel had never questioned Hetty why she was keen to help; he was just pleased she was willing to think it was her idea. He was sure there must have been some triggering incident, but she had never revealed what that was.

"Sir, I'm sure you remember that in the Bible, in Matthew chapter 25, verse 40, Jesus said, *'And the King shall answer and say unto them, Verily I say unto you, inasmuch as ye have done it unto one of the least of these my brethren, ye have done it unto me'.*"

Joel nodded. "Yes, I suppose I know about that, but...."

Hector smiled. "Sir, there are no buts; Jesus did not say help them if they are pretty girls, rich women, or poor abused girls who needed your help. Jesus just said help them. He meant everyone, and you are, sir."

Hector looked up and saw Hetty coming towards them. "Sir, I feel it important that we continue this conversation at a later date, however, Mrs Walker is here."

Hetty had heard the soft voices of the men approaching; then, they came no further. She rounded the corner of the verandah and saw Hector look up. She had seen Joel carrying something up from the wharf, and it looked like an odd shape. She had no idea what it was.

Hector gave her a micro nod as he usually did and then a small bow. He left Joel on the verandah to explain his unique gift to Hetty and returned to his work.

Joel turned to Hetty and removed the covering.

She finally saw what he had been carrying. It was a spinning wheel. "Wherever did you get that?" she asked, amazed. The upright spinning wheel was very similar to the one she had used as a child. Back in the early days, her mother had used it as a punishment, but Hetty had loved the feel of the soft fleece being spun from the brushed fluffy rolag on the top of the machine. She loved watching the yarn form as she peddled the footplate. When young, the job she hated was carding the fleece to remove dags and burrs.

Joel saw the delight on her face.

She stepped closer to him; her intention was obviously to thank him. "Joel, this is wonderful; thank you, darling." She slid her arms around his neck and thanked him with a kiss.

Joel deepened the pressure and then pulled away. "As much as I would like to take the blame for this lethal-looking contraption. Hector asked Casey to find one for you. Yes, I paid for it, and yes, I was going to ask Casey to keep his eyes open for one as well, but Hector has beaten me to it. Des apparently found one for sale. So, it's them you have to thank." He kissed her again. "But, my beloved, you are not to thank either of them like this."

Hetty gave a gurgle of mirth. "I won't, I promise." She was delighted with her gift. She drew back a little and looked around her. "Joel, was there another bundle with it?"

Joel caressed her cheek as he replied, "Ahh, no. Casey said that there were no spare bobbins nor something called a carding comb."

Hetty blew out her cheeks. Looking at the wheel, she said, "Oh, blast, I'll have to work around that; but this is brilliant, though, you darling man. I can now spin, and even if I have to hand-roll the yarn onto a stick or use the spindle to empty the bobbin, I'll work it out somehow."

Late that afternoon, Hector returned with a small item in his hand. He gave her a slight bow before handing over his gift. "Pardon Mrs Walker, but my mama used to spin, and I've been working on this for a while. I know you have been using your hairbrush instead of a comb for carding the fleece." He held out the small parcel.

Inside was a handmade carding comb made from offcuts of fencing wire that he had sharpened to a soft point. The handle was not just a flat bit of wood. It was shaped to fit comfortably in her hand. Fran had tested the handle for comfort.

She gripped the handle. "It's perfect, Hector; thank you so much. And thank you for the wheel; you have no idea how much I appreciate your thoughtfulness." Hetty saw the skill of how he had made the small comb. It could easily have been a bought one. She met his eyes. "Thank you, Hector." She touched his hand and gave it a gentle squeeze.

"My delight, ma'am," Hector turned and left her alone with her gift. Hector walked down the verandah, unaware he was still being observed. He passed Fran and gave her a slight bow. "You were right, Miss Franny; she loved it." He bowed again and walked away.

~

Two days later, Hetty was sitting on the verandah spinning while Fran and the girls were beside her, weaving. "Thank you, Fran," Hetty didn't say what for.

Fran looked up.

Hetty just lifted the comb a little and smiled. Fran looked surprised, "Oh! He wasn't supposed to say anything."

Hetty was surprised that Fran had actually had a conversation with a man. "He didn't; I saw him thank you."

"Oh," was all Fran said, but she smiled. Her eyes fell back to her work. The simple conversation was enough to please Fran. Hetty seemed to understand she did not seek any public show of affection. Having never known affection, she was still unable to accept an effusive display of thanks.

The afternoon passed with general chatter from all of the girls and children. Clara had the children practise their handwriting. Oliver, at eight, was able to grasp the rudiments of cursive writing; Ernie, at six, was writing numbers on the lines Clara had ruled on his slate. Molly had mastered writing her name and kept rubbing out her effort from the slate and re-writing it repeatedly.

During the after-hours, Clara taught the other girls to read and write. Jane was the exception. Soon all the girls were reasonably proficient at writing their own names. The days were spent working hard for Hetty and Joel.

The pile of saleable baskets was growing. Fran had also made a sizeable woven container to hold the numerous baskets. It was about a two-foot square and held many woven egg baskets. There were five stacks of twenty. Casey could now take them to market undamaged, and Des had offered to sell them for Joel.

In the intervening weeks, Joel had gone to Windsor and met again with Des; he had also met the man he was assigned to. Henry Gates was a local businessman, and Des was his man about town. Mr Gates had discovered soon after Des's arrival that he had a 'gift of the gab.' Des was permitted some freedoms as long as he could account for his time on his return. Casey had vouched for him the night he stayed with Joel, and Henry welcomed Joel by name. Casey's description of him was very accurate. "I believe you know Des Bolton?" The question was blunt.

"I do, sir; we grew up together." Joel was not sure how much Des had told him. He stayed silent; he wouldn't divulge anything about him until they had spoken more.

Mr Gates nodded and walked off.

Joel was watching him and did not hear the footsteps coming up behind him.

"Strange bod that one! Always seems sad, loves kids, but has none himself."

Joel spun around. "Hello, Des; he may well be, but he also corroborated your story. So, you are out of my hot water anyway. However, you have not told me your entire history, have you?"

Des didn't look at all abashed. "As much as is pertinent old chap." Des slapped him on the back. "How is the girls' farm? All behaving?"

Joel gave him a flash of anger. "Shh, just keep mum about it, will you? If word got out, we would be unable to keep them safe."

Des saw Joel's anger. "My lips are sealed, old chap." Des had no intention of revealing the presence of the girls or endangering them. "I am here to serve, dear Joely." He gave a mock bow. "Darn it, Joel, I would not hurt a hair on any of their heads, and you know perfectly well why. If I could undo the hurt done to each of them, I would do it. I surprised myself as my compassion was unexpectedly stirred. I scoured the colony for a female cooper. I had all but given up, and in a way, she fell in my lap. She had just arrived from London. She came at Her Majesty's pleasure, of course. The Major in town happened to mention her skills." Des paused. "Joel, just don't let on that I have empathy for the weaker sex, will you? I saw my sister in Franny. Did she not remind you of her?"

Joel nodded but couldn't trust his voice to answer. He knew Carly had died after being savagely violated and attacked by a group of youths. As two young boys, they were held tightly and were forced to watch the multiple violations. They kicked and fought to go to her aid. Carly had been raped so violently that she only survived a few hours. She had been fifteen. Fran was only seventeen, but her initial trauma would have first occurred about the same age. "I would have done anything to protect Carly. You know that, but Des, we were just little kids; we had no hope of stopping them."

"I know, but it still hurts. I still wake up fighting to protect her," Des admitted. "She was my big sister, Joel!" His hand went to his eyes and swept over his face.

"Me too, Dessy; me too." They stood silently, thinking back to that horrific day. Neither wished to remember it, but neither could forget. It was the main reason Joel supported Hetty's idea to help the other girls. It was an impassioned response to that day. He had admitted that had been something he had witnessed in his youth, but he had given her few details. He shook his head as if to scare the thoughts away.

Des said, "Enough, Joely! How can I assist you today, my good fellow?" Des's phoney persona had been erected again. He turned away from Joel.

"Leave off, Des; this is me. We know each other too well," Joel said with a touch of anger in his voice.

Des turned abruptly and faced Joel. "Fine! I don't want to remember. I took the money because I couldn't leave, so I made myself *persona non grata* by getting arrested. Now I can't go back; I emotionally flay myself daily, wishing I could change the things that occurred that day so long ago, but I can't; she's still dead. It still haunts me." He again wiped at his eyes angrily. "Carly is gone, and I was unable to help her."

"Cor Des, don't you think I feel it too? They made us watch; they were so cruel. I will never ever hurt a woman, Des. Not ever!" Joel led his friend to the verandah's edge, and they sat and talked over the horrid episode they had both witnessed. It was the first time that either had revealed their feelings. Even back then, they had hidden their emotions from each other. The boyhood bond between the two reforged over shared grief. The incident over twenty-five years before had scarred them both. Des's false bravado was now fully explained. So were the micro frowns that flashed across his brow.

For two hours, they rehashed that day and every day in their lives that followed. The choices they had each made and the reasons why. It all led back to Carly.

Then Joel asked a question that halted their conversation. "Des, do you believe in God? Hector and I have spent time over the last weeks discussing his faith. I will freely admit that I have never thought about that sort of deep belief before. But there is something so different about him." Joel didn't see the anger on Des's face.

Des stood angrily. His face was flushed and hard. He walked from one end of the verandah and back again. He stood looking down at Joel. "I'd like to say I don't believe, but then who would I blame? I blame God for not protecting her; I blame God for not allowing us to help her. So yeah, I believe in God, so I can blame Him for all the hurts I've had to live through." Des punched at the verandah pillar until his knuckles bled. Then leaned his head against it. "I wish the hurt would just go away, Joel." He almost gasped a breath. His tortured voice said in a sombre tone. "One damned night at your place, Hector wheedled the entire story out of me." He turned to face Joel. "What is it about that man that makes my tongue run like quicksilver?" Des refused to discuss his sister further. "But no more! Enough talk of Carly; she's gone, and I was responsible." Without saying anything else, Des turned and left him.

Joel had spent much time thinking about why he was in the colony. He, too, had run away from England and met Hetty the week he arrived in Sydney. They had a whirlwind romance, and he married her a month later. They stayed at her mother and stepfather's house in Sydney for some years. All their children had been born there. Now they were living on a secluded farm, far away from the morally corrupt people in Sydney. Joel did everything he could to keep the evils of the world away from his family. That his family now included emotionally wounded girls just like Carly had never really occurred to him before. When he returned that night, he knew he had to reveal everything to Hetty. He also wanted to continue his conversation with Hector. Twice now, they had been interrupted. Des's comment that he blamed God worried him. He knew God was not responsible but did not know why. He knew God didn't work that way. He thought, "Hopefully, Hector will be able to answer that question."

~

Hector was waiting for Joel at the wharf on his return home.

"All good, Hector?" Joel asked as he threw the rope.

"Yes, sir, all good; just checking you are, sir." Hector put his hand out to assist his master onto the jetty.

Casey overheard the interaction between the two. He liked both fellows. Joel had come home empty-handed, so Casey didn't stay. Joel cast off the rope and pushed the boat back into the channel. There was little current, but the breeze blew up the river, catching the small sloop and quickly carrying it out of sight.

Hector was keen to continue their conversation. "I thought we might talk as we walked, sir. I know you have questions. Did you see Des?" Hector's gentle concern gave Joel the confidence to ask the burning question.

Joel nodded. Thankfully, Des had revealed everything to Hector.

They walked but ended up on the verandah at the house. "Hector, why do bad things happen? Why do girls like Franny get abused, and those like Des's sister get murdered? Why does God allow that sort of thing to happen? I don't want to believe in a God that doesn't care. It is why we're here, locked away in our little secluded world. I'm trying to keep them all safe. I'm trying to shut out the evil, and I'd do anything to stop them from being hurt like Carly was."

"Sir, I shall answer that, but I will begin by asking a question. Do you remember the Creation story in the Bible?"

Joel nodded, intrigued at Hector's tangent questions.

"Do you remember the bit about the snake tempting Eve with the fruit?"

Again, Joel nodded.

"Have you got a moment now, or can we finish this later?" Hector asked.

"Now, Hector, I need to know why, and I need to know right now. Tell me it all." Joel pointed to the chairs on the verandah.

Hector took a seat and bowed his head in prayer. It was fine to believe for himself, but to actually put it into a few words was hard. He needed the Lord's help to explain this to Joel in a way he could fully understand.

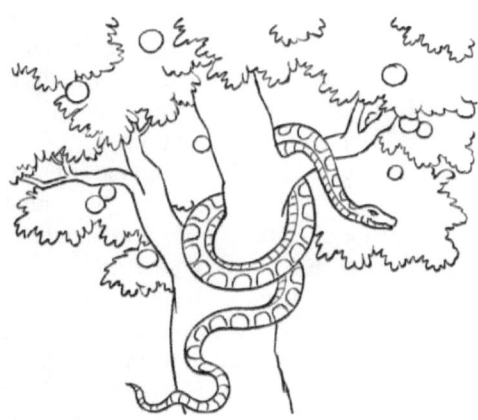

Chapter 4   Explaining the Fallen World

*H*ector felt somewhat uncomfortable sitting with Joel as an equal. He was content to be a servant. "Sir, rather than answer your questions, may I explain it as it was told to me?"

Joel nodded. "Of course, as long as you tell me." Joel felt like he was about to hear something so profound that it would be life-changing, and he wasn't wrong.

Fran brought out mugs of tea for them, and Hector invited her to join them. She sat on the verandah, leaning against the railing and listening. Hetty heard them talking and quietly sat beside Joel in the unique rocking chair he had made for her. Hector wished all the girls could listen to what he was about to say, but he was delighted that Fran had come. She, in particular, needed to hear his words. Fran was growing very dear to him. She no longer disappeared like a startled rabbit when he was around. She had even sought him out for assistance a few times. Once the four of them were settled, he took a deep breath. He knew this was probably the most crucial conversation he would ever have with them. "If I may, I shall start before the beginning," he said.

Joel nodded assent to the strange comment, then sipped his tea.

Hector started with the written word. Gone was his hesitation or his subservience. "The Bible starts with 'In the beginning', but God existed even before that. I won't get into the theology of that as I can't quite grasp the minutia myself. I shall give you five points to remember. And it was these that my grandmother taught me, and then she explained them to me. If you only believe this, it will explain much, including sin and why bad things happen."

The three sat quietly, hanging on his following words.

Hector continued, "The five points are God, Man, God and then two questions, 'What if you do?' and 'What if you don't?' If you can remember those things, it's the beginning of the understanding of God's story and why we are here. Now, I will explain what they mean. First, God existed before the Creation. He made the Heavens and the Earth and made it perfect and sin-free. This creation included all the Angels in his realm; that's the story in Genesis. One of those angels was Lucifer, and he rebelled and was cast out of Heaven with a third of the angels. Until then, God's Created realm was untainted by sin."

Joel gazed hard at Hector, unbelieving at what he was hearing. He had sat in church for years, and no one had explained it like this.

Hector smiled, "Then, next, we come to Man. God made mankind, us. We were also made perfect, which often surprises many, but it's true. The Earth was in balance, as was nature, with no floods, fires, earthquakes, and especially no sickness or sin, etcetera. As I said, the earth was in balance and good. Then, God made us a helpmate in the form of a woman. Someone to work beside him, not to be trampled on or superior to us. Equal but different. Man and woman were created for each other, complementary, and everything was still good. Then comes the but! Then mankind sinned. They were given just one rule, but they broke it. We turned, and still turn, our backs on God and go our own wilful way. Genesis tells us that the snake appeared to Eve and tempted her with the fruit of the Tree of Knowledge. Adam was not innocent, as he would have known the source of the delightful food he was being offered. Remember, God had put them in the Garden of Eden and told them they both could eat from any tree but one. They could have chosen the fruit of Eternal Life but didn't; they chose to eat from the Tree of Knowledge. That is how sin entered our world. They were tempted and fell for Satan's lie. Mankind's will from then on did not follow God's will. Bad things started happening, and the earth was put out of kilter." Hector paused to see they all followed so far.

"Go on, Hector," Franny prompted. "What happened then?"

Hector smiled at her in such a way that Hetty caught her breath. She saw his eyes soften as he looked at her, and his smile was so loving. While still gazing at Fran, Hector replied with a grin, "God gave us a way back to Him. Again, it's told in Genesis. 3 verse 15, '*And I will put enmity between thee and the woman, and between thy seed and her seed; it shall bruise thy head, and thou shalt bruise his heel.*'" Hector quoted the Genesis passage without even referring to the Bible. He continued, saying, "It was Jesus that God was talking about. That was so long ago, thousands of years before Jesus was born as a man. Only by putting our complete faith in Him, that is, Jesus, can we become right with God again. By doing this, we get washed clean and made like new." Hector watched as Fran's eyes grew wide with amazement, but she stayed silent. He directed his words to her. "Jesus came to earth as God's Son, born of a woman as a tiny baby. He lived as one of us until His task was complete. That task was Jesus's death and resurrection; He defeated the evil brought into the world by Satan. That's the meaning of the verse I quoted. Remember, Satan himself was a fallen angel who rebelled against God, so he, too, believes in God, so it takes more than just believing or acknowledging God exists. We have to do or live it too. The Devil, Satan, or Lucifer as he was first named, has been kept blind to the fact that Jesus' death and resurrection has already defeated him. Satan thinks that he still has power over us, but that is because we choose to give it to him. He lost that final battle when Jesus rose from the grave and conquered death. Jesus sits with God in Heaven as we speak." Hector paused again and checked that they were all following his words. Encouraged that they were, Hector continued, "There is a third divine being, the Holy Spirit. He is the Spirit of God and is with us all the time. He is known as the Comforter. When Jesus was alive, it was at his Baptism in the Jordan River that the three were together at once. Listeners heard God's voice, the dove of the Spirit was seen, and Jesus was Baptised. They are the three aspects of God at once. Jesus promised that He would be with us always; this is how He does it." Again, he paused.

Joel said, "Go on, don't stop now. What comes next? What are the questions again?"

Hector smiled. "Ahh, the two questions are easy. They are, 'What if you do?' and 'What if you don't?' The answer to these questions is the fork in the road of our lives." Hector dared to look at Fran. "In our lives today, we have only one choice, for most of us naturally walk the road away from God. We each have to make this decision for ourselves. It's not hard to make; we either follow Jesus, and He forgives us, or we reject Him and follow our selfish ways. Every decision you will ever make will fall under one of those two choices, for or against Him." Hector paused and glanced at the stunned faces of Joel and Hetty. He had already said much of this to Franny in snatches over the past weeks. He'd not wanted to inundate her with too much information, but now he was drawing his words together.

Fran's face shone back at his. She had made her decision but had not yet told Hector. She wished to follow. She had already prayed the prayer of forgiveness, and she felt washed clean as he had said she would. Clean! For the first time ever, she felt clean.

Joel reached and took Hetty's hand. "I know which way my decision will be. But Hector, can you explain why bad things happen? It still doesn't quite make sense. Why do things happen to some and not others? Des and I saw the same thing but chose different paths."

Hector's eyes again fell on Fran; then he turned to Joel. "Yes, sir, but it will be hard to hear. Again, I don't fully understand it, but we are victims of sin in the world. But that is not God's will for us. God allows everyone free will, which includes the sinful desires of mankind." Hector looked back to Fran. "When a man abuses a woman, he takes his physical desires out on her, but she has no say." His eyes had not shifted from Fran's beautiful glowing face. "The lust of the flesh is strong in a man and needs to be controlled, but when sin overtakes them, they give in to those desires. The Bible teaches that the physical joining of a man and a woman should be holy and good; often, it is not. It becomes abusive and controlling; this is not God's will. I can and do say that, without a doubt, this is not God's will to laud it over any other person in any form." Hector's compassion for Fran was clearly visible on his face.

Joel and Hetty noticed his gaze had hardly left her, and she didn't mind at all.

Hector answered Joel by talking to Fran. "Fran, what happened to you is horrific and not God's will. Please, do not hold all men responsible. One day you will find a godly man who will love you for who you are." He didn't trust himself not to betray his feelings for her, so he turned to Joel. "Sir, what you witnessed as a boy was wrong, but you are no more responsible for what happened than Des. You fought to be released and to assist Carly. A child cannot hope to have done anything against such evil men. Your son Oliver could not be released from my hold if I dared to grab him as you were. Mankind is evil, as we are all born in sin, and this is exhibited in many ways. Sin takes many forms; lust, murder, greed, drunkenness, debauchery, theft, etcetera; even passive observance is a sin. Sir, you did not do that; neither of you did; you fought as hard as you both could. Most sins are covered pretty well in the ten commandments. If you do not speak out against wrong, you may as well approve it. Sir, you fought for her, as did Des. Take comfort in that. Know that she is now with our Lord and is safe. Des cannot forgive himself for his sister's death, but he is not responsible for it. We talked about it the night he stayed. His life has spiralled out of control because of his hate for those youths and himself."

Hector's last words finally made sense to Joel. Des blamed himself; he had said so. Joel nodded; he knew the wall of hate was still there. Joel admitted quietly, "For me too! I still want vengeance, Hector. I want to know they are all dead, and I don't even know their names. It still eats me up when I think of what they did to her."

Hector quoted another Bible verse. "Romans 12 verse 19 says, *'Dearly beloved, avenge not yourselves, but rather give place unto wrath: for it is written, Vengeance is mine; I will repay, saith the Lord.'* Sir, one day they will stand before the Lord for judgement and must answer for their crimes. He knows exactly who they are. One day we will be there before Him too, and also be judged. However, if you have asked for forgiveness for your wrongdoings and turned your life around to follow Jesus, we are judged with that in mind. We must live as holy and righteously as possible, asking to be forgiven, not just once but often; then, our judgement will be of forgiveness rather than chastisement. That is part of the answer to the questions. It is the consequence, if you like, of mankind's sin. As those men grow older, they may one day ask for forgiveness for what they have done." Her eyes fell again on Fran. "Forgiveness for those who have sinned against you is hard but freeing. Holding on to those hurts only stunts your own growth and faith. You must hand those hurts to God and let Him deal with them. Let yourself be free."

Fran's eyes were tear-filled. She nodded her acceptance. She finally felt safe and knew she had to take the next step. That was to trust a man. She slowly put out her hand to Hector. She had not willingly touched a man for many months, yet she knew Hector would not hurt her.

Hector gently took her hand and caressed the back of her capable hand with his thumb. "Fran, we men can be caring and loving but must earn your trust again. Mr and Mrs Walker have given all you girls a chance to make a new life. Here, you are all physically safe, but until you release your own hurts to the Lord, you will never be able to accept that total healing He is offering you." As much as Hector wanted to pull her into his arms and show her his own feelings, it was the last thing she needed. It went against everything he had just said. For her to have reached out to touch him was the first step. One day at a time! He would wait for her. With a very gentle press, he reluctantly released her hand.

Hetty had sat all this time silently. She now knew a little about Des and his sister's murder. Joel had revealed more of the story after Des's first visit, but she felt there was more to it. She knew that Joel was going to see him that day. Their meeting had brought it all up again. Nothing Hector had said was new to her, but for some reason, this time, it just made sense. She was grinning and didn't know why, but she now felt at peace.

Hector may have dropped Fran's hand, but he only had eyes for her, and she was not pulling away from him as usual. She had even edged closer to him.

Hetty glanced over to her husband; Joel sat gazing at the river. He still held her hand but was deep in thought.

They sat in comfortable silence until Joel turned to Hector and said, "I want it, Hector! I want that soul-freeing peace. I want the path I choose from now on to be the one that leads me to Heaven. And I want to continue for you to teach us all too. I hope the other girls will listen, but I won't force them. I hope they will understand if you tell them as you have told us today. More than that, I want this place to become a healing haven for all the wounded girls we come across." He turned to his wife. "Hetty, my dear one, I can't do this alone, but we can do it together." He waited for her reply.

Hetty took his hands in hers. "Joel, what Hector told us today is not new to me, but I had never understood it so clearly. It was like it was all new. I wanted to help the girls, but I had no reason as to why. I just knew it was the right thing to do. I was not abused, nor did I see any actual crimes as you did, but my compassion was stirred when I met Martha. It was the same with Charity, then Franny and the others." Hetty flicked her gaze to Fran. "I want to protect you, sweet girl. I would be delighted if we can all make this place a haven for the hurt and a healing place for their souls while helping them." Hetty met each smiling face in turn.

Hector knew that he now had to warn them about spiritual attacks. He gave a brief outline to be on guard, and he had just told them to be careful, especially over the next few days. He said, "It could be anything from physical attacks, like accidents, petty squabbling, anything like that." When he opened his mouth to say something else, he froze. A piercing scream, closely followed by another, shattered the day's silence.

The four fled to assist in whatever calamity had occurred. Bess and Manda had been stuffing the top row of the wall cladding. A big snake had poked its ugly head from under the roof shingles. It was only a python, but the fright had made the elevated trestle unstable, and both girls had fallen. Manda was lying at an awkward angle; her leg was pinned under the thick slab of wood they had been standing on, and Bess was sitting up, holding her wrist. Both girls were weeping.

Fran and Hetty assisted Bess up as she was still sitting on the timber slab that pinned Manda.

Bess had a cut on her forehead and cried out in pain when she released her wrist. Fran stood with her arm around Bess while the others extricated Manda from under the plank. She was covered with overturned buckets of wadding. Bess pointed to the top of the wall, and the giant black and yellow python was still there, observing the activities on the ground.

Hector and Joel removed the scaffolding and debris, and Hetty checked Manda's legs. It didn't seem like she had broken anything, but they knew she would have a considerable bruise; she had a very sore ankle. Her leg hurt too. She was now sitting up; Faith and a flour-covered Charity were on either side of her.

Hetty went back to check on Bess. She had broken her wrist as it was twisted at a weird angle, but the bone had not poked through the skin. Hetty knew she had to set it, and it would hurt. The girls had walked Bess to the steps with Fran on one side and Hope on the other. Bess held her wrist out towards Hetty. Tears were rolling down her cheeks, but she knew that the angle it was at meant disaster unless Hetty straightened it. Bess leaned into Hope's shoulder and tried to relax. Fighting the pain would not achieve anything. She had had enough of that in her life already.

Hetty carefully felt the break and set the bones as gently as possible.

She could feel when the bones were straight. She had learned to do this when Joel fractured his in the same way. He had broken his wrist when they were building one of the out-sheds. Either she set it, or he could lose his hand, as she knew it may have started dying by the time they reached Parramatta; there, the doctor may have wanted to cut it off. Joel had insisted she try. She had Hector make him a rawhide leather splint, and she had bandaged this on, so he could still use his fingers. The splint still sat on the top of the medicine cupboard.

Hetty sent Oliver into the medicine cupboard for the splint and bandages. At nine, he was the only one of the children to be allowed into the precious supply of medicines and bandages. Hetty had shown him as she felt he was old enough to be responsible should he need to get anything. The cupboard contained a 'go' bag, as she called it. It contained bandages, tweezers, a knife and a small bottle of brandy. She also asked him to bring the leather splint. Clara took the two younger children back inside and away from Bess and the trauma occurring outside. Hetty reset the bone as gently as she could. Bess yelled, then passed out while Hetty was moving it. Hetty could now make sure that the bones were straight with her unresponsive. The break in her wrist was a little further up her arm than Joel's had been, but the splint would still work as his arm was larger. Bess was still out cold as Oliver arrived back with the leather splint. Jane appeared from her shed and brought a smoothed, thin stave that could be used as a top brace. This would immobilise the entire lower arm. By the time Bess came around, her wrist was fully bound and now in a sling.

Meanwhile, Manda was hoisted into Hector's arms and carried into her bed.

Joel came and assisted Bess, who had roused, and with Hetty's help, they walked her into the cabin, with the other girls opening doors and clearing the way of any trip points. She had chosen to walk rather than have Joel carry her and possibly bump her arm. They stopped a few times as she became dizzy, but the two girls eventually lay on their beds.

Hetty sent out the men and then checked Manda's leg to ensure she had no breaks. She didn't, but the cut on her leg needed stitching. The go bag had a clean needle and roll of fine thread in it. Hetty washed the wound and saw that it was a straight-edged cut. She wiped off the blood and then warned Manda that she would douse her leg with a slosh of brandy, and then she did the same to a length of thread and her hands. Now ready, two girls held Manda's arms, and Jane held her leg still.

Hetty knew she had to get the cut stitched as quickly as she could.

Manda expected that she would be screaming when the needle dug in, but even though she had her teeth clenched, she didn't cry out.

Hetty tried to be as quick as possible, but it took quite a few minutes to do all twenty stitches down the long gash. Hetty then noted a large splinter embedded in Manda's leg further over as she sewed. She would need to extricate that and cleanse it as well. She would also need to lance it to get it out properly. The 'go' bag had a pair of tweezers and a sharp scalpel. Manda lay still, muttering while Hetty ministered to her wounds, Manda gasped as the knife sliced into the splinter, but she knew it had to be removed. The surgery was now complete; Manda then wept. It had hurt, but Hetty's care and compassion were new to Manda. She was still finding love, and sympathy was hard to comprehend. She had battled for everything in life; this to be freely offered was new to her and hard to accept. She had blossomed in the months she had been with them, as had most of the girls. Hetty had learned that Manda's abuse was one of neglect. The poor girl had never experienced a loving home, a gentle parental touch or a caring family.

Jane had reached out to Trixi and Agnes to assist them, but Jane herself remained a closed book, as did Clara. They had rejected all attempts to get close. They both wanted to stay on the fringe of any activity but were always ready to assist anyone.

Hetty knew Jane had been hurt somehow and hoped she would open up to someone one day. Hetty left the two injured girls to the caring ministrations of their friends. Fran followed Hetty out and into the kitchen. All work had been put on hold for the remainder of the day. Charity left with a tray full of mugs of sweet tea for all the girls. Hetty washed her bloody hands in a basin just outside the kitchen door.

Hector and Joel were inside, and she could hear them talking. Hetty and Fran joined them. Both men stood at their entry and held out chairs for them. Fran chose the chair next to Hector.

As they seated themselves, Hector said, "Case in point, as we were talking about Satan's attacks. I hate to say it, but we now must be on our guard. I imagine that these attacks may increase if we are all firm in our willingness to change. I just hoped we would have had more time to prepare everyone." Hector blew out his cheeks in frustration. "Trust it to be a snake!"

Fran reached out and covered his hand with hers. His eyes fell on it then he met her gaze and smiled.

Chapter 5   The Harvest Begins

*H*etty was the first to notice a change in Franny's confidence. Some months had passed since the day when the girls had fallen from the scaffolding. Their wounds had healed, and Fran now often sang as she worked. Charity noticed and asked Hetty what had changed. Hetty suggested that she ask her for herself. Hopefully, Fran would share what had made the difference.

Hetty had noticed that Joel would meet with Hector for about fifteen minutes each morning. They spent this time in prayer. Joel was also beginning to cast off the blue devils that had plagued him for many years. The day after Hector's revelation, Hetty and he had walked along the riverbank; he had told her in full of the meeting with Des in Windsor and had poured out every detail about that fateful day when they were boys. He had spared her nothing, as she needed to understand. He was gutted that Des's life had spiralled out of control due to that incident.

Now comprehending the situation, Hetty realised Des needed them. "Can we invite him to come, or isn't he allowed?" Hetty asked tentatively.

Joel had been unsure about his friend's welcome. "I'm not really sure he'll want to talk to me again after my last visit." Joel wished that he and Hector could sit Des down and have a talk with him. "I suggested to Hector that we both go and chat with him; however, he refused. He said God would open a door when the time was right, but we must be prepared as he expects Des to fight hard. He thought that part of his problem was that he wanted to admonish himself for what happened. Des said much the same to me, so I think Hector is correct." Joel stopped walking and took Hetty in his arms. He just needed to hold her. While enfolded, she lay her cheek against his chest, thinking. They stayed in the embrace for some time. As Joel held her, he spoke softly. "Hetty, I was running away from the world when I brought you here. Your mother knew what being ostracised was like. She was an emancipated convict herself, but I wanted our children kept away from the tainted evils of the world. We saw what the people in Sydney were like, and it wasn't good. But I didn't understand that I was running from sin. I just wanted you to all be safe."

Hetty drew back a little. "We are safe, sweetheart," she said. "Only now we know we are safe in God's hands too. We are also doing His work. We didn't even realise that, but this farm is just the beginning for these girls. I don't want to hold them here, as they need to face life, but here they are secure while they heal, and they can learn. Even Franny is coming out of her shell. I found her laughing at one of Hector's silly stories last week."

Joel pulled away further. "He likes her, you know. But he won't make a move until she's ready. I think he'd like to marry her."

Hetty nodded. "She's come a long way, Joel, but if she has warmed to anyone, then Hector is the one person who has a special place in her life. However, I'm not sure if he's made it through to her heart yet." Hetty slipped her arms up and around his neck. "She has not said anything to me but shown she cares for him. A touch of his hand here and there is a huge step for her." After a reassuring kiss, they continued their walk and discussed the upcoming harvest of honey.

Jane had been busy making small barrels for the sweet substance. Each ten-inch barrel held just under two gallons. She had used all the timber she had brought, and the silver wattle was now dry enough to cut and shape. She cut the staves and then shaped each one to a rough taper; as each of the steel loops was a slightly different measurement, the staves had to be made to measure each individual barrel.

One of the problems Hetty previously had was extracting the honey from the combs. Last year, they only had one wooden hive; now, they had many. They would progressively harvest the new honey as they sold the previous batch in one consignment. Jane had made a large half barrel where they placed the crushed comb. It had small holes that drained into another collection tub. Once the honey was drained from the wax, the gooey liquid was then strained and poured into small kegs, then sealed and sold; the residue Jane planned to be poured into another large barrel and turned into honey vinegar.

Hetty explained that her honey was mainly white box honey, which was sweet and smooth. She didn't like the dark gum honey, but the black tea tree honey was good medicinally. It was also much thicker, so they had set up some hives near stands of tea trees.

Jane explained that honey vinegar was a delicacy as far as varieties of vinegar go. She explained how to make it.

Hetty looked puzzled. "Jane, dear, we do not wish to make alcoholic beverages here. Not even mead, and this is the first step to making mead wine, is it not?"

Jane smiled. "I have no wish to make alcohol either, ma'am, but to make vinegar from honey, you have to basically make mead first, then allow it to be exposed to the native cultures to sour the wine. Then it needs to sit for up to two years. Ideally, it is sold in glass bottles, but I have an ample supply of silver wattle and can make tiny tubs for the vinegar unless we can source any used bottles. If we could get those, I would then need corks."

With another product in production, they needed a storage building. Hector, Joel and the boys set to source timber to construct a supply room. Everyone had their jobs to do, and the farm prospered as everyone pulled their weight.

On a trip to Windsor, Hector met with Des; he was not too chatty but offered to assist in constructing the building. His boss was to be away for a week the next month, and he would be able to come for a few days to help with the heavy frame of the construction. That gave Joel a few weeks to source materials, set the foundations, and prepare the timbers. They had already chosen a site just above the last flood level. However, a big flood would still reach it. There was a small knoll with a flat area halfway down to the wharf where the original home had sat.

Hetty and Joel began to spend more time praying together. Each night before they slept, they now had a prayer time before turning the lamp down. If there was a decision to make throughout the day, they sought each other out and prayed about it.

In the days since Hector's talk, they had discussed their long-term plan for the farm. Before then, Joel had floated along with no goal. Money was no problem for them, as Hetty's mother had left them ample funds. Joel and Hetty's decision to bring in some emotionally wounded girls had changed the ethos of the place. Each girl had brought more skills and talents to the farm. Joel loved this. Hetty's idea of a cottage industry farm was now taking shape.

All but one of Fran's bee skeps were full and getting ready to harvest. However, that was not the harvest that Hector was really interested in. His words on the day of the accident had fallen on fertile ground. Joel's subtle change in attitude was now of friendship rather than the boss. He had even asked him to call him by name. They often talked while repairing a fence or herding the cattle or goats.

Hetty found solace with Fran. She was the closest thing she had to a friend. The girl was also blooming under the love and protection she had found on Loganberry Farm.

Hector had told Franny that Des was coming to help with the build but didn't know when he would arrive. She was to feel free to turn to him if she was afraid. Hopefully, one day she would. He would bide his time.

He didn't have to wait for long. Fran was down at the wharf when Des arrived. She had been helping to bring loads of baskets for sale in the market. She had come in the cart with Hector and Faith, and the three of them were busy unloading the full crates from the wagon as the boat pulled in. None saw that Des was on board until he jumped off. With a roaring laugh, he loudly greeted everyone.

Fran jumped and shrank towards Hector.

Des stepped away from her, forgetting the girl's fear of men. He apologised, gave a quick bow and quickly left them to load their stock.

Fran was now encircled in Hector's protective arms with her head hidden in his shoulder.

As Des walked up the hill, Hector said, "He's gone, Franny," expecting her to pull away. She didn't immediately do so; she stayed with her head hidden. He felt her move slightly.

Fran looked up at him. "I feel safe here, Hector." Her voice was hardly more than a murmur, and he wasn't sure he had even heard her correctly, but she still didn't draw away.

Hector replied quietly. "Then stay as long as you wish. I will always be here for you, Franny, and whenever you want," He started affectionately rubbing her lower back. He was sure she could hear his heart almost galloping with joy.

"That might be often, Hector." The cornflower blue eyes that met his glinted with amusement. "Would you mind?"

Hector's heart was already beating a tattoo; it now skipped with joy. "Do you mean that?" he asked excitedly. He felt her nod. "I'd be delighted." He held her a little tighter.

"So would I, Hector." He wanted to stay like this forever, but Faith and Casey had been watching them. Her hands that had sat on his chest up until now soon wrapped themselves around him.

Casey cleared his throat. "Have you two decided not to help? Poor Faith can't lift all this by herself, you know."

Reluctantly, Hector relaxed his hold on Fran, and they turned to load the stock.

Casey also had a large box to unload and some lumber and smithed hardware needed by Joel to construct the new building. There was also a case of empty ginger beer bottles. "Got no idea why you want these, but Des has been collecting them for you. There's a bag of used corks, too," Casey said.

Hector hopped into the small craft and manhandled the crates onto the wharf. Faith and Franny pulled the heavy box onto the jetty. They hastily loaded the new stock into the boat, and Casey set off again.

Hector and the girls managed to get the heavy crates onto the back of the cart. There was much giggling, but they eventually loaded everything. Hector folded up the back of the tray and shot home the bolts.

Faith had climbed up on the seat; she sat to the side, realising that Fran would now wish to sit next to Hector. He walked around to the front and assisted Fran in, pulling himself up after her. He took the reins and set off to the building site. They would leave the box there so they didn't have to move it again. The three managed to heave off the big chest and then unload the lumber, but it took time.

Faith jumped off the cart as they passed the house, but Fran offered to assist Hector in grooming the horse. Hector wondered if she knew the effect she had on him. She probably didn't, but he didn't mind. He may have sown the seed of his interest, but she still had to make the first move. He knew that every step had to be at her pace. He drove the cart into the stable yard and was about to hop down when Fran moved quickly and secured the horse to the hitching post. They quickly unharnessed him. He had not done much work, so he didn't need a brush down. Hector took him into his stable then they pushed the cart back into its corner. He was about to return to his other duties when he turned to find Fran standing a little closer than he expected. Her request stunned him.

"Hector, will you kiss me, please? It was nice in your arms, but I want to know how I will react if you get closer. I won't let any other man that near to me, but Hector, if anything is to come of, well, us, I need to know before anything starts that we can't stop." She put her hand on his arm.

His eyes dropped at her gentle touch. He covered her hand with his own. Her unexpected question had made him gasp. "Are you sure, Franny? I've wanted to do this for so long, but I don't wish to do anything to upset you."

Her eyes sparkled, and a smile hovered around her lips. "Yes, I'm sure."

He slid an arm around her waist and drew her close.

"You won't upset me, Hector. Please…" She was now entirely in his arms and gazing up at him expectantly.

Hector lowered his head, brushed his lips gently over hers, and then lifted them from her, awaiting her reaction.

She smiled. "Nice, but I meant a proper kiss, Hector."

Stunned, he said, "Are you really sure?"

She nodded.

Hector accepted her invitation to fulfil his dreams and kiss her rosebud lips. He lowered his head again and gave her a proper kiss, as she called it. As he did so, her arms snaked around his neck as she stepped closer. Neither drew apart. The kiss deepened, and they both lost track of time.

Hector was about to let his hands wander but realised whom he was holding. He slowly relaxed his embrace, allowing her to move back a little. He was sure she could hear his heart racing. "Like that?" he asked with a grin. "I hope it was better than just 'nice' this time," he chuckled. He had thoroughly enjoyed himself.

"Hmm, yes, just like that, and I liked it too." Her eyes were like shining blue lights. "I liked it very much, Hector. I feel so safe with you. I know you will never hurt me." Rather than pull away, she stepped closer again and rested her head on his chest with her arms around him. "So safe that I could stay here forever."

Hector intended to take any relationship slowly; therefore, his following words were as much a surprise for him as for her. "So will you? Will you stay with me and marry me? We will have to live here as I'm bonded to them for life, but it's a good life, Franny."

"It will be a good life anywhere with you, Hector. And I'm happy to make my life here too. But are you serious? You know my background; I'm soiled goods, dirty, used, abused and unwanted."

Hector brushed his fingers over her cheek. "And my sweet, you are forgiven and washed clean too. Franny, my dearest love, you don't even know why I was convicted." Hector wondered how she would take the news that he had been sent here for killing someone. He also knew that he might never let her know if he didn't tell her now, and she needed to know.

"I don't want to know, Hector. Whatever you did, you too have been forgiven, don't forget that." Her blue eyes were still sparkling with happiness.

He adored the way her mouth moved as she spoke. Her lips were so expressive. He loved everything about her. Simply everything! Hector blew out his cheeks and said, "I have to tell you, Fran. Then it's up to you to decide. I won't hold you to anything, but I need you to know everything about me before you answer me." He pushed her away from him and sat her on a bag of grain. Hector was not a man to beat around the bush, so he came straight out with his conviction. "Franny, I killed a man. Admittedly it was in self-defence, but he's dead, and I did it."

She realised he was right; she needed to know. "Oh! You had better tell me, Hector, but it won't change my mind. You are no longer that man." She patted the grain sack, and he sat next to her. Close but not too close.

Her lips were still reddened by his kiss. A curl had escaped and sat on her cheek. He was tempted to tuck it behind her ear. He swallowed hard as he shook off that desire. Without further ado, his story poured out. "I had been walking home from work one day when three men set upon me.

We fought hard as they attacked me. I used my fists to the best of my ability, and one man fell. Unknown to me, he hit his head when he did. The other two assailants escaped. It all happened so fast. I fled home, pleased that I had escaped alive but not knowing what had occurred to the fallen man. He died."

Fran was spellbound. "But why did you get arrested? You did nothing wrong. He died, but you didn't kill him." She took his hand in both of hers. Looking directly at him, she said, "Keep going." Realising there was more to tell.

He nodded and continued his story. "I later discovered that one of the three men was the mayor's son from a nearby area. I had not recognised him, but he apparently knew me, as did one other man; he was the ringleader. I still have no idea why they set upon me, but it was the mayor's son who fell and later died. They twisted the story and said to the magistrate, who was the dead man's uncle, by the way, that I had attacked them." He frowned at his retelling. Somehow, it didn't sound so bad when he told her. He shrugged and continued. "When the constable came some hours later and questioned me, my mother, who was ill, had just finished patching me up, so I had only a few bruises and cuts to show for the fight. She was used to my cuts and scratches, as my job was assisting the forester on a significant local estate in Kent. I had only come from Scotland to help on the estate eighteen months before. Mother had joined me just weeks after my arrival. The Duchess there, well, she is Scottish too, and she was from my town and, being mother's cousin, she knew of our need. A week After the incident, I was arrested."

Hector paused for a while, thinking of the man who visited his mother. He shook off the uncomfortable thought and said, "You see, my father deserted my mother before I was born. She presumed he died somewhere overseas as he never returned for her." He shrugged. "Anyway, I needed work, so I took this job. I felled trees, coppiced woodland, and repaired briar hedges and dry rock boundaries at home; therefore, I had those forestry skills. I am generally an outdoor man, so I used my arms a lot. My weapon of choice was just myself. However, I rarely fought, but I'm not a weak man. My work made me strong. That may have been why I was attacked, for sport. You see, I had found out some of the antics of the young fellows in the local village were, well, not honourable, trust me. You know what young men are like in that situation. Egging each other and pushing them to do things they otherwise would not even consider."

Fran nodded and wiggled closer to him. She wanted to feel protected again. She snuggled under his arm as he finished his story. "So, they turned the tables on you, and you were arrested."

"Yes, in essence, yes, just like that." Her understanding of the saga was not yet complete. "Fran, there's more to the story. The mayor's son's friend came and spoke to me. He apologised and tried to give me money to go away. I thought the magistrate would just dismiss the case, so I refused. By then, I had been released and was back at home. Some months had passed since the incident, and by now, Mother's sickness left her bedridden, and I was the only person she had to look after her. However, a man occasionally visited her, although he had not come since the attack." Hector shook his head to make those memories flee. He had seen their activities.

Hector paused. "Mother died the day after I was rearrested. I was found guilty, and within weeks, I was on board a convict ship bound for Sydney. I could not even go to her funeral. In a way, I'm pleased she didn't know the outcome. The duchess arranged her funeral for me as they were related. I heard that my mother was buried on the estate where I worked. I had no other living family nearby, and the dead man's friend, Mitchell, had much more to lose than I did, not just money but also a position in society and family. I had nothing. At home in Scotland, even though I was young, I also worked as a preacher for the Church of Scotland. That was initially to please my grandmother, but I realised I believed what I was saying. However, it also meant I was not at home often, which suited me just fine." Hector could not yet tell her about his home in Scotland and all he had left behind. That was a story for another day.

Fran sighed. "So you took the fall for him. You sacrificed your life so that he wouldn't lose his." Fran lifted his hand and held it to her cheek.

Hector gazed down at her. "Sort of, you see, he had lost his best friend. He knows the truth and has to live with that knowledge all his life. I have a clean conscience but am convicted of murder; I will have the tag of a murderer all my days. The Lord knows the truth, though. I thought that was all I needed until now, but I wished you to know. No, I need you to know that before committing to any relationship. You will be marrying a convicted murderer." The arm that he had wrapped around her pulled her closer. The trusting blue gaze that met his pulled at his heartstrings.

Fran said, "I don't care, Hector. I trust you, and from me, that is unbelievable. I was given seven years for stealing, but mine was intentional. I had heard I would be transported if I stole something valued at a shilling or more. I was in an abusive job and regularly used by the man who had employed me. I was so young, and he was so much bigger than I that I had no chance to fight back." She turned, put her head against his shoulder, and softly told him her story. "I am an orphan, an ill-begotten love child, as they called us at the orphanage. I have nothing but this to say who I am."

She pulled a much-knotted old string from down her dress, and a tiny gold key hung on it. "My mother had it around her neck when she was found. They never knew her name as she had no identification on her. She was at a hospital to give birth; then, the hospital sent me to an orphanage after she died from my birth. Matron gave it to me when I got my first placement. I had never known affection and thought that my new master touching me, as it was when it started, was him caring for me. It didn't take long before that touching went further. He attacked me violently. I had no idea what he intended to do before he… well, you know." She turned into his shoulder again, wrapping her arms around him. "Hector, I was just fourteen. It was my first placement, and I was scared. The matron had given us a very sketchy education about babies, but I knew what he kept doing to me was wrong as I had been placed there from the orphanage and was told in no uncertain terms that I could not go back no matter what. Matron told me I was a love child, but I didn't quite know what that was either. When I did find out, I didn't think it was a good name. It is a horrible name, considering my father, whoever he was, abandoned us, and my mother died giving birth to me. I had nowhere to go and no one to turn to." She touched the long string around her neck. She pushed the key back down her dress. "That key was the only thing my mother had on her when she died, but she wore no wedding ring and had not recently removed one." Her voice had a catch. "I had no other option than stay, Hector. Being born with a pretty face is a curse. He used me for a couple of years but became even more abusive as I got older. He even hit me a few times and once knocked me out. Since then, I was used as a plaything by any man who wanted me until I came here." She sniffed. "Anyway, back to my first placement. I had no choice in what he did to me, so I did the only thing I could to stop it. I stole a yard of lace-edged fabric. I made sure I was seen and arrested on the spot. I never had to return to him. In gaol, a lady named Elizabeth Fry brought me some clothing, and she asked another lady to try to protect me. All that worked while we were in Newgate Prison, and then they moved us onto the Hulks before our transport. We had more freedom there, but Hector so did the sailors and guards. I learned not to fight as I would be bashed, abused, and sometimes even tied up while they violated my body. They liked it rough, so I lay still until they had finished using me. I became like an empty shell. I tried to think of something else while… You know the rest, so I won't repeat that." She gave a half sob. She was amazed that Hector had not already pushed her away; she wrapped both arms around his waist and cuddled into him.

Her vile abuse gutted him. He held her tightly, trying to bring her comfort. He could not imagine what she had gone through. He absentmindedly stroked her cheek. He felt her take a deep breath, then heard her murmur, "Then Mrs Walker found me soon after I had lost the child and brought me here and… and, then, I met you. You were different from other men. You didn't paw me or manhandle me; you respected me and gave me space. I learned to trust you very quickly. When I am with you, I feel safe and protected. I want to feel safe like that forever." She lifted her tear-stained face to his again. "If you still want me, I'd love to marry you."

"Oh, Franny, we are a good pair, both running from the world's evils, and I praise our good Lord that we can now be together here in safety." He again accepted the invitation of her rosy lips, drawing her as close as he possibly could.

Joel had noticed that neither had reappeared after returning with the cart to the stable. There was silence as he approached the barn and saw Des waiting outside the door. Motioning for Joel to keep his voice down, Des wiggled his finger to follow him. Some distance away, Des said, "Seems Hector has won the fair lady's heart. They are inside pouring out their stories to each other. I didn't mean to listen, but I was intrigued." He shrugged and looked a little embarrassed.

"What do you mean, 'won the lady's heart'?" Joel asked, stunned.

"Short version is, he proposed, and she accepted. The long version, well, that isn't important. They are in there now, sealing the deal. I expect you will need to take them to Windsor to get hitched." Des sighed. "So, I lose another young lady."

Joel's eyes flashed with momentary anger. "Des, leave well alone; she was never yours to lose." Joel was exasperated with his bombastic friend but thrilled for his servants. With their backgrounds, they deserved any happiness they could get. "Stay here, will you."

Des nodded and watched his friend walk into the stable.

Joel wondered what his reception would be. He wasn't left to wonder for long. Joel found them tightly wrapped in each other's arms.

Soon, Des heard the sounds of three laughing adults coming from the stables, making him chuckle. Fran had turned to Hector for protection when he had arrived. Something had indeed been brewing between them for some time. Fran and Hector emerged arm in arm and smiling.

Des winced. To see others happy still hurt; hearing the laughter was one thing, but seeing them so joyous was just unpleasant. He felt like lashing out and making a nasty comment to them but held his tongue. For once, he wished them no harm. He remembered Hector's words from the last visit. Joel had said he could come, and he wanted to hear more of what Hector had started to tell him; however, he refused to admit this, even to himself. He shunned long-term relationships or any form of commitment, especially with women. He didn't mind male friends but often intentionally hurt them to keep them at arm's length. He never wished to care for another person again. It hurt too much when he lost them, and he always did.

Chapter 6   Vine Weaver's Wedding

The engagement of Hector and Fran was greeted with joy by all the residents of Loganberry Farm. Hector treated her like a lady. He would ask to take her for an evening stroll along the riverside, and he never overstepped the bounds of propriety.

Fran, who had never had such respect, was confused that he didn't touch her. She thought that he would have made a move to take her to bed or at least fondle her now that they were engaged. One day she could not hold her words. He saw a tear roll down her cheek as she turned to him and asked, "Are you having second thoughts, Hector? You have not touched me since the talk in the stable." Fran was afraid he had changed his mind. "You have not even kissed me."

Hector was surprised. "Oh no, sweetheart, but with what you have been through, I refuse to be included with those who have abused you. We shall wait until we are married before I touch you like that. Trust me, I'm finding that hard, but I respect you so much, so we will wait because I love you. I shall respect your wishes if you find the physical touch distasteful after we are married. But, sweetheart, we will work that out later. If you find the intimate side of marriage objectionable, at least I will have you near me. I love you, sweet Frances. To have you near me is what I desire in any way I can. Do you know that Frances means 'free one'? And Rea is…, well, you are my ray of sunshine."

Fran was stunned; no one had ever said that to her before. "Truly?" she asked.

Hector nodded. "Truly, you are my free ray of sunshine." He bent and gave her a quick kiss.

Franny was relieved. "That won't happen, Hector. I know what that side of marriage entails, remember. So you haven't changed your mind?" She was put at ease but asked, "Hector, can I stay with you tonight?"

Hector was a little taken aback. She did not understand how he felt about marriage. He gently explained, "No, sweetheart, for that treat, we wait until we're joined in marriage and trust me, it will be a wonderful reward." He gently took her in his arms. "I will relent and kiss you occasionally, but more than that will have to wait." His kisses quenched her desires a little but did the opposite for him; he found it hard to release her. He knew they still had to apply to be married, and as they were both convicts, he knew that permission could take months. At least he could see her all the time and even take her for walks. It was more than he could have done at home.

Fran and Hetty now sat in on the morning prayer sessions, and Des joined them when he was with them. He had even begun to ask questions. He had noticed a change in the attitude of everyone except himself; he still inflicted pain and punishment upon himself whenever he could. Hector, however, had seen a subtle difference. The brashness was beginning to subside, as were the sly remarks and jibes. He also now considered his words before he spoke.

Des had only planned to stay for a couple of days to do the minimum of work and return to his life of leisure. But Des had stayed for a week and assisted in completing the construction of the storeroom. As it was halfway to the river and should be well out of the average flood's reach, the knoll was some twenty feet lower than the house.

Hector had said nothing, but Des watched him. Even when he took Fran for a walk, they remained in full view of the house all the time, and he never did more than kiss her. Sometimes they even took one or two of the other girls or children. Des was frustrated; Hector was squeaky clean. Obnoxiously so, but you just could not help but like the man. There was something about him that was almost too good to be true. When Des overheard that Hector had been convicted of murder, he punched the air. Then he heard that he had taken the fall for someone else; Des was totally confused. His jaw dropped; why the heck would someone do that? The more he knew about Hector, the more puzzled he became.

Two days before Des returned to Windsor, his curiosity overcame him. He said to Hector, "Why? Why take the fall for someone?" Des admitted he had overheard him talking to Fran.

Hector took Des down to the wharf, then told Des what he had said to the Walkers and Fran. He repeated his five points; God; Man; God, and the two questions. When Hector then explained that bad things happened because of sin, not because God did them, Des turned and gazed at Hector. He stood, spun on his heel, and walked away without a word.

Hector let him go keeping his eyes on the river. Hopefully, he would return. Des was walking up and down the river edge, obviously battling with that revelation. Hector's attention was drawn when he heard an anguished cry. Des had been gone some time. Hector now watched him with a frown on his brow.

Des fell to his knees, then onto all four. Now leaning on his hands, Des wept. Hector could see his shoulders shaking as he sobbed. Des poured out his hurts to God. A tortured cry of "Why God, why?" drifted to Hector's ears. All this time, he had taken the fault on himself. He had always known that he could have done nothing to help his sister, yet he still carried that guilt all his life. When Hector explained that was the exact thing that Jesus had done for him, it hit hard. Jesus had fought for him and given His life for poor, unimportant Des. He also realised it was what Hector had done for his abuser. His fragile life collapsed around him. His shallow life of self-flagellation was pointless and also extremely selfish.

Hector let him wallow in his self-pity for some fifteen minutes before hoisting himself up and going to him. Des was now in a foetal position on the ground, and he was still lamenting his pointless life and the death of his sister. Hector walked over slowly and silently lowered himself to Des's side. He sat quietly with just a hand resting on Des's shoulder. The sobbing stilled, and the silence grew.

"I stuffed up my life, Hector, big time," Des eventually uttered.

Hector smiled; his words had hit home. Des would need many more talks but needed a listening, non-judgemental friend. Hector sat silently, waiting for him to be ready to talk.

Des slowly pulled himself up. "What comes next? How do I dig myself out of the grave hole I have buried myself into all these years? How did Joel deal with it?" Des pleadingly begged Hector to answer his questions and tried to remove the eternal ache from his heart.

While Hector sat beside Des, he prayed silently about what to say next. What were the words Des needed to hear now? The word forgiveness came to his mind. He subtly nodded at what he knew was God's instruction to him. Des did not only have to forgive those who had done the crime, but he had to ask for forgiveness for himself. The conversation that followed outlined what he needed to do. But his first suggestion was that Des was required to forgive the youths who had perpetrated the crime that caused his sister's death. This atrocity would be by far the hardest thing for him to achieve. He had carried that hatred for decades and now must release it. Although Hector knew Des had made the first move, it would take time. The deep discussion continued. Hector was now answering Des's question rather than imparting more information. "You must forgive, Des. Both them and yourself, only then can you move on."

"I can't, Hector! How can I do that?"

Hector replied, "You can and you must. Do you think that God will let them off scot-free?" Des shook his head. "Then leave it to Him."

More questions followed. An hour later, they slowly returned to the house. Joel and Hetty had watched the saga unfold from inside the front room. They knew that Hector's gentle words would break through, whereas Joel's angry ones bounced off him.

Des returned to Windsor a changed man.

Fran had even hugged him. She could see that the brashness he had surrounded himself with had been a shield to keep the world from reaching him. She knew that feeling all too well.

~

Over the next three months, Des returned often. He would collect the stock personally and stay a night on each trip. He could not get enough of the family now; with each visit, another layer peeled off the barrier and false bravado he had built around himself for so long.

Finally, permission for the wedding to proceed arrived. The new church being built in Windsor was to be the venue. It needed to be completed as the walls were only half-built, but weddings and other services were already held there.

On the first week of September 1821, Hector Macdougal took Frances Rea to be his lawfully wedded wife. The church could not be consecrated until finished, but Reverend Samuel Marsden solemnised their marriage. Everyone from the farm had travelled to Windsor for the ceremony, most just for the day. However, Hector had travelled down the day before and stayed with Des that night.

After the wedding, Hector arranged for one night at the only inn in town before they returned to the farm. His quarters in the stables would become their home. However, they would have their wedding night away from prying eyes.

Joel had asked Casey to bring the large sloop to take the rest of the family and girls to Windsor for the day. The wedding was late morning, and Hetty gave Fran a new gown. It was cream with some crocheted lace on it. She had made a new straw bonnet for the service and trimmed it with delicate vines. Molly had picked some tiny white flowers that morning, so these were poked into the edge of the ribbon.

Hetty wanted to give her something to show that she had been renewed. Fran refused white but accepted the lovely cream gown. Months ago, they had started having a small service on Sunday mornings. Hector led this and taught them more about the Bible and their budding faith. As he mentioned earlier, he did this in Scotland before moving to Kent. His grandmother had encouraged him to voice his thoughts and faith, honing his beliefs; admittedly, it was only in the chapel at home and nearby village, but it was often enough to receive a license to preach. Fran would be able to wear her new gown for the services.

As Hector and Fran waved farewell to their extended family from the Windsor wharf, Fran took her husband's hand. "We're married, Hector. Can you believe it?"

Hector looked down at her stunningly beautiful face, yet he saw so much more than her beauty; he saw into her glorious soul. She was his dream girl. "I can, my sweet, beloved wife and I have never been happier." With no one around, he slid his arm around her waist and drew her to him. "Would you like to take a turn along the river or head to our room?" He didn't want to hurry her or press her to become his wife in more than just name. However, as much as he wanted her, he would never force himself on her.

Fran looked up shyly at her new husband. "I think I'd like to go to our room, Hector." He felt like running and dragging her into bed.

Her bonnet was trimmed with tiny tendrils of a native vine that looked like delicate ribbons. One of the small flowers Molly had picked had come unstuck and hung over the edge. He carefully removed it and tucked it in his jacket's top pocket. Her hat was interwoven with some native flowering blossoms. She looked adorable, yet, he wished to strip her as fast as possible.

Nevertheless, that was different from what he would do. He had himself under control and hoped he could restrain himself. As they arrived at the inn, they walked sedately upstairs, and he opened the door for her. As they entered, she untied and removed her floral bonnet, carefully placing it on a chair, and turned to Hector. "I want us to become man and wife in the full sense of marriage, Hector. I want us to be one."

Hector stepped to her and took her in his arms. Before he kissed her, he stood looking down at his wife. He said one simple word, "Sure?"

She nodded; even now, he was not going to force her.

"Your wish is my command, my beloved, but I have a confession. I have never been with a woman that way, so this will be very special for me." His smile had spread to his eyes.

They retired to the big feather bed. The next hour was the most beautiful experience for them. Both had prayed for healing for Franny; however, they had no idea how healed she had been. Their first time together was like she had never been with a man, even to a spot or two of blood on the sheet. Knowing she had already born a child, neither had expected this. She had been completely healed.

Hector was so careful not to frighten her; although nervous himself, his actions were done for her consideration. He was surprised at her gasp as he had to push to enter her. She showed no fear or stress but responded to his loving with everything she could muster. Their marriage thus consummated; the discussion that followed amazed them both.

God had healed her entirely; neither had known that could occur. They lay in each other's arms in absolute adoration for the other. Hector now knew that side of their marriage would be pleasurable for both. His anxiety about how she would cope with the physical side had worried him. He lay with her cradled in his arms, discussing the miracle.

Fran still didn't like being looked at by other men, but with Hector, she was happy to uncover herself to his gaze. He had never seen an unclad woman, and both had to get used to the new intimacies of marriage. Her perfect feminine form made him wish to unite with her again, yet he did not move. She saw his desire building and encouraged another joining. Neither wanted to pull away; they fell asleep, still entwined.

Eventually, hunger got the better of them, and they decided to dress so they could eat downstairs. After dinner, they returned to their room and made the most of their short time together. They knew they had to return home tomorrow but now had their entire lives together. Hector was over the moon that he had not frightened her and that their marriage was everything he desired.

As the little sailboat neared the wharf, Fran started giggling. "Look, Hector, they have made us a wedding arch out of vines." She was leaning back in his arms, relaxing. She had just had two of the most fabulous days she could imagine, hardly believing she had only left the day before. She was now returning as a married lady. She would be allowed to spend the rest of her days in his care; she was delighted. However, she was itching to get home and tell Mrs Walker about the miracle.

When Hector saw the vine-covered arch, he smiled. "Well, you are a vine weaver, my love. It's appropriate and beautiful," Hector whispered to her.

A few days before the wedding, Hetty had taken Fran for a walk along the flat near the river. Hetty realised that Hector had been as good as the words he preached and had not encroached upon Fran until they were married. With Fran's background, Hetty was worried about her reaction to his physical advances. She knew Fran had never had a caring and fulfilling intimacy with a man. She had been used and forced, but Hetty wished to let Fran know that when the intimate side of marriage was performed with the one you love and within the bonds of commitment to each other, it was completely different. Hetty had used the term 'joys of marriage' to Fran, and she wanted to ensure that this was something Fran looked forward to, not recoil from. Fran could not wait to return and let her know all was well.

As they pulled up to the jetty, Joel and Hetty welcomed them. Joel caught the rope and flicked it over the bollard, and Casey tied up the rear one.

Once moored, Joel and Hector handed Fran out of the sloop, and she walked straight into Hetty's waiting arms.

Hetty whispered, "All good?"

Fran's adamant nod and shining face reassured Hetty. "Yes, thank you, Mrs Walker, but I want to talk to you later, please," Fran whispered, grinning.

Hetty's eyebrows raised, but she gave a smile and a nod of assent.

Hector joined Fran and slid his arm lovingly and possessively around her waist. As they walked towards the waiting girls at the arch, he stopped and whispered to Fran, "Happy, my little ray of sunshine?"

Her blue eyes shone with joy. "Absolutely, husband mine."

They reached the archway just where the jetty started, and as they stood underneath it, the girls showered them with petals and leaves. The girls had thrown a few of these in Windsor but picked every flower possible here. The floral confetti was like being married all over again.

All the girls, Jane included, were squealing with joy; then, in unison, they called for a kiss. "Kiss her, kiss her."

Hector was usually undemonstrative; he looked down at his wife in his arms; he cocked an eyebrow when she said, "Give me a good one, husband mine." Fran chuckled just before demonstrating how a 'good one' was done.

Amid cheers and whistles, the two eventually came up for air. Fran hid her head against his shoulder. He had not even kissed her like that in private. She was now looking forward to being alone with him as soon as possible. She clung two-handed to his arm as they walked up to the house. She was skipping with happiness.

Hector was laughing at her evident joy. "Come on, wife of mine, let's settle into our quarters." He held the door of his room open for her and froze, then gasped. In the short time they had been away, Joel had arranged for a new double bed to be installed, and new curtains covered the windows. They had whitewashed the room, and he hardly recognised his previous cramped quarters. A new door had joined Des's old room to his, and they now had a sitting room and a bedroom.

Joel walked to his side. "Des came after the wedding, and while we were away, he brought a couple of friends. We decided you needed a proper big bed, and the girls did the curtains and whitewashing. We hope you like it."

"Sir, it's wonderful, but you didn't need to do that for us." Hector was overwhelmed.

Joel smiled. "No, I didn't need to, but we wanted to do it as a thank you for what you have done for us. Call it a wedding present. Des will sleep in the drying room when he comes now." Joel and Hetty looked around at the refurbished rooms; the blue gingham fabric looked lovely and fresh. It was neither girly nor strictly masculine. It was the same colour as Fran's eyes.

Fran took Hetty's hand and walked into the sitting room. "Mrs Walker, I have to tell you, I'm so excited. You know you told me about the joys of marriage and all that, well that bit is perfectly fine, but you know my history and that I bore a child. When we were together for the first time, we found I had been fully healed. I mean, like everything had never happened." She threw herself into Hetty's arms. Her face was aglow.

"Truly?" Hetty was amazed.

"Yes, even to the marks on the sheets. God washed me clean, Mrs Walker. Completely made new." Franny released a huge sigh. "Hector is so wonderful. He said if things were uncomfortable or if he made me fearful, then he wouldn't insist on that side of our marriage. Did I say Hector was wonderful? He needn't worry about that, though." She giggled, then blushed.

"Franny, that's wonderful, truly wonderful, so everything is good?" Hetty asked quietly.

Franny nodded and did a little skip and hop on the spot. "And now you have done this for us. Mrs Walker, we have never ever had so much space for our own. In the orphanage, I had to share a pallet bed with up to three other girls. I suppose I was lucky, as at least I had a blanket. Hector didn't even have that. Before his Mama came, he slept in the foresters' hut, often in a different one each night. Hector only had what he wore." Franny swung around with her arms outstretched, "Here, we almost have our own home. Something we never thought we would have. Thank you so much!" She threw herself joyously into Hetty's arms again.

"I think it's time that you called me Hetty. One married lady to another, Martha does, as does Charity." Hetty smiled down at her shining face.

"Truly, Mrs Walker? I mean Hetty." Fran threw her arms around her for a third time. "Thank you, for this means now I have a friend. I have never had one before, you know!"

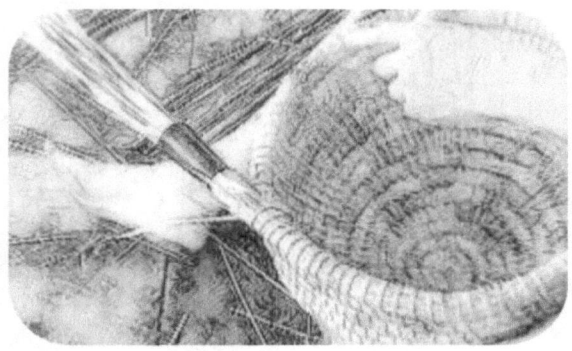

Chapter 7   Rushing Down the River
Four years later

The smell of roasting meat was wafting down the hallway. Usually, the smell was something that Franny adored. However, as she had previously discovered, her metabolism was definitely out of kilter, and this was the third time she had experienced these nauseating feelings. Their nearly three-year-old daughter, Skye, had added to the female population of the farm. She was named after the island where Hector's mother, Sarah, was born. Hector's grandparents had been staying with family on the island when Sarah had arrived early; the family had been visiting from their home in Edinburgh.

Fran was standing on the front verandah and holding her stomach. They had been married for a year before their family started. He was overjoyed when she told Hector she was carrying his child. Hector had mollycoddled her for the entire seven months from when she realised her interesting condition to their daughter's birth. She now had to tell him he was to be a father again. Today Fran walked to the verandah railing and watched the new water mill turning. She waved to them. Typically, she was basket weaving with Hannah, Dawn, and Faith, but they were down grinding a large grain order today. The fresh river breeze fluttered the curls at the base of her neck. As she watched the girls work, a thought occurred to her. She was happy, delightfully so. Hector was a wonderful husband, and their life together was good. Skye was a lovely little girl, and she had plenty of help.

Fran's hands fell to her stomach again; she knew she had to tell Hector soon. Fran thought about the hundreds of baskets she had made since her arrival. The stock of these still grew daily; they now made a twice-weekly delivery to Windsor. Many farmers purchased them for their produce. The bee-skeps were also hugely popular. However, this meant the need for rushes grew. There were few left nearby, and they had an order for more skeps.

The business was doing so well that Joel and Hector now had to go further up the river to source both vines and rushes. They could sell as many skeps as they could make, though the various vine baskets were the most popular. They didn't have to last long; they just needed to be firm enough to hold fruit and eggs for sale at the markets. Fran didn't like flimsy wicker ware, so her baskets were all made to last for some time. Fran had recently tried a different sort of vine that she thought she would try to weave. Although she had used this vine to make the first skep, she gave Des a sample on his regular weekly visits and asked him to find out what it was.

Hector had become adept at bringing home new plants for the girls to try and use. Hector had discovered this strange leafless vine entangled in various bushes in the area. The name Des came back with was *Devils' twine* or *Dodder-laurel*. It had no thorns and was supple. It could also be untangled and used as twine for the skeps.

Young gum trees were a particular favourite host habitat for this unusual plant. Fran decided to try braiding some. Her deft fingers plaited and twisted the long vines into some of the most unique shapes and quirky baskets. The top opening of these new freeform baskets were loops of the plaited vine, and the actual basket was a natural handful of dodder-laurel pressed and shaped with a bowl and a rock. Then she braided the tops, turning the excess into a handle.

Oliver and Ernie were now old enough to plant hunt with them. Joel would still not let the others harvest the rushes as he had to stand waist-deep in the quickly flowing river. He was a strong swimmer, and even though Hector could swim a little, the current was often too swift for him, particularly after rain. Both boys were in and out of the shallows, but Joel would make them all stay out of the water until the flow slowed. If they wished to swim, not far away, there was one small shallow, rocky section of the river that was like a billabong where they swam in hot weather. In past years, they had lost their small jetty a couple of times with a quick flash flood, but the flat on the river edge was the only thing inundated to any extent.

They were now in drought. It had been years since the rains had fallen hard and heavy enough to make the river rise further than the flat. The debris from the 1819 flood had overgrown so much that the river's edge was often hard to access. The last big flood had left a layer of rich river silt on the flat below the house; Joel kept the grass in this area short for the children. So, for some years, the greened flat was nice short grass, and Joel let the children use this area as a play area. It was somewhere to kick a ball and run around, and friends occasionally camped there.

As they grew older, Oliver asked if he could plant some pumpkin seeds he had purchased at the Windsor market. These had been a resounding success, and the area often had some or a variety of melon or pumpkin growing. As there was very little expenditure on this venture, they did not have any significant crop loss if a flood occurred. They bartered or bought what grain they needed and stocked up when prices were cheap.

Two years ago, Joel decided to try to make a small watermill near the edge of the river. The wooden paddles were the easy bit. Hector found an old turpentine tree that had washed downstream decades ago. It had seasoned well, and with Jane's help, she had made a suitable water-driven shaft to drive a grinding stone. They had purchased a second-hand small grinding wheel set from an old mill in Sydney. It had upgraded its millstones and sold the old ones. As Joel was the only bidder, he bought them for £1. It took much effort to get them to the farm. He originally intended to bring them in by boat, but the possibility of them falling overboard was too great. They eventually came up on the rough two-wheel track from Emu Plains.

In the past years, Hector, Joel, Des, and a few of his fellow convicts from Windsor had finally cleared the horse track while the girls had gone to Martha, now in Emu Plains, for a weekend trip. They now had proper access to Richmond, Windsor, and Emu Plains. Until this was constructed, there had always been a very circuitous route into the farm; it had taken hours. Now it was a fifteen-minute run to the main road. It still needed much work, but Hector and Joel would clear another section every time Jane needed timber.

The she-oak saplings were a perfect size, weight, and strength for Jane's mill shafts. She cobbled together various timbers to make some with cogs turned by the paddle wheel. The effort put into this meant they no longer had to pay to get their grain milled. Soon other nearby farms were bringing their grain for processing, which became another source of income. The river water did all the work. Two girls usually ran the mill with ease, one to pour in the grain and another to scoop out the flour. Jane had made a clutch so the grinding wheels could be disengaged when not in use. It was also mounted on a cart, and Hector took the wheels off the sides. They could re-attach these wheels and pull the wagon safely when a flood was imminent; they could always replace the water wheel and shaft. Every year, the cart needed to be moved for maintenance and thorough cleaning anyway.

They kept their food stock in big square bins she had made, but they had found a snake in one and rodents eating the wood in another. The farm didn't have a pottery kiln, but they did have a cooper. Therefore, Jane volunteered to make some full-sized kegs. She had been experimenting with the gum sap and found that when she had a heated barrel, she could rub the outside with collected black pine or gum resin and seal the keg. On the inside, she tried painting with hot beeswax. She usually did this when making kegs as it sealed them. It was the last thing she did before adding the final hoop to seal the cask top. In this case, the lids would be removable as they would need to access the grain and refill the barrels from the grain sacks. She recessed the staves so the lid fitted snugly. However, she would need to buy more steel or hoops to make a set of grain storage kegs.

Fran smiled at the thought of the girls; all of them were happy and contented. Hetty had called this place a haven, and it certainly was. She was still watching the girls work the mill when she felt Hector's arms slide around her waist.

Hector had noticed her hasty departure from the kitchen. Concerned, he followed and asked, "How is my darling wife?" Hector kissed the dark curls at the base of her neck as he cradled her from behind.

She turned in his embrace and slid her arms around his neck. "Ahh, she is well; actually, Hector, my darling, we both are."

It only took moments before he realised what she meant. "No! Are you expecting again? Are you sure?" When she nodded confirmation, he picked her up and spun her around.

Hetty heard Fran's giggle and came to see if she needed anything. She also noticed Fran's quick movement onto the verandah when the roast was pulled from the oven. She had also been ill like that when expecting a child. If Fran were in an interesting condition, then Hetty was thrilled. She saw Hector swing Fran around and then kiss her. Smiling, she knew her supposition to be correct. Hetty was sad she had not fallen with a fourth child. Joel had been so sick soon after Molly was born. His throat had swollen, and so did his private parts. That had been the year before they moved to the farm. They had all caught the illness, but Joel's sickness lasted the longest. However, the three children they had were perfect and healthy. What more could she ask?

Girls from the Female Factory had come and gone over the years, so their extended family kept growing. Of course, the first to leave had been Martha. She had written six months afterwards that she went to say that she was now married to a wonderful man named Jack Turner. He was granted a Ticket of Leave soon afterwards, so they moved to Emu Plains and built an inn. They now had two little boys and a little girl, and she was expecting their fourth child. Then there was Charity; she was still with them, as was Fran. Trixi, Agnes, and Manda had stayed until they finished their term, then returned to find paid employment in Parramatta. They had all found jobs at the Government Dairy making cheeses for Government Stores. Two were now married to soldiers of the 48th Battalion, and Manda was engaged. All returned for visits and sometimes camped on the flat beside the river. As tempting as it was, Joel never let them stay close to the water's edge but on the slightly elevated rise, out of flash flood danger. Many had visited over the years. Hetty particularly loved Martha being close and welcomed her unexpected but usually well-timed visits.

Other girls had come and gone over the past five years. All had been needy in some way. Some had been abused like Fran; others were just timid. Hetty's compassion for what they had gone through made relating to them relatively easy. Some had been abandoned or even sold at the market. Hetty had purchased them. All the girls who came through their doors listened to Hector's talks. He didn't like to call them sermons, although he chuckled and told them his name literally meant to 'heckle or bully,' though that was the last thing Hector ever did. However, no one ever left Loganberry Farm unchanged. When they did, Joel made sure that safe positions were sourced for them. Then as they went, others came.

Des Bolton was still working for Henry Gates; he was given more and more freedom. He was now a frequent visitor. It had been over six years since his first visit. He had asked for Sundays off when possible, so he could come and hear what Hector had to say. The brashness and bravado were utterly gone, and he did everything he could to help on the farm. The friendship between Joel and he had been rekindled, and not once did he make a move on any of the girls. It had taken time, but Des had earned their trust; he was humbled and changed.

Early in January 1826, Des had come for a visit to assist in some rush collection. Henry Gates was away for the week in Sydney, and he had some free time. Joel had let Des know that they had an order for twenty bee-skeps; this meant a need for many rushes. The only problem was that they had used all the rushes near the house. Des had told them on his last visit that he knew of a small creek that was now unnavigable as it was choked with rushes; therefore, Joel had given him some money to hire the larger sloop. The three men were to head off together, and they would harvest as many as they could.

There had been little rain for many months; the water levels were low, making harvesting easy, if somewhat muddy. It also meant the leeches were hungry. Hector hated the beasties. Joel still did most of the cutting; Des frequently joined him in the water as both were strong swimmers. The skies were clear, and no rain was expected. The three men set out on their journey with enough food for an overnight expedition. Grose River was downstream from their farm, and Nutmans Creek branched off that. There was a mass of rushes that were a fair way up the creek from the main river channel. They hoped to bring a sloop full of rushes home and dry them for use. They had packed short-handled sickles and a large bundle of hessian sacks. Hector's job was to carefully place the cut rushes in the bags and make sure they were straight. Des and Joel would harvest.

The girls stood on the verandah and waved farewell. Oliver and Ernie were on the wharf, and Oliver would be the man of the farm while the men were away. It was the first time fourteen-year-old Oliver had been left in charge. He was so proud that his father thought him now responsible enough to look after things, even if it was just for one night. Joel had given his son an extra hug as he hopped in the boat. Ernie arrived just as they left, and Joel said he was proud of them both. The ship pushed away from the jetty. "Be responsible for your mother, sister, and the girls for me, Ollie. You are the man of the house now, son. Ernie, help where you can. Remember, I love you both."

Fran was due in three months and was already beginning to feel uncomfortable. It was hot and, for once, humid. Hetty promised Hector that she would not let her do any arduous work. They had a massive bag of dodder-laurel to convert into whimsical baskets for the market. These baskets were far more robust than they looked and easily held a dozen or more eggs. They lined them with dried moss. The twists and natural knots in the thin vines grabbed onto each other and made a strong base. However, they had to dry them before selling, or they would not hold their shape. Fran, and now Molly, added plaited straps for a firm top and handles.

Molly had delighted in learning the weaving skill from Fran. While her brothers were often with the men, she couldn't wait to finish her lessons with Clara and join Fran. At ten, she had even designed a few of her styles of baskets. Years before, Molly had found a grapevine washed down the river. Hector had planted it, and it thrived. She had cut off a long length of the errant vine to use as a handle for a dodder laurel basket she had just finished. They couldn't wait for the men to return so they could get started on making the new bee skeps. In the meantime, the women got busy preparing the twine they would use to sew them.

For the men, the trip downstream was reasonably uneventful. The sloop was well-balanced and had room for a lot of material. They had thirty empty hessian bags on board, which should be enough to fill the order. They were relaxing and laughing as they sailed. Hetty and Charity had packed enough food for six people, but as they all had healthy appetites, they didn't complain. After two hours of sailing on the virtually still river, they reached the fork. They had to negotiate their way into the narrow, almost blocked entrance of Nutmans Creek as it was not navigable very far; they would need to hack through the scrub to reach the rushes further upstream. However, this was why they had come, so that didn't worry them.

Joel had not been up Gross River before and looked forward to a bit of exploration while there. He noticed it was silting up fast in the years since they had lived on the river. Soon Casey would be unable to negotiate the shallows beyond Agnes Banks. The first thing they had to do was find a suitable camping spot. This wasn't a hard decision, as there was only one convenient place soon after they turned into the creek. Once they set up camp, built a fireplace and unloaded the bags and tools, they left the boat and set about collecting the rushes. Des and Joel were knee-deep in the water and throwing the cut plants to Hector, who filled the bags. By nightfall, they had eighteen bags already loaded into the sloop. Hopefully, they would be finished by mid-afternoon the next day, if not earlier. The men enjoyed their outing, as none had had much male-only time before. After spending a couple of hours telling stories around the campfire, they lay in their swags on the beach. The stars were bright, and the evening warm.

Des was woken pre-dawn by a chorus of birds and a kookaburra sitting in the tree above them, calling a wake-up song. "Leave off, birdie! I want to sleep," Des groaned. It was just first light, and Des crawled out of his swag to stoke the coals for a desperately needed mug of tea. Joel and Hector were stirring, but neither was up. Des gently nudged them awake. They packed up camp, only leaving the billy on the river rocks that circled the fire. Half an hour later, they set to work. Hector was the first to notice that the sun had disappeared. Mid-morning, he looked up and saw a single cloud pass overhead. It wasn't that black, so he went back to work. He wondered, though, if a cloud burst had occurred upstream. They had cleared most of the rushes near the camp the day before, and now they were working on a wide area a couple of hundred yards up the riverbank. There was a steep embankment on this section of the creek, so Joel and Des had to walk through the water a little downstream to get to the rushes.

After a few hours, Joel and Des had cut an enormous pile, and Hector had been busy carting the filled bags to the boat. He had taken more full bags and returned to the camp to collect the last couple of the bags he had forgotten to bring. He had already taken ten full sacks back.

Des needed to relieve himself and was some distance from the creek when he heard a shout from Joel. As he had been squatting, he couldn't see the stream. He finished as fast as he could and returned to his friend. Des was horrified that the previously low creek was now a raging torrent. A flash flood had come down the narrow channel in the few minutes he had been gone. Joel was nowhere to be seen, but Des could see that some of the embankment had collapsed. He then saw an area where Joel had obviously tried to climb up the embankment as his sickle was embedded in the grassy edge. Des grabbed it and went looking for Joel. As he looked back around the curve of the creek, he noticed that a large boulder had dislodged near where Joel had stabbed the dirt, but Joel was nowhere around. Des began to panic. Where was Joel? At the top of his voice, he called to his friend. "Joel, Jooeel, hey, JOELY, where are you?" Although he shouted at the top of his voice, the rushing water drowned him out. There was no answer, no returning call. All Des could hear was the raging water. Surely Joel was fooling; he had to be nearby. Des continued to call as he bushbashed downstream the few hundred yards towards the boat and camp. The water level was already easing.

Hector had seen the water rushing past and was thankful he had been near the sloop. He was busy holding the now nearly full boat from washing away. He added an extra rope to the hired sloop and tied it to a huge tree, hoping it was strong enough to keep it safe. He stayed to watch it.

As Des approached Hector, he asked, "Is Joel here?" Des desperately hoped he would be. By the time Des reached him, the flood was already receding.

"No, he's with you, isn't he?" Hector saw the horrified look on Des's face.

Des blanched. "He was, but I left him in the creek cutting rushes while I went bush to relieve myself. I was only gone for a bit when I heard a yell. He's gone. His sickle was stabbed in the bank, but no Joel. Cor, Hector, where is he?" Des threw Joel's sickle into the boat. With the water falling, Hector grabbed a spare rope and returned to where they had been working. They were halfway there when Hector saw Joel. They stopped, frozen to the spot. Joel's blue drill shirt bobbed in the water and was stuck on a branch. He was floating face down in the rushes on the far side of the creek.

The water had nearly returned to the original level, so both men waded into the creek. They reached their friend at the same time. Des flipped him over, but both could see he was not breathing. His forehead had a large section caved in, and he was dead. The boulder must have dislodged and hit him as he attempted to climb out.

Des stood looking at his friend. A bloodcurdling scream emitted from deep within Des. "NOOOOOO, not Joel, why God, why him too?" He pulled him into his arms and hugged him, sobbing as he did so. Joel's limp body dripped blood into the water.

Hector gasped; he was stunned and in shock. He was biting his lip. Joel was dead. There was no miracle survival, no missing person, just a senseless, accidental death.

Des gently released Joel and closed his eyes. He was now sobbing, and his tears flowed unchecked down his cheeks. He finally realised that they now had to get Joel home. With an arm each, they towed Joel back across the creek. The flood had cleared the channel, and it was now easy to walk back to camp in the shallows pulling Joel's body with them. Doing this was easier than carrying him through the scrub along the bank. When they arrived back at camp, they carefully hoisted Joel into the sloop, gently placed him on top of the bags of rushes, and then covered him with a blanket. The trip back was made in absolute silence. The shock was now setting in. Occasionally one or the other would sob. Neither spoke. No words could explain their grief and the horror of what they now had to report to Hetty and the children.

Joel Walker was dead.

Chapter 8   Homeward Bound

*T*he trip downriver yesterday had taken only two hours, but the trip home felt like an eternity. They were returning with heavy hearts and travelled against the wind. They had to tack all the way in the main channel. Hector even pulled out the oars and started to row so they could get back faster. He was fighting tears.

At the tiller, Des didn't hold back; he let his fall, swiping them away angrily. They both knew there would be many more to follow.

It was mid-afternoon by the time they came into view of the jetty. Fran was the first to see them, and they saw her stand and wave. She called for Hetty as she appeared next to her.

Hector readied the rope, hoping Oliver and Ernie were nowhere nearby. He didn't want them to see their father.

Hetty realised something was wrong when she realised only the two men were in the boat. They saw her hurrying down the steps to the jetty, and Fran and some others followed her. By the time they reached the wharf, the boat had tied up. Both men were out and standing with their backs to the sloop.

Hector didn't want Hetty to see him yet.

Hetty knew something had happened. "Where's Joel?" she was already weeping. Her voice hitched as she asked, "Where is he?"

Des walked to her and pulled her into his arms. Both were now weeping. Hetty saw a covered body in the boat. "No," she said softly. "No, not Joel!"

Hector had Fran in his arms, and they stood silently. He had no words. What could he say? Although he wasn't to blame, he said, "Sorry," but it was so inadequate.

Des finally found the words. "There was a flash flood in the creek, and it caught Joel. He tried to pull himself up the embankment, and a boulder must have dislodged and hit him. Neither of us saw it happen. Oh, Hetty, I'm so sorry. I should have been with him. I should have protected him. I heard him call, and he had vanished when I returned. I went back to Hector at camp, but he wasn't there. We found him face down on the other side of the creek. It should have been me, Hetty. Why wasn't it me?"

Hetty was numb. Joel couldn't be dead; he just couldn't be. Then it hit. He was dead; she was alone. He was her life; no, he had been her life. Now he was gone! Overwhelmed, she crumpled.

Des caught her before she hit the wharf. "I'll take her home, Hector. Can you stay with…" he was going to say with Joel, "…stay with the boat?"

Hector nodded. He said, "Fran go with him and stay with her. They will both need us, sweetheart. I have things to do."

Fran looked at her husband's tear-stained, grief-stricken face and nodded.

"Franny, keep the children away," he said as she was about to leave. Again, she nodded.

Hetty was gently placed on her bed by a grief-stricken Des. He had wept all the way to the house. Fran told the girls, and word spread. Silence fell.

She roused as Des left. Fran sat with her. Nothing could bring Joel back. Fran could bring her no comfort.

Des knew he had yet to bring Joel up to the house. He told Clara to keep the children in the schoolroom. They were not to be told anything yet.

Two girls harnessed the cart and horse and took it to the jetty. Hector had left it ready as they would use it to bring the rushes to the drying room. Bess realised what had occurred and threw in a blanket to cover Joel.

When Des and Hector put Joel's body into the boat, they lay him on the bags of rushes, and Des covered his face with his large handkerchief and then a blanket. He was now stiff and hard to move. Thankfully, they laid him reasonably straight and put his arms across his chest. Des had already closed his eyes.

With as much reverence as they could muster, Joel was placed in the cart and taken with great respect to the stable. The weather was hot, so they realised they had to bury him that afternoon. One of the topics of conversation they had in the past weeks was about death and burial. Joel had said he wished to be buried on the farm. They didn't expect it to be for many years. Some months before, he had shown Hector where he wanted to lie. On the way down the river, Joel pointed it out again. It was next to a large rock platform on a small knoll overlooking the river. It had deep soil nearby and was a beautiful spot. They didn't have a coffin, so he would be buried wrapped in the rug that now covered him.

When Hetty stirred, she went with Fran to tell the children what had happened. Oliver gasped; at fourteen, he was now the man of the house, but he was still just a boy. Hetty gathered all three children to her, and they wept together. After some time, Hetty turned and said she wished to see Joel before they buried him. She needed to say goodbye. The boys followed her. They were old enough to make that decision for themselves.

Molly was made to stay with Clara. She didn't quite understand that her papa was dead and she would never see him again.

On arrival in the stables, Hetty climbed into the cart and pulled back the blanket from her beloved Joel's face. The rock had crushed his temple and half of his forehead.

Des had not looked at his best friend's face again until now. He gasped at the horrific damage. Even if the flood had not washed him away, Joel would not have had a chance. He must have been dead before he hit the water.

Hetty re-covered the damaged half of the face with the handkerchief and called the boys to say farewell.

Leaving the family with Joel, Hector grabbed some tools and went to dig his grave. Jane joined him, as did Des, and a little later, the boys too. It was the last job they could do for their father. Casey arrived as they were still digging. He hobbled up to the house as no one was at the jetty, and he had a delivery.

Charity told him what had occurred, and he assisted with Joel's burial.

Fran and Hetty wrapped his body securely into the blanket. It was all they could do for him now.

Joel was buried just before sunset.

No one wanted to eat, but Charity had cooked some oat biscuits and left them on the table. They were barely touched.

Hector had made Fran eat some bread and butter, nearly making her ill. The house was eerily silent. There was no laughter or conversation at all.

Joel was gone!

Just before sunset, Hector went and unloaded the bags of rushes onto the jetty; they would move them tomorrow. He left everything in a big heap. He didn't care.

Casey and Des stayed the night in the timber drying room.

Hector's heart hurt. His one consolation was that he knew Joel believed firmly in his final destiny. He would see him one day in Heaven.

Casey was silent; Des knew he had known Joel well. He saw him wipe his eyes a few times.

The two men poured out the entire story to Casey.

Joel's passing was a hard loss to everyone.

Casey had yet to head upriver and do the deliveries he had not completed. Des would return to Windsor tomorrow with the hired sloop. He would register Joel's passing and tell Casey's wife what had occurred and why her husband had been delayed.

Life would be very different on Loganberry Farm

Was Oliver old enough to run the property?

Would Hetty stay?

What would happen to Hector, Fran and the girls if they sold the farm? Joel's death left many questions for everyone.

Chapter 9   Life Goes On

*H*ector bore the brunt of the work on the farm while Oliver and Ernie did what they could.

Des also came often and helped with the heavy work. His owner, Mr Gates, was currently in England, and Des was a little less confined than he would have been if he had been in Windsor. He managed to get most of his work done in double time, and he also purchased a horse. The sturdy white steed would bring Des with great regularity. He could come and go at will. He was nearly always there by dinnertime on Friday evening and would help Hector do what jobs needed two men.

Fran's baby was due around Easter. She hoped it would be a boy, and they had decided to name him Joel, but he would be known as Joey. Fran was sick of being so big and found weaving difficult as the baby got in the way. Molly became Fran's hands and feet; she was her shadow. Skye and Fran had become Molly's security.

Hetty had withdrawn from the children somewhat, and Molly needed someone. Hetty was often seen sitting on the rustic rocking chair that Joel had made for her, rubbing the smoothed branch arms. Most evenings, she would silently take her mug of tea out onto the verandah and sit watching the river. It was as though she was waiting for Joel to return. She knew he never would, but she still watched and waited in silence.

Things came to a head one Friday evening when Des was late arriving. Hetty became stressed. "Des said he'd be here. Something must have happened to him too. Where is he?" Hetty was pacing the verandah for over half an hour before he arrived. She threw herself into his arms and yet flailing against his chest. "Where were you? Why are you late?"

He didn't have a chance to answer before she sobbed on his shoulder. He scooped her up and sat on a bench seat with her cradled to him. As her sobbing didn't ease, he held her tighter. Having denied his emotions for decades, he had wanted to keep her like this for years, but even now, he knew she didn't see him as anything more than Joel's best friend. He kissed the top of her head. She would never know. Maybe one day she could return his feelings.

But Hetty did; she felt the endearment and looked up at him. "No, Des, no!" She jumped off his lap, a look of both horror and surprise on her face.

"Hetty, I'm sorry, it was just one for comfort. No more than that, I assure you." Des's heart crashed. He did not wish her to pull away from him altogether. He would figuratively take a step away from her. He would always be there if required, but if that's all she wanted, then so be it. To be near her would have to be enough. He stood to leave.

Hetty was so confused. "No, please, Des, don't leave me either. I need you; I want you close, but I need time. You are my one link to him. Can you give me time?" She pleaded to stop him from going but was confused by her raging emotions. Her grief won out.

Thankfully no one else was nearby. Molly was with Clara, being put to bed. The boys were on the flat kicking a ball. Fran had put Skye to bed in the stables, and the girls were all in their dormitory.

Des was as conflicted as she was. His feelings for her had grown over the years, but more in the last weeks. He respected and honoured Joel and would never have said a word inappropriately. It was part of his anger when they first met. Hetty was everything he had ever dreamed of in a wife. "I want to be here for you, Het, as long as it takes." He put his hand to her and drew her back to him. "I will be whatever you need and want me to be." He didn't know whether he should take her in his arms again. He was so uncertain of what to do.

Hetty wasn't; she wrapped her arms around his waist. She held on to him as tightly as he now held her. He wouldn't kiss her again; she would have to ask him to do that. He would wait. He was now sure that one day she would be his. In the meantime, he was her best friend and her support.

After that evening, Hetty and Des would drink tea together on the verandah each night he was there. Des never overstepped the bounds of propriety again, but sometimes Hetty would hold her hand for him to clasp. It was enough for the moment. Her heart was still Joel's.

~

Hector had arranged to have an Easter service on the verandah. They would often have it on the flat, but with Fran due to deliver their child at any minute, he refused to let her leave the house. They could not attend church in Windsor, so Hector set up his usual service area.

Hetty sat beside her through the short service and noticed Fran squeeze her hand regularly until Hector finished. As Hector said the final words, Fran grasped Hetty's hand tightly. "The baby is coming, isn't it?" Hetty asked.

Fran nodded and put her finger to her lips. She waited until Hector packed up and left to put things away. "I've been having pains all morning, but they are getting stronger." As she spoke, another contraction hit. "Oh, that was stronger, but still a good fifteen minutes apart. This is my third time doing this, Hetty."

Charity went to prepare for the birth, and she heard a wagon approaching. She waved to the welcome visitors.

Hetty had managed to get Fran standing. They were walking through the house and about to head to the stairs into their quarters when a "Cooeeee" sounded from the stable yard.

Martha and Jack Turner had arrived with their four children. Hetty waved a welcome. "Oh, Martha, talk about timing; Franny has just started her labour pains. We're going to need you, dear girl." Hetty greeted her friend with a big hug. Clara came and took the Turner's children into the schoolroom to play. Martha and Hetty managed to get Franny up the stairs to their room. Her waters broke as she was on the third step. Jack, Oliver, and Ernie set about unharnessing their horse.

Hector came as she cried out. He asked, "Is it time?"

Fran grinned at him. "Yes, sweetie, I tried to hold on but made it through the service."

Hector was about to scoop her up in his arms when Martha stopped him. "She'll be quicker if she walks, Hector. It hastens the labour." Martha had delivered numerous babies, including a few belonging to her friend Maureen Murphy. "I've learned some tricks since I was here, Mrs Walker. I've also made friends with some of the indigenous women. I've watched and even helped them give birth; they do it squatting. It hastens things amazingly."

Hetty said, "Call me Hetty, please, Martha; you know that."

Martha smiled and nodded.

Hector stayed with her as he had done last time, but the birth was much less painful for her in a squatting position. He was in a chair and wrapped his arms around her; she could brace herself on his legs as she pushed. With Hector holding Fran, Hetty and Martha delivered Joel Hector Macdougal at ten o'clock in the morning. It was three months to the day, and even the hour, from when Joel had died.

Hetty caught the baby boy. She wept as she cradled the child.

Martha handed her a cloth, and she wrapped the infant and held him until the cord emptied. Martha tied a string twice and cut the cord. The babe was now free; rather than ask for the child, Fran said for Hetty to have the first proper cuddle.

They had to wait for the afterbirth to come, and in the meantime, Hetty gurgled and cooed over the new baby, totally ignoring Fran and her needs. Her face glowed with happiness for the first time in three months; Hetty walked around the room with the tiny babe. Baby Joey had given her a reason to live again.

Fran delivered the afterbirth, and Martha removed it and cleaned her up. Hector knew the pain this entailed, and hearing her screaming in such agony nearly broke his heart. He had yet to see his son, let alone hold him, but Fran was even more important to him now.

By the time Martha had her cleaned up, Hetty had realised that the child's parents had not yet seen their son. Reluctantly she handed the baby to his mother.

Hector caught her sad glance. "Ma'am, we must share this child; what do you think?"

Hetty's face brightened, and she nodded, but she stayed mute.

Hector continued. "Well, we're not going anywhere, are we?"

Franny was tired, but she knew everyone wished to see the baby. She was exhausted, and she just wanted to sleep. Soon, Joey had been fed and was now asleep in his father's arms. Hector was delighted.

Skye was introduced to her brother. She frowned, then declared, "He is all right, I suppose, for a boy. Can you have a girl next time?" Skye had inherited her mother's cornflower blue eyes, which flashed with frustration. "At least Aunty Martha has girls I can play with." She kissed her mother and ran off to play with Jenna and Vicky, Martha and Jack's two daughters. Her parents watched her leave and then chuckled.

Hetty wished to sit holding the sleeping babe but knew she could not take him from his father. Later, there would be time for many cuddles; he would become her special child, her little Joel, not Joey. Joel would live again through him.

Martha put a hand on her shoulder and pointed to the crib. Reluctantly Hetty put him down and left him with his parents. Fran was already asleep.

Hector was sitting protectively, watching them both. He had a son, not that he didn't cherish Skye; he did. He adored her, but he never thought he would have a son. He had learned how to change Skye when she was born, so when Joey awoke, Hector carefully picked him up and took him to the changing table. He had everything ready, the flannel napkin was beside him, and he unclipped the pin and eased off the napkin. Joey released a golden stream straight into Hector's face and neck. Gagging, Hector flicked back the wet cloth and waited. With one hand on the baby, he wiped himself with another dry napkin before attempting to change the child.

Martha arrived just as he finished. His shirt was wet, with a fine line of urine down the front.

She giggled. "He got you, didn't he?"

Hector didn't need to ask what she meant. The baby's urine had left wet arches on his shirt. "Yes, and it's vile. Skye never did this," he said in a matter-of-fact tone.

Martha chuckled. "No, it's a boy thing. I was coming back to see how they were. I see she's still asleep."

By the end of the weekend, things began to settle back to normal. Des had gone back to Windsor. The Turners returned to Emu Plains, and Hector was left with the bevy of women, Oliver, Ernie, and baby Joey. Hector was walking around grinning; he could just not get used to having a son.

Fran was up and about within days, but she was forbidden to do any work. Skye was slowly coming around to having a brother instead of a sister.

Hetty took to looking after baby Joey as much as she could. If he cried, she would attend to him at the first whimper. She changed his napkins and threw herself into mothering the child. It became so pointed that she would only reluctantly hand him back for feeds or at the end of each day. His birth had dragged her out of her melancholy from the loss of her own beloved Joel. However, Molly suffered. At eleven, the little girl was at an awkward age where she needed her mother, but her mother treated her own three children as though they hardly existed.

Fran took Molly aside and explained that her mother still missed her father. It was not that Molly was loved any less, but the grief and sadness in Hetty were profound. It would ease in time, but she suggested that Molly become a runner for her mother until she was better. Helping wherever she could. Fran felt a little put out herself, and she was rarely able to hold her son during the daylight hours. Hetty did everything for him. She would stand and watch over him while he slept. She became very possessive.

At night, Oliver could hear his mother weeping. Everyone knew what the problem was, but no one could bring her Joel back.

Hector tried to stand in as the head male, even for the children, but he also consulted Oliver on everything about the farm and took him under his wing to teach him how to run the business.

When Oliver turned fifteen, he missed his father waking him on his special day, and he hit out at Hector and stormed off by himself.

Hector stayed silent, understanding his hurt.

~

A week passed, then a month.

Hetty became more and more attached to Joey as he grew. She responded to questions and laughed at the jokes, but the Hetty they knew of old was gone. When Joey was asleep, she would wander around as though lost.

When Des came on the weekends, she kept him well beyond arm's length. No hugs or welcome, just the nod of her head, and she would walk off, leaving him bemused. Before Joey was born, there was always a warm hug for Des, but no longer. He had even caught a few dirty looks from her. If he moved towards her, she would step out of his way, turn her back to him, and then walk off.

When Joey was over a month old, Hector said he was taking his family to Windsor to have him Baptised. Des had made the arrangements the week before, and the Baptism was arranged for the seven o'clock Sunday morning service; this meant that the family had to stay overnight. Des had offered his rooms, and he planned to stay at the farm while he was away. The Macdougal family caught the boat back with Casey. They would return on Sunday afternoon.

She watched as the ship sailed out of sight. From the moment they left the wharf, Hetty sat in the rocking chair and rocked back and forward impatiently. She drank and ate but would not communicate with anyone.

A pall had fallen over the farm. Oliver, Ernie, and Des did what they could to lighten the mood at dinner; Hetty hushed them and chastised the three of them. Molly remained quiet. The girls all scattered when they had finished eating. All of them were concerned; none knew what to do.

~

In St Matthew's church in Windsor, Reverend Cross had arranged to do the Baptism during the service. The godparents were Des and Oliver as Godfathers, but as neither was present, Hector and Fran answered as proxies for them. After the sermon, Reverend Cross called them to the font near the entry door.

Skye sat still in her father's arms as Fran passed their son to the minister. Skye watched everything with great interest. As Reverend Cross tipped the baby backwards, Skye asked in a not-so-quiet voice, "Papa, are they going to bathe him or drown him?" She didn't keep her voice down, and everyone ended up giggling.

Hector hugged her. "Neither, sweetheart." He shushed her with his fingers on her lips.

As she watched the procedure, her eyes grew bigger and bigger. She pulled her father's hand from her mouth. "He's going to drowned my brover. He is Papa; stop him!" She knew that Mr Walker had drowned and she had never seen him again. Skye had grown to like the giggling, gurgling, happy baby with the big blue eyes and dark red wavy hair. He was her 'brover', and she became quite protective. "Don't drowned him, please, mister. He didn't do nuffing wrong. He's just a little tacker, and he's mine. Please, mister, don't do it." She was pleading now for his life and struggling to get down. Two big tears dribbled down her rosy cheeks.

Reverend Cross was almost laughing aloud himself. He looked up and cupped her chin gently. "I won't hurt him, sweetheart. I promise this is what Baptism is." He set to explain to her. "See, I pour a bit of water on his head and say some special prayers," which he proceeded to do. "Then, I sign him with a cross like this." He drew a small cross on Joey's forehead in oil. "Then I say some more prayers." He looked at her intense gaze. "Now he's part of God's family."

The little girl's gaze and frown met his. "So, no drowning?"

Reverend Cross was now biting his top lip hard, trying not to laugh. "No drowning, sweetheart, there, see, that's all done. Now we welcome him into the church family." The minister walked with Joey in his arms into the aisle and introduced the newest church member to the congregation.

The small voice piped up again. "Papa, now that man is stealing my brover now."

Hector's smiling eyes met Fran's, and both chuckled.

Reverend Cross returned before she had everyone laughing, as he was trying hard not to do it himself. He gave the sleeping baby into his mother's arms. The family returned to their seat. He continued with the service and started the preparation for Holy Communion. Skye was happy that her brother had been returned and remained quiet for the rest of the service.

On leaving the church, everyone welcomed them. Hector was known to many, but Fran had rarely stepped off the farm. It was how she liked it. The beautiful woman she had grown into made many stop and stare at her. Hector kept forgetting she was still only in her early twenties. Fran stayed near Hector with their two children held close.

They had three hours to pass until luncheon was to be served at the inn, after which they would return with Casey. He was making a special trip so they wouldn't have to stay a second night.

The return trip on the small craft was speedy as the wind was behind them. The July winds were chilly, and Joey was tightly wrapped and cradled in Fran's arms to keep him warm. Skye sat on Hector's lap, snuggled in his greatcoat. His body heat kept her warm. Turning the last bend, they saw someone on the verandah waving; others joined them. Fran placed the sleeping child in his basket. Soon there was a line of people heading to the jetty.

Even after returning from their honeymoon, everyone had not come as quickly. Hector wondered if something had occurred. His heart was racing as they tied up. What had happened?

Des was beside Hetty, who was almost jumping up and down. "He's back, Dessy; they have brought him back." Hetty clutched his arm in excitement. It was the first time she had touched him in weeks. Des had known of her infatuation with the baby, but not that it was an obsession. She had poured all her grief from the loss of Joel into the adoration of his namesake, Joey. He looked nothing like Joel, even as a boy. Des knew that Joel had been fair-haired and had light brown eyes; Molly and Ernie were his colouring. Joey had dark red wavy hair and Fran's huge cornflower blue eyes. Nothing about him reminded him of Joel but his name. That was enough. Hetty reached out for the baby's basket as soon as the boat had tied up. She reached in and scooped up the sleeping child. Ignoring the protests from Fran, Hetty walked back up to the house with the babe in her arms. She had not even acknowledged his parents.

Des held both Fran and Hector back as the others joined Hetty. "We have a problem, folks. She has not left her rocking chair since you left. She sat where she could see the river, watching for your return. She was up at dawn and took up her place, and she has barely moved all day."

Fran had wondered if this was what would occur. She murmured, "I'm hardly allowed to hold my own child, Des. I don't know what to do."

Des turned to watch Hetty walking up the hill. Jane followed behind with the baby basket. Clara had Skye in one hand and Molly in the other; all the staff were concerned.

Casey couldn't help but overhear. "You need Martha Turner. She'll sort her out in a breath. Martha knows how to deal with her, for they are friends."

The three turned to look at him.

Casey was one of the few who knew how Joel had died. They had told everyone else he had been killed in a flash flood, which in a way he had, as he wouldn't have climbed the embankment if it had not occurred. Casey had helped lower his friend into the grave. The night of the burial, he had stayed with Des in the stable. Hector and Casey had sat with him for hours. Des was almost inconsolable with guilt that he had not been there to help his best friend. Casey also knew how Hetty had taken possession of the baby in the past weeks. He also noticed that it was the only topic of conversation she discussed. He said, "I have to go up to Emu tomorrow. I'll let them know. Jack has to make a collection from the ford. I'll get him to send Martha as soon as she can come."

Chapter 10 Honey Harvest

*J*n the three days since their return from Windsor, Hetty had become even more possessive of Joey.

Fran and Hector were barely allowed even to hold him during daylight hours. Hetty would bring him to be fed, hover nearby, and then take him away. Fran was beginning to fret, but they had no idea what to do. Fran wanted her baby. She needed to cuddle him and breathe in his clean baby scent. Fran and Hector began to retire early, just so she could walk up and down in their rooms at night, holding him while he slept. She tried to make up for the daylight hours when she could hardly get near him.

Hector would finally get Fran to put Joey in his basket and come to bed. Then one night, she lay in his arms, silent and almost unresponsive. She was deep in thought. Eventually, he felt her lift her head towards him, "Hector, what are we going to do? It's getting to the point that Hetty won't even allow her own children near her, and Molly is feeling her rejection badly. We can't let her go on like this. She's getting worse."

Hector was worried too. "We can only pray, sweetheart. Only God can break through to her now. Casey said he would try to get Martha to come; however, I don't know if Hetty will listen to her." Hector was worried too. Hetty's behaviour was not normal. Hector knew that Franny had now recovered after the baby's birth, but he made no move to stir her responses. That could wait. At the moment, they had a bigger problem to sort out.

That Friday night, Des appeared as usual. Hetty was still shunning him, but Oliver and Ernie greeted him warmly. Hector lined up a list of jobs, and the four would tackle them together.

Molly had worked out that if she wanted her mother's attention, she had to become a helper for the baby, and then Hetty would give her a nod of thanks and even a smile, but no more.

Hector knew Des was hurting too, but there was absolutely nothing they could do. He also knew Des's feelings for Hetty went deep. He had realised some time ago how Des was drawn to her as far more than just his friend's wife. A suspicion of how Joel died had momentarily flashed through his mind, but when he saw Des's reactions when he saw the body, it put paid to that idea. His grief was genuine. Moreover, he had heard Des calling for Joel and thought Joel was hiding. No, he did not doubt that he had done anything to his best mate. Hector never even voiced that idea to Fran.

Martha and Jack appeared mid-morning on Saturday.

Hetty welcomed them with Joey in her arms, as was usual. Joey was no longer a tiny babe; he should have been allowed time to kick and roll on the floor. He was barely allowed out of Hetty's arms.

Hetty gave her friend a quick welcome kiss but refused to pass over the child when Martha asked for a cuddle.

Fran did not have to explain anything; Martha saw Hetty's absolute obsession with the baby. Martha met Fran's concerned face with an understanding look and a smile.

Jack, Des and Hector sat on the cart in the stables discussing what they should do. Jack looked around to make sure Hetty was not in earshot. "Martha wants her to come and stay for a while, but I have no idea how we will get her to return with us."

Des knew this had to be sorted before she got any worse. He knew that he would have to jeopardise the chance of his life with her, but he would make her listen. "If she won't go voluntarily, I'll have a long talk with her. If worse comes to worst, I shall make her go, even if I must drag her there myself and abandon her at your place." He didn't say how, but Hetty must leave. Even for a few days, but preferably a couple of weeks. He loved her too much for her to be left in this state. This was far more than normal grief, more than even depression. Her possessiveness of the child was becoming dangerous for the little boy. She was now stifling his development.

How they all survived that day without saying anything, they didn't know. Fran was putting on false bravado, but Molly was the one to set the ball rolling. Hetty had insisted on cuddling the child through the meal, even though he was asleep. She rarely lifted her eyes from his cherubic face.

Molly just started weeping silently, then a hiccough. "I'm sorry I grew up, Mummy, I'm sorry I didn't stay a baby, but I miss your hugs." After that comment, she left the table and ran to her room. Most jumped slightly when the door slammed, but all remained silent. It was as though Hetty had not even heard her daughter; she shrugged and looked down again at the sleeping child.

Martha saw and motioned for Fran to take her son. Fran nodded and then yawned; she said she would retire early. She reached for Joey and nearly had to fight to wrest him from Hetty's grasp. Finally, Hetty looked at her and released the baby. She was bereft.

Martha saw tears come into Hetty's eyes as Fran and Hector left the room. Martha put her hand out to Hetty. "Walk with me, please."

As the child was gone for the night, Hetty had no excuse.

Martha gently guided her out to the verandah. Martha walked Hetty to her favourite chair but did not let her sit. She took Hetty's other hand and stood looking directly at her. "Dear, you have to let him go. The babe is not your Joel; he's gone. You are not only hurting yourself but Franny and the babe too. Franny is fragile enough, and you are turning her away from you. She needs to look after her own baby."

Hetty's chin dropped to her chest. "But…"

"No buts, Hetty, he's not your Joel." Martha knew that she must get her away. A break would be hard, and she knew that time away from the farm would be good.

Hetty shook her head.

Martha took her chin. "You know I'm right, Hetty dear, you have to let him go, and I'm not talking about the baby."

Those words hit hard. Hetty broke. She had cried often since Joel's death, but it seemed as if her heart had finally broken this time.

Des had been hovering nearby, and Martha motioned for him to come. He made it to her side as her knees gave way. Des lifted her gently and sat on the bench seat as he had done before. He was careful not to show her affection this time, but it was lovely to hold her close again. He realised she had no idea who cradled her or where she was. Her shoulders shook as she sobbed, and her breath came in deep gasps. Her hands clasped together as if praying. She leaned into him, releasing her grief. Her anguish was so great that it was as though her soul was draining.

Des clung tightly and let her emotions play out. She needed this; she needed to release Joel to God's caring hands. He could be hurt no more. Thinking of his best friend, he began to weep too. He realised that he had been refusing to let him go as well. He rested his cheek on Hetty's hair and mourned his friend. He still wished he had died instead of Joel, but surely the good Lord had a purpose in letting that happen. He had no idea what it was, but Hector had not been wrong so far. His tears finally flowed as he no longer cared if anyone saw him. He now battled his survivor grief.

Martha stood silently at the railing with her back to them. She bowed her head in prayer. Jack joined her, and they stood and waited. Hetty needed release.

It was nearly six months since Joel died, and she finally let him go. It took Hetty a long time before her hacking sobs subsided enough to realise who held her. She had felt her hair wet from his tears and realised Des had been weeping too. For once, she did not pull away but relaxed against his chest. "I'm going away for a while, Dessy," she murmured into his shoulder without looking up. "I'll go and stay with Martha and Jack for a bit,"

Des felt like weeping all over again. He knew she needed this but didn't want her to go. He nodded. Her following words took his breath away.

"Dessy, will you wait for me? Will you stay and help Hector and the boys?"

Martha could hear them whispering but not the words they spoke.

Des wished to kiss her but said, "Yes, Het, I'll be here as often as I can." She was now sitting with her arms wrapped around him; he brushed a tendril of her hair from her cheek. That loving gesture typically would have elicited a pull away from him, yet she didn't move. He showed no more care than that. He was there; that was enough. Now was not the time. Hopefully, now she could release Joel.

~

Weeks later, Hetty was still with Martha and Jack and had sent no word of when she would return. However, Martha reported Hetty's progress to Casey, who passed the information along. Hetty was doing just fine. She had wept a lot, but that, too, had eased.

During that time, Fran had kept the cottage industry moving along. The next honey harvest had been due only a short time after Hetty left, and this was a job that Hetty usually oversaw, but Fran and Jane had helped her often enough to know how it was done.

All the other girls but Clara and Jane were new as a month after Hetty had left, the three sisters had been offered positions together at St Matthews Church of England rectory in Windsor. Knowing they would be safe there and that other girls needed a haven, they swapped places.

Des took the three sisters on to the next stage of their lives. Bess had gone to a position in Richmond the year before, and no one had come to replace her. The four new girls from the rectory would fill their vacancies.

Fran was anxious, knowing she had to cook until the new girls came. Hopefully, that would not be long, as she hated cooking.

Molly was now proficient at weaving and kept working while Fran prepared meals. Fran confirmed that she was a far better weaver than a cook. Her bread was edible but didn't rise properly; her porridge was lumpy, but at least it was hot, and she didn't cook the pudding through properly. However, their tummies were full. No one complained much.

Again, Hector was impressed that she didn't protest; she just did what was required. He admitted to her that he would not have known how to make porridge.

Since Janey Brien had left for England with Perry and Katy White four years before, finding out who now needed their help was more complex. Consequently, there had been few replacements; therefore, Hetty had been reluctant to let their existing girls leave. Major Grace occasionally sent along a girl or two, but that was rare.

The exchange of girls this time came about as Des had asked the minister's wife to let him know if she heard of anyone in need.

Mrs Cross knew of Hetty Walker's work with the abused girls and had met her a few times over the last eighteen months. She had liked the Walkers and was sad when she heard of Joel's passing. Six weeks after Easter, Mrs Cross visited the Female Factory in Parramatta while looking for replacement staff for the rectory. She had seen four girls clinging together and asked about them. On being told they were in a fragile state and prone to the vapours, she requested that they be assigned to her. However, at the rectory, where visitors were frequent, the girls were so timid that they would jump at any new sound and hide whenever anyone came to the door. Although all were good workers, they proved useless working at the very busy church residence. Mrs Cross contemplated returning them to the prison before remembering Des Bolton's request. She sent her houseman to find him.

Des came as beckoned. He was introduced to the girls and saw their nervous state. He suggested a swap with the girls from Loganberry Farm. He had spoken to Oliver and Hector about finding a safe placement for the sisters.

Before Des finalised the exchange, he knew he also had to run it by Oliver, Hector, and Fran. It was Fran who had mentioned the sisters were interested in getting married one day, which meant leaving to meet new people. The sisters' time of servitude was nearly up, and being young, they wished for their own families. Ideally, they wanted to stay together, but they all knew the time would come when marriage would draw them apart. For them all to be placed together at the rectory would be ideal.

Thanks to Hetty Walker and Fran, each was far more confident. They had been kept safe as well as reunited.

Oliver approved the swap; however, there were many tears of farewell. They were sad they could not say thanks and say their goodbyes to Hetty, but they would only be in Windsor. All promised to come and visit after they received the certificates of freedom.

Des had not ridden to the farm for weeks as he was bringing bags of vines with him on each trip, so he needed to come by boat. Des escorted the three sisters back in the boat with Casey on Sunday afternoon, introduced them to Reverend and Mrs Cross, and left the girls in their care.

Once settled into their room, they pitched in and helped straight away.

On meeting the sisters, Mrs Cross adored them and hoped they would stay. Two days later, the four rectory girls, Mary, Catherine, called Kitty; Bertha; and Mildred, known as Milly, left Windsor with Casey on his regular run up the river. Des assured them they would be safe with the friendly, one-legged skipper.

All were timid and had been emotionally hurt, if not physically abused. When Des asked if any of them could cook, two had nodded in the affirmative. Thankfully, these girls were capable in the kitchen. After a weekend of eating Fran's bread, it was one of the first things he had thought about. He remembered how Fran had felt about him and acknowledged their fear and concerns. He treated them with respect but kept his distance.

On arrival, Fran showed them their quarters and told them they were to share with only Jane and Clara.

Some years before, Hector and Des had whitewashed the inside walls of their room. Later they sourced some lengths of chintz. The floral curtains had made the dormitory a lovely feminine retreat. The four entered in pairs; they stood frozen, stunned at the beauty of their new surroundings. Here, they would be protected and have safe accommodation; they had mattresses, curtains, and even new clothes to wear. Jane had kept some of the new mob caps from the market stock. It was one item that had sold very well over the years. They were simple to sew and part of nearly every woman's attire, from plain, serviceable calico ones to fancy, frilly ones with poke front brims. All women wore a head covering of some sort.

Hetty had insisted on the girls all wearing clean clothing and bathing regularly, so there were always some gowns for the girls to wear. The gowns were only made of drill or surge, but they were nearly new, and there was a large hanging space filled with them. All the girls but Jane were approximately the same size, so they shared the loose-fitting dresses. The three sisters had taken some gowns with them, but Mrs Cross said they would be given new uniforms, so they left most of their dresses for the new arrivals.

Hetty had left no instructions about any work on the farm; she had just left. On her departure, she had not been in any fit state to think about anything.

Des and Hector politely deferred to Oliver for decisions but guided him on what needed doing; he grew in confidence with his role as a farmer. He understood that even though he was the boss, he, too, needed instruction. Hector was often sought out for advice.

Fran oversaw the work for the new girls; she had picked up the reins of being the charlatan of the homestead.

Tatting had been another skill they had each wished to learn, but until Mary came, they needed a teacher. Mary had previously done some basket weaving and knew the various techniques required; Kitty was inexperienced but willing to learn. She could, however, tat and also make lace. Fran set her to make lengths of lace to trim some of the new mob caps for sale.

Jane had taken control of the honey harvest and had that down pat. She had made the harvest keg soon after her arrival; this was a sizeable open-topped half-keg, where the large combs of honey were folded, crushed, and the honey drained from them. It was a bumper crop this year. Hive by hive, they smoked the bees and moved the queen bee into a new skep, then waited until the swarm found her and vacated the old skeps. Then it was simple to break out the honeycombs from the empty hive and crush the full comb into the harvest keg. However, they sat this in the sun, covered with muslin and let the honey drain from the squashed combs.

They had nearly one hundred small kegs of honey at the end of the harvest. Jane was surprised she had made so many barrels; she kept herself busy.

Knowing how many skeps they had, she also made a large barrel for excess honey to keep it safe until required. She also suggested that they could supply refills if people wished to return empty barrels. Des had a sign made up for the markets, and soon named mini kegs were being returned for refills. They charged half the price for a refill than a new full barrel. They were thrilled because they had only collected twenty small drums the first year Fran had been there. They decided not to send word to Hetty about the success of their project. That could wait.

Oliver had learned to record the stock and sent only a few barrels of the delicious white box honey to market at a time. They put the rest in storage. From the dregs, Jane and Fran showed Mary and Kitty how to set it in the sun to ferment, and make it first into mead, then into vinegar. At only sixteen and seventeen and being city girls from London, they knew little about farm life. Thankfully Milly and Bertha were more experienced.

Milly was an excellent bread maker and set a batch to prove soon after she arrived. She had seen the remains of Fran's effort and had giggled. On questioning, Fran had discovered her cooking skills, so Milly became the designated cook. Bertha investigated the stores to see what they had available to feed their new family. Both were in their mid-twenties but had seen a lot of the seedy side of the world, and neither had had much choice in their lives nor freedom to have any other lifestyle than they were forced into. Here they were safe and unmolested.

Hector had seen Hetty doing the books for years, and he had insisted that Oliver learn his mother's system, initially to give her a break. Thankfully Oliver had, and this was a way that he could keep tabs on the farm work and turnover.

Fran kept up the basket weaving. She wished she had some grapevines, the one growing on the riverbank was clipped regularly, and she used the off-cut vines, but there were never enough of them. They planted other short sections to see if they could get more grape vines growing. However, she found that the native vines that Des was now bringing her were equally as good. Des now arrived each week with bags full of fresh native lianas. Over the past years, they had cleaned out most of the close ones from the trees around their farm, much as they had with the rushes. Des knew that they needed vines to make more stock. Oliver had given Des £1 in coins to pay others to collect long lengths of native vines.

To keep the books straight, as much as Des was happy to pay for this himself, he handed Oliver an account with each delivery. At a penny per bag, the £1 lasted for a long time as that was enough to buy two hundred and forty bags of vines. Des knew they were best used as fresh as possible. Casey would normally deliver any mid-week loads if he had room in the boat. He could leave them unattended on the jetty and be on his way before anyone could make it down to meet him.

Fran discovered that one load of vines included an off-cut roll of fencing wire. Des had found it covered in mud and embedded in a riverbank. He wondered if it could be used as ribbing for baskets, so he sent it along for her use. Des had later arrived with some of the thick vines, and she had an idea to make heavy-duty baskets that would last a long time. The wire would be cut into yard-long lengths and used as ribs to hold the vines in situ. Hector had to assist with cutting off the lengths of wire and finishing off the top. The fencing wire was too tough to weave, but the wire ribs meant it should last a long time. These baskets were two feet across and were strong enough to hold firewood or other heavy-duty items. Fran used the thick ends of the lianas to weave these. They had previously discarded them as they were too chunky for their ordinary baskets.

Molly's deft fingers made tiny baskets for nicknacks and berries. Egg baskets were still a popular item, as were rectangular shopping baskets.

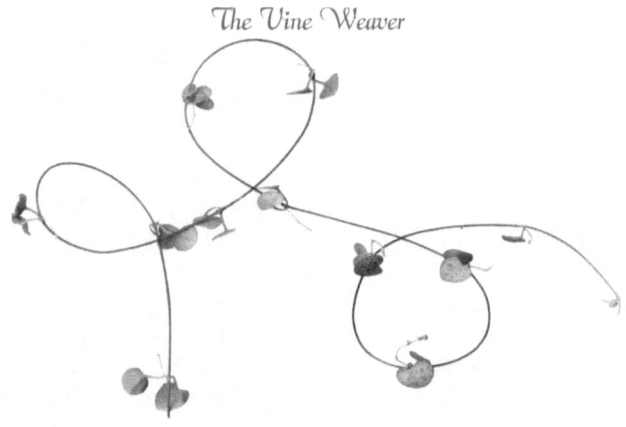

Chapter 11 Twisted Tendrils

One evening, some four months after Hetty had gone, Fran and Hector were walking along the riverbank; she noticed a long blade of flat-leaf grass and absentmindedly plucked a handful of the blades. She wove the fresh stems into a small basket as they sat, relaxing and watching the water run by.

Hector sat watching her, entranced at her dexterity and the swiftness of her work. With no tools, she had a completed square-weave basket soon sitting in her hand. Unlike the baskets with ribs, this one was leaf over leaf, woven in a multitude of small squares and the tips rewoven back down the sides. She now had a small open topped square sitting in her hand.

While she worked, they discussed Hetty's return and wondered if she would have changed. Once Fran had finished the small basket, she turned to her husband. "Hector, do you think there is a chance that Hetty might not even come back?"

Hector was lying on the short fresh grass. Ernie had seen a brown snake there a month or so ago, and Hector had suggested that the flat be burned off. He knew that Joel had planned to plant pumpkins again this year, but it had been just one of the myriad things that had not been done. With Joel's death, the birth of their child and then Hetty's problems, they had completed only the essential work.

Four weeks ago, they set fire to the knee-high dewy grass. The fire had only burnt the grass on the flat as he'd hoped, and now the new soft green shoots were still short and pleasant to lay upon. He eventually replied. "I think she will, Franny, but things might have to change when she does. Joey may have to become a communal baby for some time, sweetheart." He didn't know what to expect when Hetty came back. She would have to return at some stage, but he had no idea what she planned to do with the farm. "I think we must cross that bridge when it occurs." He thought briefly before adding, "Sweetheart, she may even wish to sell up." He reached out for her.

She lay back in the grass next to him. "My time is up, Hector, so I can have you assigned to me, but where would we go? What would we do? I'm so happy here, with you and with this family. I've never had a family before, and they have all become special to me." Placing the tiny basket on the grass, Fran snuggled to her husband's side. "I suppose I should collect my Certificate of Freedom paperwork sometime."

Hector looked down at the beautiful woman now cradled in his arms. She had blossomed into what he called an exotic flower. Franny was still fearful of strange men and rarely left the property. Whenever she did go to town, men's eyes followed her as she passed. Fran didn't like it. She had begun to walk with her head down and the brim of her bonnet shading her face. She had even taken to adding a veil to some bonnets. Hector, however, could gaze adoringly at her whenever he wished. Her blue, blue eyes still made him catch his breath. "Franny, that's only one possibility; Oliver may wish to take on the farm himself. It's going well, and with no crops, there's not much to lose if a flood or bushfire happens. We've cleared the scrub from the back of the house and outbuildings, so there is little nearby to burn. Thanks to your input, my love, Hetty's cottage industry has now made the farm almost self-sufficient." He knew that the sales of the cheeses, honey, baskets, sewing, and numerous other crafts that the girls made brought in a more regular income than a grain crop could have done. They had bought more goats and three more dairy cows with calves at foot.

Once a year, Joel had hired the bull from the next-door farm and then would leave him to please himself with the cows for a month. It rarely took that long for the bull to cover the herd, but two cows had not calved one year when the bull had only stayed for two weeks. Hector had returned the bull a few weeks before Joel died. Most of their eight cows were now ready to drop. All would calve this year. Hopefully, most would drop heifers, but the bull calves would be butchered or sold on the hoof. He did the same with the mares and sold their offspring. Hector dropped a quick peck on her cupid lips, "Quite honestly, my darling love, I'm happy here too. I have no desire to see things change. I could lie here forever with you in my arms."

She lifted her chin invitingly.

It was an invitation he willingly accepted. After their long kiss, both lay on their backs gazing heavenward.

After a while, she said, "I'm happy wherever you are, Hector; it's why I'm so sad for Hetty. I think how I would feel if it were you who died that day instead of Joel. Des is still beating himself up that he wasn't with Joel when it happened. He said Joel probably would not have died if he had been at hand. I corrected him and said they both probably would have been caught in the flood and drowned, even if the rock had not hit Joel." Fran reached out and stroked her husband's cheek. "Hector, there may be another complication to Hetty selling up; it's Oliver. Have you noticed him watching Mary?"

Hector's sleepy eyes flew open. "No, he's a little young, isn't he?"

Fran chuckled as she leaned over him. "He's sixteen, sweetheart, as is Mary. It never occurred to me that…" She left that unfinished for a while, occupying his lips with another kiss. "It just never occurred to me that he would be interested in one of the girls. I forgot he's almost grown up." She paused again; she knew she had to tell Hector what he had to do. "Sweetheart, I don't think Joel ever spoke to him about those sorts of things. You know, the boy talks. You or Des are going to have to talk to both the boys. The new girls are fragile as it is; if the boys misbehave with them, oh Hector, we could have a real problem."

Hector groaned. "You're kidding, aren't you?"

With a chuckle, she said, "No, and I have to talk to Molly about woman's things. She's old enough to start her monthly flow soon, and I know Hetty won't have told her anything. Molly is beginning to find her gowns tight around the top, so she's maturing as well."

With these thoughts still in mind, the young parents knew they must return to the house. They had relished the time out while their children slept. They tried to manage a short break from the daily chores each day. Most days, Clara kept her eye on the children as they went for their walk.

Hector leaned over and brushed one of the black curls from her forehead. "Before we head back, Mrs Macdougal, I'm going to kiss you just because I can." Franny giggled and reached out for him. His kiss was both possessive and passionate. He groaned with desire as he released her. "Please make your excuses and come to bed early tonight, darling."

She jumped up and brushed the debris from her skirt and hair. "Your wish is my desire, husband mine. We could always have an afternoon rest ourselves."

"Hmm, tempting!" Hector removed a few twigs from her hair and then bent and picked up the discarded woven basket. "Let's see how these sell. This plant may be another source of weaving. I haven't seen you do this sort of weaving before. It's different." The tiny basket sat in the palm of his hand.

Fran had forgotten all about her weaving. "It's what I call square weaving, as it is different to vine weaving. I just wondered if this plant would break when woven. There is plenty of it around, and it grows fast; it's a sort of blade grass. These may need to be dried before selling. They are also normally more fragile than vine baskets. I would suggest we market those for selling things like strawberries or raspberries. For those, we could even use fresh ones." A look of joy swept across her face. "Hector…"

He knew that look. "What wonderful idea have you thought about now, my sweet?"

Fran chuckled. "You know me too well! Strawberries, my love." Her comment didn't need much explanation

Hector gave a gurgle of joy. "You never cease to amaze me, dear wife. You arrived here so frightened and scared of any male…"

Fran interrupted, "Except you, darling man; I was never frightened of you."

Hector kissed the top of her head as they walked. She fitted under his arm so well. "Okay, most men, then. When you said you could weave, I don't think even Hetty knew what she was letting herself in for. You turned a tiny idea Hetty had into a full cottage industry. Yes, she had one hastily cobbled-up beehive, and when she got twenty small tubs of honey from her hive, she was over the moon. After you had settled in, the first group of girls came, and then Jane. Sweetheart, I found it hard to keep up with all of you. I'd finish one job, and you would have six more for me to do. You shed your fear, or so I thought, until the day Des arrived. Now, here you are, my wife, mother of my children, and, in essence, running the entire place yourself, with us all at your bidding. Now you want us growing the berries for your new baskets." He saw the flash of interest in his joke.

"Oh, could we? Could we ask Des to find us some strawberry runners? And get some raspberry canes or even blackberries. And Hector, what are loganberries? I have never heard of them, but that would be wonderful to have some of those." Her thoughts were beginning to wonder what else they could put into the small baskets.

"Loganberry was a name Joel made up. We could try to make one of our own, a 'cross' berry between a raspberry and blackberry; however, my love," he chuckled, "I demand some attention myself. An afternoon rest sounds tempting." Hector smiled at her absent-minded comments. She was always thinking about what she could do to help anyone else. Even when Hetty kept taking Joey, she never complained. She had been hurt; she just wanted to cuddle her own child. Even now, he knew she wished to get back to him. Then at night, he knew she had to bathe Skye and tell her a story; then, he would join them to say prayers and put the children to bed. Only when they were asleep would he have her complete and undivided attention. He adored his family life and the small routines of his children. He had much more here than he ever would have had as a forester at home. And that had been preferable to what he left behind in Scotland. He still had no regrets about leaving there. Here there was no coppicing, no briar hedges.

In Kent, he had had to trap the vermin and many of those he gave to the poor to eat. He refused to think of his life before that time. His oppressive grandfather in Scotland had no love for him. No, he was happier here on the Hawkesbury River, and so was Fran.

With that thought, he grabbed Fran and swung her around until she was giggling hard; he joined her laughter with his deep-throated chortles. Her joyous laugh was something he needed to hear. As he placed her gently down, he bent to kiss her. There was a whistle and a cheer from the watchers on the verandah. Hector acknowledged the cheers and said, "We can't disappoint them, sweetheart." They both waved, then enjoyed a passionate embrace that delighted all the watchers. Fran was nearly breathless but didn't care. She knew Hector loved her. She now understood what being cherished meant. He would never take her for granted nor hurt her. Yes, she felt cherished. It was a word she had learned to love.

The light moment of joy lifted the spirits of them all. However, their kiss also made Hector realise he had to talk to Oliver sooner rather than later. As they walked home, Hector saw Oliver move towards Mary as they stood at the railing. Hector whispered something to Fran, to which she nodded, and they decided to head home quickly.

Hector's conversation with Oliver the next day caught them both by surprise. Hector hadn't realised Oliver was old enough to be interested in a serious relationship. He had no idea what to say to the budding man.

Oliver missed his father; having said that, what he asked Hector, he probably would not have voiced to his papa. The young man even surprised himself. A wide-eyed teenage Oliver asked Hector. "Hector, what does it feel like to be in love?"

Hector groaned inwardly; he could no longer shelve the conversation. "My mama died when I was young too, Oliver. I remember her saying, '*You don't marry a girl you can live with; you marry a girl you can't live without.*' I was like that with Fran, and your parents were the same. Your mama adored your papa so much that she finds life hard without him. Oliver, Mary is traumatised from her experiences in England, in prison, on the ship, and in gaol. If you put one step wrong now, she will flee from you. Before you do anything, become her friend. You are just both only teenagers and far too young to be married, but having said that, you are now the man of the farm, and you will have to grow up quickly. But give Mary time; she's not going anywhere. Become her friend and let her heal. Franny and I are here to talk too, if required; please ask if you need questions answered." Hector waited for his explosion; it didn't come. He'd just clipped the young man's wings.

Oliver, though, was thrilled with his answer. As Hector said, he knew sixteen was too young for him to marry, even with his mother's consent, but Mary wasn't going anywhere.

Hector was willing to stand in the role. Oliver was sad that his father was no longer around to answer his queries, but Hector had not told him no, just not yet.

They had a big tree trunk to saw up, and it would take most of the day. They worked the two-handled saw together all morning. As they cut, Hector said, "You know they call these things a 'misery whip'." He was puffing as hard as Oliver; between breaths, he said, "…And I know why." Every few minutes, they took a break. When they did, Oliver shot more questions at Hector.

By lunchtime, Hector realised it was time for Oliver to know the absolute basics of how a woman's body worked. He gave him a brief fact-of-life talk that was quite detailed. To which Oliver initially blushed but listened in awe. Hector was sure this was something that Joel would have handled a lot better than he did, but Oliver needed to know why Mary and the other girls were so afraid. He also needed to understand that the physical act that had violated them could also be something beautiful if done in marriage with love. He told Oliver that the physical side of a relationship, or as it was known, the joys of marriage, was beautiful when done together with love and commitment. If he forced her against her will, she would withdraw from him, and he would have built a barrier he would be unlikely to be able to scale.

Oliver's reply was just, "Oh!" He thought deeply before saying. "So, just friends and let it build from there?"

Hector was pleased the lad had grasped what he said, "Yes, no more for a couple of years. And even if she wants to sneak off with you, you must resist. Oliver, you must respect her and be her role model and friend. You must learn to treat her as a lady, forget her convict status. You know of both Fran's and my convictions. Even Janey Brien was innocent. It was Janey who helped your mother find the first lot of girls and my Fran too, yet all of us will stand equally for judgement before God. None will be exempt from that. We all must answer for both our words and our actions, and as it says in Matthew 12 verse 36, '*But I say unto you, that every idle word that men shall speak, they shall give account thereof in the day of judgment.*' Be careful, Ollie, that you don't become part of the problem rather than the solution." He didn't often use his pet name but wanted to lighten the conversation. Hector then added, "In Luke 6 verse 37, it says, '*Judge not, and ye shall not be judged: condemn not, and ye shall not be condemned: forgive, and ye shall be forgiven*'."

Oliver was horrified. "Gosh, Hector, I don't want that to happen. No way! I have no intention of hurting her. Can I ask a favour? Will you keep your eye on us and make sure I don't do anything to blow it?" He was imploring Hector for guidance.

Hector put a caring hand on his arm. "Of course, lad. And Ollie, ask anything you want to whenever you need to. Also, we must both have a chat with Ernie. At nearly fifteen, he'll need our guidance too. Make sure you directly answer his questions, just as I have with you today, for he may not wish to come to me."

Oliver nodded with a big smile and a nod. Ernie had already been asking him such things. Now he had some answers.

Mary was sitting alone on the verandah with Fran. The conversation between the two women was along the same lines. Mary had started the conversation by calling Fran, Mrs Macdougal. Fran put paid to that as soon as Mary uttered it. "I'm Fran; I was a convict until recently. I am now an emancipist, but Hector still is serving his term. We are on equal footing here, dear."

Mary nodded, then fell silent while she worked. She had different design ideas for baskets and used the thick stems as the ribs and then wove those with the thinner vines; sometimes, she even used unravelled dodder-laurel for the sides, making them look much finer weaving. Jane had offered to make bases, but Mary declined politely. She had found that a wooden base sometimes broke, whereas a woven one was a little more flexible. Mary sat weaving for a while before saying, "Franny, I'm scared. Not like before I came here, but…" She stopped and looked at Fran. "…it's Oliver." Mary hoped that Fran would understand what she meant.

Fran wanted and even needed her to voice what she was feeling. "Is he becoming a problem, love?" Fran asked, hoping she would elaborate.

"Yes, and no, Fran, you see, I think I like him, and I know he likes me, but I'm a convict, and he's the farm owner." Fran caught Mary's shy fleeting glance.

"Ahh! I was wondering if what I suspected was the case. Oliver Walker is a wonderful young man. I wish you had known his father. Hopefully, you will meet his mother soon. Mrs Henrietta Walker is the most amazingly kind and compassionate woman. She is warm and loving and sorely misses her husband. As such, she's currently staying with her friend Martha Turner in Emu Plains. Hetty is having a tough time coping with the loss of Mr Joel. His death hit us all hard, but her in particular." Fran was determined not to mention anything negative about Hetty. Even though she had become possessive over Joey, she had not hurt anyone other than herself. Fran adored her and wished her well. Her obsession with Joey was a symptom of her grief; that was all. They all wanted her to be well again and to come home.

Mary nodded as she concentrated on the weaving. "Jane told me about her, Fran. She said she almost took Joey from you."

Fran should have expected this but was surprised that it was how Jane saw the situation. "Not really, Mary, it was just a sign of her grief, for I love Hetty dearly. Nothing she did hurt anyone but herself. Joey was born exactly three months after Mr Joel's death. She simply poured out all her love into the baby. The only issue with that is that he was a little slower in sitting up and crawling, but nothing lasting. Our concern was for her and only for her. Martha was the first girl she helped, and as friends, they came and took her for an extended holiday. I hope that tells you a bit about her. You see, Martha and Jack Turner were both convicts, as was Hetty's mother." Fran let that sink in as she flicked a few more strands of vine over the ribs. "Martha loves her as a sister, but we are all worried about Hetty." Fran glanced up at her weaving companion. "Mary, you are only sixteen. Yes, you had a bad start, but so did I. Very similar to yours, if you must know. I lost a child, and I had no idea which one of the fifty-odd sailors who used and abused me had fathered it. Mrs Walker, as she was to me back then, rescued me the week the child was born dead. She promised to keep me safe, so I came with her. Here I met Hector." Fran told Mary of her emotional healing and then about her physical recovery. For most young unmarried girls, you would not even discuss the actual marriage act. But like her, this girl had been severely and violently abused. Kitty had known her story as the four girls had arrived on the same ship. Kitty was attractive too, but not the beauty that Mary was. Yes, Fran knew precisely what Mary had endured. She had therefore reached out to her the day after she arrived. Fran could see her reaction to every male. She knew that fear all too well.

Kitty had heard Mary crying the first night and told Fran. Mary had poured out her heart to the caring lady who had cradled her lovingly. She had only been twelve when her abuse started. She had worked in a laundry at a big house, and her abuser had been one of the housemen. He had been caught in the act and was dismissed on the spot. She, too, had been reprimanded, but she had been sent back to her parents. With no food there, she was arrested for stealing food and then transported.

Fran's advice to Mary was to befriend Oliver. If nothing more came of it, then at least she had a good friend.

Mary nodded, agreeing to her wisdom. She knew what that side of marriage entailed, she wasn't that keen on it, but Oliver had shown her only kindness, something that had been in short supply in her life. While they talked, Fran had sent Molly to Kitty and Clara; they were sitting on the far end of the verandah. Molly was now learning how to tat. Lace was not only expensive but time-consuming to make. If Molly could learn this skill, they could teach the others. This was an activity they could do indoors around the fireplace at night or when it was too wet or cold to work outside.

In the three weeks the new girls had been at Loganberry Farm, Kitty had become quiet, very quiet. She had been almost bubbly when she arrived and when she saw the lovely room they were to share. For the first weeks, Kitty was the talkative one. Now she rarely said anything. With everything happening on the farm, Fran didn't worry too much.

Mary was the one who alerted Fran to Kitty's problem. "Franny, she thinks she's having a baby. She was 'had at' the week before we left Windsor. She was getting water from the back well late at night, and someone must have jumped the back fence or something, or maybe they could have been sleeping in the back of the stables because she didn't see a thing. She got jumped and tossed to the ground, Franny and he did bad things to her; now she's expecting a child. She said it was like a ghost as she could feel him and what he did to her but saw nothing, just the dark night. I only found out about her condition last night. I wondered as she hadn't had her flow, we normally have it together, but she's missed twice now."

"Mary, you keep weaving, and I will take Kitty for a walk." Fran was shattered for her. She'd been so concerned with Mary and Hetty that she'd not given as much care to the other three girls.

The upshot of the walk was as Mary suspected. Kitty was with-child. She figured she was due about April the following year. She poured out her story to Fran and then dissolved into tears and fell to her knees. "Why, Franny? Why me? What have I done to have this happen to me?" Kitty begged for an answer from Fran.

Fran knew her anxiety. She had asked the same questions and told Kitty, "I asked the same thing, sweet girl, when I was in the same way. But Kitty, know that this child you carry will be loved and will have a great purpose. Here, you will be supported and accepted. We will help you every step of the way. It happened to me, too, Kitty, but my child died. I'm sure Mary told you that."

Kitty nodded but kept weeping.

Fran took her hand. "Sit with me." They sat on the riverbank, and Fran repeated what Hetty and Hector had said to her. She was loved, forgiven and accepted. "Carrying a child out of wedlock is not your fault. Others may shun you, but not here on this farm."

Kitty's big eyes were filled with tears. "Are you serious, Franny? I can stay. Won't I get sent back to the Factory? That's what they told me would happen if I got knocked up." The matron at the Female Factory had read them the riot act. She was puzzled how the girls there kept falling with child. None were prepared to report her husband. He would come in after lights out, drop his trousers and with his hand over their mouth; he would take his pleasure with whom he wished. One or more of his friends, or even the warders, often came with him, and they slaked their lusts. If the girls reported them, the girls would get the blame for being provocative, and they would be demoted to third grade in the gaol, then made to break rocks while being put on bread and water for up to a month. "It's not fair, Franny; we get abused, and then it is us girls what has got to pay the price." Kitty was weeping on Fran's shoulder.

Fran totally agreed with her; it was so wrong. She had wished she'd had a caring shoulder to cry on back then. Janey was the only one nice to her, but she lived off-site. However, her care made a big difference. She said, "No, Kitty, life is not fair. We will cope, though, dear, and we will love the little one when it arrives." When Fran had given birth to her child, the doctor would not even come when they called him. Her child had never breathed. She tried to kill herself soon after that. Now she looked back at that incident; if she had not been carried out on a stretcher when Hetty arrived, she would not be here today. Fran shook away those memories. "Kitty, somehow God will get the glory from this."

"I don't see how, Franny; I have this unwanted thing growing in my belly, and I don't even know who the man was. It was dark, and I didn't see his face. When I turned to where I knew he should be, there was nothing, just blackness, like a ghost, but I could feel him. Mrs Cross knew something had happened as I came in crying and covered in dirt. I said I'd been attacked but couldn't admit I'd been 'had at', too. She didn't really dislike any of us, but she didn't understand Franny; she didn't know what we'd all been through. She was kind, but she didn't understand. When we arrived here, we was welcomed and given such a pretty room to share. There was only Mr Hector and the boys around, and we were safe from more abuse. Now that night has come back to bite me." She dissolved in tears again.

Fran sat and hugged her.

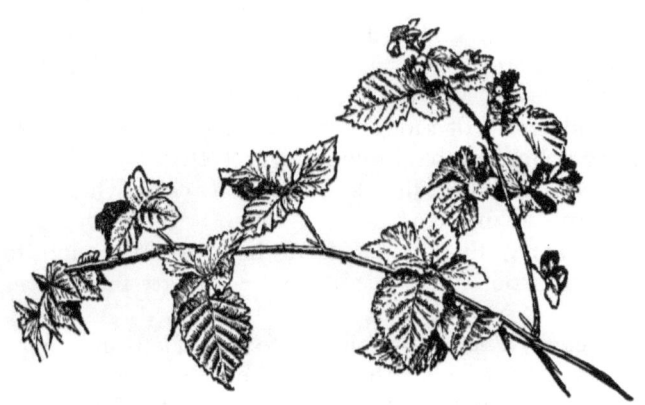

Chapter 12 Vines Bearing Fruit

*T*he November harvest of the new fruit they had growing was in full swing when they heard a wagon coming along the road. Molly's cry alerted everyone. "Mama's home."

Hetty had returned. She didn't know about the new girls and therefore didn't know that Kitty was now some five months along; Kitty, being such a tiny frame, her condition was now apparent, and she was wearing Fran's maternity gowns.

The welcome Hetty received allayed her fear of reprisal from everyone.

Molly was the first to greet her, flying into her mother's arms. She welcomed her with a kiss and a hug.

Hetty kept hold of her daughter's hand as she hugged the boys. Then the four drew into a group hug.

Oliver was now over a head taller than his mother, and his muscles had grown as he and Hector had done a lot of manual labour in the intervening months.

Ernie was now at eye level. His voice had not fully broken and alternated pitch, while Oliver's was rich and deep. He now sounded very like Joel. The timbre of his voice made Hetty start. It was as though Joel were speaking.

Rather than weep, Hetty giggled. "Oh, Ollie, you sound just like your father; how he would have loved that. Ernie, you are his image and how you've grown, and Molly, my sweet, you are so grown up. Look at you all, how I have missed you, but I am better now. I am so sorry I was not there when you needed me, but Martha and God have made me well again. However, I will need your help." She kissed them all again. "Now, where are the rest of our extended family?" Hetty looked around and saw new faces, and some were not there.

"Welcome home, Mrs Walker," Fran said.

Hetty had a wave of sadness cross her face. "What's this Missus bit, Franny? Am I so abhorrent that I'm no longer 'Hetty'?"

Franny nodded. "I didn't know if you wanted me to." She was enveloped in Hetty's loving arms.

"I'm so sorry, Franny; I missed him so much and took your precious child from you. Will you forgive me?" Hetty pulled away a little. "Please?"

Fran smiled. "There is nothing to forgive, Hetty, nothing at all. We all miss him, you most of all." She kissed her. "Now we have news. The three sisters have gone, and we have new faces. I will tell you all soon, but one, Kitty, is expecting a child in a few months." She stumbled over the words, but Hetty needed to know the status quo before meeting them.

Hetty merely nodded.

Hector greeted her and then helped Martha down from the wagon seat. She had stayed seated until Hetty welcomed her family. The four children stood waiting until they were told they could do more. Jack was lifting his children down one at a time.

Martha was also expecting another child. She was due in six months, so she was not yet showing; however, Jack was already mollycoddling her. He would not let her jump down from her seat.

When Martha had let Hetty know her condition, she knew it was time to go home. Hetty also realised she was looking forward to returning. She was ready.

The one small person Fran knew Hetty wished to see was Joey. At now eight months old, he was having an afternoon sleep. Fran knew whom Hetty was looking for. "He's asleep, Hetty; you can have a long cuddle later." She didn't elaborate. "Now, Hetty, you have some new faces to meet."

Hetty nodded and smiled. "Thank you, Franny."

Mary, Kitty, Bertha, and Milly were introduced; this was the first time they had met the person they had officially been assigned to. Even though Fran and Hector had assured them that Hetty was adorable, they all expected an absolute tartar, but the petite lady who had arrived made them all release a sigh of thanksgiving.

Hetty was in a fancy, over-frilled gown. Her hair was different from how she had worn it before. She now had a fringe that curled naturally, and her long brown hair was pulled back into a tight bun on the back of her head. Her smile was genuine, and her voice soft and loving. Hetty was just as everyone had described her, but they could not believe someone could be so nice. No one could be as sweet and caring as she was supposed to be. None of the girls had met anyone like her before.

Hetty gently touched her hand to each new cheek, kissed them, and then welcomed them.

She was back to the beautiful person she had been before she lost Joel. On his daily trip, Casey had taken word back to Des that Hetty was back.

The big test for Hetty was to be Friday evening. Des was due again.

Friday arrived, but there was no Des. He had not come with Casey. Hetty thought he would ride instead, but he didn't come.

Casey's trip on Saturday brought news that Des would await an invitation before arriving from now on. He had presumed his welcome for the past six months, but now he would wait for an invitation.

Casey carried a two-word note back to him. *"Please come! H"*

If Hetty had written more, she would still be writing.

It was close to a year since Joel had died. She had done much thinking in the months away. She decided she really wanted Des to be part of their life, but more importantly, she wanted him in her life for herself. She questioned her motives. Had enough time passed since Joel's death?

Casey only did a Sunday run each week if he had to. He wouldn't do the run if Des didn't need a lift back.

On Monday, Casey carried a note from Des to Hetty. It contained just one word. *"Sure? D"*

Hetty's reply was a fraction longer, *"I'm sure I need you, and Des, I want you. H."*

She was nervous putting it on paper, but she wanted him near and needed him to be sure of his absolute welcome.

Des didn't send another note; he came.

He rode his horse and arrived mid-afternoon on Friday. He was very hesitant as to how he would be welcomed. He wanted to take her in his arms and kiss her silly, but he would bow over her hand and be as distant as she wished.

In the months she had been away, Des had worn a new shortcut track through the scrub just behind the bee skeps up near where Joel was buried. He tipped his hat to his friend each time he passed by. He still missed him.

Hetty wasn't expecting Des until that evening. But she wished to visit Joel's grave and also check the new hives and make sure they were not in the sun.

The clip-clop of hoofs made her heart leap. The rider could be no one else but Des. She had wished to be alone when they met, and thankfully everyone else was busy.

Des had already seen her in the distance before she heard his horse.

She stood still, waiting out of sight of the house. Her heart was racing. Her eyes were fixed on the oncoming figure. She hoped she had not distanced him from her. His notes were short and gave nothing away about his feelings.

What she wanted and what she knew she should do, were vastly different. She dreamed of being greeted by Des jumping from his horse and sweeping her into his arms. She had dreamed of the deep, passionate kiss they would finally share; she had dreamed of a life together and being cherished as she had been with Joel. But that was a dream.

Des would greet her coldly, bow over her hand and kiss it. Des would not overstep the bounds of propriety because now Des was a gentleman.

She stood waiting with her arms folded over her stomach, trying to quieten the nerves.

Des drew his steed up beside her, and she took the reins.

She said nothing; she didn't have to. The tears rolling down her cheeks said it all. She put her arms out to him, and he jumped off his steed and drew her into his arms. Her face was uplifted, asking to be kissed. He then played out her dream.

When Des finally lifted his lips from hers, a teary Hetty clung to him; he said, "I missed you so much, Het."

Her eyes were glistening from her tears. "I couldn't push you away anymore, Dessy," She lifted her face to his. "I missed you so much."

He thumbed away an errant tear from her cheek; then, Des accepted her invitation for another kiss. His passion was apparent; he held her crushed against him. When he lifted his lips from hers, his lips were as red as hers; but both were grinning. He unapologetically said, "I should not have done that, Het. For we are not engaged."

Her face glowed with happiness. "We are not setting a good example, are we?" she said as her eyes dropped longingly to his lips again.

He complied but gave her only a peck on her lips. "No, but there is a way we could sort it out, Het. Is it too early to ask you to marry me?"

Her smile made her eyes twinkle. She shook her head.

Des didn't know if that meant it was not too early or that she wouldn't marry him. However, her following words left him in no doubt. "Ask me, Dessy."

He dropped to one knee and asked her the question he had wished to ask her for a long time. "Henrietta Sarah Logan Walker, will you do me the honour of accepting my hand in marriage?" He had no ring, and he had little money. He was still a bonded convict, but he had temporarily forgotten that. He did have a full heart.

Hetty, nodding, pulled him back to his feet. "Yes, you wonderful man, yes, I'll marry you."

Des shouted with joy and crushed her into his arms again. This kiss was one of his dreams, for this time, she was promised to be his forevermore.

Neither had noticed Des's horse had vanished; it had walked down the hill and into the stables with its reins dragging on the ground. Hetty had dropped the reins soon after Des had dismounted.

As the horse wasn't sweating or injured, Hector waited a little while before following Des's normal pathway to the farm. He had seen him pause at Joel's grave each time he came. He was sure what had delayed him, and it wasn't Joel. He had seen Hetty walking to check the new bee skeps. He smiled; hopefully, his friends would have finally sorted themselves out.

Hector noticed that they were oblivious to him watching them. They were so tightly wrapped in each other's arms that Hector wondered how Hetty could breathe. He looked around his feet for a twig to step on; even the loud cracking sound did not disturb their occupation. He turned to leave them alone.

Des finally lifted his head a few moments after he heard the twig snap. With another quick kiss on Hetty's cherry-red lips, he called to Hector. "Come and congratulate us, Hector, for we are engaged."

The joy in Des's voice was enough to make Hetty giggle, blush then hide her head on his shoulder.

Hector shook Des's hand and wondered if he should kiss Hetty's cheek or her hand. She put out her hand and then pulled him close for a kiss on the cheek. "Wish us well, Hector, for this could not have happened without you. Thank you."

Hector looked at his friends. "I do wish you well and hope that all the permission is processed without issue." He saw Des start.

Des's face blanched. "Darn, Hector, I forgot about that. I'll ask when I return home. Reverend Cross should give me a reference, and I'll apply for a Ticket of Leave immediately."

Des was walking with his arm around Hetty's shoulder. She fitted snugly under his arm. He was also looking around for something.

Hector smiled, reminding them of his missing horse. "If you're looking for your valiant white charger, I had put him in his stall and given him a good brush down. Yes, I know you were otherwise occupied," Hector replied with a grin. "It's how I knew you had arrived safely."

"Thanks, Hector, we were, um, busy," Des chuckled. "To say I was fearful of my welcome was a vast understatement."

Their return to the house arm-in-arm gave away their not-so-secret secret in a second.

Fran was the first to see them. "Have you seen the children yet?"

With that question, Des guiltily dropped his arm from around Hetty. "No, Fran, I have not." He told Hetty, "I will ask Oliver's permission, my sweet."

"Ask them all, Dessy; look, they are coming back with Clara." Hetty pointed with a lift of her head to the three young people just stepping onto the verandah. Des did just that, and soon they were surrounded by three delighted young people.

~

Life on Loganberry Farm settled back into the routine for the rest of the weekend. After many months, the joy of life had returned to everyone, and they once more heard laughter around the dinner table. Des and Hetty were seen on a few long walks along the riverbank. They rarely went out of sight of the house but often stopped under the shade of one or the other trees along the route. They often spoke of Joel and also of Carly. She was why everything had occurred.

Des reluctantly mounted his white horse on Sunday afternoon and returned to Windsor. He took his parting with Hetty in private and then left along the narrow pathway back to Windsor. As he rode, he thought, "I am so blessed. I have such a lenient boss." He was allowed much free time as long as his boss's business didn't suffer. Mr Gates knew he had taken responsibility for the Walker farm after his best friend died. He knew Mr Gates was in Sydney until mid-week.

On Monday morning, after Des completed his initial chores, he saw Reverend Cross and obtained a reference. Then Des breezily wandered down the barracks office and applied for permission to marry. He'd not heard of one being refused, so his entry into the office was with confidence. The Major had often sought his help with obtaining items for his men, so this, too, was almost a formality. Major Morgan signed the documentation, and Des only had to get the last signature. Mr Gates was due to return on Wednesday. He set about the week's work and had the itinerary for the week's chores well underway by the time Mr Gates arrived home. Upon his boss's return, Des requested an interview, and once booked in; he had a wash, shaved, and fronted up at Mr Gates's office on time. Early that morning, he had asked Major Morgan to wait an extra few minutes before shutting the afternoon despatch box so that he could add the signed request. Des felt ready for his meeting. Nervous but excited.

However, Mr Gates was in a non-talkative mood. There was no cheery greeting.

Des realised that something didn't sit right; this meeting didn't bode well after all. Des had forgotten to pray about any of this. His heart sank as he entered the immaculate, timber-lined office.

Mr Gates looked up and gave a nod of acknowledgement. He liked everything dotted or crossed precisely; this was why he liked Des. Des knew how to do things the way he liked them.

Des took the seat that his boss pointed to and sat quietly. He held the documents firmly in his now sweaty hand. He knew to speak only if invited. He waited.

Mr Gates finished what he was doing, then looked up and asked, "What's this about, Bolton? I was going to call you in any way."

Des took a breath and asked permission for him to be married. He handed over the sheet that needed signing from the Major but not the actual permission document. He also withheld the reference from the minister.

Mr Gates flicked it open, read it and looked up and said, "The Walker woman, I presume. You've been up there nearly every weekend, haven't you?"

"Yes, sir; however, she has not been there. I have been assisting her young sons and yardman with some bigger jobs. She only returned this week after several months' absence." Des was as nervous as a schoolboy.

Mr Gates looked down at the document again. Then he tore it up. "You're assigned to me and are not going anywhere for four more years."

Des's heart sank; no, it crashed. He had not prayed. He had not even asked for God's guidance about the engagement; he had just presumed. Guilt flooded through him. He blanched and was now lightheaded. They were not allowed to marry. His dream of Hetty being his wife was stripped from his hands again. He felt like weeping like a young schoolboy getting the cane. He knew that Mr Gates was talking to him, and he had not heard a word. His eyes were fixed on the wastepaper bin that now held his torn-up passage to happiness.

Shaking off his melancholy for a moment, he forced himself to focus. "Sorry, sir, I missed your instructions." Des tried to sound apologetic, but he was beginning to become angry. Angry at himself and also angry at Mr Gates, the word 'pray' came to mind. He did. He silently shot Mr Gates a begging prayer. More importantly, his ears finally tuned in to what Mr Gates said.

Mr Gates had a massive folder in front of him. Flicking it open, he said, "Bolton, I have a new project starting, and you're instrumental in it. I have taken a selection out at Bathurst, west of the Blue Mountains, and I'm sending you to oversee the set-up. I have bought a flock of sheep, which will arrive over the next months. I want you to fence the property and then drove the flock from Sydney when they arrive. You will be leaving next week, so you can have the rest of the week off and say farewell to your woman. Dismissed." Mr Gates returned to the file.

Des was gutted. He stumbled as he walked out. He managed not to flatten his boss. He wished he could reach out over the desk and hit him. He made it into the back garden before letting out a bloodcurdling roar. He knew he had to tell Major Morgan to seal the despatch; then, he would pack and leave for the remainder of the week. He would spend every moment with Hetty that he could. He had absolutely no choice; he was a bonded convict for four more years, four long lonely years.

By dusk, Des was riding down the narrow pathway past the beehives. He paused in the spot where his heart had sung only days before. Now it was crushed. He was not looking forward to telling Hetty that he had to leave.

Chapter 13 Banished

*H*ector was the first person he saw. The etched lines on Des's face told him something was terribly wrong, not to mention that it was Monday. "You okay, Des?" Hector asked, concerned.

"No, I'll tell you later; I must tell her first. Where's Hetty?" Des waited briefly for his friend to give directions to her.

"In her chair, Des. Did you get permission?" Hector figured he hadn't.

Des was so choked up that he couldn't answer. He shook his head.

"Damn!" Hector uttered under his breath.

They walked together to the house.

Hector had an idea, and he wanted to be close at hand when Des told Hetty his news. He let Des walk to her first; he would give them ten minutes together before following his friend's footsteps.

Hetty was weeping in his arms, Des's head resting on hers. They didn't pull apart when he approached. Des gave him a flash of anger but knew Hector would not encroach on them unless he had a reason.

Hector waited.

Des finally pushed Hetty from his arms. She was as shattered as he had been earlier in the day.

Without waiting, Hector barged on with his idea. "I want to talk to you both before you say anything to anyone." He motioned for them to sit and listen. "I'm licensed in the Scots Kirk at home and permitted to marry folk. The laws here don't allow me to do that because I'm from the Church of Scotland. However, in the eyes of God, I don't think He would be too fussed. I can perform what is, in essence, a clandestine marriage." The seed now sown, he waited for their reaction.

Hetty's glance flew from his face to Des's. "Could we, Dessy? At least we'd have this week, and I could come and see you in Bathurst too. My stepfather was Scottish, Des. I'll claim that."

Des was shocked, "But it wouldn't be legal, Het." Des wasn't sure this was such a good idea.

Hector filled in a little that he thought they should know. "In the eyes of God, it would be. Even at home in Scotland, everyone is supposed to be legally married in the Church of England. My church is not allowed to do the honours. However, we still do marriages like Roman Catholics, Quakers, and the like. In Scotland, you only must declare in front of witnesses that you are man and wife to be married. However, some of us were permitted to perform such unions. I only did a few before I left for England. Scottish law sanctions marriage with all the rights according to the church. So, all the couples in Scotland are not legally married according to English law, but we're not in England, are we? You would, in essence, have a clandestine marriage like in Gretna Green and over the anvil. Married by the rights of the Scottish Law, but with no certificate or registration, as I have none to give you."

"Please, Dessy, we can marry tonight, then we can at least have the week before you leave." Hetty still had tears flooding her eyes.

"But it's not legal, Het. I couldn't do that to you." Des was really concerned.

"It will be right before God, Dessy. There are no denominations in Heaven, only many Christian believers. Joel said that to me once; I have no idea who told him. I'll keep the name of Hetty Walker until we can marry legally or at least register our marriage, but I will know I'm your wife," Hetty pleaded with him.

"If you are sure?" he said the words as a question.

Her pleading gaze was lifted to him. "I am! I am absolutely sure. It's not what we wanted, but it's better than nothing." Hetty wrapped her arms around him. "I don't want to waste a moment more, Des, let alone four years."

Des smiled and nodded. "Okay, let's get married." He wondered what Mr Gates would have to say to that. He already had permission from the Major, so there would be no issues with his convict status. It was only a problem with his owner.

Hetty turned to Hector. "How long will it take you to get ready, Hector?"

Within the hour, Hetty was dressed in her best gown. She had had a bath, and Clara had done her hair. Clara had hairdressing skills she had kept hidden. With everyone assembled on the wide verandah, Oliver walked his mother out. Ernie and Molly stood as attendants for the bridal couple.

Hector married them, but there were no documents to sign. He knew that at some stage, he would have to add them to a marriage register somewhere for the union to be official. Hector knew that God would work that out too. That was a problem for later.

~

They had a week together before Des had to return to Windsor on Wednesday, then he needed to travel first to Parramatta and then to Bathurst. Hetty and Des parted in private in her bedroom as she could not bear to see him leave.

The lone horseman left. He rode past the big rock by Joel's grave and once again tipped his hat. Des refused to allow Hetty to return with him, but he promised to write and tell her when she could come and visit. It could be the entire four years that he would be away, but he would return to her. Their parting was bittersweet. Their week together had been so short but filled with love.

Only if something happened to Mr Gates would Des be free to be reassigned to Hetty. He promised that he would return as soon as he could. Des still had Reverend Cross's reference and the Major's permission letter. Thankfully he had not handed them over to Mr Gates. Des was sure he would have torn those up too.

The following day, Mr Gates travelled with him to Parramatta and collected an assignment of new convict men. Mr Gates had asked for an allocation of twenty, knowing that he'd probably not be allowed that many. At least Des was free to choose who was to work with him.

Des went and met the potential convicts that Major Grace had suggested. He found eight with farming experience, including a blacksmith and carpenter. There were two other unskilled men he chose as they were big beefy men who could work hard. Des willingly acknowledged he didn't know one end of a sheep from the other. However, that was not his job; he had to arrange to fence the entire new selection. Thankfully, he had helped Joel do that often enough to know what was required. He had also helped build the storage shed, amongst other chores for Mr Gates. With his mind still on the magical week he had spent with Hetty, he was now waiting for Mr Gates to sign out the chosen men.

Major Grace caught his eye and noticed Des was very quiet; they had met many times with Joel at his side in the years since Hector's breakthrough in Des's guilt. On various trips to Parramatta for Mr Gates, Des had pumped the Major about his faith.

Major Ned Grace stood out from the other soldiers, and now Des knew it was because of his strong faith. They now had that in common and discussed it often. On this visit, Ned noticed that Des did not seek him out for conversation, and he was puzzled and went to his side as Mr Gates engaged in conversation with the warder of the men's gaol.

Des, however, was oblivious to Ned's concern for him. His mind was back on Hetty. He hoped she could come for a visit. He knew the road across the Blue Mountains was traversed frequently now. If the children travelled with her, she'd be safe. Oliver was now his height. He also knew Hetty wouldn't leave them again. If she came, they would too. He loved them all dearly as though they were his own family. He jumped when he heard the quiet voice ask about his well-being.

Ned asked, "Des, what's occurred? You seem to be very preoccupied."

Des's startled gaze turned to the fair-headed soldier beside him. "Hetty and I were married last week by the Scottish Law because Gates wouldn't sign the papers. His was the last signature I needed. I don't wish to leave her, Major, but I had no choice."

Ned was astounded. "You mean Mrs Walker? Didn't she only lose her husband last year?"

Des nodded. "Yes, she had a rough year since Joel died. He and I were childhood friends, as you know. She's been away with Martha Turner in Emu Plains for some months, and I've been helping her children and Hector Macdougal with the farm. I don't want to leave her, Ned, but can't say no. I'm bound by law to go." Des gave Mr Gates a glare of almost hatred. "If I ran, he would know where to look." Des gave a tilt of his chin towards his owner. "I know God is in control, but I don't have to like it."

Ned placed a caring hand on his shoulder. "I can't change things, Des, but I can pray for you."

Des nodded his acceptance of that offer. "Do that! I need it."

Ned had a thought. "You don't have the other papers on you, do you?"

As Des refused to leave them unattended, he nodded.

Ned saw Gates coming and put his hand out. "I'll fix this end." He shoved the documents in his coat pocket and smiled a welcome at the approaching man.

~

Early in 1827, Hetty called Fran into her bedroom one morning. It was nearly three months after Des's departure and their magical week together. Hetty admitted her suspicions of her growing condition to Fran and then fell into her arms, weeping. "He's not even going to know he's going to be a father." At thirty-five, she had never expected to have another child. She had never conceived again after Molly was born. However, their week together had been fruitful, but Des was gone, banished miles away, beyond Bathurst. It was on the far edge of the land allowed to be settled. Mr Gates could hardly have sent him further away unless it was to return to England. With no way to even contact him, Hetty could not even write. Her only hope was that she could go and stay with Martha for a while, as Des said he had to come east to collect the sheep when they arrived. He would have to drove them through the ford at Castlereagh near Emu Plains.

Joel had now been dead for over a year. Hetty marked the day sitting in the rocking chair and praying. She was both happy and sad all at once. Now she missed both Joel and Des, knowing she could not have either. Hetty and Des had been married for over three months, and it was nearly as long since she had seen him.

That month also saw the birth of Kitty's child. Emmy was a shock to them all. Her baby's skin was much darker than any other child they had seen, even darker than the local aboriginal babies. Kitty fell in love with her little girl when they laid Emmy in her mother's arms. Her double-dimpled cheeks and dark, tightly curled hair were adorable. However, Kitty immediately knew who her father was. There was only one dark-skinned convict in Windsor, and he worked at the rectory as an outside man; this would explain why she had not seen him approaching. His dark skin on a dark night would have made him virtually invisible. He had been convicted in London for attacking another woman, but he was a gently spoken man and, up until that night, had never laid a hand on Kitty or any of the girls. He was employed to do the heavy labour in the rectory and rarely conversed with any of them. She had seen him pause and watch her while hanging the laundry, but he had never even spoken to her. He was usually chopping wood. He was tall and handsome, but she had never even smiled at him. She had occasionally let her eyes flick over his glinting body, and the perspiration trickled down his back.

Hector knew he had to now report to Reverend Cross about the extent of abuse to Kitty the night she had been attacked. If the convict had done this twice, he might try it again. Even Mrs Cross was no longer safe. Reverend Cross had to know whom he was harbouring.

Hector and Fran escorted Kitty and the well-wrapped baby to the rectory. With her very dark skin, Kitty had dressed Emmy in the prettiest pink outfit with a frilled hat. Hector had said he wished to see Reverend Cross and discuss a Baptism. It was an ulterior motive, for as soon as Reverend Cross saw the child, he would understand the situation. Kitty had already told them about the attack, just not exactly what it entailed or that he had violated her.

Omara Kaylim was often bare-chested and stood an impressive six-foot-six inches tall. When he was brought into the office and challenged, he remained silent, even when he saw the beautiful child Kitty held. He stood erect and mute, but his eyes rested on the baby. The Major came in and arrested him soon after the group's arrival. The evidence was overwhelming, even in the lack of a confession. So, Major Morgan clapped him in chains and marched him past Kitty. Omara tried to pull around to see the little girl again. "I'se sorry, missy, I'se be sorry, youse be so pretty," he said as he was dragged passed her. "I jus' wanted to touch you, missy; I'se real sorry." His words were as good as a confession. "Look after her, missy. Please care for my daughter."

Kitty cuddled her baby; she fully intended to do what she could for her child.

Major Morgan jabbed Omara in the back with his musket. The baby was proof of his sin, as no one else could have fathered the child; however, his words had just condemned him. Omara was taken directly to the magistrate, and his words were repeated.

Reverend Cross followed them out and vouched for the timidity of Kitty and the other girls. To his knowledge, Kitty had never even spoken to the prisoner.

Mrs Cross also vouched for Kitty's character and told the magistrate that she had not stepped outside the rectory property for the short stay. However, they did admit that they knew about the attack but not how far the man had taken it.

Kitty was brave in facing her abuser but also felt sorry for him. He had never hurt her before but had no right to touch her. She had not encouraged him in any way. Even his abuse of her left no external marks or bruises.

Omara was sentenced to one hundred and fifty lashes.

Hector gasped; surely, he could not live through that. At forty lashes, his back would be almost shredded; at eighty, if he still lived, he would be unconscious and possibly would have been for some time. He would be taken down, sent to the hospital and returned to receive the remainder of the lashes in another one or two sessions.

That afternoon, all the other convicts in the barracks were lined up and had to watch the punishment. All knew what this man had done. Word had spread quickly through the rest of the inmates; he had molested an innocent girl at the rectory and fathered a child.

Omara was tied to the whipping post with his legs splayed. He remained silent, barely flinching when the first scourges hit. The timbers of this contraption were smoothed by frequent use over the decades.

At forty lashes, the crowd was splattered with his blood, and he gave his first shout of anguish. Little flesh was left on his back by the count of eighty, but he remained responsive. The flaying continued; somehow, he remained conscious for another sixty lashes. The vicious scourging continued, stripping the remaining flesh from his bones. They should have stopped when he passed out, but the man with the whip delivered the last ten scourges, with Omara finally unresponsive. The gooey pulp of his bloody flesh was highlighted against the darkness of his remaining skin. The ground at his feet swam with his gore, and his bladder emptied as he passed out. No one had ever lasted for one hundred and fifty lashes and survived. Omara had, but he was an extraordinary man.

The crowd had fallen silent as they watched the determination to endure his punishment. When Omara was taken down from the whipping frame, he was like a giant rag doll. All the watching crowd silently watched the big black man's strength and fortitude. Few had known he was even in town, but now, few would ever forget him. If any had seen him, he had walked by them with his head down, humbly and non-threateningly. Now they just felt sorry for him; after all, he was a convict like them. They all knew that if he survived the whipping, he would be put onto a chain gang or sent to the coal mines.

Somehow, he did survive, and Kitty was informed that he was sent to Newcastle. When Kitty heard about his new sentence, she sighed with relief. She knew that she would never see him again, and she was pleased he had not died, but Emmy would never meet her father. Only God knew what sort of life Emmy could have in a primarily white European settlement. He would have to open a door for her. She would need to find a place where she felt comfortable.

Emmy was an adorable child, and back on the farm, her extremely dark skin caught the attention of some of the local indigenous women. Up until now, they had refused any contact with the family. However, some of the tribe had first seen the baby when returning from Windsor. As Emmy grew, Kitty began to take her down to the river edge with Fran's two young children. Fran was with child again and a month or so further along than Hetty. So, she could no longer walk far and certainly not down the steep path to the river.

The first time one of these women came out of the woods, she frightened Kitty. The woman was virtually naked, wearing only a small tassel back and front. Kitty had never seen an unclad woman before. She didn't even have a mirror to view herself, so she was quite shocked and didn't know where to look. Kitty wanted to run away but had to stay and protect the three children she was watching. The woman carried a baby about Emmy's age and placed a wooden *coolamon* cradle on the ground. It contained a sleeping naked child much the same age as Emmy. The woman put her hands over her heart and pointed to the baby, and then she pointed to Kitty and did the same.

Kitty pointed to Emmy and said her name, then to herself and repeated her own name.

The woman copied but spoke so fast that Kitty could not hear her. The woman put her hand to her chest and said what sounded like, "*Dharug Eloira.*"

Kitty presumed that was her name but couldn't say it, so she called her Laura. So again, she pointed to herself and again said, "Kitty," and then to the baby, "Emmy," and to the woman, she pointed and said, "Laura."

Laura giggled, shrugged and nodded, saying, "Laura," patting her chest and then pointing to her baby. *"Garung Carrigal."*

Both babies soon woke with a whine, then a gurgle. They saw each other and reached out to touch the other child.

Kitty thought she would call the baby "Carrie" and said her name. The babies were so similar that both mothers laughed at the children's actions. Emmy was the darker of the two.

The meeting was not the last the two young mothers would share. For some time, it became a daily occurrence. Laura and Carrie would appear from nowhere when Kitty was anywhere near the river.

Kitty thought to bring a spare blanket and lay it on the prickly grass for their comfort. It was made from the wool Hetty had spun. It was thick and warm. She asked Hetty if Laura wanted it and if she could give it to her.

Hetty agreed willingly. Hetty and Fran watched the regular interaction from the verandah while they worked. Both were excited to see they had finally made friends with some of the 'ghosts of the bush,' as Hetty called them.

Hetty's mother, Sarah, had known the previous family who owned the homestead. When they lived nearby, before Hetty was born, Hetty had visited her mother's friends for some years and had loved the position of the new house they were building. It was she who told Joel the property was for sale. They had no hesitation in buying the farm after the flood. They completed the partially built house on the hill and moved in, but they had never again seen the local people who had once inhabited the area.

Since the big flood just before they bought the farm, the locals had been on walkabout, rarely being seen anywhere. Hetty was sure that it was only from fear, but she knew them to be a kind and gentle people. Hetty had eventually told Joel about them, and with encouragement from Hetty, they regularly left out some small offerings of flour, a spare tool or two, or some honey. They would often find a bark bowl of sweet pink apple-flavoured fruit or even some freshly speared fish in place of their offerings. So, even though they never saw them, they never had a problem with them. Now, finally, Kitty had made the breakthrough, a personal connection.

One afternoon, after they had sat on the bank for some time, as Kitty stood to leave, she offered the blanket to Laura. Kitty had been doing some basketwork while watching the children play, and Laura wanted to learn. She would sit and watch Kitty, giggling as she would battle with a thick vine. She offered a finger to hold it in place as she worked. Soon the two girls were regularly seen working together on the riverbank.

~

A month after Laura's first visit, she beckoned towards the bush, and three more girls joined them. They carried huge armloads of thick vines and offered them to Kitty.

The gift of these was wonderful. Kitty wondered what to give them, and Laura motioned to the old pliers with cutting blades she was using to trim the vines. Without asking Hetty, Kitty reluctantly did the swap.

They had received an order for some laundry baskets and wondered how to obtain enough thick vine to make them. If Laura and her friends could bring more vines, they could make bigger, stronger baskets. Laura introduced her friends as they arrived, but again Kitty did not understand the names. She called them Anna, Maree, and Noree.

The girls giggled joyously as she obviously had got their names wrong. Kitty shrugged and held up her hands in resignation and repeated her names for them.

The new girls sat happily with Kitty, Laura, and the children as they worked and played. Maree was now watching the small group of little ones play. They had five little naked babies sitting in the lush green grass, plus Fran's two very white children.

Laura and Anna decided Kitty needed some language lessons while busy weaving. Anna gabbled to the other girls and walked to the water. Scooping up some water, then pointing both directions along the waterway, she said, *"Yandhai,"* then again, putting her hand in the water, said, *"Deerubbum."*

Kitty repeated the words but wasn't sure if this meant water or the river's name. Her pronunciation of *"Dee-rub-bum"* set the girls off giggling again.

Laura patted the riverbank, and they pointed to the land around them, *"Yarramundi."*

Kitty exclaimed, "Yes, yes, *Yarramundi*, I know that one. That's the land we are on." She also grabbed some of the gravel near her and repeated the word.

Laura was excited that Kitty recognised a word. The four girls giggled again and nodded.

Kitty decided it was time to return, but there was so much to carry and look after the three children. She wondered how to get it back to the house.

Laura turned to Maree and gabbled. Maree clapped her hands to get the attention of the two older children and beckoned them to come. Soon an unusual procession made its way up to the house: four near-naked, nubile, indigenous girls, Kitty, and a rainbow assortment of various coloured children wended closer.

Fran and Hetty watched the unusual procession. Hetty had been thrilled at the breakthrough Kitty had made. She had a special gift ready for Laura; she knew that metal axes were something they highly valued. Martha had told her they would sit at the ford near her house in Emu Plains and make stone axe heads from the grey river rocks. Hetty and Fran met the girls at the kitchen door with the axe wrapped in a length of calico tied with a ribbon. She did not doubt that the men would take the axe, but the cloth and ribbon Laura should be able to keep. As expected, Laura's eyes nearly popped when she saw the gift. The other three girls stroked the pretty mauve silk ribbon. Laura placed her hand on Hetty's arm and grinned. Hetty took that as her thanks. However, this simple act of trust propped the door of friendship firmly open. From then on, the four girls were frequently welcomed at the house. They would often arrive with vines, rushes or some other valuable supplies. A youngish man was often seen sitting on the rock shelf near Joel's grave, watching over them protectively. Hetty gave them some items that she knew they would use. A camp oven and a large empty tun-size barrel were accepted willingly.

~

Over the following weeks, the bond between the two groups solidified. Laura came one day with a special coil of bark fibre. She showed them how to make a fishing line. The end product was a two-ply twisted line that was surprisingly strong. Later, Laura taught them how to knot nets for fish catching. Hector wished to know from which plant the fibre had come. He hobbled after her as she walked along the verandah. Laura pointed to the shady tree ferns near the stables and also towards a tall cabbage tree palms at the back edge of the river flat. Then she turned and looked at Hector, touching his brow.

Some days earlier, Hector had attempted to climb a tree to reach some vines and fell; he was not hurt other than a big cut on his leg. Fran was no medic and cleansed it as best she could. Hector doused it liberally with rum, then bandaged it. After a couple of days, it had grown red and angry. It was now covered in pus, and he was feeling quite flushed.

When Laura arrived, she saw he was unwell. Now she insisted that he show her his leg. She unwrapped his dressing; she shook her head when she saw it. She grimaced and said, "Tch, tch," then motioned for him to stay there and left.

Hector sat and rewrapped it to keep the flies away.

An hour later, Laura returned with a strange bundle wrapped in paperbark. She led Hector to Fran, and they sat on the verandah as Laura treated his leg.

Hector had just doused it with rum again, and it was oozing yellow pus. He was beginning to feel quite ill and very lightheaded, so he thought he had nothing to lose, allowing Laura to treat it. "Do your darnedest, lass," he said to her somewhat wanly.

Fran uncovered his rough effort at bandaging.

Laura carefully laid her bark bundle beside him. From it, she took a stone scraper. She scraped off the remaining pus and cleaned it as much as possible. Hector gasped with pain as she scraped off the ooze. She made it bleed, and once she was happy it was clean enough, she picked up the puff fungi she had brought. Before Hector could stop her, she puffed the yellow powder-like substance directly on the wound. She then picked up the inside layer of paperbark she had brought everything in and placed it over the wound. She tied it on with some of the string they had made. Happy with her handiwork, she stood up. Being unable to give verbal instructions, she made the sign of sleep.

Hector realised that he had to keep it on until the next day. He nodded, to which Laura grinned, then giggled again, and then went back to weaving with Kitty.

Much to Hector's surprise, his leg didn't hurt much for the remainder of the day. He even started feeling a little better. He didn't remove the bark bandage and was careful not to dislodge it as they slept.

Laura returned mid-morning the next day with another bundle. Much to the surprise of everyone, when she removed the bark from his leg, there was no pus. The wound was red, but the pus was gone. However, she cleaned it again with the cleaned stone blade and then treated the wound again, only this time, she produced three similar fungi. She pointed to two and threw them away. She used the third one; they could see no difference between them. Now warned, they would not treat themselves in case they used the wrong one.

Hector's leg was fully healed within the week; this was the final barrier between the two groups.

Laura had done something for them without being asked.

Hector admitted to both Fran and Hetty that he had been worried about the visits of these people. He realised how wrong he had been. He started making some more tools for the tribe to keep. He wasn't a good blacksmith, but his basic tools worked. The first thing was a large axe for the man who watched over the girls. Laura was presented with the tool as a 'thank you,' she shook her head and walked off.

Hector was now worried he had offended her. Puzzled, he stood watching her leave. She returned a few minutes later, followed by the tall, skinny man clothed only in a loin-tassel, back and front.

Hector realised that she wanted him to give it to this man. He was probably her husband; he'd sat up on the rock while the girls were at the house.

She gabbled his name, and it sounded like *Billynudgewoi*. Hector called him just Billy, and both laughed at the name, but the tall man nodded with a smile. Hector took the axe in both hands and, with a bow, presented it to the tall Aboriginal man. Billy accepted it and then beckoned Hector to follow him. All the others stood watching from the stable yard. The men walked up the roadway a little and towards a small sapling; the man shoved the new tool towards Hector. Hector took it and showed him how to use it.

Three cuts and a wedge were visible in the tree.

Billy took the axe and tried it for himself. He stood in precisely the same stance as Hector had, settling his feet firmly, and swung the weapon. The sapling fell in six thuds. They watched as the man flipped the axe upside down, checked the blade, and heard a shout of surprise as he cut his finger on it; he realised it was still sharp. Double dimples popped in both of his cheeks. He whistled, then made a sound like "Oi!" and stuck his bleeding finger in his mouth. Moments later, he chuckled.

Hector pulled something from his back pocket; it was a sharpening stone. He showed Billy how to sharpen the axe.

Billy's teeth gleamed in the sunlight, and Hector noticed that his brown eyes were two different shades. He shook his head and walked away from Hector. Billy turned and beckoned for Hector to follow. About one hundred yards down the track, Billy headed back towards the riverbank. Hidden amongst the shrubs was a big flat rock. Hector had seen this before but had not known what they used the rubbings for. Billy bent and showed Hector that this was his sharpening stone.

Hector saw long, smoothed grooves where many stone axes had been honed and sharpened over many years. He ran his fingers over them and felt the grain of the rock. He dug out his sharpening stone and compared it. The grit was much like the one he inspected; Billy stood watching.

Billy gently touched him on the shoulder and pointed to another, smaller rock. There were more groove marks, but the rock formation was much coarser; this was the first stage of shaping a stone axe. After that, up to ten of the tribe were regular visitors for some time. Often, they would appear daily; then, they would be gone for days, if not weeks. On each visit, they brought something. They left with food, tools, clothing, or blankets.

After this interaction, Laura and Billy often came with Carrie.

As Laura chattered to Kitty, Hetty overheard that Billy was from Pemulwuy's tribe, the Bidijigal people. He had the same mismatched eyes as the infamous older man did, and Hetty wondered if the relationship was much closer. She doubted she would ever know. Hetty was spinning madly as her growing condition hindered much other activity. Her baby stomach was now pronounced, and she stayed well hidden from Casey or other visitors. She had forgotten how ungainly one became at this stage of her confinement. Fran was even more cumbersome.

Chapter 14 Discoveries

Six days after Fran gave birth to their second son, Alistair Hector Macdougal, Casey arrived with a letter from Martha informing them that Des would be heading through in a week.

Skye was a little disappointed that she had a second brother, but she had learned to love Joey, so she wasn't too upset. The baby, Alec, as she called him, had his father's red hair.

When Martha finally heard that Des was heading to Sydney to collect the first flock for Mr Gates, she sent word to Hetty. Des had been gone nearly eight months. He would pass through twice and hoped Hetty would come to see him at Emu Plains.

Excitement flooded through the household; Hetty was determined to travel to Martha's place to meet him. He would be there in mid-July. She wished to tell him herself about their baby before it arrived. As she was so large with child Hector and Fran insisted on accompanying her, worried she would have the baby early. They had to stop for her to relieve herself frequently.

As it was winter, Hetty wrapped herself in a large overcoat to stay warm and hide her advanced condition in case they met anyone they knew. They had managed to keep news of their illicit marriage well under wraps. All would have realised that Joel died too long ago for him to be this child's father. Travelling this late in her condition over bumpy roads was inconvenient, but she was determined to go.

Clara, Jane, and Oliver were left in charge while Hector was away. Hector, Fran, and their children would only stay one night and then return. They would collect Hetty again in two weeks unless they heard otherwise.

Des was travelling through to Sydney to collect the promised stock.

He hoped his note had reached Martha and Jack and that Hetty would meet him at Emu Plains. He missed her so much. Their week together had been short and sweet. Leaving her had nearly crushed him. However, knowing that he would be free in just over three years was all that had given him the strength not to abandon his job and return to Hetty. He knew he could no longer be the irresponsible man he had spent many years perfecting. Des noticed that in the intervening eight months, Jack had finished building the inn. There were new stables out the back and a large yard with a corner sand-roll area for the horses.

As Des rode into the stable yard, movement at the kitchen door caught his eye. What he saw made him turn in his saddle. Hetty was heavy with child. "Hetty! My darling Hetty, my love," he hopped off the white steed and flicked the reins over the hitching rail. He strode to Hetty and gathered her gently in his arms. "My darling love, how?... no, don't answer that; I know how. I supposed I should ask when are you due." His mind doing a quick calculation.

Hetty smiled at her husband. He was as surprised as she had been at her condition. "I'm due within the month," she said as he gazed up at him. "I've been hoping I would see you before its arrival."

Des silenced further comments with a long and loving kiss. Eventually, he lifted his head and said, "In a bit over three years, I'll be a free man, love. It can't come soon enough, but I want to be near you; I won't run away as I would only be hunted down. We'll start afresh then, my sweetheart."

Hetty gave his cheek a loving caress. "I know, but Dessy, I have an idea. Is there somewhere I could stay in Bathurst if I came up for those three years? Hector and Fran can run things with Oliver, as he's getting close to eighteen. Molly can come with me. What do you think?"

Des gave her a quick peck. "I think that's wonderful, but Het, Bathurst is a primitive place, and the farm is worse."

Hetty didn't answer immediately, although a frown crossed her brow.

Des saw it. "Het, what are you thinking?"

She had not seen her two brothers for years. They had crossed the mountains some twenty years before and gone westward to farm. They had visited their mother in Sydney before Hetty married. However, the two handsome men were not strangers, as she presumed. She had remembered them well as they did her. She knew they had taken up land selections over the Blue Mountains, and both grazed sheep. However, she had no idea where they were other than it was somewhere near Bathurst. She said, "Des, my half-brothers, David and his wife Bessie, and Duncan McLean, went west. I don't know exactly where they took up their selections as I was only young when they went. I don't know them well, but I could find out where they are and write to them. I was wondering if Mr Gates's selection is anywhere near theirs."

Hetty continued her story as they watched Jack grooming the sweating steed. "Neither of them writes to me, and I don't have their direction. I'm not even sure they are still alive. I gather from your gasp that you know them?"

The discussion that ensued was enlightening to both.

Des unbuckled his saddlebags from the saddle and then stood arm-in-arm with Hetty as they watched Jack take the horse to be washed. "I do, my love, David is next door to the South, and Duncan is some miles west on his selection *Duncan's Reward*; he just calls it his reward," Des laughed. "David named his place *Wambool* Station; it is the local name for the winding river that runs through his place. Sweet Hetty, I did not realise they were your brothers. They are fine, upstanding men. I should have guessed."

David McLean's selection adjoined Mr Gates's along the long boundary, and they had often worked together. Duncan's property was some thirty miles further west with a shared back border. David's and Mr Gates's properties were so vast that the residences were some fifteen miles apart by road. However, Mr Gates's selection was named *Narrowgate*, as a play on his name and for the valley where it sat. The main entry into the property was through a narrow pass between two hills. There was a shorter track over the escarpment that bordered the properties. Des used it when he visited, but it was only suitable for a single rider. David's selection was lush pastureland along the river edge. The Fish River flowed into the Macquarie River, so Des knew it well. He had helped David fence the boundary. He had been impressed that David did most of the work himself as he refused to have convict assistance. The two brothers only had each other to help. Both had a pack of working dogs that did the work of six men. They also caused a lot less stress than a team of convicts. But they couldn't assist with fencing. Des was surprised that Hetty had never mentioned either of them before. He quizzed her.

After chatting briefly in the cool outdoor area, Hetty escorted Des back to the stables. "My only problem is that I hardly know them, Dessy. Since I grew up, I have only met them a few times, but they are my half-brothers, and they may help us. I know David remarried after Bessie died, but I have not met his new wife."

As they spoke, Jack had put the saddle undercover and left the saddlebags ready for Des. Jack had taken the horse for a roll in the sand before brushing him down.

They meandered towards the house.

Martha greeted him and suggested that they wait in the sitting room in front of the fire. Fran and Hector were currently minding the children. Fran was bathing all the children down in the cellar. Martha's baby, Cathy, was a month old; Fran and Hector's son, Alec, was two weeks younger. With eight children in the house, it was surprisingly quiet. Martha's brood was well-behaved and adorable. Skye and Joey loved having friends their age and were content to share their bath with their friends.

As they were all downstairs, Des drew Hetty into his arms again as the sitting room was empty. However, he didn't kiss her; he set one hand on her distended stomach and was surprised when the child kicked him. Astounded, his head jerked up, and he said, "Did you feel that?"

Hetty chuckled. "Yes, of course, you should feel it from my side." Joel had had much the same reaction when he had felt Oliver move for the first time.

Des didn't move from her side. "Now, what were we discussing? You had an idea regarding your brothers."

Hetty smiled. "Yes, I wondered if I could come and stay with David if he's the closest; then perhaps I could see you occasionally?" She lay her head on his shoulder.

Des was still in awe that he could hold her so. For her to wish to be near him made his heart race. "You would do that, my beloved? David's place is far better than my accommodation, as I am only in what they call a shepherd's box. It's barely big enough for me. Mr Gates is building a homestead, not that I'll be allowed to sleep there. I have an elevated bark shack with a pallet bunk. It's hot and uncomfortable in summer, frigid and leaks in winter, so it is unsuitable for you, my love, not even for one night, not that we would fit in together."

Hetty leaned as close as she could. Their child came between them. "It would not be until the babe arrives, but if you sound out David, see what he says. I'll come up as soon as I hear back from you." Hetty looked up at him. "Dessy, make it soon."

Des could only stay one night, but they made the most of the togetherness. He left at dawn the following day. It would take a week, at least, before he could return.

Hetty refused to go home until she saw him again. Hopefully, the child would arrive early so he could see it before he returned to Bathurst.

~

It was ten days before Des returned. He had two hundred sheep with him and six new convicts to assist him.

The droving of the flock of sheep had taken him longer than planned, as the flock was recently off a ship and in relatively poor condition. As he knew of no pens or sheepfolds along the route, they had to keep their eyes on the animals constantly. Each morning they did a headcount and needed to round up any stragglers.

When he returned to Emu Plains, Hetty greeted him with their daughter in her arms. Hetty was quite sure what name Des would choose but remained silent when anyone asked. She refused to call her anything other than little one, so he could name her. Even though they had had so little time together, Hetty knew one particular name was suitable.

Des's smile showed his delight at seeing his daughter. "What's her name, Het?" he inquired.

Hetty bit her lip before saying, "I have left her for you to choose, Des. Though, I'm quite sure I know what you will select." A playful smile was his response.

Their eyes locked. Des said with an understanding grin, "Caroline Henrietta then, Het. But she will be known as…" he paused and smiled again; he nearly choked on the name, "…as Carly. My own Carly."

Hetty grinned again. "I wondered, Dessy, Carly was why you and Joel both came here. She is the reason for so much, including our being together. So, Carly, she shall be."

Des slid his arm lovingly around his wife and child. He couldn't believe it. Hetty held the babe to him, lovingly taking the tiny cherub in his arms. He ran his finger over her hips. "Carly, I shall protect you the best I possibly can all my life. I shall be very protective of you, my girl, so be warned." He pushed back the blanket a little and saw her shock of dark hair. His sister had hair like that. "My Carly would have turned forty this year, Het." He kissed the top of his daughter's head.

Leaving the flock to the new shepherds for the night, Des took the opportunity of spending the night with Hetty. Although they could not be together intimately, they lay cradled in each other's arms. They had no idea how long it would be before they saw each other again.

~

It was six months before Hetty felt she could take her daughters and Ernie and travel to David's property. David had written excitedly with an open-door welcome. He explained that both the sheep properties had been purchased with family money, so she had as much right to it as he did. He had made two rooms ready for the family.

Hector and Fran were instructed to oversee the farm under the auspices of Oliver's authority. Although he was too young to have the job himself, Oliver was still not eighteen, but he was keen to have the final say in what the farm would do over the next three years. There was not much he would change, but it was nice to have that authority if he wished to do so. Hetty had also given her blessing to his relationship with Mary. However, she suggested he wait some years before moving to more than friendship.

Ernie had initially resisted his mother's idea to go with her until he realised it meant travelling across the Blue Mountains. It was something he had always wished to do. He would also meet his two uncles, whom he didn't even know he had.

After a week-long journey, the family arrived in Bathurst safely and settled in for their extended stay.

Meanwhile, work on Loganberry Farm continued unhindered and unabated. The new square weave berry baskets were filled with succulent homegrown strawberries, mulberries and raspberries, then packed and prepared for transport. The previous year, Hector had sourced whatever berry plants he could find. He already had a mulberry tree growing on the river's edge, but it only fruited in October. The vines and trees thrived in the lush river soils. Even Molly's grapevine was a surprise. It was now of a size that it bore nice bunches of plump green seeded grapes. They were sweet and juicy.

Jane had suggested that rather than planting the thorny raspberries and blackberries in the ground, they use some half kegs to avoid them running wild. The plants loved their new homes. They had placed the tubs in the courtyard between the stable, dormitory, and house. The raspberry canes produced berries in this warm spot for far longer than expected. The clump that Hector had sourced already had some second-year canes, so the tub was producing only six months after planting. The blackberries only had one or two berries this first year, so they made a couple of mixed berry baskets.

Hector loaded the cart and took the produce to the markets in Richmond. It was closer than Windsor. This was the first time that there were enough berries to sell.

With the Aboriginal girls now sourcing and supplying vines, productivity once again picked up. Over Summer, Laura and her friends often sat on the verandah weaving with Fran and the other girls. It was cool, and they would try to learn new words from each other.

When the near-naked girls arrived for the day's work, Oliver and Hector would vanish. It was hard for them to pull their eyes from the nubile female forms displayed so innocently, so rather than try to keep their gazes from them, the men fled, only returning when they left.

Jane was still making her small honey barrels but needed new hoops. One day, out of the blue, she said, "Hector, I'd like to go to Richmond and talk to the blacksmith. I wondered about taking Mr Oliver and a sample of what I want." This trip was the first time Jane had asked to leave the farm in the years since her arrival.

Hector asked her why she didn't just want him to go for her as usual.

She hedged his question. Jane was one of the two girls who had never opened up about her past. All they knew about her was that her father had taught her to make barrels of all sizes. She was a closed book.

Hector thought that maybe she was unsettled, so her request was a surprise. He knew she was serving a long sentence but didn't know why; Jane was approaching thirty fast. Being so tall and well-built, when she arrived, Fran had thought she was older than the mere twenty-one years that she claimed. She had been with them for nearly eight years.

Jane didn't explain much, but looking Hector in the eye, she said, "Fear can keep you safe, but Hector, it can also imprison you. I have been imprisoned by my fear of what could happen if I left; therefore, I have never done so." She paused before saying, "I don't wish to go to Windsor but to the blacksmith at Richmond."

Hector looked at her and tipped his head to the side. "And...?" he questioned.

With a resigned sigh, Jane knew she would have to answer him. She explained her dream, which was so vivid that she believed it. "I'm not one to be fanciful about anything, Hector. You should know that by now. However, I am only telling you because if it is true, I shall return with a severely injured man." Her glance at Hector reassured her to continue. "I had a dream of an explosion in Richmond. A man will die if I don't go," she explained bluntly. She did not reveal whom her dream involved.

Hector believed in words of knowledge and knew she was right to act on her vision. "Then I shall come instead of Oliver. I shall also prepare a room for him in the timber drying room. It's warm and will be away from the other girls."

They set out two days later.

In good faith, Hector had made up a bed for the unknown man in the drying room. The nights in September were still chilly, and he would be warm there. Fran and Kitty told Laura and her friends that a sick man might join them. He was a man who would probably have burns. All might be required to nurse him.

With a frown on her brow, Laura nodded her understanding, then vanished. Hand signs were still mainly used, but they were finally beginning to understand a few words of each other's language. Fire was a word that had been taught early.

Hector and Jane departed while the others waited anxiously at home. They did not know what or who they would return with, but they hopefully were prepared. Fran found a torn sheet and washed it, then tore it into strips for bandages.

After a few hours, Hector and Jane arrived at the smith's forge in Richmond and discussed the new thin hoops Jane required. The barrels were only to be eight inches high. The narrow hoops she needed had to be purpose-made. Soon after arrival, Hector heard her make a slight gasp. He frowned in wonderment.

Jane had been stunned to see the man working the forge, for she knew this man had trained as a cooper, not a smith.

The man had not seen her; she had ducked her head as he turned. However, her eyes were drawn back to him. Her heart had skipped a beat.

Remembering her dream, she looked around the forge and saw a quenching barrel of water and a blanket. The man had just brought in a large coal shuttle and shovelled some into the forge. Moments later, an explosion occurred. This coal contained pockets of volatile gas, which then ignited and exploded. The new coal had caused a few minor eruptions in the last few days; none were as significant as this.

The chunks of coal that the striker, Nate, had just added had lots of these pockets, and the fire blew up, covering him with fine-burning coal shards. When the blast occurred, Nate was leaning over the forge, so he caught the full flareup on his face, chest, and arms.

The senior smith stood immobile, unsure of what to do.

Without thinking, Jane grabbed the blanket, dunked it in the water, and used it to extinguish his clothing. Then she took the quenching bucket, carefully doused Nate's smouldering hair, and sloshed it over his burned skin.

Nate's screams filled her ears, just as in her dream.

While Hector sent the smith for the doctor, Jane carefully poured water on the burnt areas of his face and arms. After some minutes, Nate collapsed in agony. Jane sloshed him with water, ensuring the coal fragments were fully extinguished. Once he passed out, she removed the small chunks of coal from the burns on his face and arms. Jane and Hector managed to get him onto the cleared workbench.

On arrival, after taking a quick look at his patient, the doctor said, "He'll die; nothing I can do." Then he departed, leaving Nate unattended.

A young woman had trailed behind the doctor, apparently his assistant. She said she was used to bandaging wounds. When she heard the patient had burns, she grabbed a jar of thick dark honey and bandage rolls. She carefully smeared this dark sticky substance over the melted skin, which had already blistered and some had broken.

Nate was a mess. Thankfully he had still not regained consciousness. On the smith's return, he realised Nate could no longer work and left again to report the accident to the Major. His striker was now useless, so he would ask for another convict to take his place. One was much the same as another.

When the Major arrived, Hector asked that Nate be reassigned to Mrs Walker. The Major agreed, filled in the paperwork, and wrote, "Unlikely to survive" beside his name. The smith was assigned another convict immediately.

Hector and Jane loaded Nate into their cart and took him to the rectory. They stayed the night at the rectory while caring for the injured man. Reverend Cross always had spare places for them when required. The overnight stay also meant that Jane could catch up with her friends. All helped where they could, taking turns sitting up with Nate for a few hours throughout the night.

Early the following day, they loaded up the still-breathing but unconscious man. Jane was determined not to let him die now; she climbed into the cart with him and cradled his head in her lap while Hector drove home. Mrs Cross had given Jane a short length of muslin to keep the flies from his face. The doctor had allowed the nurse to apply more thick tea tree honey; however, sadly, this attracted flies, and Jane fought to keep them away from her patient and his burns.

The cart slowly traversed the track to Loganberry Farm two days after leaving the farm. Oliver saw them first and noticed Hector alone in the front seat. Jane sat in the back, keeping her eyes on Nate's face.

Hector gently pulled up in the stable yard and flicked the reins over the hitching post.

Fran and Oliver were the first to arrive. One look at Jane's face was enough to see her concern. She had not lifted her eyes from the bleeding immobile body beside her. She was kept busy brushing the flies from his muslin-covered face. Thankfully he was still unresponsive.

Fran gasped when she first saw the man; his face was unrecognisable as human. It was just an oozing, gooey, red mess.

Jane's teary face pleaded with Fran. "We have to help him, Franny. His name is Nathaniel Jamison. He was father's apprentice, and I didn't even know Nate was here." Jane's glassy eyes returned to the living corpse beside her.

Hector took his wife aside and suggested she tell all the others to stay away. The sight was gruesome. The entire top half of his body was burned raw. How he was not dead already, they didn't know. "We must get him into his room before we treat him."

At that moment, Laura and her husband appeared. The man looked into the cart, then passed his spear to Laura, and in one careful movement, Billy lifted the unconscious man and carried him into the waiting room. He tasted what was on his face, smiled, and then wiped off the excess with some paperbark that Laura handed to him.

Billy turned to Laura and gabbled something. She vanished up the path, then quickly returned carrying something. He started smearing Nate's face with a gooey substance. Having seen how the treatment of Hector's leg had worked, they let him continue. Over this, he peeled off thin layers of paperbark and stuck it over the burns. There was little more they could do. Hector had not even expected the man to have lived through the trip. How he had, amazed him. Nate still didn't stir, but soon, his breathing was no longer rasping.

Jane sat beside him, holding his unburned fingertips. She refused to leave his side for more than a few minutes. Fran realised that there was more to her care than just her dream. Nate meant something to her. He stirred enough to drink, then slept again. Every few hours, they roused him and gave him more fluids.

Laura and her husband came daily for a few days and reapplied the unconventional treatment. On the fourth day, Laura came alone. She had a container of moving soil in a small wooden coolamon.

Hector was horrified at what he saw. Fran almost screamed. Out of the soil, Laura dug a gigantic white witchetty grub. She proceeded to squash this into the now-familiar paste. She once again spread this on Nate's burns. The redness was already going, and there seemed to be virtually no infection. Only one small area on his shoulders remained full of pus. Laura put some yellow puff fungi on this and covered it with more bark.

Hector, Fran, and Jane watched on, amazed.

Nate had yet to wake fully, but his sleep was undoubtedly more comfortable; they could rouse him to drink, and then he slept again. He lay on towels that needed to be changed regularly, but his wounds responded to the treatment.

As Jane was content that he was now on the mend. She went to bed and slept. Fran sat with Nate and prayed.

On the sixth day, Nate finally stirred; the burns were already beginning to heal. The last of the pus had also gone, and he finally fully awoke. He opened his eyes as Laura's breasts wobbled in front of him.

The girl was again smearing the gooey substance over his face, arms and chest. She gasped when he reached out and touched her. Laura called for Jane, "Jane, him wake."

Jane came immediately. Nate saw her and tried to speak. He realised he could not smile and then put his hand to feel his face. It hurt, and he didn't know why. Jane explained what had occurred, and Nate finally remembered the fire. He remembered feeling that his face was hot and burning. He finally croaked, "Jane, my Janey." He reached for her hand and then fell asleep again. She couldn't be there; he must be dreaming again…

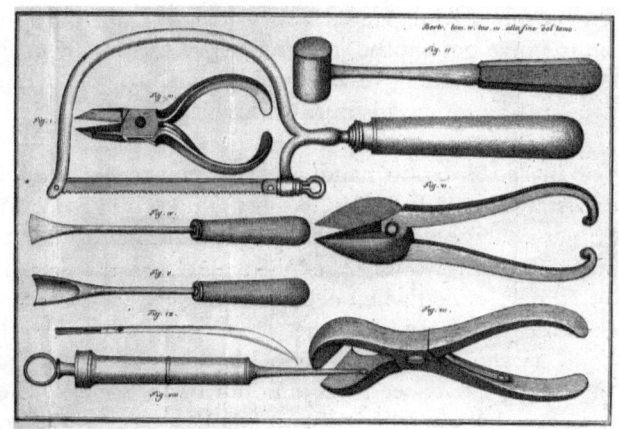

Chapter 15 Healing Times

Over the next week, Nate recovered enough until he could sit up unaided.

He still had no idea where he was or why Jane was there. She had refused to answer his questions.

Laura continued with her treatment.

None dared to tell Nate what it was. It worked; that's all he needed to know for the moment. He was finally well enough to speak, and Hector dressed him in clean trousers and assisted him to the verandah to watch the girls working on their weaving. Hector placed him in Hetty's rocking chair.

Nate watched silently as the baskets took shape before his eyes. Each was a different size, shape, and even material. One girl was making bee skeps; another one was making vine baskets. Mary was busy making berry baskets, although sometimes she was doing some tatting. The long roll of lace-like loops was then sewn onto mob caps for sale. Kitty was embroidering some flowers onto these trimmed caps.

Clara occupied the children in her classroom.

Jane kept her distance. When she was near him, she still avoided all questions.

Nate watched silently until Hector returned, followed by Oliver. "What is this place, Hector? Why are they all so hard at work making stuff?"

Jane had not told him anything. She had retreated back into her silent world. She was currently shaping staves for small casks and knew that she would have to work hard to catch up on the time she had taken off nursing Nate.

Hector explained. Then he revealed to Nate that he had been reassigned here as they had expected him to die. It had been a technicality so the blacksmith could get another convict striker as soon as possible.

Nate only commented, "So I don't have to go back? Truly?" Tears flooded his eyes and ran down his burnt face; he relaxed and lay back in the seat.

Hector placed a caring hand on the unburnt section of his arm. "No, you are to stay here with us. Mrs Walker is presently away, and her son, Master Oliver, is in charge. I am a lifer too, Nate," Hector didn't want him to ask any questions, nor would he explain much of the situation on the farm. That would be revealed when necessary.

After three more days of the silent treatment from Jane, Nate caught her hand as she was leaving his side. He had woken to find her sitting next to him. She had been weeping but had a smile on her face. As soon as she realised he was stirring; she stood to leave. He grabbed her hand, "Don't go, Janey; please don't leave me again."

She snatched her hand away and walked to the door. She stopped with a hand on the doorpost, she leaned her forehead on the timber, and her shoulders shook with her weeping. She had thought she could gaze at his face and him not know of it. She had been wrong.

Nate saw her hesitation, "Janey, talk to me, please. It was not my fault. Don't blame me, please."

At those words, she spun around. "Blame you? How could I blame you when it was all my fault? I did not know the evil a woman could do to another because of false love. Nate, I am not worthy for you to even speak to." She turned to leave again.

This time Nate didn't stop her. He lay puzzling over her words. Surely, she could not blame herself for the death of the obsessive lunatic who had pursued him so relentlessly. He had never encouraged his neighbour, Cecile, but she would not take "no" for an answer. She shadowed him and frequently appeared in places where he least expected it, trying to get him to compromise her so he would have to marry her. Her ploys failed. Cecile had become such a problem that he had needed to tell both Mr Matthews and Jane about her.

Nate remembered the day he asked Jane's father for her hand in marriage. Her father had willingly given Nate his blessing. He had been so nervous. Although he was sure of Jane's reply, he was still shaking when he proposed to her while they were shaping staves for a large oak barrel. He had been overjoyed when she had agreed. As Jane had no brothers, Mr Matthews said Nate would take over the business one day.

It suddenly struck Nate that Jane was blaming herself for Cecile's death. Considering both of them had been convicted for her murder, he thought this was probably not surprising. However, he knew that they were completely innocent. They had both been visiting the minister to arrange their wedding when Cecile had died, but she had left a letter that they would be responsible should she be found dead. In hindsight, Nate realised that Cecile had thought that if she could not have him, then no one else could either.

Nate struggled to rise from his bed. He still could not put any load-bearing weight on his arms. He groaned in agony at the effort, and it brought Jane to his side faster than he could imagine.

"Nate, you must not exert yourself. Wait for Oliver or Hector to assist you." She tried to stop him from rising.

He took her arm and gently drew her to him. "No, my Janey, we need to talk. I can't bear being so close and having this wall between us. We are both innocent. It was the ravings of a crazy woman that sent us both here."

Resigned that a conversation must occur, she sank down beside him. Jane could no longer hold back her tears. "But I wished her dead, Nate. I told her to her face that I wished her to blazes. You and I were getting married, and there was nothing she could do to steal you from me. I told her to leave us alone. Then the next day, she was dead. I may as well have pushed her myself."

As much as it hurt, he drew her into his arms, his heart hurt more, but he would not let her go again. He refused to be this close and not claim her as his own. He had no idea she had been so near for eight years. He didn't know where she had been imprisoned; he had presumed she was still in England. They had spent so many years apart and must work out some future as they were now assigned together.

Hector heard the voices travel through the stable wall and knew Nate was awake. He appeared to assist and saw Nate lift her chin and kiss her gently but lovingly.

Nate saw movement at the door and greeted Hector. He did not withdraw his arm. "Sweetheart, we have company."

Jane lifted her teary head from his bandaged body. She did not want to move, yet she knew she must leave him so he could dress. She gave Hector a nod as she passed him but remained silent.

With one raised eyebrow, Hector looked at Nate.

Nate smiled in reply. "It's time to tell you everything as I dress." Hector helped him with his trousers, but Nate refused a shirt as it stuck to the burns. Nate explained their long-term engagement, innocence, and arrest for murder. The minister who could have vouched for them had been killed on the way to visit a parishioner soon after they had left him. He was their only alibi, as no one else had seen them at the appointed time at the rectory. In a letter found at her home, Cecile had named them both as being responsible. She had been found floating in the river. They were arrested and presumed guilty. The judge would not believe their protestations of innocence. They were damned by her words and both convicted to life terms. Nate had even wondered if Cecile had been responsible for the minister's death. There was no way he would ever know. However, it was odd for a wheel to come off the minister's new gig.

Nate had not seen Jane again. That had been nine years ago.

Hector smiled in understanding. He had let Nate tell his story uninterrupted, occasionally nodding and sometimes agreeing with what he was saying. His story also explained why Jane had felt strongly about going to Richmond. He explained her dream and their trip and said he understood the emotional tie one had for a loved one. His grandmother had told him of someone whom the Scots called fey. He told Nate that he called it a Word of Knowledge and declared that such a gift was from God.

Once he had his trousers on, Nate did not try to stand. He and Hector sat talking on his bed for some time. Nate did not understand why Jane had blamed herself to the degree she did. He could vouch for her being with him; there was no question of her guilt, or his for that matter.

Hector admitted that Jane had never spoken of her past. She had made friends with the other girls but had thrown herself into work rather than socialising. Hector also admitted that sometimes he had to stop her from taking on too much work. Some days in summer, she worked until she almost collapsed. She had kept on working through the heat of the hottest days.

Nate knew her work ethic. She had always wanted to prove she was equally as strong as any man and often had many more staves shaped than he had. He knew she was tireless. However, Nate was gutted as Jane still held him at arm's length most of the time. "What do I do, Hector?"

Hector had wondered about just this question. "If what I saw is an example, then I suggest you take things day by day. She obviously still has feelings for you. However, as you are here to stay, I would not rush her. I have no idea what she went through before arriving here, but a friend of Mrs Walker's sent her." Hector looked at the injured man with a frown on his brow. His words were said with great compassion. "Nate, only the emotionally crushed or violently abused girls were permitted to come here, so that may be the reason, although she was also sent because of her coopering skills too."

Nate nodded as the full meaning of Hector's words hit. But he smiled. "She's still doing that? I never thought she would touch the tools ever again." He had not seen her storeroom of barrels on the far side of his building. He had once walked through the coopering room and even heard someone working there but had not realised it was Jane.

Hector nodded in answer to his words. "She is almost obsessed, Nate. If we get an order for a hundred mini barrels, she has them done in less than half the expected time." Hector paused, thinking hard about what to do. Frowning, he said, "Nate, talk to my wife. Fran might be able to get her talking now. Jane will need a shoulder to lean on as I feel that she will now open up. My Franny is good at that; she came as one of Mrs Walker's first rescued ladies." He saw Nate's eyes wide in surprise.

Nate said, "All of these girls too? They were all abused?"

Hector nodded. "Yes, Nate, all of them to some degree, including my Fran; this is a healing haven. A place where the girls are safe from further abuse." He paused, letting that sink in. After a moment, he said, "In the meantime, let's get you up and outside; Laura is awaiting you."

Nate groaned, his skin was still red and raw in places, but the deep burns were healing. "Does that girl ever wear clothing? It's, um, very distracting." He was still unsteady on his feet as he had been flat on his back for so long.

Hector shook his head and chuckled, then said, "Keep your eyes closed, laddie."

Jane was nowhere to be seen when they emerged. Hector thought it was not like her to have not started work; however, her workshop was empty. Hector let Nate lean on him as they walked to the verandah into his usual chair. Now Hector knew their back story; he and Fran had something specific to pray for and, hopefully, a way to assist. They had spent many hours talking with Jane over the years about her faith. Nate's arrival had brought on a change in her. If Fran knew the problem, she could have a base to start a conversation with her. Hector settled Nate in Hetty's rocking chair, leaving him to watch the girls work.

Laura soon appeared and treated him. He still had not asked what was in the ointment, and no one volunteered the information. If he knew what it was, he would be horrified. They all decided to stay mum over the ingredients. Squashed witchetty grub puree smeared on one's face, and the body was not conducive to good mental health.

Laura made him close his eyes as she did her work. He would have, anyway. The cream was soothing and took away some of the pain.

Hector quietly left them; he beckoned Fran to join him. They retired to their room in the stables to discuss the unfolding situation privately. He filled her in about what he had discussed with Nate.

Fran gave him a quick kiss and left him to search for Jane. Now she knew the problem; she hoped Jane would open up to her. Fran knew just where to look. Since Nate's arrival, after finishing work for the day, Fran had often seen Jane heading up the hill towards Joel's grave. She would go anywhere to avoid people. There was a large flat sandstone rock that overlooked the river. The rock seat on the ledge was hidden from the house, and she could be alone. It was here that Franny found her.

Jane had seen her coming; she knew it was time to clear the air. Her hiding years were over.

Fran sat beside Jane on the low rock shelf near the back of the prominent outcrop and then waited.

It was almost as though time stood still, but the river kept flowing, the breeze still blew, and the birds still sang cheerfully. Life moved forward in the typical day-to-day way of life. The world kept on turning, but Jane's life stopped. It had frozen one day, nearly ten years ago. Her life had all but ceased. She ate, breathed and slept, but her life was merely a void.

Without even acknowledging Fran's presence, Jane started talking. "It's as though the last nine years didn't happen. I had no idea that it was Nate whom I needed to bring back here, but I should have guessed. He's the only one I have a connection with like that." She hardly took a breath before her entire story flooded out.

Fran just had to sit and listen while holding her hand.

Jane paused and looked at Fran. "I still love him, Franny, but I don't deserve him. I wished his neighbour Cecile was dead so often that I was thrilled to hear she had died, but we had nothing to do with it." Jane sniffed. "What do I do?"

Fran wished Hector was here; he seemed to have the answers, not her. She said the first words that came to her. "Talk to him, Jane. You have to tell him how you are feeling. You have to talk it through, and Jane, pray with him. You have learned the power of prayer."

Jane nodded; she knew that was a long conversation she didn't want to have. Yet, she also realised that it was now inevitable.

Over the next week, Jane and Nate were seen together often. During that time, Jane did little work on the casks.

Hector explained to Oliver what was happening.

Knowing the state of his own heart. Oliver agreed and said Jane would not be pressured to finish any work. Jane was too valuable to their farm for her to want to leave. Not that she legally could.

Neither Jane nor Nate let on about their discussions, but Jane had obviously decided that her future with Nate was happily unavoidable. She started up her work again and was often heard singing to herself. Nate was determined to help her if he could, but he knew he still had to keep his wounds clean. The skin on his face was growing back. His arms and the backs of his hands were still delicate, but he could use a spokeshave and rasp to shape the staves as his palms were unburnt. He knew his forearms might be left with some scarring, but he would survive. He had nothing to prove in life, and a few scars were worth the cost if he could have Jane back in it.

At the end of the month, their engagement was officially back on. Nate knew that their conversations had been successful when she appeared wearing the engagement ring he had given her nearly ten years before. He had no idea where she had hidden it all these years, but the fact that she had kept it thrilled him. He'd had little money when he proposed, so the ring was only a small cairngorm stone set in a silver band, but she had kept it, which made his heart soar. He had even less money now, so he could not have replaced it.

Life on the farm settled back down to manufacturing baskets for the markets. Jane still didn't have the hoops she had gone to Richmond for, but she had Nate. He was feeling much better and planned to make the hoops himself. By the time he had been on the farm for a month, he was well enough to do some light smithing work. With Hector's assistance, he placed an order for the coil of steel banding required.

Thanks to Hector, Nate found he could buy a roll of hoop metal from Thomas Tindale, the blacksmith in Parramatta. He only needed a small fire pit to heat and rivet-weld the joins of the small hoops. Both were skills he had; having done his first apprenticeship as a cooper and eight years as the striker and blacksmith's assistant at Richmond, he could now turn his hand to most things.

While they waited for the order to arrive, Jane and Nate got busy making staves, plus bottoms and tops for the new size of tiny barrels. Over the years, Jane had built up a supply of small lengths of the silver wattle that were too short for the average-size staves. These timbers had knots or insect holes in the wrong places; otherwise, the wood was solid.

Jane had made a squat barrel with the hoops she had but thought smaller, narrower barrels would look good.

After a few weeks, the coil of half-inch-wide steel arrived.

Hector and Nate had made a small forge pit and borrowed the tiny bellows from the kitchen fire. They were able to source the essential tools required, and soon various lengths of steel hoops were awaiting use. After making the first set of bands and assembling the initial test barrel, they fired up the forge again, and the two men, plus Oliver working the bellows, decided to make up two-thirds of the coil into the small hoops.

They had made enough small staves to make close to fifty of the small, eight-inch barrels. Each barrel needed three pairs of riveted thin hoops or three wider ones. Nate wished he had now ordered two widths of the banding, but he found some of the original coil she had brought with her years before. They had to make do with what they had, which was the one-inch wide steel, so each tiny barrel needed only three hoops. Nate hammered all the lengths into curls on Hector's anvil and then sealed the rivets in the fire, thus closing the loops.

Nate could not hammer for long and showed Oliver how to shape the curves on the round end of the anvil. Each was measured, and holes were punched in the correct places.

Jane could chamfer the staves around each slight difference in measurement. They just had to make sure the rivets sat flat on the timber. These could be heated in the fire and set on the barrels to fix them in position. They did this by hammering down the hot hoops with wooden wedges. As Jane had been doing these for years without assistance, she had worked out a way to keep everything in situ while she worked.

Each size of hoop sat in its own basket. Working together, they set a circle, and then Nate kissed her. After over two hundred hoops had been placed on forty small barrels over the week. The laughter and fun emanating from the cooper's shed brought Fran to watch. Rather than stand back and melt away, she entered the shaving-filled workroom. Beside Jane were rows of finished headers for top and bottom use for the small barrels. On the far wall was a line of nearly finished micro kegs. They yet had to have the bung holes drilled into them, but they looked fabulous. All had been sealed internally before the top header was added.

Fran could smell the beeswax used to line the insides. She had seen Jane seal the outsides once. Jane had even made a treadle clamp machine with a foot treadle, a little like a lathe. After sealing them with the hot pine resin, she would polish them with shavings. She would hold a handful of shavings to the spinning barrel, adding a sheen to the timber and polishing the hoop. The lovely pale wood would take on a reddish hue from the resin and then a shine from the shavings.

Nate swept up the shavings and placed them in a basket so she could grab a handful at a time. His hands were too raw for this job, but the sweet smell that filled the room was almost delicious.

The forty-eight, eight-inch barrels had taken less than a month from start to finish.

Nate had finally discovered the ingredient of his ointment and refused further treatments from Laura. He would only allow Jane to apply anything else to him if he knew the complete content list. The thick dark honey was permissible, but it made him very sticky. It also attracted flies.

Fran produced a sweet-smelling oil that he didn't mind using. It was a mix of rose hip and geranium oils. Fran insisted that he helped make it, so he knew what was in it. She had thickened it slightly with beeswax. This ointment eased the scars.

Chapter 16 Bathurst Happenings

*H*etty and the younger children had been gone for eighteen months. It was now 1830, and Carly was nearly two and loved seeing her father each week. Hetty loved reconnecting with her brothers and loved the life that David had built for himself at *Wambool Station*. David and his wife, Matilda, welcomed the extended family. Ernie was able to pull his weight and assist his uncle. They had three daughters, all of whom were much older than Ernie. Their eldest daughter was married and had moved onto another property, and David loved having the assistance of his nephew.

Des came over when he could, but of late, Mr Gates was currently visiting, and he had been unable to get away for the last few weeks.

David had heard of stirrings of unrest in town and some surrounding areas. He insisted that the ladies stay close to the homestead.

Governor Darling had visited the area with his family the year before and had been shocked to find two men bathing naked in the river near the crossing. Horrified and disgusted, the Governor had ordered they be arrested without further questioning. It seemed that the two men had been consigned to take a load of wool clip to Sydney, and being hot, they went for a swim. They had received fifty lashes each, and the fleeces were confiscated. The repercussions of this incident were just beginning to manifest. John Lipscombe was the squatter on the other side of David, and Ralph Entwistle, one of the swimmers, was assigned to him. John wasn't happy that the government took his fleeces after all his hard work and blamed Ralph. When Ralph started stirring up trouble, the authorities tore up his Ticket of Leave in September. He and a few other discontented convicts started raiding properties to show his ire.

David had not let his family know, except to say they were not to leave the house yard for any reason. Des kept him up to date with what was occurring. Ralph was a bit of a larrikin but otherwise had seemed a likeable bloke. Des had worked with Ralph often in the year before the incident, repairing other adjoining boundary fences. Then he, another convict, and David had mended the fences on David's boundary. They had got along well, and he had enjoyed working with them. Hopefully, that bond would keep their properties safe.

At sunset on the last day in September, Des came from *Narrowgate* and reported the beginnings of what would become a significant concern. Ralph Entwistle now had over fifty followers, and the first person they turned on was the overseer on Lipscomb's farm, James Greenwood. Greenwood was shot and killed, and the gang, now called bushrangers, fled. They vanished into the bush.

Des was seriously concerned for his family and wanted to ensure their safety. He stayed the night before needing to return to work. He wished his time was up and he could take his family back to *Loganberry Farm*, but he only had over six months left to serve. His parting was harrowing.

Hetty didn't want him to go and clung to him, weeping. Carly saw her mother crying, so she wailed too.

David eventually had to hold Hetty as Des rode away with his heart heavy. Both men knew of the killings on other properties but had not told the women. Hetty knew something was wrong when David had taught Ernie how to shoot. They kept the guns close to the doors; shot and powder were near each weapon. Carly was told to stay well away from them. Hetty and Molly kept their eyes on her.

Two days later, the news was brought to David by a visiting farmer that officials had formed a posse in Bathurst and set off after the gang with Aboriginal trackers' assistance. Ralph was still the ringleader, and now for some reason, he had a swathe of white ribbons tied around his hat. The group was called the Ribbon Gang due to Ralph's adornments.

Des came over again the following weekend. David had gone out to see the stock and insisted that Ernie remain on guard. Finally, Des and David sat the women down and explained the situation. Ernie was left at home with them as David still had to work. At nearly eighteen, he was now the only protection for the farm.

Pastoralist William Suttor and his brother Charles led a posse hunting for the bushranger's hideout. A shootout ensued on the Abercrombie River, and the bushrangers fled south. The trackers reported that half had headed out of the area and others towards the Abercrombie caves. Hard on the heels of the bushrangers, the posse and trackers came across a trail of destruction at each homestead, they came across. Now joined by a military cohort from the 57th regiment, they followed the path into the caves. The trackers reported that there should only be about twenty men remaining in the gang.

Now cornered, the bushrangers shot to kill. The following hours saw over three-hundred shots fired. Two of the gang lay dead, and many on both sides were injured. Yet, somehow, the gang slipped out and circled back. The posse returned to town to regroup and reconsider their position. Unbeknownst to the bushranger gang, some trackers followed them to a bald hill outside Bathurst. Again, the posse found them, and another gunfight ensued. Lieutenant James Brown lost two of his men and five horses. Furthermore, the Ribbon Gang claimed victory.

On return to Bathurst, Lieutenant Brown called for reinforcements. They were soon joined by a vast military contingent of one hundred and thirty armed soldiers from the 39th regiment from Sydney. Meanwhile, a bevy of mounted police was despatched from Goulburn, and Lieutenant John McAllister commanded them.

The Ribbon Gang were now moving through Cowra, Galong, and Boorowa. Leaving a trail of destruction as they ransacked homesteads, they were not too hard to follow. On leaving Boorowa, the two groups met. Lieutenant McAllister was shot in the thigh, and others on both sides were wounded. The troopers retreated to quarters in Bong Bong, taking three wounded gang members with them. Now demoralised, the posse soon rounded up the gang. Many had fled; others surrendered.

By the end of October, the rebellion was over. The remainder of the gang were now in gaol in Bathurst and ordered to stand trial. Ralph Entwistle, William Gahan, Michael Kearney, Patrick Gleeson, Thomas Dunn, and John Shepherd were immediately convicted of the murder of James Greenwood. The remaining bushrangers, Robert Webster, James Driver, Dominic Daby, and John Kenny, later joined them on the scaffold. When the judge said that the sentence would be publicly carried out on November 2, peace returned to the area, but the memory of the devastation they caused remained. Many had gathered to watch the murderers do the dance of death on the gallows.

Mr Gates was due the next day, so Des needed to be back for his arrival. Des rode across to give the family that bit of good news. Once again, he spent the night with them before returning to *Narrowgate*. He valued every moment he could with Hetty, and they had slept little this night. Much of the time was spent talking, but they enjoyed the intimacy of marriage a few times throughout the night.

Hetty knew Des had exactly six months until he gained his freedom and they could return home. She hoped Mr Gates would only stay briefly as Des was rarely able to visit while he was there. Des kissed Carly before leaving, telling her to be a good girl for her mother. Their parting was sad but not tearful, as the bushrangers were now gone. Ernie was once again allowed to head out with David and the dogs. Hetty and Matilda were again left in charge at the homestead. David and Ernie rode a boundary fence from different directions, then met in the middle and rode home.

On arrival home on the second day after Des's departure, they were met by Mr Gates himself. He had come to ask why Des was not on the property to meet him. Mr Gates revealed he had known of the secret marriage and was not impressed with the unconventional wedding. Major Ned Grace told him he had recorded the Scottish ceremony in government files. He knew they also now had a daughter. Des had admitted this to his boss soon after Hetty had arrived in the area. However, Mr Gates expected to see Des at the homestead. He was surprised to see Hetty's panic and then her tears. He realised something must have happened to him and waited anxiously for David and Ernie's return. David knew the shortcut that Des used between the properties. He led Mr Gates and Ernie up the narrow pass and down the rocky trackback to the *Narrowgate* homestead. Half a mile from the homestead, they saw Des's horse at the bottom of the gully. It had fallen and was dead, but where was Des? The three started calling for him. Ernie brought up the rear and heard a groan from behind a large boulder, half-hidden by shrubs. He called out, "Over here, Uncle David, and he's alive."

Des had been thrown from his horse and was lying at an odd angle. He had broken his leg as there was an extra bend where it should have been straight. He must have lain there for nearly two days. Ernie was down on his knees beside him with his water bag. Des roused and drank thirstily. It took the rest of the day to manoeuvre Des back to the homestead carefully, but he was alive. They could only move him on a stretcher, hastily made from two hessian bags and slung on two saplings. The path was too narrow for anything more than a horse or for men to walk wider than single file. Ernie was sent to tell his mother that Des was alive. He was to escort her the fifteen miles by road, and she was to bring their wagon to the *Narrowgate* homestead.

Des was ensconced in the Gates homestead by nightfall, and Hetty had cleaned the wound and set his leg as best she could, but it was a mess. One of the bones was sticking through the skin. Thankfully it had been protected from the dirt by his thick trousers. Mr Gates was in awe of her ability, skill, and willingness to try to fix the grey, ugly mess. But Des was in a bad way. She had liberally doused everything with Mr Gates's special proof brandy.

Although Mr Gates liked the man, he knew that this would take more than the six months he had remaining for him to heal. He needed another overseer. Once Des was settled and asleep, Mr Gates took Hetty aside. "I will sign him over to you for his remaining six months. I need an overseer, and you need your husband." He saw a flash of joy cross her face. "Yes, yes, as I said, I know of your illicit marriage and that you still go by the name of Mrs Walker. Des is now a changed man from the dissatisfied, unhappy and colourful, liquid-tongued man I first met. I don't know what altered him, but he's a better man for it, whatever happened. Take him home, and I hope he survives for you." He paused before adding, "I married once, but I lost my wife when she was carrying our child. I'm sorry; I lashed out angrily when he asked permission to wed you. It would have been our anniversary that day, and it hurt."

Hetty felt sorry for him; she didn't know what to say. She also knew what had caused the change in Des but remained silent. She, too, liked the change in him, or she wouldn't have married him. She recalled her first meeting with him, where she had shrunk from his presence.

Des was in and out of consciousness for the next few days. Hetty now had to sort out how to get her severely injured husband home to the Hawkesbury River. Only there could she get the help he needed. Des may yet lose his leg, but she would do everything she could to stop that from occurring. Whatever happened, she wanted to be at home to nurse him, as she could access the special help she needed there.

~

A fortnight after the injury occurred, the slow-moving wagon turned the final corner of the now smoothed track to Loganberry Farm. They arrived the week before Christmas. Hetty and Ernie were in the back, holding Des still. He had been in and out of consciousness for the past two days. Prior to that, he had been in severe pain but lucid. Molly, at fifteen, was driving the wagon. Carly sat beside her sister but kept her eyes on her silent father.

While on a two-day stopover at Emu Plains, they had sent a message through to home that Des's leg was in a bad way and that they would be home in a day or so. The wound where the bone had stuck through the skin was a worry. Hetty had cleaned it as often as possible but realised he was still in grave danger. If he had to lose his leg, Hetty wanted someone skilled to perform the surgery. That would only occur if her plan failed. The doctor from Richmond could visit him at home, but hopefully, her first port of call would be Laura and Billy.

The faces that met them showed concern. Next to Jane was an extremely tall, scarred man-mountain she did not recognise. Hector introduced Nate as Jane's fiancé and said he would fill her in later. He still had some reddened scars on his face and arms; otherwise, he was all but healed.

Laura and Billy stood behind the welcoming group, both still virtually naked. Billy was standing on one leg, with his foot resting on his knee. He had a long spear in his hand. Laura now tended to cover herself if anyone else visited, but today she was in her natural state. Billy usually just cleared off when visitors came; today, he didn't. He had watched Hetty's care of all his people and knew he would be safe.

Billy pushed through the small group and walked to Des when the vehicle stopped. Hector took the reins from Molly and then assisted the girls down.

Hetty sent them straight inside to Clara, leaving the adults to see to Des's injury. Hetty had thought she would have to send someone to hunt for Laura. For them to be here on her return was beyond her wildest dream. Billy looked at Hetty, who gave him a nod, then, without waiting for further instruction, pulled back the cover and saw the splint. He turned and gabbled to Laura. Even though with child again, she took off into the bush. Oliver, Billy, Nate and Hector had carried Des into the main bedroom on the stretcher he had been on since leaving Bathurst. Even at Martha's place, they left him in the wagon tray rather than jar his leg.

Ernie led the way to his mother's room, opening doors as he went. Hetty followed with Fran in their wake. Having seen what Billy did for Hector's leg, Hetty was hopeful they had some treatment for Des. The wound was not healing, and Des was still in agony with each movement. So she knew it needed to be immobilised a lot better. Hetty had exhausted her healing skills. She could now only hope Billy and Laura could help.

Laura returned with an armload of paperbark and some string and gently held another puff fungi.

Hetty only had rum to douse the wound and then cover it to stop the flies. She didn't know what else to do. She had not dared to tell David why there was such urgency to return home, considering Des was so severely injured and shouldn't really travel, but David didn't like Aborigines.

On her return to collect their possessions, Hetty had made her farewells to her brother and sister-in-law, loaded their wagon and left to collect her husband. Now they were home.

While the unusual pair worked, Nate was introduced to Hetty and the children, and he explained his story. The smile on Jane's face told Hetty all she needed to know. Jane was happy, so Hetty welcomed Nate and turned back to Des. She would deal with them later.

Billy stood back and put Laura to work on the immediate need, cleansing the pus-filled wounds. Des had gashes from his fall, as well as the broken leg. All needed attention. Laura undid the linen bandage and removed the splint. There was a vile smell when she undid the final wrap. They knew what that meant; the skin was dying; hopefully, Des was not. The skin, thankfully, was still red and inflamed but not black. Laura finished cleaning the ugly wound. Hetty brought in rum, clean cloths, water and soap. Together they washed the injuries until they were just raw skin. While the girls were working on the abrasions on his shoulders, Billy felt Des's leg.

The trip in the wagon had jiggled the bones, and while Des was still out cold, Billy straightened his leg again. Even unresponsive, Des groaned in agony. Billy looked at Hetty's sticks she had used as splints and nodded, then walked, beckoning Hector to follow with an axe; he left.

Laura kept her attention on the injured man. She had now covered the raw wounds with the fungi powder.

Hector and Billy returned fifteen minutes later with a tube of tough bark from a tree. When Billy returned, Laura stepped back and let him take over. She held Des's foot steady as he bound the break with paperbark, secured it with twine, and wrapped it all in the hard sheath of bark. The curved sheath was thick, sturdy and would form a sleeve that would encircle Des's leg, keeping it immobilised. He tied it all with the thick twine. He added Hetty's splints to add to the strength. The entire treatment took less than half an hour.

Des roused some hours later and had a long drink. For the first time since the break, he was not in as much pain. He looked around him and realised where he was. "You brought me home, Het," he said as she came to his side, "I'm in your room."

"I did, and you are now virtually a free man, Dessy. Mr Gates signed you over to me, and this is now our room." She bent over, kissed him gently, and then brushed the hair back from his damp brow. "I brought you home as some people here can help you. They have already done their first treatment. Billy reset the leg, and Laura has done her magic on it. How does it feel?"

He frowned, thinking about the pain level. He said, "Surprisingly, not as bad." Des certainly didn't look as pale. He was not sweating nor shivering, and his speech was clear. Hetty had no idea if this was natural healing or because of what Laura and Billy had done. Either way, she was thrilled.

Twice a day for the next week, Laura treated his wounds.

When Des first saw them walking into their room, his first reaction was shock. He found it hard to tear his eyes from her voluptuous breasts that wobbled delightfully as she worked, and eventually, he just closed his eyes to avoid the temptation. His shoulder responded well to her treatment; Laura again applied a gooey ointment to the wounds.

When Fran saw what she was putting on him, she giggled. She left the room, unable to retain her mirth. The squashed witchetty grub cream once more did its magic. The deep cuts and scrapes healed quickly. Each day Des said he felt better. He could even sit up without feeling dizzy.

Billy would not let him out of bed by himself, but after the first week, Hector and Billy assisted him onto the verandah. There he could observe the activities of the household. Des noticed that some new thicker vines were being used.

Hetty had mentioned that Laura and her friends had brought a new native liana; he didn't realise the vast difference in designs they could achieve with different thicknesses of these native vine species.

Over the following weeks, his healing continued apace. The soft tissue injuries were nearly just a memory, but the bones in his legs were still mobile. He was unable to put any weight on his leg at all.

Chapter 17 Looking Forward

*J*ane and Nate had an idea. Nate asked, "Feel like throwing together a small surprise for our boss, love?"

Their coopering ability came with other skills. Both knew how to make wheels. They set to work in their workshop using dried timber; they made four wheels. They had everything they required for the project, as the barrel strapping could be used to make the outer hoops for the new wheels.

Hector had already added leg support to one of the dining chairs, making Des more comfortable. Hetty's rocking chair wasn't suitable as Des had once over-rocked and bumped his leg. His roar of pain brought everyone running. It was this incident that made Nate put his plan into action. Silver wattle was not the usual timber used to make rims for spoke wheels, but these wheels were not for heavy use on a cart but a chair. Each rim section or felloe would hold two spokes, four of which were required for each wheel. The spokes needed to fit into a central hub, and then the tops fitted into the four dove-tailed felloes and were held together by a riveted steel band. Nate made a pair of large wheels mounted on a fixed axle for the back, and Jane made a smaller pair for the front. However, the axle for the smaller wheels was trickier as it needed to turn. The large wheel rims were wrapped in rawhide leather bindings so they were easy on Des's hands and the floors. When everything was ready, they took Des's dining chair as it had arms and converted it to add the wheels, and then they adjusted Hector's extended footrest.

Des was thrilled. His leg was sitting on a frame that kept it elevated; now, the bones just had to knit, which would take time. Even the puncture wound on his leg where the bone had stuck through had responded to

Laura's fungi treatment; it had nearly closed over. He could now carefully move around the house without bothering anyone else.

Some weeks later, Laura came with a coolamon of six of the round fungi, held it out to Hetty then waved farewell as she left. They were going walkabout for a while. Fran said she had done this last time they went for a few weeks. It was like a spare medicine bowl if needed. They knew to use paperbark for dressings and tea tree honey for minor wounds.

Hetty felt uncertain about how she felt about treating him herself. Now she had no option. Laura would not be around, so his healing was now in her hands. Was she ready?

With Des unable to assist Hector, he called a meeting at the kitchen table. Des, Hetty, Hector, Fran, Nate, Oliver, and Ernie were summonsed. The boys were now twenty and eighteen. Oliver fell to thinking as they waited for Fran to join them; he could legally run the farm himself the following year and be allowed to marry. He had done what Hector suggested and made friends with Mary. He more than liked her and knew her to be his future. He just had to wait until he was old enough. Now his mother had returned; although she had already given her blessing for them to court, they had to look toward the future for the farm.

Hetty and Des found settling into the new surroundings more complicated. Considering they had been married for over four years, they still had little time together. Their first week was a whirlwind. Since then, they had snatched a night or two here and there before the accident occurred. Des was in the main bed, but Hetty could not share it because of his broken leg. Carly shared with Molly, and the boys were still in the same bedroom. Nate was still sleeping in the drying room as there was nowhere else to go. Until Hetty's return, Jane had been procrastinating about setting a date. Hector suggested he perform a Scottish marriage for them too, but Jane still said no.

Fran guessed what the problem was, and one day, making sure that no one would interrupt them, she took Jane back up to the big rock shelf, where they had previously had other discussions. "Jane, Nate wants you to fix a date. You can't keep him on tenterhooks for so long."

Jane shook her head. "I can't, Franny; I can't let him touch me that way." She sniffed. "He'll know!"

Fran realised what worried her; she asked, "Was it the convict ship or the gaol?"

Jane's words were tortured. "Both! I was asleep both times. I had no say, but I was violated and am unclean." Jane's voice broke. "We didn't... you know... I don't want him to find out. How can I come to him now with my background?" She put her head onto her knees and sobbed. "Why did all this have to happen? We were innocent; no, we *are* innocent. We did absolutely nothing wrong. If the minister had not died, we would not even be here. We would have been happily married and had a family of our own. Now I cannot even look him in the eye and tell him what happened."

Fran had seen Nate coming quietly up the path just before she had taken a seat. She motioned for him to stay quiet and swapped places with him while Jane sobbed. Before he sat down, he had heard what she said.

Jane was oblivious to the fact that Nate heard her words. "I love him so much, Fran, but I'm fearful I shall pull away from him if he touches me that way. What do I do, Franny? How do I tell him?" She felt a hand start rubbing her back comfortingly.

"You just did, my sweet. Do you think I didn't know?" Nate said with great care.

Jane's eyes flew open, and she gasped as she turned her tearful face to him. She expelled a long-drawn-out "No," to his words.

Nate lovingly flicked a tear from her cheek. "I figured out what had happened soon after I woke up. You no longer wanted me to touch you, and I knew it was not because of my burns. My dear, I saw what had occurred to other convict women on my ship. The situation in the gaol was no better, and the guards even boasted of their nocturnal activities." He saw the women also withdraw from physical touch after being violated. "Janey, my love, I do not love you any less, just the opposite, in fact. You see, if you had felt no shame, you would not have been the Jane I fell in love with so long ago. We made the decision not to be together that way before we married. We both held ourselves back from that side of things, but the evils of this world have tainted us both. We have both seen and experienced things that neither of us dreamed existed. We have to use these evils for good rather than bad. Jane, we can overcome this together." He drew her into his arms. "Will you let me?"

She nodded. He knew what had occurred, and he still loved and wanted her. She didn't withdraw from him but turned into his shoulder and wept afresh. Only this time, it was with relief. He loved her still.

Nate sighed with relief. "Then we set a date?"

She lifted her face to him. "If you are sure…?"

Nate caressed her cheek. "I am and always have been, but are you?" he asked. She was no petite lady, but his size was so large that she fitted comfortably into his arms.

Uttering a watery gurgle, she said while nodding, "Yes, yes, I am, more than you can ever realise, Nate. It was all that was holding me back."

Her watery giggle gave him the confidence he needed. He lifted her chin and silenced her for some time before saying, "Then let's get married as soon as Hector can do it. We'll get permission later, but I've waited long enough for you."

She was nearly as giddy as a schoolgirl. "Yes, please, Nate; today by choice, and Hector can certainly do the deed."

As they walked down the hill hand in hand, Fran and Hector met them in the stables. "So we have a wedding to plan?" Fran asked Jane.

Jane gave a shy chuckle and said, "I had no idea you had gone. He heard me. You are so naughty, but I couldn't have told him otherwise. So, I suppose I should thank you."

Fran hugged her. "Jane, most of the girls here have had similar things happen to them. Look at Kitty, and you know the stories from the other girls. You are not alone in what happened to you."

While Nate was still speaking to Hector, Jane continued. "I never listened to the other girls, Franny. I shut myself away in my hurt heart and closed my ears to everything around me. I didn't want to know anyone or them to know what happened. I felt dirty. I knew about Kitty, of course, but didn't seek details."

Fran drew her to a bag of grain, and they sat talking while the men were still conversing. "Me too, Jane! I gave birth just before Hetty came to the gaol. I thought about killing myself but couldn't bring myself to do it. However, I did try to scar my face so the men would leave me alone. Then Hetty came and brought me here, and that's why I have rarely left."

Jane nodded. "I know; I told Hector just before we went to get Nate, 'Fear can keep you safe, or it can imprison you.' I have let it imprison me, but no more. I will marry Nate and try to be the best wife I can be. We are both 'lifers' due to no fault of our own, but we can now spend our life together as we had always planned." She looked toward Nate and saw he was waiting to interrupt them. She reached out her hand to him.

Nate grinned as their eyes met. He joined their conversation, "How about this afternoon, sweetheart? Ready to marry me and become Mrs Jamison at long last?"

Jane rose and nodded. Smiling at his question, she replied, "Ten years late, but yes, absolutely." She took a long deep breath and then gasped with a horrified look. "I have nothing to wear, though, Nate."

"You look beautiful as you are, my love." Fran and Hector may as well not have existed. Nate drew Jane into his arms and brushed his lips over hers before deepening his kiss. In Nate's massive arms, the junoesque lady looked almost petite.

Hector and Fran left them alone. They had a wedding to prepare.

Hector arranged the ceremony for two that afternoon. In the hours before that, the tack room had to be cleaned out, and all the leatherwork moved into the wood drying room where Nate had recovered. They would build another tack room later.

As all the beds were box beds, they moved Jane's bed into the tack room and pushed it next to Nate's. The two horsehair mattresses were also the same thickness, and rather than put them side by side, they turned them to ninety degrees and made a double bed for them. Fran had done this with their bed as it was more comfortable than having a split in the middle of them. They were delighted. Hetty had been spinning and had knitted a large oversized double blanket for sale, so she gave it to them as a gift. They had single sheets, which the girls sewed together, and soon their new quarters were ready.

The wedding was to be on the verandah so Des could be there. Oliver was to give her away. She was so much taller than all the other girls, so she could not borrow a new gown from them; however, Hetty loaned her a beautiful shawl to wear over her Sunday dress and a length of lace from her wedding to Joel. Hetty had not even worn it for her marriage to Des.

When Molly handed her a posy of hastily picked flowers, Jane felt like a real bride.

Oliver and Jane were about to walk from the sitting room onto the verandah when they heard wheels on the track. They put proceedings on hold for their unexpected visitor.

Hector's eyes nearly popped when he saw who it was. He had met this man the year before in Windsor while collecting supplies. None other than the Reverend John Dunmore Lang had come to visit. When Hector realised who it was, he asked the bridal couple if they would mind a change of minister. He knew Reverend Lang was legally permitted to marry couples throughout the colony and often did the services without the government's permission.

Puzzled, they both replied, "No, we don't mind."

Everyone waited while Hector saw to the visitor's horse and buggy. When they returned, Hector introduced the unexpected visitor to Hetty and Des, their children, the girls and Fran then finally, the statuesque bridal couple who dwarfed everyone else.

With little time wasted, the service continued with a new minister. Reverend John didn't ask about permissions; before God, they would be legally husband and wife.

Soon Nate and Jane were legally married. As the reverend had often done this sort of service, he carried an official marriage register with him. He added their names, and they signed where he pointed. Both were educated, and they could read and write well. Hetty and Des witnessed their marriage.

Hector also asked the reverend if, by any chance, he had a spare line in the register for 1826, as he had never registered Hetty and Des's marriage as he had no way to do so.

The minister flicked back to the appropriate year and found that no marriages had been performed after October. As he started a new page each year, he quickly added them in for November and had them sign. He also filled out a certificate for them. Fran and Clara signed as witnesses as they had both attended.

With both marriages duly registered, they settled down to enjoy a special afternoon tea. After a short while, the reverend gentleman took Hector aside, and although they remained in sight, he spoke to him privately.

Fran saw that Hector was stunned, but he shook his head. For each question he was asked, he said no. Fran wished she knew what was happening, but he had not called her over. Hetty gave her a questioning look, but the reply was a shrug. They would have to wait.

Eventually, Hector turned and called to them both. Trying not to look too eager, the two ladies joined them. Hector swallowed and said, "Franny, Reverend Dunmore Lang has asked if I would lecture at his new college. I have refused. Hetty, I am assigned to you for my life; having said that, even if I were free, I do not believe I am called away from here." Hector looked stressed as he spoke. His beseeching looks worried Fran.

Fran felt this man, who had arrived unannounced and uninvited, had encroached upon her husband's kindness. It was not that she didn't like him, but this was her home, and she didn't want it upset.

The minister said kindly, "Hector, I'm just Lang; Dunmore was my mother's name. I use it as many have heard of her family." He smiled a little bashfully. "Now, Hector, I have heard of your good works here. You too, Mrs Walker, or should I say, Mrs Bolton. As you are now legally married."

Hetty almost blushed. If only he knew why they started this haven, he might have been horrified.

However, the minister continued, "What you have done for these young girls is admirable, saving them from their abominable situations."

Hetty gasped, and her eyebrows flew up in surprise; maybe he knew already. She mumbled, "Thank you, sir."

He continued. "However, I am looking for those of my faith to teach at my new college. Hector's reputation precedes him. Having stayed at the rectory in Windsor, Reverend Cross has only good words to say for him. Mrs Bolton, when I met Hector last year, I was struck by a sense of peace in him. Not many have this demeanour, especially in this hell hole." Looking back at Hector and Fran, the reverend said, "I despise the transportation system, especially for such as you folk, but please do not get me started on this little hobby horse of mine. Hector, the offer is open and will remain so if you decide to change your mind."

Hector said, "Sir, we understand poverty is not a crime in Scotland. Therefore, things like theft of food are not punishable like in England."

All eyes were on him as he spoke. Reverend Lang said, "I know, sir, and I agree. It also explains the excess of Irish felons. The English hate them and will accuse them of anything they can. They also dislike our church; hence I wish to start our own college. Will you reconsider your answer?"

Hector felt Fran squeeze his hand, and she gave a subtle shake of her head. If she thought he looked concerned earlier, she looked panicked. "Thank you, good sir, but there is no need. My answer is final. We shall not be leaving here." Hector waved his hand around the area. "This is our home, sir, and this is where our good Lord has called us to work."

Hetty gave a long sigh of relief. She would have released him. He knew that, but she would have hated breaking up their unique family unit.

Although disappointed, Reverend Lang seemed to accept Hector's answer. "I'm saddened, Hector. However, I do understand. I have a gift for you, though." The minister handed Hector a blue-covered book. "This is a copy of the sermons of Reverend John Scott. It is not even out yet; this is a draft copy that I thought you might like. I figured you could use this for your services. Scott gave me two advance copies; it's due for release next year."

Hector thanked him for registering both marriages. Reverend Lang stayed for another hour before departing for Richmond.

~

Three months after Des arrived home, Hetty had a big surprise for him. The night before his accident, they shared a loving night together. They had rarely had such intimate time since the week of their marriage. They had been so stressed up until then due to the danger they faced. Their relief was so great with the bushrangers' capture that they had slept little and that night had manifested in her conceiving another child. Hetty had yet to tell Des. She was both ecstatic and nervous. She had stayed silent longer than planned as he had been so sick. As she was ill that morning, she knew the time had come for him to be told. Des had wheeled himself out onto the verandah and was just about to pick up his tools and start work when Hetty came and moved them away.

She took his hand. "We need to have a little chat, Dessy." Hetty moved her chair so she was looking directly at him. "Des, dearest Des, the night before your accident, we had a night I shall never forget." That night of lovemaking was one she still dreamt about. She swallowed, wondering what to say next. She was about to continue when he interrupted her.

His tear-filled eyes searched her face, and he said quietly, "You want me to leave, don't you? I'm useless now and can't help on the farm. It's why you married me."

The look on his face made her cry out, "Oh no, Dessy! No, it's not that all; we are having another child." She blurted out the words, not caring who heard them. She was on her knees before him, hugging him.

The look of sadness in his eyes fled, and joy swept across his face. "A child? Really, so I have not worn out my welcome?" He swiped away an errant tear. He gathered her to him, relieved that she still wanted him.

Now sitting beside him, she chuckled against his shoulder, "No,

Des, I need you so much. You will not get out of being a father to your two children." She carefully hugged him again. His leg was still in the splint frame, so she had been sleeping on a small cot in their room. She was horrified that he thought she would want him to go because he couldn't work. His words of dejection made her determined to return to their bed that night. She did! She realised she had rarely expressed her love for him.

By the time Des's sentence had expired in July, he could move around the house on crutches that Nate had made for him. His leg was still in a splint, so he used the chair around the house. Hector and Oliver refused to allow him outside work, but at least Des could sit in a chair normally. So he wasn't bored; Jane had taught him how to whittle. She set Des to make more bobbins for Hetty's spinning wheel. Jane had made three, but Hetty would have loved many of them. He set about this chore with glee. This new craft kept Des occupied, and he knew he was doing this for his beloved, and he sat near her while he worked.

While Des was busy, Jane began making a swift for Hetty. This was a ball winder to turn a hank of yarn into wool balls. It involved many arms, hinges and much experimentation. Jane was making it for Hetty's birthday. She had also made a bobbin frame that held all her full bobbins of spun wool. From that, Hetty could easily make two, three or four-ply yarn.

Months passed.

Being six months with child, Hetty spent much of her time spinning next to Des. Hetty found carrying a child at nearly thirty-nine was vastly different from twenty years younger. She was only eighteen when she married Joel, and Oliver was born the following year. He had been in Sydney only for a few weeks when they met. She had stepped in some foul-smelling lump of muck, and he had assisted her in her odoriferous predicament. They had lived with Hetty's widowed mother until Molly was two. Then her mother died.

Although Governor Macquarie had cleaned up the infant town, the place was still one of rampant debauchery. It was still dirty and smelled. This was evidenced by how Joel had met her. The buildings that were taking place were done mainly by convict labour. They didn't mind that so much, but the filth of the streets and the stench were nauseating in the summer heat. As they sat, Hetty told Des of those early years.

His three years in Bathurst gave him much time to ponder his past life. As they now had time, he, too, opened up about his wasted years, as he called them. Hetty renamed them. They were the years when he learned how not to live. It's why he was so different now.

Chapter 18   Unexpected Discoveries

*L*ittle baby Bolton arrived at noon on a blustery August day. Lewis was born with little warning as Hetty felt her first pains after a late breakfast. Her previous confinements were extended labours, lasting many hours. The baby had other ideas; he entered the world less than two hours after Hetty's first contraction. Des was determined not to miss this birth.

Hector had pinned him down some weeks earlier and told him he would not regret sitting with her. Hector had been with Fran each time and found the experience extraordinary. Fran, Kitty, and Jane helped with Lew's delivery. Jane wanted to know what was before her as she had just realised her own interesting condition. She and Nate were expecting a blesséd miracle in six months. Hetty had said she needed to push only two hours into her labour. As Fran was not expecting this so early, so she had not checked to see if she was ready to deliver. Fran lay Hetty on the bed. Sure enough, she could see the baby's head. Hetty sat up in time to say, "Basin quick," before she threw up.

Des had just enough time to get himself into position sitting on the edge of the bed. With Hetty squatting between his legs, Lew was born. His hasty arrival had caught them all by surprise; however, he gave a lusty cry as soon as he was born. Des and Hetty watched their son turn from a grey blue to a healthy pink.

Fran tied, then cut the cord and handed the child to his parents. Soon after delivering the afterbirth and then feeding her son, Hetty fell asleep. Des sat cradling his son, unbelieving that his life was back on track. The week before the birth, he and Hetty had been wondering what to call the baby. They considered Frances Sarah for a girl after Franny and Hetty's mother. But for a boy, Des wanted to thank Hector somehow for his words and wanted his son's name to be meaningful and preferably Scottish. He would have to think about it for a while. Maybe Hetty had an idea; however, she had fallen asleep.

On waking the following morning, Hetty asked Des if he'd made any name decisions. He told her about his thoughts, and she suggested Lewis. She said, "It means 'famous battle', which was, in essence, what you have gone through, the battle for your physical and spiritual life. It is also the anglicised version of my father's name, Louis." The couple had battled through various things to be together. Des had said that Joel and his sister Carly would always be a part of their relationship because they would not be together without them, but they would not name their son Joel. Lewis Desmond Logan Bolton was duly called. He was Baptised six weeks later. Life settled happily on the farm.

~

Twenty-one months after Des's accident, Carly held Lewis's hand and walked along the verandah, giggling. Lew would turn one next week, and he had discovered the joys of being upright at ten months old, but his balance was still off-centre a little. Carly adored her little brother and was usually on hand to help him balance. Oliver was astounded that he had a brother twenty-one years younger than himself. His eyes rested on Mary, and she returned a shy smile. Soon it may be their turn.

Des's recovery had taken time, but months after his accident, he could now walk unaided. His leg still ached in wet weather, but he exercised it daily to ensure he regained strength. He received his Certificate of Freedom from Mr Gates only months after his return. As Hetty had not left the farm, Hector took Fran to Windsor to receive her overdue paperwork from the Magistrate.

Hetty had asked that Hector's assignment be transferred to Fran, and they were awaiting receipt of the paperwork before they told them. Hopefully, Casey will bring it soon. As the sloop was due through on its trip upriver, everyone was hurrying their meal to load up the stock for the new markets in Emu Plains. These days Casey brought new orders for honey and baskets to be sold from Martha's Inn. The business was booming.

Since Nate's arrival, the variety of stock had increased fourfold. Laughter was heard echoing from the cooper's shed and all around the farm, and it was not all from their children. Jane had delivered their twins as easily as Hetty had produced Lewis. Leonie and Liam Jamison had arrived six months earlier. Both were large babies considering they were twins. Each was over six pounds, and the arrival of a second baby had been a massive surprise as Jane had not been that big. Her height had helped her carry the weight and hide the size of the twins. Des and Hetty set about building them a better set of rooms behind the dormitory. They now had a three-room cottage under construction. Having two children meant that the old tack room was far too small.

More girls had gone, Bertha and Milly had taken other placements, and three new girls, Abigail, Frederica, and Helen, known as Abby, Freddy and Nell, had arrived. Thankfully all could cook, and they took turns at this chore as the others spent time assisting in some of the other cottage industry crafts. Each brought new ideas and skills. Abby had been a milliner before her arrest for petty theft, and one of the crafts she wanted to try was to plait the local grasses into long lengths and make straw hats. It took her only a short time to try a variety of grasses before finding one suitable. Soon a long length of flat plaited fibre was being rolled into a coil. From this, she could sew the flat plaits and make hats. Her first design was a poke bonnet lined with some off-cuts of chintz from the cabin curtains. Mary had added some tatted lace edging. The girls each had added some trimming or a ribbon and gave it to Hetty for her birthday.

Fran had not thought of making straw bonnets, but she thought of a wide-brim hat for men for work, which would be good with the heat of summers here. So straw hats were another item that was added to the market list. Abby found various grass types that would suit her new craft. While she was fiddling with a brim section one day, Freddy picked a leaf and tore it into strips. She tested it for strength and went to find Hetty.

Freddy showed Hetty what she wanted to do. "Mrs Walker, is there any chance we could make some paper? I know how to do it, and then I can decorate some cards with quilling, but instead of quilling with coloured paper, I'd use dried leaves. Look, they dry to different colours and shades. I'm sure I could even dye some." Thus, another cottage craft was born. Gift cards were soon being made and decorated.

Nell was just like Fran; she wanted to hide and didn't like men. She was happy in the kitchen with her arms deep in the warm, freshly ground flour. The peaceful life on Loganberry Farm helped the new girls settle.

Clara had taken Hector and Fran's children into the classroom with Carly and Emmy. Knowing her seven-year term was well and truly expired, Hetty had often asked Clara if she wished to leave, and she had refused each time. She shook her head and walked back into her safe little world of the children's classroom. Clara was happy here and had no desire to be elsewhere. She wouldn't give her reasons, but this was now her home. Children came, grew and left; Clara said she would never have any of her own. She told Hetty that it was a decision she had made years earlier, well before she was convicted and ended up as a convict in New South Wales. One day she might tell Hetty, but not now. Whenever the topic arose, she would fall silent and slink away to the classroom.

After today's conversation, Hetty saw Clara standing at the classroom window with her hands on her stomach, watching the children playing outside on the grass. Hetty walked away and realised there was much more to Clara's story, but pushing her was useless. One day she would find the right person to tell; it would not be her. Not even Fran could break through her resistant shell. Hetty glanced out the windows she was walking past and wondered what else Clara was watching. Nothing, in particular, caught her eye. It was two o'clock, and the sloop was on time. She could see it coming down the river. Des was waiting on the jetty for Casey to pull close. He wanted to ask Casey to keep his eyes open for any mail for them. It had been weeks since any letters arrived; Des expected the paperwork to have come by now. He wanted to give Hector his transfer papers. He would, in essence, be free. Casey told Des he had double-checked the mail in town to ensure the packet had not been overlooked. They loaded the order for Emu Plains, and Casey took off, waving farewell.

At ten the following morning, Casey arrived early and shouted from the jetty. He had two well-dressed gentlemen with him, and they alighted from the sloop. From his vantage point on the verandah, Des realised one looked far too familiar. His heart sank, and with a resigned sigh of receiving unexpected visitors, he waved and beckoned them up to the house. Why was Mr Gates coming to visit?

Hetty had not dressed for visitors and quickly changed while the men walked up from the jetty. She arrived beside Des on the verandah, somewhat flustered. Des was senseless and in agony the last time she saw Mr Gates. "Why is he here, Dessy?" she whispered to Des as she slipped her hand into his.

"I have no idea, love, but I hope it's a quick visit." Des had a false smile on his face. "And before you ask, I have no idea who the other chappie is." They stood, watching the two well-dressed, middle-aged gentlemen approach.

Mr Gates spoke as he arrived. "Mailman," he called cheerfully. "I've come to see how you are, Des. I had heard from Casey that you had recovered fully, and I was stunned that you had actually survived, so I have come to see for myself." Then he chuckled. "However, I do have mail for you, although I have brought one letter with a man attached."

Des saw a frown cross Hetty's face; this was not the place for uninvited men, and neither had been invited. He gave her hand a quick squeeze of agreement.

Mr Gates introduced the man accompanying him. "May I introduce Mr Sidney Grey, from Kent, in the motherland. This is Mr and Mrs Bolton; although to confuse people, Mrs Bolton has kept her previous married name of Walker; in a way, that's my fault." He smiled at her.

Des welcomed them and confirmed their names. The introduction did not explain the other man's identity or why he was there.

Mr Gates pulled out a small mailbag from inside his coat pocket. "I really did bring mail, Des, but I came to bring Mr Grey as he is looking for someone whom I think lives here. He has some news for him. Is Hector Macdougal here?"

Des didn't have to answer as Hector arrived with Fran on his arm. Hector had heard they had visitors but had no idea who had come. He turned the corner and froze, horrified at who he saw standing on the verandah. Abandoning Fran, he turned and started to go.

Mr Grey saw him and called him back. "Hector, leave if you must, but take this." He held a letter out to him.

Flashing the man with a look of anger, Hector reluctantly took it, turned on his heel, and then departed, leaving Fran with the unwanted visitors. Fran stood watching her husband go. Her mouth was agape. She was unsure what to do and was about to follow her husband when Mr Gates caught her wrist.

He asked abruptly, "Who are you?"

Panicking, Fran tried to snatch her hand from his grasp. "I am Hector's wife, Frances Macdougal. Who are you?" She was as abrupt as the other man had been. She angrily tried to pull from his grasp; she wished to follow Hector and see what that incident had been about.

The man persevered. "No, no, who were you before you married?" He still held her wrist but was not hurting her. The look on his face was as though he had seen a ghost.

"My name was Frances Rea." She lifted her chin proudly and said, "I was an unwanted love child, a foundling, and I have no idea who I am or who my parents were." Realising Fran was near panic level, Hetty went to Fran's side and held her other hand. Hetty asked, "Why, sir?"

Mr Gates then asked, "Where and when were you born?"

Fran answered curtly. "I was born in a hospital somewhere in London in September 1803."

"Oh no!" he exclaimed and fell into the closest seat. His forehead was now beaded with perspiration.

Hetty looked concerned. "Sir, is there a problem?"

Mr Gates stayed mute; he was gazing at Fran shaking his head. His eyes misted.

Des said, "Sir?"

Other than once, Mr Gates had never been unkind to him; but he had never known him to show emotion like this. Hetty gasped; she remembered that Mr Gates had told her he had lost his wife and child. Mayhap, there was more to the story.

The other man ignored them and stood watching Hector vanish from sight. Hector reappeared on the other side of the buildings as he climbed the hill at the back of the house and vanished again. When Hector disappeared, Mr Grey returned his attention to what was occurring around him but didn't move.

Mr Gates glanced at Hetty and then again at Fran. "Sit down, everyone, please. I think I have a story to tell you. Mrs Macdougal, please sit here." He patted the chair next to him. Fran would not release Hetty's hand. She wanted Hector, but he obviously had his own problems, so she sat where he said. He waited until everyone was settled; he turned to Hetty. "When Des had his accident, I mentioned to you, Mrs Walker, that I had lost my wife. It's an ambiguous term, isn't it? One presumes she died. When in reality, I literally had lost her."

Hetty gasped and nodded. Fran looked puzzled. Des needed clarification, he glanced at the other visitor, and Mr Grey was absentmindedly gazing at the river, clearly not listening.

Hetty heard the girls arriving to work. Kitty came first, and Hetty waved her away. She said, "Work elsewhere today, dears."

Seeing the confusion his words had caused, Mr Gates said, "I'll explain as I think my search has finally ended. Mrs Macdougal, I shall address my words to you as you need to hear my story. Early in 1803, I was just twenty-one. I fell in love and quietly married a lovely lady named Julia Penwick. My father was overseas, and the marriage was legal as I was of age. It was duly registered, and we had eight wonderful months together before I, too, had to take a business trip. Julia was in our flat in London and six months along with our child. I had no wish to leave her, but the trip was important for our business. If Father had been around, I would have sent him." He got up and paced the verandah for a while before returning to his seat. He continued his story with a deep sigh. "The time I was absent blew from the expected six weeks to twice that. I knew Julia was close to her time when I was heading home. Again, I was delayed for a week by the weather this time. All this while, I had been in regular contact with her, but on my return, she was gone. Gone as in she wasn't there, literally vanished, but she had taken nothing with her. Fresh food was left on the bench; even the milk was fresh. Only one set of her clothing was missing, and her reticule. There was no note, nothing. She had just vanished. There were no signs of a fight, nothing." He wiped his hands over his face as though the memories severely upset him. "I hunted high and low. I visited every single hospital bed in the city. Nothing! I knew she should have had the child by then, so I started looking for that, but I had no idea if it was male or female. Due to our marriage being, in essence, secret, she dared not wear a ring; she kept it on a blue ribbon around her neck, with a key for this." He pulled out what looked like a gold fob watch from his vest pocket. He heard Fran gasp. Her hand flew to her neckline. He looked up at her, intrigued, then frowned, followed by a smile as he watched her action.

Fran hooked her finger around the string she wore and pulled out the small item that hung from it. Hetty had never seen this before, as Fran had always hidden it well. Hector was the only person who knew it existed.

Fran kissed it every night as she took it off. The string had been replaced numerous times over her life, but apparently, it originally had hung on a ribbon that had broken. She had no idea what colour it had been, as she had never seen it. She said, "This is all I have from my mother, sir."

His face was almost glowing with happiness. He reached out to touch the unique key as it swung from the string. She saw a tear fall as he fingered it. She lifted it from her neck and passed it to him. Surely this man wouldn't know the secret of her background, would he? He inserted the tiny key into a small slot on the side of the fob; with double action of pushing and twisting, it sprung open. The item was not a watch, as all expected, but a locket with two porcelain miniature paintings. One was of an image that could well have been Fran but with she had dark blue eyes; the other was a younger version of himself. "This is your mother, Julia Gates, and your key proves that you are indeed my daughter. I know this for two reasons; first, you are the image of your mother, but with my eyes, and second this key will open no other lock. I have not seen these pictures since I departed from my wife, as she had the only key." He gazed at the beautiful miniatures. His finger caressed the picture of his wife. "I loved her so very much."

By this time, Mr Grey's attention had been caught, and he was leaning backwards against the verandah railing listening intently. When he heard Mr Gates's words, they heard him gasp. Then without a word, he turned and walked away from them. His departure was instantly forgotten. The four people on the verandah returned to the revelation unfolding before them. Frances Rea Macdougal was, in reality, Frances Gates Macdougal.

Fran was stunned. "I'm your daughter? You are my father?"

Mr Gates smiled at her. "Yes, I believe you are. You are my only child, for I never remarried, hoping I would find my wife and my child one day." He sniffed, then blew his nose. "You say Julia died? Do you know how?" he pleaded with her. "I still hunt for her on every visit to London. I have never given up my search."

Fran shook her head. "Not really; I was told she was taken to a hospital. I gather there must have been some accident just outside as she was found injured and on the doorstep of the place. I was born that day, and she died. I was taken to the closest orphanage straight away. I was only told when I left at fourteen. There was a letter from the hospital with the key enclosed. It was all she had on her; no ring or anything else, just that." She pointed to the key. It had not yet sunk in that Fran was legitimate, no longer a love child that was unwanted and abandoned. She had a name, a father who had searched for her all her life. She had a mother who had cared enough to want her born in a hospital. The news that she had a father was enough. She would ponder on all that entailed later. She sat with a silly smile on her face; her eyes were twinkling with joy.

Mr Gates then handed her the locket; she sat gazing at it. She was so like her mother but had her father's cornflower-blue eyes. She had always wondered which of her parents had such eyes. Now she knew. She, too, traced her finger over the face of her mother. A soft smile teased her lips. She looked up and met his watery eyes with her own. "I'm your daughter! I have a family." It was a statement of acceptance. She wanted to tell Hector; he needed to know; however, right now, she needed to get to know her father. She didn't weep; she just sat with a smile from ear to ear.

Des had only ever seen Mr Gates show anger on the day he had asked permission to marry Hetty; he had been refused, and even then, he had not explained a reason. He had given an abrupt "no" and moved on. Des reached for Hetty's hand and gave it a gentle squeeze. His frown showed concern and puzzlement.

Hetty saw his face. "The day you asked for my hand was their anniversary, Dessy," she whispered. Des's face lightened; that explained much. Des nodded with understanding but remained silent.

Mr Grey saw that the group he was with was well-occupied. He realised that they would not notice if he left them. As he had seen the direction that Hector had gone, he followed. He walked through the maze of outbuildings in the backyard. Female voices were coming from some rooms, but he walked past them all, totally oblivious to anything else but his quarry. He was on the hunt for Hector. He followed a well-worn path up the hill and saw a large rock platform above him. As he walked, he prayed. What he had to say would be hard for Hector to hear, but he had to listen. Hector had to know. As he drew closer, he saw Hector sitting on a stone shelf with the opened letter in his hand. His face was one of shock and resignation.

Hector heard the approach of someone; he turned and gave a half-smile. This conversation could not be avoided. He motioned for Mr Grey to sit beside him. It was the last place he wanted him, but there was nowhere else to sit, and they needed to talk.

"Did you read to the end?" Mr Grey asked.

Hector nodded. He had a lump in his throat that stopped him from answering.

"I have another letter which I will give you after we have talked." Mr Grey saw a wave of grief pass across Hector's face.

Hector finally found his voice. "I thought it didn't worry me, you know. My murder conviction, I mean. But this..." He waved the letter, "Whatever brought this on? Why did he confess?" The letter was from his accuser, Mitchell Grey. The man had finally had a conviction of spirit and had come clean about what had occurred. He had confessed to the court that it wasn't a murder but an accident and that Hector was the innocent party. The letter admitted that Hector had taken the fall for his actions. There was also a document of exoneration.

Mr Grey put his hand on his shoulder. "Mitch is dead, Hector. He died last year, and I knew he was eaten up with grief about something, and it was only shortly before he died that he confessed to me what had happened; I was able to get the ball rolling, and he had a bedside confession to the Magistrate, who was James's uncle, by the way. James was the boy who died. Hector, you have been absolved."

Hector nodded, stunned. He was free.

"There's more, though, Hector, and that's what the second letter is about. As you know, I was not around when all this occurred. If I had been, things would have been different. But, lad, now I must tell you why; it will be hard to hear. Hector, it's now my turn to confess." Mr Grey sounded sad. He wished he had been able to help Hector years before.

Hector saw a wave of melancholy cross the man's face. He said, "Go on; it can't be any more astounding than this." Again, Hector waved the letter and document he held.

With a half-smile breezing across his lips, Mr Grey said, "Don't be so sure, but it will explain Mitch's actions on that fateful day." He took a deep breath and started his story. "On the day he met with you, Mitch set out to right what he saw was a crushing wrong that had been done to him. Mitch was wrong, but it took years for him to admit that. He lost his best friend and his peace. He was never the same after that last conversation with you. Now, I shall tell you why." He paused, looking over the majestic valley before them. While he collected his thoughts, he watched as the river flowed, carrying various bits of vegetation with it. Behind him, a bird chortled happily, but both men ignored everything around them. "When I was young, I married while I was in Edinburgh at university; I met and married a wonderful girl. We had six fabulous months together before I had to return home. I had bought her a small cottage and left her unlimited funds to live on. I planned to return after I had told my family about her. She came from a good family, but they were upset that she had married a *Sassenach*; that's an Englishman, as you know. Being staunch Scotsmen, they were livid. Her father refused to allow her even to use my name and insisted that she return to her family home, but she wrote and told me she had refused. My plans to return to Edinburgh were put on hold when I was reluctantly sent to serve in the Navy under Admiral Cornwallis. I had intended to resign my commission when I returned south but was called up as soon as I arrived. I wrote and told her I would return as soon as I could. I had told my father of my marriage, and he, too, was livid. I was the eldest son and should have married someone of his choosing. However, it was *fait accompli*, and he could do nothing about it. It was legal. Oh, but Hector, my beloved, was so strong-willed. She was wonderful."

Hector wondered why he was being told this but sat quietly, letting the man unload.

Mr Grey continued, "I had no idea that my time in service would take me away for years. It did. On return from the failed battle of Quiberon, I was seconded to the other frigates, and, well, to cut a long story short, I ended up on the Ivory Coast, and then we were sent to the West Indies for nearly six years. Of course, I wrote as often as possible but heard nothing back as she could not contact me. Hector, it was eight years before I returned. The house was empty and had not been occupied for years. My man of business saw the bills were all paid, but the mail had piled up inside. My letters were all there on the floor, and no one knew where she had gone. She had moved only six months after I left." He wiped his brow, stressed over what the memories dredged up. "My searches drew a blank, so I decided to brave her family. I fronted up and humbly asked for her direction. To say I was given a short shift was an understatement. I was grabbed by the collar and quite literally thrown down the steps. I was still no wiser as to where she was. I did, however, know she was alive as her father said she didn't wish to speak to me. I was shattered." He wiped his eyes before continuing. "I stood looking at the door that had been slammed shut in my face. I wanted to see my wife; I missed her. I hung around for a week, trying everything I could to see her, or if not, then her younger sister Fiona. Not a glimpse, Hector, nothing! Having no other choice but to leave, I returned home. I now knew where she was, so I wrote. I had no idea if she ever received them, but I sent money and vowed my undying love. Once home, I had one more hope. I discovered that her cousin Susanna was now the Duchess of Gracemere and lived not far from me in Kent. I had met her a few times in Scotland, but I was now in awe of the incredible woman that she had become. It was through Susanna that I first met Sarah and Fiona in Edinburgh. The three girls were at a party together. Susanna was only sixteen when Sarah and I married; Sarah was two years older than her."

Hector gasped; Sarah was his mother's name and the same age; her sister was Fiona and Susanna Bland or Susanna Lockley, Duchess of Gracemere, as she was now, was her cousin and two years younger. Things about the story were now beginning to gel. Hector turned his full attention to Mr Grey.

"When I returned home from Scotland, my life had been put on hold long enough. I told my parents I refused to remarry and told them not to push me. By then, my younger brother was married and had a son, Mitchell." Mr Grey looked at Hector, ensuring that Hector saw how all this fell into place.

Hector just nodded, so Mr Grey continued the saga. "Mitchell, as you know, was an undisciplined lad who had everything he could want except the position of heir. Quite honestly, Mitch was a spoiled brat. He had far more than was good for him, and my father denied him nothing. That was more out of spite to me. Then one day, years later, I received a letter from Susanna. She told me Sarah's father had died. She also revealed that Sarah had a son, my son. He was nearing twenty. Hector, I never knew. I had no idea she was with child when I left her. I tried everything possible to find her but was blocked at every move. Susanna had been sworn to secrecy by her uncle as he had threatened Sarah, and as soon as he died, Susanna wrote to me. Hector, son, I went directly to Scotland and brought Sarah back. Susanna had already given you a position on her estate only weeks before, and now you know why, and then I had to work out where you could live; I found the small cottage on the edge of the Gracemere estate that was closest to me. Mitch was already causing problems, so I could not yet acknowledge you for your safety. We had eighteen wonderful months where I saw her as often as possible. You know what Mitch was like first-hand. I did not trust him with your mother's life. He ran with a bad crowd, and rumours abounded of their antics."

Hector nodded. Now he understood something that had puzzled him for years.

Mr Grey continued, "What's more, Father still refused to allow me to acknowledge you both as my family, but I saw her every day I could, for our love had not died. She poured out her sadness to me, and I to her. The wasted years of our parting were even more tragic when she fell ill only a couple of months after she came. Then one day, somehow, Mitch found out about you. He must have overheard Father talking to me, saying he would never acknowledge you as his legal heir. I told him he had no choice as you were my legitimate son."

Hector nodded again and took a deep breath; he knew what was following. He pre-empted his father by saying, "This explains Mitchell's attack on me. I never knew why it had occurred."

"Yes, Mitchell took it upon himself to secure his own future. His friends stupidly thought that if they roughed you up and you vanished, all would be well. Mitch didn't expect you to fight back or for James to die. When you so graciously offered to take the blame, he was stunned, but he was thrilled. Hector, I had no idea of any of this, for I was overseas again for some time. Your mother had died by the time I returned, and you were gone. Susanna didn't even know where you had been sent. I did not find out for years that it was you that Mitch had had a run-in with. Admittedly, I was so grief-stricken over the loss of your mother so soon after I had found her that I wasn't thinking straight. Hector, I'm sorry I failed you both; I should have come and told you who you were as soon as I knew about you. I know you saw me coming and going from your cottage more than once, but I was merely following your mother's request not to reveal myself until we could be together. I inherited the estate when my father died two years ago, he did not name you in his will, but he did not need to; I was his heir. Then just before Mitch died last year, he finally told me what had happened and where you were. I thought you must have returned to Scotland when your mother died. I looked there but couldn't find you."

The pair fell silent for some time, both deep in thought. Finally, Hector said, "I would have returned there when she died, as I had nowhere to go. However, I was not too fond of Scotland; it was not conducive to my happiness. Grandfather was full of rules and restrictions. He told me you abandoned my mother and that you were dead. I have had a good life here, sir, and I have a wonderful wife and three children, with a fourth on the way. You are correct; I had seen you coming and going but thought you were using Mama, so I was furious. I wish I had known. I wish that you had told me who you were. Today, I thought you had come to continue the saga of my conviction. I had no idea, sir, none at all."

"Sarah told me you were happy, settled, and a good son. I pleaded with her for me to at least reveal who I was. She refused." Mr Grey glanced at his son. "Are you not angry with me? Or with Mitchell either?"

Hector quickly turned to him with surprise on his face. "No, sir, anger is pointless. I am disappointed that I did not have the chance to get to know you so many years ago, and I do wish you had told me, but then I wouldn't have my Franny. For that alone, it has all been worthwhile. My work here has been at His calling." Hector pointed heavenward. "Our work with the many young women brought here for healing is rewarding. My Fran was one of them; she is a queen amongst women. How she survived the horrors of her life…" He shook his head. "Then she chose me, and well, I am astounded. She has more compassion in her fingertips than I have in my entire body. She knows what to say to the other girls." Hector suddenly thought. "My name, it's not Macdougal then, is it?"

Mr Grey shook his head. "Yes, and no! Your mother had you Baptised in Edinburgh as Hector Sidney Macdougal Grey. She had it done against her father's wishes." He dug into his coat pocket and pulled out a parchment envelope. He handed it to Hector.

Hector glanced at the handwriting on the envelope and recognised it. His mother's exquisite script met his eyes. He knew it would contain the truth of his birth. He didn't want to read it just now, though. He tucked it into his pocket. "I shall read this later, Father. Will you come and meet my family?" Mr Grey stood, and as he did so, Hector put his hand out to shake. When Mr Grey took it, Hector pulled him into his arms. Hector muttered, "I have never had a father's hug."

"I hope you will have many of them in times to come, my son," his father replied.

Chapter 19 Family Introductions

*H*ector's return to the verandah was greeted with joy by Fran. She was up on her feet and in his arms as soon as he drew close. "Hector, you know my key; I found out what it fits; come and see. Also, I have someone I wish you to meet."

Sidney Grey had yet to reappear as he had needed to use the facilities and was a little delayed. The men had talked non-stop as they dawdled down from the rock platform. Twice Hector had stopped and hugged his father. Each time he said, "I do wish I'd known, Father." His heart was light when they arrived at the stable block. Hector had walked off and left the visitor because he had recognised the man as his mother's lover. He had not wanted to face him. Unbeknownst to either of his parents, Hector had arrived home twice and seen them in each other's arms. Hector only knew the man had vanished just before his mother became ill. When Hector was arrested, and his mother was very sick, he felt horrible leaving her utterly alone. As he was being dragged away, Hector encouraged his mother to contact her cousin, Susanna. It was from Mitch that he discovered the man's identity. There was much Hector had not understood. Nothing had made sense. Looking back, Hector realised that Mitch also knew a lot about him. He had no inkling that the man who had visited his mother had been his father or that he was legitimate. Now he had to tell Fran and also that their names were wrong. Hector was biting his lips, trying hard not to grin. He was busting to tell her, but she, too, was excited over something, and he graciously let her speak first.

Fran was nearly bubbling over, "Hector, darling man, this is Mr

Gates, Des's old boss, but I think you have met before?" She lifted her eyebrows in query.

Hector nodded and let her continue. He turned and gave the man a slight but polite nod of acknowledgement. This man had caused sadness for Hetty and Des, but neither looked upset. He turned his attention back to his wife.

Fran's voice bubbled with excitement. "Hector, look," Fran had a beautiful fob in her hands. With a flick of her wrist, she turned the key that she had worn under her gown, and the fob flicked open. He saw it was a locket; she handed it to him. Inside were two paintings; the woman looked astoundingly like Fran, but the eyes were wrong. Then he realised that it wasn't her. Something was slightly different in the smile and shape of her face. He frowned and looked up at his wife for an explanation. "Hector, this is of my parents." She let her comment sink in.

Hector looked at the man in the picture. An older version of him was sitting next to Fran. His confusion departed. "You are her father, Mr Gates? Seriously?" Hector threw his head back and laughed. Soon he was nearly doubled over with merriment. This was not the reaction anyone expected. Hector was still laughing when Sidney Grey arrived. Biting his lip, Hector regained control. "My dearest love, this is wonderful news, but I have some for you, too." He beckoned the visitor over. "May I introduce this gentleman properly?" Hector introduced his father. "This is Mr Sidney Grey of Kent, England; I believe you know that. It was his nephew Mitch who was responsible for me being here. However, far more importantly, he is my father. My real name is Hector Sidney Macdougal Grey. He brought news that Mitch had admitted the attack and that I have been exonerated." His face was lit with joy.

All eyes turned to the debonaire gentleman who returned to the verandah. He shrugged and then smiled. What else could he do? He said, "I came myself as I couldn't really put that in a letter, could I? It's taken me this long to find where Hector was. So I came as soon as I could. It's not like I could write, 'Hello, I'm your father, and oh, you are legitimate' despite what your grandfather thought."

Mr Gates also roared with laughter. "Well, you have missed that I am your daughter-in-law's father; her mother and I were married too." An idea struck him; he grinned before saying, "Sidney, this means we share the grandchildren." His bushy eyebrows flicked up, and he turned to Fran, "Where are they, dear girl? I can't believe I have…." He looked at them both. "I have no idea how many grandchildren we have?"

Fran reached for Hector's hand. "We have three, with another due in about five months. Skye, Joey, and Alec are nine, six, and four. This one is due in January." She said, rubbing her almost flat stomach.

The two men looked at each other, smiled, and in unison, they asked, "Can we meet them?"

Soon, the two new grandfathers met their three grandchildren. Both were astonished at how the day had turned out. Fran had to explain to the children what a grandparent was. They knew no older people and were shy of the two gentlemen. Des was the most senior person they had met; he was only forty-two. Both new gentlemen were nearly sixty, and both were greying at their temples; both also had huge silly grins plastered on their faces, and their eyes danced with glee. Neither had ever expected to have grandchildren nor ever see their offspring again. Henry Gates didn't even know if he had a son or a daughter. To find she had been so close for so long, and he had not known, made him somewhat sad.

While the children met the men, Hetty and Des had retired to their room; they had a quiet discussion about where the men would stay. Des took the opportunity to open his mail. Sure enough, the contents were the transfer of assignment for Hector to Fran. He smiled, as it was now obsolete. Rather than tear it up, Des refolded it and put it away for later. He would give it to Hector anyway as a souvenir of his life. If what Sidney Grey said was true, Hector was now free. Des's old room sat empty on the other side of the stables. It could be set up as a room for Oliver and Ernie, and the men could take the boy's room. They had no guest room as they never had guests. That night the boys often slept on the floor in the sitting room as they did when the Turners came, but they had no idea how long these two would stay.

Sidney and Henry stayed for three days during that visit. On return to Windsor, they sat and discussed their unbelievable link and their shared family. They discovered they had much in common. The conversation also turned to their beloved wives. Only to each other could they discuss the loss of their spouses. Neither had looked at any other woman. Neither had even thought that their offspring would be found or, if they were, that they would have children. From then onward, the men visited the farm weekly, staying for a night or two each time. By the third visit, their grandchildren would be seen waiting anxiously for the sloop to bring them. It did not take long for Henry to be called 'Papa' by Fran. Sidney and Hector had already settled on the more official 'Father'. Grandfather names were, however, more controversial. Henry somehow gained the moniker of 'Papa Hen'. Sidney became 'Pop'.

~

Fran and Hector's second daughter, Julia Susanna Macdougal Gates Grey, was born a little earlier than expected, as she arrived in December 1832. Hector again was with Franny for the birth.

Both grandfathers were waiting in the sitting room like expectant fathers themselves. This was the first time that either were involved with the increase in their family. Sidney had moved from the hotel into Henry's home in Windsor, but they had also paid to have the small store room at the other end of the stable fitted with two beds so they could stay when they wished.

Soon after the appearance of the grandfathers, Oliver eventually asked Mary if she would walk out with him. Her shy reply was a simple nod. Since she had been at Loganberry farm, she too had matured into a confident young woman until Oliver appeared anywhere. She would blush, fall silent and get on with whatever she was doing with her head dropped. Oliver had finally proposed on Christmas morning, and Mary again nodded her acceptance; only then did he kiss her. She could not believe that he wanted to marry her. When Oliver announced their betrothal at Christmas luncheon, no one was surprised. The other girls clustered around Mary and congratulated her. Oliver sat with a silly grin on his face; he caught his mother's glance and returned her smile.

Ernie knew now was the time to move on with his own plans. His Uncle David had written to him, and he had thought much about what his letter contained. He realised that with Oliver getting married, it would be a good time to write back and put his life in order. After luncheon, Ernie asked to have a private chat with Des and his mother. The three retired to the verandah with a mug of tea each, and Ernie revealed the letter's contents. "Mother, Uncle David wrote to me a few weeks ago. When I was in Windsor, I collected the letter but haven't known how to tell you. With Oliver's engagement, I think this could all dovetail in together." Ernie paused; telling his mother he would leave the farm was much harder than he realised.

Hetty asked if David and Matilda were well, to which Ernie said yes and filled them in on the news of *Wambool Station*.

Finally, Ernie blurted out, "Mother, Uncle David wants me to come and live with them with the idea of me taking over the farm. His three daughters are now all married; they are there alone and… and… Mother, he wants to give me the farm." Phew, he had said it.

Des glanced at Hetty to gauge her reaction; it was not what he expected, although he knew this was a possibility. Hetty reached out and took her son's hand. "Ern, David spoke to me long ago when we were still there. I did not know how you felt and asked him to wait a few years before he said anything. Since their youngest daughter's wedding earlier this year, he has struggled to cope. Ernie, go with my blessing. I know you love the place and the work. But please know you will always have a home with us too."

Ernie's face lit up. "Mother, you knew and never said anything?" Ernie was thrilled.

Hetty smiled. "Des and I discussed it after we came home. We thought it was something your father would like too, not to mention that it's keeping *Wambool* in the family. You have as much right to it as they do; both realise that. Uncle David purchased it with family money, as did Uncle Duncan with his place. You have more right, as most of the money came from my father, not theirs." She glanced at Des, then added, "Lew may wish to take over Duncan's place one day as he has no children. He wrote to me and made that offer when Lew was born." She had not mentioned that all their children would be well provided for.

Des gasped. She squeezed his hand. They would discuss that later.

The upshot of the conversation was that Ernie would stay until Oliver and Mary married; then, while they were on a honeymoon, Des, Hector, Nate, and he would convert their room, and then he would leave.

They planned the wedding for February 1833 at Saint Matthew's in Windsor. Reverend Joseph Docker was the incumbent there now. Reverend Cross had left a couple of years before to go to Newcastle, and now Reverend Docker was to leave. This wedding would be one of his last before he retired to his new farm; he had only been there for five years. Henry Gates had made the wedding arrangements, followed by a lavish affair at his home in Windsor. He said it was his reparation for not allowing Des to marry Hetty. Des gave Mary away, and Molly and Clara stood as attendants for her.

The festive occasion was a massive celebration for the town. A spin-off from this was the discovery that Oliver Walker of Loganberry Farm owned the newly opened Loganberry Store in town. Everyone knew the farm's name as the market stall had been a famous attraction for many years. The December before the wedding, Oliver had decided to open a shop in town and employed two more convict girls to run the store. They had lived at the rectory for a while as the building was prepared. Oliver had bought a small cottage; the girls moved into the backrooms, and the shop was now in the converted front sitting room. The four men from the farm had utterly refurbished the cottage and fitted out the room as a shopfront. Their cottage market industry had grown and moved onto the next stage.

Henry Gates oversaw the day-to-day needs of the girls. He was now family and relished the involvement with his extended household. He took Des aside at the wedding and talked about Hector and Fran. At seven and five, their two boys, Joey and Alec, were too young to know their future, but Henry was already thinking of their heritage. Henry had had many conversations with Sidney about the future inheritances due to the children. Joey was heir to Sidney's home in England, and he had been uncertain of mentioning this idea to his family. Henry also had no one to take over his farm, or his import-export business or even his home. They had put their heads together and decided to approach Hector and Fran after the wedding.

Henry and Sidney asked to see Hector and Fran inside. Fran had just fed Julia and put her down to sleep. Hetty and Clara watched over the other children.

Sidney started the conversation as they had planned. He had not revealed everything to Hector as he knew the ramifications of what he had to say. Sidney took a deep breath before saying, "Hector, it's six months since I told you of your history. However, I have not revealed all. With Oliver now married, I have to start to think about heading home. It won't be soon, but I must return. Hector, I want you to come with me. Not to stay unless you wish to but for a visit. I wish you to meet the family."

Horrified, Hector jumped up and paced the room. "No, I don't want it; I don't want to go back. This is my home, here on Loganberry Farm, with Franny and the children." He was still pacing the room with a deep frown etched on his brow before turning to Fran and kneeling before her. "I don't want to go, Franny. I want to stay here with you. I won't leave you; I don't want history to repeat, as I might get stuck over there."

Sidney realised that Hector thought that he meant for them to separate. "Hector, no, no, you have misunderstood. Fran is to come too, as are the children." Sidney dug into his pocket, pulled out a document, and passed it to Hector.

Hector flicked open the seal and read the official-looking certificate he held. He looked at his father and said, "Thank you, but I still don't want to leave."

Sidney smiled at his son's words. "Maybe so, but don't you think you should let Fran decide?"

Fran had no idea what they were talking about until Hector handed her the document. It was an Absolute Pardon in the name of Frances Rea Macdougal Grey. She gasped. Although she had served out her time, she was still not permitted to leave the colony. This document allowed her to return home. She sat gazing at the paper in her hand, wondering what to say. She didn't want to go either, but if Hector had responsibilities there, then as long as he didn't leave her anywhere for long, she would brave the world and travel with him. She reread the document three times before a thought occurred to her. Directing her gaze at Sidney, she asked, "Sir, if Hector is your only son, then Joey is his heir. That's why we have to go, isn't it? He has to know, as it will be his."

Sidney nodded. "I have a suggestion. Joey will be old enough to be at school soon. They start boarding at eight in England, and what I was thinking is that next year we all return and set that ball rolling. We will all travel together, Henry too, and meet all the family and enrol Joey into school for the September start. I will stay and care for him there, and you can return here."

Henry occasionally nodded throughout Sidney's speech. "Sidney and I have talked long and hard about this, Fran. I was going back next year for business anyway, but Franny, dear, I also have a suggestion. As you know, you are my only child. You will inherit all I have, so I plan that Alec will become my heir here. I know it should be Joey, but this way, the boys will each have a substantial inheritance. If you have more sons, they will be included where needed. The girls will get ample dowries from us both. Trust me; we have spent much time discussing our grandchildren as we are so proud of them all, as we are of you both. Therefore, we only want what is best for them. Separating them from their parents is something we will try to minimise. They will, however, have two grandfathers who adore them and protect them as much as we can. With ships now much quicker than ever, they can make trips home and back in months rather than years. The eight-month trips of yesteryear are a thing of the past. Four months is the norm now; I imagine it may well be down to weeks by the time they are old enough to travel alone. Sidney and I are keen to work together in whatever way you decide, as we are both determined to stay closely in contact with you all, even if it means us travelling ourselves. I love it when you come and stay with me in town, but I know you are far more content in your converted stable rooms."

Fran nodded.

Hector could not believe what had happened. Their comfortable life on Loganberry Farm was being torn from their grasp. As they were no longer convicts, Hetty had no say over either of them, but she was like family. Here they were both safe and comfortable. They had little, but they needed little. Having said that, Hector knew he could not shirk his responsibilities. He knew God didn't put them here for a comfortable life. Hector walked to the window and stood looking out at the festivities going on in the backyard. He knew he had to go to England, but it was the last thing he wished to do. He was no longer needed on the farm as Des, Oliver, and Nate could handle everything. Hector knew he didn't have to decide now, and the required proposal needed much discussion with Fran. He turned back to them and said, "We'll talk it over and let you know our decision later. There is obviously plenty of time, but I promise you that I will not go if Fran is at all unsure or unhappy. If it means I must forfeit everything, I will, as I have nothing now. Franny has already been through too much. I promised her safety and security. If we go, which is a huge if, we will not enter society but stay on the fringes. I must have you understand that." He turned to Fran. "Franny love, we will discuss this privately, but be assured one skerrick of hesitation from you, and the trip will not be contemplated." He knelt before her again. "You are my world; if you are perturbed even by the thought, then that will be that!" He hoped she would agree, and they could stay on the Hawkesbury.

In the time Hector had been thinking, so had Fran. Hector had been her world for the past eleven years. Now it was time for her to be his support. Fran reached out to stroke a wayward lock of his red hair into place; then, she caressed Hector's cheek. "Darling Hector, you have helped me and protected me for so many years, but something Jane said when Nate wanted her to set a date for their wedding has just come to my mind. Her words were, 'Fear can keep you safe or imprison you.' My darling Hector, fear has imprisoned me for too long. I will be all right with your Father, Papa, and you by my side. It was not society I was fearful of; it was what men would do to me. Then one day, you told me of the bible passage, Psalm 118, verse 6; '*The Lord is on my side; I will not fear: what can man do unto me.*' With three men to guard me and God beside me, I shall no longer be afraid, darling Hector. Sweetheart, we shall go back for a while, maybe even a year, but then we will come home, for this is where our hearts are. However, we will need to ask Hetty if she wants us to continue to live with her. With their place growing, it may be time for us to move in with Papa here in Windsor. We can oversee the shop from there." Fran leaned closer, and regardless of their fathers watching, she kissed him squarely on the lips. "I seem to have grown brave after becoming a mother to four fearless Australians."

Hector returned her peck on his lips with a deeper kiss. "Are you sure, sweetheart?" His eyes looked into hers. He knew her mannerisms well enough to know her every mood. "Even if we make plans, we can cancel them until the last minute. Will you promise me you will tell me of any concerns? Any at all!"

Fran gave a half-laugh, nodded and said, "Of course, I'm not sure, and I'm somewhat concerned, but I know we have to do this. I feel at peace about the trip, Hector; we must return. I promise, but I won't change my mind because we are not just doing this for you or me; this is Joey's destiny. Alec will also receive an education, and the girls will have a future beyond any I could have imagined. However, I will not allow an arranged marriage for any of them, but I will vet their friends and partners like an overbearing mother hen. They are being offered all the things we missed out on and how different our lives would have been if various situations had not happened as they did." Fran was now concerned that Hector would not go.

For a third time, Hector kissed her. "True, my beloved, but if it had not all happened, we would never have met, making my world a much sadder." Hector stood and looked at the two older men; he said, "Father, Henry, it looks like we are going to England."

Chapter 20 Setting up the Future

With much discussion over the following weeks, plans were made to return to England towards the beginning of spring. Part of the delay in their departure was a hold-up in signing the Power of Attorney of Henry Gate's estate and business over to Des while Henry and Hector were away. Des knew how all of his enterprises worked and could keep everything running as he previously had done, but Henry now had fingers in many more pies, and he wanted to make sure Des knew the ins and outs of everything. Henry took Des to Sydney and introduced him to the stock manager there, Thomas Tibbs. Henry also gave Des letters of introduction to his shipping agents and the various captains who were currently absent. Des had not realised that in the years since he had left, Henry had purchased some trading ships and chartered others, and therefore his import-export business was flourishing. Henry's absence on this trip could be for a few years, and knowing that he now had grandchildren to provide for, he wished to ensure all was looked after well. Henry named Hector and Des as joint guardians for the children in case of his demise.

Sidney Grey planned to do the same once he returned to England. In the meantime, he left a dual witnessed letter with Harry Moffatt, the Justice of the Peace in Parramatta, outlining his wishes. This was, in essence, a codicil for his existing will in England.

With Oliver now married and running the farm, including the new shop in Windsor, Des and Hetty decided to visit Ernie and David while Hector and Fran were still around. They realised they would need to remain at Loganberry Farm with the girls after the Grey family left. At Henry's suggestion, they would stay at *Narrowgate* homestead rather than with David and Matilda to ensure everything was running well there. They would finally get to stay in the master bedroom.

When they arrived in Bathurst, Des didn't initially let on that he would now act for the owner while Henry was absent, but word soon filtered to the staff. Des had spoken to Henry before leaving, and with his permission, he set to right some inadequacies of the homestead and the running of the property. The early discovery of his new role came about as one of the first things Des did was to build dormitory accommodations for the shepherds and convicts. Admittedly, it was only a sizeable single long room, a log cabin; but as it had full heating facilities and large shuttered windows, all the men were thrilled. Built off the side of that, Des added a large mess room with a kitchen and a giant table where they could comfortably relax, and then he designated one of the men as a cook. George Blinkhorn had recently been injured, and rather than be sent back to prison; Des looked around for other work for him. Discovering that the man could cook, he set him to work in the new staff kitchen. George was popular with everyone, so his friends were thrilled he could stay. With the improvements, the morale of the place lightened considerably. Des knew what life in a shepherd's hut was like, which wasn't pleasant. They were still used as an overnight option rather than in the main quarters. He also purchased some of David's trained sheepdog pups and added them to the farm. Then he removed all the chains of the convict workers. He had worked beside most of these men for years; he knew that with good treatment and plentiful food, they would cause no problem. He was right.

Darcy Paisley, the overseer and manager, responded enthusiastically to the greater responsibility thrust upon him. Darcy was delighted when Des said he would stay and assist with the shearing and the wool clip. The early timing of the clip meant that they would return to Loganberry Farm just before the family sailed in spring. Trips to David, Matilda, and Ernie were frequent, but they always took the longer route, as did the family on their visits. However, Ernie would ride over via the track at least once weekly to see his mother. He made care to watch for snakes.

Des had told him that a giant brown snake had been the cause of his horse rearing and the reason for its fall down the cliff. Carly and Lew were under the constant eye of Molly, who, at eighteen, was like a second mother to her half-siblings. Duncan came and made himself known to his heir and used the time to get to know his family. Des insisted they stay close to the house unless he or Ernie were with them. He still had memories of the trouble caused by the rogue bushrangers. He was also still overwhelmed that the small child, Alec Grey, as he was now known, was to inherit the farm, and Lew would inherit *Duncan's Reward*. Henry Gates had spared nothing when building the magnificent two-storied homestead on a hillside. Des had laughed when he saw where he had chosen to build until he spoke to some of the local trackers. The valley was known for flash floods; Henry had listened to the wisdom of where to position his home. David next door had done much the same thing, but Duncan had built near his creek. Des knew that Duncan would probably lose his home one day, just hopefully not his life. David had tried to tell him, but he wouldn't listen. Des and Hetty were much less experienced in what the area did during floods, so they left the discussion alone.

However, it did worry Hetty, as she had lost Joel because of such a flood, and she didn't wish to lose a brother as well. She had a good dig at Duncan before they left, and he revealed that he had seen evidence of floods well above his roof height. He admitted he had already put in the foundations.

They had been in the Bathurst area for three months when news arrived that Mary was expecting a child. Oliver had asked his mother about when she was returning, as he wanted her there when the baby came. Hetty and Des planned to return in early September after completing the shearing. Oliver and Mary's little one was due in November, so they didn't need to adjust their plans. They wrote back, assuring Oliver that they would be there. The wool clip was a good one, and as soon as it was finished, Des packed up his family and headed home. Duncan, David, with their families and Ernie came and farewelled them from the homestead verandah. Hetty didn't know when she would see her son again, but it was time to cut her apron strings. She saw David put a hand on his shoulder. Ernie was nearly a man. He had to make his own decisions now, and David was there to guide him.

The passage to England was delayed, mainly due to a lack of suitable cabins. Sidney Grey managed to book five suites on the British Sovereign in November 1834. She was not the fastest ship on the seas, but she was a comfortable three-masted vessel of 350 tons. Captain Browne welcomed them all aboard and showed them around the ship. There were only a few other first-class passengers. One was a widow and her five-year-old child, returning after her years in the colony. The Honourable Mrs Amelia Black and her daughter Esther, known as Essie, were travelling to England. It didn't take long before the two women became friends. Fran and Amelia met over the interaction of their children.

Once at sea, there was only one room the children could relax in, and that was the extra cabin Sidney had booked, especially for that purpose. Essie was soon invited to join Fran and Hector's children. Due to the children's chatter, the two mothers soon discovered that each had served time. Soon both women were consoling each other, knowing what they had each gone through at the hands of evil men.

Fran spent many hours telling Amelia about the refuge that Hetty Walker had started. It wasn't long before they found mutual friends in Martha and Jack Turner. Amelia had spent a year living with them, and it was where Essie was born. Amelia had heard about Mrs Walker through Martha and knew of her work. She was thrilled to find that Fran was one of the girls rescued by Mrs Walker. Amelia was alone on the voyage and needed a friend. She relished the companionship of another lady for the long trip. Hetty Walker's work was often the topic of conversation between the two. However, Fran was amazed to hear what Amelia had been doing. She had been working with the Governors to improve the conditions of the convict women in the gaol in Parramatta. In essence, they had both been doing much the same thing from different angles. Amelia's work just helped many more.

As Fran had only three men for company, she gravitated to Amelia whenever possible. They discovered there was only a year difference in their ages but a world away in their upbringing. Fran was very fearful of what was in front of her. Her new status was vastly different to what she had left. Neither had a staff of any sort, although a ship's maid often watched the children while they were asleep. They had juggled cabins, so the children were on either side of the playroom. One maid could watch them all.

Amelia also confessed that she was returning with great trepidation; she had an unknown future in front of her. There was much she didn't say about her family, as she didn't know where they were or why they had abandoned her. Her brother, Jimmy, had been corresponding with her, but even that had not been regular. She mentioned that she would be living at *Meldon Hall* in West Sussex and noticed that Sidney's eyes nearly popped. "Do you know of it, sir?" she asked innocently.

Sidney's reply was one of interest to her. "I do indeed, Mrs Black. I know it well. The Earl, Sam Garney, is causing a delightful stir amongst the peers of the realm. He and his friend Perry White, the Earl of Collingsford, spent years in the colony. The Earl started the idea. If you ever meet Perry, you will know. You can't miss him, for half his face has melted. He was seriously burned in a fire that killed his wife's father. However, a nicer man you could not meet. So, if you get the chance, grab it. Mrs Black, Katy, the Countess, served time too." He added the last few words and looked at Amelia to gauge her reaction. He saw her smile. "Do you know what he's doing with the house, madam?" Sidney tried hard to hide his grin.

Noticing his restrained mirth, Amelia gave a slightly naughty smile. "I do indeed." Her eyes were almost dancing. "I am going there to teach their adopted, illegitimate children, parented by those same snobbish peers. Sam and Anne were the rejected by-blows of two of the aristocracy, and their parents all but abandoned them. Most poor mites are in similar situations to most of their staff. Up until Earl Sam took them in, the children sought to live life however they could scavenge. Sam is remedying that. As I have a past that is, um, socially unfit, to say the least, I will fit in well." She smiled at him as she spoke.

Her reply gave him heart. "Oh good, as I fully endorse his work and have employed some of the others he assists. Did you know it's not just the young children he helps?"

Amelia nodded. She glanced at Fran but remained silent.

Sidney continued, "He has put Christ's words of helping the blind and the lame into action. Only he does it quite literally. Wait until you see the place. Many, like me, have changed our way of thinking due to Earl Sam's example. Before heading home, I will take my family there, so we shall meet again." Sidney was thrilled, yet he was unsure if she knew about the reformed harlots and streetwalkers Sam was training as maids; or the size of the house she was going to. It was immense. He was wondering how he was going to introduce Hector to Sam. He knew the place because one of his business associates, Marcus Ryan, lived next door. Sidney and the family could now visit Amelia to ensure she had settled in well. He said, "We will also visit Hector's cousin in Kent before heading in that direction. They live near Maidstone."

This time it was Amelia's turn to show her interest. Her home was Pittford Manor in Aylesford, not far from there. She knew many locals and hoped it would be someone she knew. "I know the area well, sir, as my home is not far from there. May I enquire whom you know in the area?"

Sidney smiled at her enquiry. "My wife's cousin is Susanna Bland, or was; she is now Her Grace, Susanna Lockley, Duchess of Gracemere. I'm sure you would have heard of her."

Amelia's gasp intrigued him. "I know of her, sir. I have reason to wish to see her myself soon, as I have messages from a family member." Amelia's heart was beating a tattoo. What were the odds of these people being related to Ned's mother? She had promised not to let on much about him, but now she knew she could at least trust them with her friendship, for this man to be distantly related not only to Ned's mother but also that they knew Earl Sam, as well as Ned's friend Perry, was something that should not have surprised her. She had seen God's work too often for her not to realise He was now providing her with safe travelling companions.

~

The five months passed with many sightings of whales and a myriad of sea birds. The various ports of call broke the journey, and the families became good friends. Amelia recognised Hector's aura of peace as a sign of his deep faith. She sought him out and asked for his prayers. Over the months, they prayed together as a group, bringing both ladies comfort and solace. Many times while at sea, Fran wished she had changed her mind and not come, but she didn't voice her fears to Hector. She still was sure that Hector was needed there. She would stand beside him and be the wife he required, even if she was quaking in her shoes. Amelia had secretly been giving her etiquette lessons on board. Skye, at eleven, needed to learn quickly. Essie, at five, knew more than she did. Although older than Essie, Joey and Alec were also ignorant of what was required of them. Fran listened intently to all the instructions, trying hard to absorb everything.

The lessons had come about as Amelia had started teaching the children. While Amelia was teaching the girls to curtsey, she discovered that Fran didn't know how to do more than a servant's bob. From then on, Amelia included Fran in all the lessons. Fran didn't realise how much she didn't know about how to behave in England. She wasn't sure she wanted to learn either. Nothing like this was ever taught in the orphanage. Who knew there was a right and a wrong way to walk across a room, how to curtsey to the correct degree or even how to sit down? Amelia took particular interest in grooming Fran for what was ahead of her. As Fran's place in the world changed, she realised she had no choice but to learn to live in her new world. She shed many tears, but Amelia was a kind and loving teacher. Amelia had also taken Hector aside and given him some basic lessons in deportment and behaviour. With Amelia taking them in hand, Hector realised how much he needed to learn and approached his debonair father for assistance. He had no idea how to tie a cravat properly, bow over a lady's hand at the various levels depending on their rank, and even hold Fran on the dance floor. Henry also watched with great interest, absorbing the lessons himself.

Hector was aghast. "Father, how did I let you talk me into this? I have no desire to learn all this clap-trap," Hector said mournfully. Hector, too, wished he had stayed back on the Hawkesbury River. "Father, I said we are not entering society, I mean at all, ever. Therefore, I don't need to know this stuff." Hector had always prided himself on being clean, efficient, and well-dressed. His red hair was always immaculate. He felt gauche, uneducated, and ignorant compared to what he was now learning.

Sidney smiled. "Yes, you do! Son, even though you are not entering society, you must learn to behave in certain ways. When you meet the Duke of Gracemere, you must know how to greet him and how it's different to an Earl, a Baron, or a mere Mister; each one has its form of address. What happens if Sam or even Perry's father comes for a visit? And then there are the presentations to the family...." Sidney saw a wave of fear wash over Hector's face.

After a few nocturnal discussions with Fran, they threw themselves into what they termed the 'education of the socially naive.' Some days Fran would return in tears, trying to remember all she knew she had to learn. "I can't do this, Hector; I'll just stay at Sidney's house and hide. I'm nervous about making the wrong move or saying the wrong thing. I just wish to remain invisible. I can't remember how low to bow to a Lady or...."

Hector cut her off, chuckling. "You curtsey, I bow! I know exactly what you mean." He drew her gently into his arms and comforted her. "Sweetheart, it's overwhelming, but darling, we don't have to learn it all at once. The children enjoy it, and we must follow their lead." He bent and gave her a long, loving kiss. As much as he wished to stay and continue their intimate interlude, he would do that later. He said, "I have a treat for you to get our minds from it. Tonight it is calm, and Captain Browne suggested that we go outside and see some of God's magic. Coming?" He was now holding the door open for her, and she followed him onto the deck. Hector led her to the railing and slipped his arms around her waist. Drawing her close to watch the magic start, Hector said, "The captain said it would take a few minutes until our eyes adjusted, but we are to watch the waves." They leaned on the railing with her cradled in his arms. His love for her was almost overwhelming him. His emotions were close to making him weep. He murmured his love for her as they stood watching. Then the magic dance of the bioluminescence started in the bow waves.

Fran saw it first. "Oh Hector, look, the sea is alive, it's frolicking, and oh, darling one, this is just what I needed to see. God is in the tiny things, as much as He is in the stars." As she turned to look at his face, she saw the myriad of stars behind him. "Hector, look up; there are so many stars visible and bright tonight."

Hector, however, couldn't lift his eyes; he was too busy gazing down at the beauty cradled in his arms. Everything he did and would do was for her and their children. Yes, he was pleased he now knew his father, but since his marriage to Fran, he was happy. He had not known that had been missing in his life. He had been happily single until she arrived. Her way of thanking Hetty for saving her was to throw herself into doing everything she could to make money and saleable items for the farm. Fran had turned a tiny idea of Hetty's into a thriving business for everyone. In the process, she had unlocked his heart. He had not even realised that he had locked it tightly away. With his mother gone, he had harboured anger towards the man who had visited her, then abandoned her when she needed him most. He still wished his parents had told him while she was alive, but the past couldn't be changed, only learnt from. Hector bent down and kissed her forehead. "Sweetheart, the beauty God made is not just in nature but also in my arms." As they were now wholly enveloped by the darkness, he lifted her chin and gently kissed her. She slid her arms around his neck and responded to his caress passionately. There was much promise in her response. The bioluminescence continued to dance with the two standing at the railing above it, totally oblivious to the beauty around them.

"Hector, you really need to look up." Fran pulled away slightly and looked up at the stars as they shone down on them. Above them, the heavens started fireworks of their own.

Unbeknownst to them, their fathers had come on deck to see the display. The two men had heard them murmuring and sat in silence and waited. As the heavenly light show exploded above them, both gasped at the awe-inspiring display. Hector heard their fathers and called for the men to join them. He didn't release Franny, but they all stood watching both above and below. Soon they heard more footsteps. Captain Browne had seen them come on deck and escorted Amelia to join them. He explained what they were watching. "The sea lights are a regular occurrence. I don't have a name for it, but I often see them in the waves, especially on a calm dark night like tonight. One day they will have some magical name for it, but to me, the phenomenon is from God so that we can see our way through the darkness. The shooting stars happen only a few times each year." He never tired of watching either of them.

The Captain encouraged the first-class passengers to see the spectacle. For these both to occur at once was what he considered a blessing. He had found the people that were on board this trip amazing. Over dinner at the captain's table, they had slowly revealed some of their past. Mrs Black had remained silent, but he initially thought the situation was tragic for her to have lost her husband. After some weeks at sea, he found that the man, Mr Black, had been abusive and was killed by his horse. He discovered that Mrs Black had been relieved rather than grieved. The Governor and Anne Deas Thomson had accompanied her on board, and his friend, Major Ned, had introduced them to the captain and the doctor. Then he presented Amelia as The Honourable Mrs Amelia Black and mentioned that he was the child's Godfather, so he knew her well.

At the end of March, England's shoreline finally came into sight. After a week of travelling up the Thames River with the tide, they finally neared the wharf in London. The ladies said their final farewells before docking. Amelia assured her friends that she was being met and that she needed to have said her goodbyes before disembarking. After the last breakfast, she found Fran and hugged her. They parted with a kiss assuring each other that they would meet again soon.

Once the ship docked at the quay, they watched Captain Browne carry Essie down the gangplank and saw Amelia greet two tall, handsome men. One took Essie in his arms, and just before Amelia left, she turned and waved a farewell. Then they were gone. They knew they would meet again at Earl Sam's place. Sidney had to arrange transport to his London home and suggested the family stay on board until this was done. He disembarked just after Amelia and Essie and quickly left the dockland. Fran released a long sigh. With Amelia now gone, she had to take a deep breath and face what was before them all. Hector knew what she was feeling. He was equally concerned at what was before them. He had been happy as a forester; for him to return as the legitimate son of a very wealthy landowner was not appealing to him.

Chapter 21   Further Revelations

Sidney returned, collected his family, and took them to his London house. He had had time to let his mother know she was about to get a house full of visitors. He also had not let Hector know that his mother was still alive. He had tried to find the words, but she had never come up in conversation. He had time to kiss his mother before he left. "I have to go, Mother, but be ready, as you have a grandson and his wife but four great-grandchildren." He heard her gasp as he left. Sidney collected his family and Henry from the ship in a fleet of carriages and a luggage brake with servants. He had sent instructions for his mother's luxurious travelling chaise, the town carriage, and the staff carriage to head to the docks. Sidney travelled back in the town carriage and took a deep breath before he alighted. He had to tell Hector now. Walking on board, he drew Hector into the ship's library and shut the door behind them. "Hector, you would think I would have had time and the opportunity over the past months to tell you one more thing. I have a confession to make."

He saw Hector wince.

Sidney continued with a half smile, "No, do not stress yourself; it's nothing bad, but it's about someone I should have mentioned. My mother, your grandmother, is still alive. She is in her seventies and is otherwise well. She is an astounding lady, and I admit I'm somewhat in awe of her." Sidney had the courtesy to look somewhat embarrassed.

Hector had raised an eyebrow when he heard the news and then threw his head back and laughed. "Is there any more family I should know about?"

Sidney nodded and said he would show him the family tree when they reached the house. He said, "The size of the family is not vast, but many are still alive, like my brother, Clayton, and we remain in contact."

Hector re-joined Fran and let her know of the revelation. She would soon meet her grandmother-in-law. For some reason, Hector was nervous, more than he had been on his wedding day. However, this was just one more thing that was unavoidable. He shrugged off his attitude, then stood tall. He bent and whispered to Fran, "Let's go and meet this harridan!"

Fran chuckled, then gave him a quick kiss before collecting their children. "I'm ready. Let's brave the world again."

Sidney and Henry already had their luggage in hand. They saw it loaded onto a large luggage brake carriage. The boys were under the charge of one of the ship's maids, and Skye oversaw Julia. The small child didn't want to go with her sister; she demanded her mother. She'd had enough of the floor moving, enough of small rooms, and not being able to play outside. Julia plonked herself on the cabin floor and would not move. Fran arrived as she was about to turn over and throw a complete tantrum.

Hector stood at the door and watched the antics of his family during the hustle and bustle of packing. He didn't hear his father and Henry's arrival behind him.

"You are so lucky, you know. You have been able to spend every moment with your family. That's a blessing neither of us has had. Make the most of every second, son." Sidney put his hand on his shoulder and asked, "Ready?"

"Yes," said Hector as he picked up his youngest child.

Sidney chuckled. He had learned that Hector was not one to waste words.

The arrival at the considerable facade made both Hector and Fran gasp. They were perfectly content in their two rooms above the stable. For them to live in such a magnificent edifice was greeted with trepidation. Fran leaned over to Hector and whispered, "Can we go home now?"

With a slight chuckle, he just said, "No, I'm dying to meet the harridan that scares my debonair father so much." He took her hand and assisted her out of the carriage.

Walking to the impressive door, they noticed their children and fathers had already entered. They were greeted by a butler dressed in full grey livery, with black and silver epaulettes and shiny silver buttons. This man threw open the door, and they followed him upstairs, where they heard their children's raucous voices coming from a door to their right. The sight that greeted them was the toddler, Julia, standing before an awe-inspiring woman who was seated at an angle on a longish stool. Hector presumed that this was his grandmother and that she seemingly had just met her match. The words they heard made Fran giggle, "I'se Julia 'dougal Grey, who is you?"

The older lady was in deep negotiations with the intrepid child. "I, miss, am your great-grandmother, and my name is Lady Juliana Grey, and it is very similar to yours."

Hector saw his father was nearly in stitches. Henry had to turn his back as he was laughing so much. They had missed the introduction of the other three children, but Julia had challenged the old lady on meeting her. She had never met a woman that was so old and did not realise that she had to respect her elders.

Lady Juliana summonsed her son. "Sid, you did not let me know how adorable my great-grandchildren are; undisciplined but adorable." She bent down and took the small child in her arms. "Now, child, you will listen while I tell you who I am." She put her fingers on the girl's lips. "I am the matriarch of the family, and you, my dear girl, are the baby, so you will listen and behave while you are here. You will learn to be a lady, obey the rules of society, and be a good girl and do what you are told."

Julia frowned and pulled the old lady's fingers from her mouth. "I don't fink that is going to happen. I'se only here for a holiday, then I'se going home, but I'll try to be good."

With a start like this, the introduction of Hector to his grandmother passed without further incident. Lady Juliana had put Julia down and given her attention to her grandson and his wife. With Skye's assistance, a maid took the four children to the nursery. Peace reigned!

After fifteen minutes, Lady Juliana dismissed them all with a wave of her hand and told them to return for tea. Hector could not wait to get out of the room and ask his father how she had a title, and he didn't. "Father, who was she? I mean before she married."

Sidney smiled in acknowledgement of his query. "Son, Mother was the daughter of the Earl of Riverdell. Her brother Edmund is the current Earl and has no time for any of us, including his daughter, Christina, who married a ne'er-do-well and moved to the colony too. He considers that they married beneath their status, which in fact, they did. My father was only landed gentry, so although not titled, he was well-to-do; hence the Earl's and my father's objection to my marriage. I will tell you more about that later." He glanced at Hector to gauge his reaction.

Hector had stopped walking, "My great uncle is an Earl?" He was stunned. "Are there more revelations I should know about?" He shivered; he again wished that they were back on the Hawkesbury.

Sidney nodded. "As I said, a few, but they can wait." Sidney encouraged them to follow him to their allotted rooms. "I've put you in the royal suite; it's overwhelming, but it's got the most space, so I thought you'd appreciate it. We've never had royalty here, so it's incorrectly titled, but you will see why it's named so very soon. It was Father's idea, of course."

They walked with Sidney up the stairs, Henry following silently in their wake. He had no idea of Sidney's status or link to the aristocracy. He was new money himself and, as such, not in their league, even as just part of the gentry. He may be able to buy them out ten times over, but here he would never be more than middle-class. Henry thought he wished he was also back in New South Wales, where life was so much simpler. He also knew he had to be very careful about conducting his business from now on. Not that he'd ever had crooked dealings, but some were dubious. From now on, everything had to be entirely above board. The past eighteen months had taught him that the value of money was nothing compared to family. There was no way he would ever jeopardise them. Plus, the marketing of his produce had always been a bugbear for him. Sidney had offered some introductions while in London and would take every opportunity available. Sidney was willing to put in more than a good word for companies to purchase his wool clip. Another of Sidney's partners was Marcus Ryan, who owned some progressive woollen mills. Marcus had a farm in the Hunter Valley, and they shared a friend in Ned Grace. This potential link could open the door for permanent sales.

They had climbed the wide carpeted staircase, stopping and often gazing at the various portraits while Sidney explained who they were. Fran was becoming more and more fearful of what lay before them. Hector could tell as her grip on his arm tightened considerably. He thumbed the back of her hand comfortingly, but it did little to ease their worries.

Sidney opened a door halfway along a long corridor. "I chose this one for you as it looks out onto the mews rather than the street. Behind the mews is the communal garden where the children will be taken to play." He walked to the window and pointed to a tiny scrap of fenced green grass. He seemed pleased to be able to offer such a small mercy. Fran was horrified. It was minute; their children had grown up with unlimited acreage to roam around. She sighed; they would have to make do.

Sidney left them to settle in, then escorted Henry to his room across the corridor. "You are close by, Henry, but as I know you've been to London often, I hope you don't mind a street frontage room, but you are close to Franny. Our suites are down the other corridor, so you will all have privacy. Skye is next door, and the other children are in the nursery. She may wish to move up there with them, but that will be her choice." Sidney opened the door of a lovely airy room furnished in forest green. The bed was a four-poster with dark green velvet drapes that matched the curtains. The room was more extensive than Henry's sizeable living room in Windsor. If he thought his wealth was vast, it was as though Sidney had just put him in his place. This room was neither overdone nor ornate, just perfect taste. It was undoubtedly a man's room. A male servant stood quietly to one side, waiting for instructions; he had already started unpacking Henry's luggage.

Sidney introduced the man. "Giles here will be your valet for your stay. The bell pull is over there." Sidney motioned to where a long cord hung on the wall. "I'll leave you to settle in and will come and collect you in half an hour." With that, Sidney left Henry with Giles.

In Fran and Hector's room, once the door shut behind their fathers, Fran turned to Hector for comfort. "I can't do this, Hector; I want to go home; I want to be who I was before, just a nothing."

Hector knew this feeling well. He drew her into his arms for mutual comfort. "Franny, you were never just a nothing, but I have just discovered that my grandmother is an Earl's daughter and sister. How do you think I feel? We're in this together. We'll do what we have to do and then go back home. The hardest thing about that will be leaving Joey here with Father. I'm not looking forward to that. I didn't ever want to be the absent parent; now, it looks like life will be repeated. Sweetheart, we have to trust that God has this in hand. We know that we can't do this in our own strength. We also know that the trip between countries won't always be a four-month journey. Recently the *Sophia Jane* shaved weeks off that, and soon more steamships will be making the trip in a matter of weeks. We will return, even if only to see Joey." Franny took comfort in Hector's strong arms, but his words were more for his benefit.

With her head still on his chest, she said, "It's the things I know we will have to do, the society things, Hector. Your grandmother is not the sort of person to say no to. I don't think she will accept our refusals." She rubbed her cheek against the rough wool of his so familiar tweed jacket. His following words enhanced her feeling of security.

Hector loved how she turned to him for safety. This time it was for mutual benefit as he was also very unsure of what the next year would bring. He kissed the top of her head before saying, "Franny, if she thinks she can push us around, we will just leave. I'm prepared to give up everything and leave if things become too uncomfortable. Nothing is worth losing my family or upsetting you and the children. You are all too precious to lose for the sake of wealth or position in society."

Fran lifted her lips to his, and with his assurance, she pulled away and said, "We had better get ready to meet her for tea." Her wardrobe was sadly lacking; Amelia had inspected her clothes on the ship and told her she didn't have a tea gown. Fran agreed; even with what her father had bought her, she knew she didn't have much fit for London.

Neither had much time or inclination to look around the room. It was vast, vivid and overwhelming. They knew they had little choice but to stay in the red gilded, over-ornate room, but at least the bed looked inviting. "We'll christen it tonight, sweetheart," he said naughtily to her as she started to remove her travelling outfit. He was about to caress her when he realised a maid was in the next-door room. "Until later, darling one," he quickly kissed her before pushing her gently towards the internal door.

They had found that all the luggage had been unpacked and hung in a dressing room next door. A maid waited for Fran to assist with her attire change and then re-did her hair. Fran felt decidedly uncomfortable. She had never had this done other than on her wedding day.

Henry and Sidney were waiting to escort them back downstairs. They returned to the sitting room late as Fran had insisted on seeing where the children were. Sidney expected this and informed his mother of the potential delay.

The nursery was beyond the comprehension of all three visiting adults. The four children were entranced with the myriad of toys, yet as soon as the door opened and they saw their parents, they dropped what they were doing and enveloped them. Little Julia was taken into her father's arms as she explained the fairyland they now had to play in. "My darling Ju Ju, will you be happy here with your sister and brothers for a while? Mama and I must return downstairs, but we'll see you soon." He turned to look at his father for confirmation.

Sidney gave a nod.

Julia nodded, then wiggled to be put down.

The four children each demanded their parent's attention as to what they were doing. It was difficult to leave them, so they were later than expected. The tea tray was already waiting when they entered.

"Sit, dear ones, while I pour," Lady Juliana said. With the elegance of a queen, the regal lady poured the tea, and a maid handed the cups and a plate around.

With no free hands, Franny had no idea how to hold both the cup and her plate and help herself to a cake as the maid offered it to each person. She was so out of her depth. Amelia didn't cover this in her lessons. She ended up setting the plate on her lap and placing the cake on it. Hetty had small tables next to each chair at home, but she didn't have fragile tiny china cups; they used mugs that held a decent amount of tea. She looked at the small amount of tepid, milky fluid in her delicate cup and wished to have one of Hetty's large pottery mugs with sweet black tea. Hopefully, she will be offered a refill.

While Fran was gazing into the depths of her milky tea, she heard Lady Juliana ask, "Franny dear, I was wondering if you would be interested in accompanying me to an at-home at Lady Devonshire's place tomorrow?"

Franny lifted her horrified eyes, met her grandmother-in-law's ones, and then turned to her husband. Her eyes filled with tears. She shook her head but remained silent.

Hector knew her dilemma. He knew he had to nip this in the bud before she made any plans. "Grandmother, we shall not be socialising at all while we are here. We shall attend no social functions, balls, teas, soirees, or other fiddle-faddle. We are simple country folk and want none of the society who have hurt us so badly. I have assured Franny that she will not be forced, and if we are, we shall return home on the next available ship. Father, do I make myself understood? Nothing, not one! No presentations, nothing!" As he finished speaking, he adamantly turned to his father. "Nothing, Father, or we leave, is that understood?" Hector waited for his father's answer.

"Perfectly, son! Franny, I have not had time to let Mother know. I will ask you if I may fill her in privately on your situation?" Sidney watched Franny nod and saw her relief. "Mother, when I tell you later of their history, you will understand their reluctance to enter society. I have promised they have my full support in this, so please, no exceptions."

Lady Juliana frowned but accepted her son's explanation.

Sidney then turned to Hector again. "Hector, you must return to Scotland and see your mother's family. That will be your priority after you have settled."

Hector frowned. "Why would I wish to go to Scotland, Father?" He could not fathom why the great need for him to return to the country of his birth. He had lived in a great grey stone Keep, some distance from Edinburgh. This building was all but a castle and had been his home for his first eighteen years. His grandfather rejected him, and he saw his grandmother as weak and refusing to stand up for his mother or himself.

Sidney looked to Henry, who encouraged him with a nod. "Hector, you need to go because your cousin, Fiona's son, Callum, is not fit to run the estates, and he drives them into the dirt. He is only supposed to be the estate manager, but he's a spendthrift, a gambler, and a drunkard."

Hector was puzzled. "I don't understand; why can't Uncle Fergus deal with him?"

Sidney swallowed, "Why Hector? Because your Uncle Fergus is dead. He died without legal issue, although I believe there may well be a by-blow or more in Edinburgh. So, it is all yours! You are now the Baron, the eldest child of the eldest daughter. I'm sure you know how inheritance works in Scotland. If there is no male heir, the daughters can inherit. As her older brother Fergus died without a legal heir, Sarah would have inherited, had she lived, but you are her son, and therefore you must assume the role." Sidney paused before saying, "Plus, your other grandmother wishes to see you before she dies."

Hector was horrified. He grabbed his chest as though it hurt. He gave a long, drawn-out "Noo! No, Father, I won't go!"

Sidney's heart went out to his son. He knew he would react this way. "I'm sorry, Hector, but this is why I didn't tell you about this before. I have enquired, and you do not have to stay, but this will also be Joey's one day. I have spoken at length with your agent at *Glenview Keep*. He is quite content to run things with you as a silent partner if you will. Callum's hands will be then tied. You can write a Power of Attorney for me until Joey comes of age. However, a trip up there is required to see that the paperwork is in order and to meet the family again. We will all go, Mother included." He looked at his mother as he spoke.

The look of stunned amazement on her face made Hector smile. Her mouth opened and closed without comment.

"It seems we are all to be put out of our comfort zones, Grandmother." He turned to his father. "It looks like you have won this round, but again, we will attend no functions." Hector's gaze fell on Franny's face. What he saw made him go to her side. Tears were sliding unchecked down her cheeks. "Sweetheart, I need you with me on this journey. I wish you to see where I grew up and meet my other grandmother. I saw her as a weak woman, but now I look back, she was married to a very domineering, bigoted, and unjust man who told me my father had abandoned us and was as good as dead. I'm now guessing my grandmother must have tried all she could to keep the peace. Her name is Sile, but it is pronounced Sheila." Hector spoke the name with a definite Scottish lilt. "I remember her as a person who gave good cuddles to a small, scared boy." He thumbed away a tear from her cheek before asking, "Will you come and brave the other she-dragon with me?" Hector's pleading question elicited a gurgle of laughter from Franny.

"Considering how you have supported me all the years, of course, I'll come, but no functions!" She bent down and kissed her husband on the lips.

This action made Lady Juliana chuckle; she had overheard the words "other she-dragon", knowing she was supposedly the first, and smiled. "I think I'm going to love getting to know you two. You are unafraid to speak your mind and do what you wish, regardless of who is watching; you remind me of myself. If we are going on this momentous journey, we had better get to know each other. Come and sit beside me, Franny; unlike Hector's other grandmother, who is apparently also a she-dragon, I do not really bite."

Her comments brought chuckles from everyone except Sidney, who added not so quietly, "Often...."

Chapter 22 New Identities

The following week produced a new nickname for Lady Juliana. Julia had obviously been thinking deeply about this conundrum of two with similar names, and it stuck. She announced, "Me Julia, you Great Ju Ju." Then she climbed onto her great-grandmother's lap and told the grandam about all the toys upstairs and how small the garden they had to play in.

Lady Juliana had had nothing to do with small children for many years and was somewhat overwhelmed. Julia's tiny fingers knew no respect for expensive gowns, diamonds, or hours of painstaking coiffuring of her hair. She was Julia's great-grandmother, and the child, therefore, needed to give her great-grandmother every minute detail of every moment and movement of her life. Such things were essential to a small child and thus required to be imparted to the aged lady. When her sons were born, Lady Juliana had willingly handed her children to nursemaids, having employed a wet nurse for their care. The discovery of a small child's innocent love, and even adoration, took her breath away. She realised how much she had missed in shunning any part of her son's upbringing. Lady Juliana began to look forward to time with her great-grandchildren, even finding her way upstairs to the nursery on more than one occasion.

There were three weeks between the decision to go on the impending journey and their departure in the first week of May. Great Ju Ju had shed much of her previously austere nature. Sidney had rarely heard her laugh before; now, it was a frequent sound echoing through the house's corridors. Sidney had confided Fran's story to her the day after their arrival, and Fran had been summonsed and embraced. Lady Juliana would require nothing of her more than she wished to give. With the assurance that her grandmother-in-law knew her background, Fran sought her out often. In those three weeks, however, Juliana demanded that Fran be appropriately gowned. What passed for suitable gowns in New South Wales, where her father had purchased her a new wardrobe of clothing, were the equivalent of servants' clothing in London. Even Fran acknowledged this sad fact. But she refused to throw out her old gowns, knowing she would need them at home. Fran was about to object when Juliana informed her that she would not even have to leave the house. A dresser would come to them. "There are still some benefits of being an Earl's daughter, dear."

Sidney did the same for Hector, Henry, and the boys. Henry had mentioned getting some Shultz coats for Hector but was informed that the man had recently died. When Sidney heard the request, he said, "Sorry, Henry, we'll have to stick with John Weston. His work is better, at least to my taste. Hector's physique is such that it will set off whatever he's wearing."

Hector was acutely embarrassed. When he was measured for Weston's coats, the tailor voiced much the same comments. "I am listening, you know, Father! But I will say that whatever I get, I insist I am comfortable in them."

Once the new attire arrived, they set off on the trip north. They chose not to travel by ship, even though that was quicker and more comfortable, but Hector and Fran wished to see some of the country. They decided to travel by coach, with a minimal entourage of staff.

Sidney had arranged to meet with the agent in Edinburgh, and their arrival was at the end of the first week in May. They were to stay one night in Edinburgh before proceeding to the family home. When Sidney had written to the Scottish family, he merely said they were to expect visitors. He did not say who would be staying with them or how many. Sidney knew that Sile would guess who it was when she heard the visitors were coming from England. They had made peace before he left for New South Wales. Sidney had gone there shortly after Mitchell died and told Sile what had occurred. She was thrilled about discovering where Hector was and that he was now free. Sidney had also promised that if Hector returned to England, he would bring him to Scotland as soon as possible.

The journey north took two weeks. However, they knew the mail coach could make the trip in forty-five hours when the roads were good and the nights were clear. But they turned their journey, made with three carriages, into a sightseeing trip. They stopped at Cambridge, Stilton, Colsterworth, Grantham, Doncaster, Boroughbridge near Harrogate, Darlington, Newcastle-on-Tyne, and Berwick, and finally, they drew to a halt in Edinburgh. Travelling with four children made the journey legs short by necessity. Julia often wished to travel with her mother or Great Ju Ju. The little girl often chose her great-grandmother by choice now. The old lady discovered the joy of having a child fall asleep in her arms or on her neck. However, she learned the inconvenience of slobber dribbling down her front and found she didn't care. She had an assortment of cloths at hand to catch whatever mess Julia made.

Sidney was amazed, knowing his mother usually insisted on immaculate attire. This cleanliness was difficult to sustain when travelling with a not-yet-two-year-old.

On their arrival in Edinburgh, they were met by the agent who dropped the final bombshell. On meeting Hector, he greeted him with a deep bow and the use of a title. "Lord Glenview, Lady Glenview, may I take this opportunity to welcome you home." He bowed low over their hands and Fran's stunned face, so he did not notice the looks on the visages of the two people as he was now almost prostrated in front of them.

Hector's eyes were wide open, but he kept his mouth shut. He had failed to recall his grandfather's status. Riordan Macdougal, Lord Glenview, had little time for his grandson; therefore, Hector had forgotten the name that was now theirs. He squeezed Franny's hand and gave her a gentle shake of his head. While still reeling with shock, they followed the agent into the office with their fathers tagging behind them.

Lady Juliana, and the children, escorted by her maid and Sidney's valet, decided to walk up to the castle on the hill. They all needed to stretch their legs.

In the agent's office, the four visitors settled themselves. Fran was already uncomfortable as the man stared at her almost lustfully. Therefore, Hector sat on the opposite side of the room from Fran to make the agent's all-too-obvious gaze directed at his wife all but impossible.

Being the perceptive businessman, Henry asked to look over the estate books and accounts as the others talked. Before entering, Sidney had asked him to check that everything was in order, giving Henry an excellent excuse to see that things were running as they should. He noted many entries with Callum's name on it. Henry marked each one with a question mark. Much of this was vast sums with no explanation for its distribution. This spending would have to stop as it was draining the reserves in the bank. The books showed that the income had declined in the past twenty years. Little or no investment was revealed in these accounts since the death of Hector's grandfather, although various large sums had been taken out by Hector's grandfather in his final years. He presumed that Fergus must have also been a wastrel, as there were various entries under his name. The name Hamish also had appeared in the book until two years ago.

After some time, Henry shook his head and said, "Tch tch, this is not too good, Sidney! Callum is bleeding the place dry. Little has been done as per improvements, and if this were a business… well, if this continues, it would no longer be viable. While we are here, I may take some time to cast my eye around and see what can be done."

Sidney nodded acknowledgment, as did Hector.

The Agent sat listening. He had done his best, but Callum was a spendthrift, and his uncle, Lord Fergus, always had just paid off his accounts without question. His grandfather had not been much better. He was thankful this would now stop. He knew Callum was not going to like it. Mr Rory Featherstone reached under his desk. "My Lord, sirs, I have another book Mr Callum does not know of." He passed Henry the second ledger and let him peruse that.

Sidney didn't know what it contained but said to Hector, "It's what I thought, Henry. Hector, does Henry have your permission to investigate change?" Sidney wanted Hector to voice his wishes in front of the Agent.

"Of course, Father, Mr Featherstone, please draw up appropriate paperwork so my father-in-law can act on my authority for improvements, and my father can act as Power-of-Attorney for myself and my heirs. Of course, you will be still doing the day-to-day business, but my father will handle the big decisions. That includes Callum's affairs. Henry, am I correct in thinking that his access to funds is an issue?" Hector and the two older men had already discussed this at length on the journey northward. Mr Featherstone, however, needed to know all were in agreement.

They had not noticed Henry had fallen silent as he read the second book. Henry had glanced at Mr Featherstone, who leaned over and pointed to an entry. Both men smiled.

Hector sounded far more confident than he felt. Knowing what was set before them, they bid the agent farewell and left for *Glenview Keep*. The ancient castle was half an hour out of Edinburgh.

Sidney still remembered quaking in his shoes and his rejection when his father-in-law had all but cast him down the front stairs. It still stung. Until Susanna had told him, Sidney had no idea that he had a child, let alone a nearly teenage son. Now his son was the owner. Sidney smiled to himself as that thought floated across his mind. Justice! How Hector's grandfather would hate that. All those years he had missed from his son's life. Sidney just wished everything had been different. He could have had a wonderful life with Sarah and their family. They probably would have had more children. Now his daughter-in-law and mother were to meet his wife's family for the first time. He knew Sarah always adored her mother, and if his last visit was anything to go by, she was right.

Hector was the only one relaxed about returning to his boyhood home. Having two young sons of his own, he knew of every haunt and hiding place in the old tower and all the tiny nooks he wished to show them. Growing up in an ancient turreted castle was a small boy's dream. He knew they would love it. Skye was old enough to be shown some of the ancient treasures and jewels housed in the magnificent edifice. The three-story stone Keep, and the original round tower was a wonderful playground for the young. The old moat at the back was a worry, with Julia being so adventurous and undisciplined. He would make sure a maid always remained with her.

Their arrival at the castle was met with little surprise as the Agent had written the day before. Hector's grandmother had been informed of three coaches of visitors that would stay for an indeterminate time. Lady Sile had worded up the staff about how many were arriving but not whom. Hector knew Callum would be livid and would not take kindly to being ousted by a *Sassenach*, well, a half *Sassenach* and one who had been an Australian convict too.

Sile could not wait to see her grandson again. Hector had always been a favourite, but she had been unable to show any partiality due to his parentage. Unbeknownst to Hector, she had fought many battles with his grandfather over his future. She insisted he not be sent to an orphanage when he was born; her husband wished to get rid of what he termed a mongrel child. Now Hector returned as heir. She smiled and waited for their entry into the ancient, fire-warmed room.

Hector recognised the butler from his time at the castle.

The kilt-clad butler in the Macdougal red tartan showed them into the heated room. "The Right Honourable, The Lord Glenview; The Lady Glenview. Their children, The Master of Glenview, The Honourable Joel Macdougal Grey; The Honourable Skye Macdougal Grey; Master Alistair Macdougal Grey; Miss Julia Macdougal Grey; Lady Juliana Grey; Mr Sidney Grey and Mr Henry Gates." He announced each one in a sonorous voice with a thick Scottish lilt. After they had all entered, he stood to attention and awaited instructions. Receiving an order for tea, the butler bowed the family inside and departed. This dear old man had been one of Hector's protectors as a young lad. Angus Macdougal, a distant family relation, had greeted Hector with a beaming grin and a handshake when he arrived before remembering his station and who this young man before him now was. Hector had taken a moment to offer his thanks and had given him a special two-handed shake.

Fran gasped when she heard all the titles. Hector had explained, but to listen to them spoken for the first time was a shock. From an abandoned orphan to a titled lady would take time for Fran to grow accustomed to the transformation. Oh, how her life had changed.

Hector saw his grandmother sitting in her familiar winged armchair close to the fire and covered with a woollen blanket. It was over twenty years since he had seen her, and she'd aged dramatically. "Hello, *Seanmhair*," he said, surprised that he even remembered his pet name for her. He turned to Fran and said to her, "The word means Nana." Then he introduced everyone else and finally the children.

Lady Sile offered Lady Juliana a seat near the fire, apologising that she was unable to stand as she had twisted her ankle. "Please sit, everyone;

we are all family, and I refuse to stand on ceremony. I am going to do away with protocol and insist on Christian names. My Gaelic name is Sìle, but please call me Sheila, as most of my friends do. Children, I suppose I am your great-grandmother."

Sidney assisted his now tired mother to the armchair closest to the fire. Juliana willingly rested her cold and weary legs. She was chilled through and had had enough of travelling. Sidney, Henry, Hector, and Fran took seats on the settees nearby. Fran then instructed the children to sit quietly on the floor and stay still. Julia, of course, would not do as she was told; she heaved herself up and waddled over to the new face. "Hello, I'se Julia, are youse sick?"

"Not sick, sweet child, but injured. I took a tumble last week and did myself an injury." She pulled the blanket back a little and showed her great-granddaughter her bandaged ankle. "See, just bandages; nothing is broken."

The small child put her hand on the old lady's ankle, closed her eyes and said a prayer. "Poor, Great She She, ouchy! I kiss bettera like my mama does for me." Julia bent, kissed the bandages, and stood, saying, "It will get goodera now." The small girl didn't realise she stood centre stage for everyone watching. "Now, can I have a huggle?" Julia put up her arms to be picked up by her newest great-grandmother.

Sheila lifted her great-granddaughter onto her lap. Lady Juliana chuckled and said, "She'll twist you around her little chubby fingers. She has done so with me. She informed me she had never seen someone so old and then asked me if I knew Adam and Eve." Juliana tried hard not to show her mirth, but Sheila didn't hold back. She threw her head back and released a joyous laugh. Little Julia snuggled onto the warm lap and settled to sleep.

Hector did not ever remember hearing her laugh before. This homecoming was not as he had presumed. He also expected more of the family to be around; none had yet appeared. "*Seanmhair*, where is everyone? I expected the house to be full as it was in my childhood." Hector saw her facial expression fall.

"They left soon after you did. Your grandfather managed to ostracise most of them. Of course, he could only countenance Fergus, Callum and his equally odious younger brother, Hamish, before he left for. Canada. Sarah went to stay with Fiona in Edinburgh for a while when you left." She saw Hector shake his head. Sheila continued, "As you know, Callum was a handful for Fiona and her husband, Andrew, even then. Suffice it to say; your grandfather spoilt both boys. Hopefully, you are here to deal with Callum. So, you are the heir since Fergus died three years ago." She looked down at the sleeping cherub on her lap. "Hector, the Bible says in Proverbs 13 verse 24, '*He that spareth his rod hateth his son: But he who loves him chasteneth him betimes.*' Children need discipline, not thrashings as your grandfather did to you, but they must have boundaries. Fiona never disciplined Callum or Hamish or set boundaries for them." She looked again at her great-granddaughter and then lifted her eyes to Hector. "I'm so sorry, laddie, but I had to walk a fine line while your grandfather was alive. I can see that your children are well disciplined, except mayhap for this little one, but I will excuse her because of her age. How old is she, by the way?"

Hector looked at his youngest daughter, now curled up on his grandmother's lap. She was deeply asleep. "Julia is nearly two and is a precocious little imp. As Lady Juliana said, she has everyone twisted around her little finger. *Seanmhair*, she met you less than half an hour ago and look at you now. You terrified me when I was little, but nothing stops her." Hector smiled.

Sheila gazed down again at the sleeping cherub in her arms. Like Juliana, she had little to do with her children when they were small. Her husband had insisted on a wet nurse for each of them, and having no say in the matter, she gave in without a fight. "I shall enjoy what little time I have you all for, my dears." She sat stroking the child's cheek and playing with her dark curls.

Lady Juliana knew precisely what she was feeling. She had rediscovered her heart over the past month. It was like scales falling off and emerging from a fugue state. Juliana was surprised as she had thought that appendage was well dead. She looked around the room at her family with new eyes, and she met Sheila's gaze from across the room, and both smiled knowingly.

The success of the visit to Scotland still hung on to Callum's interview. He was often, if not usually, in Edinburgh living it up, and Hector knew he would come home in great anger when he found his allowance had been cut off. For years Callum had presumed he was heir to Hector, wherever he was, not knowing Hector had two sons. Callum's allowance was now zero, as were his expectations. Hamish had left for Canada years before realising he would have no inheritance.

~

As Hector expected, it didn't take long. Callum came only two days after Hector's arrival. There was no doubt that he had returned home when the sound of his angry bellow echoed through the halls.

Sedately, Hector went and found his father when he heard the once familiar voice shouting at full volume.

"Where is that illegitimate *Sassenach* who calls himself the heir?" Callum stood at the bottom of the grand staircase and shouted. He paced the hall floor and waited impatiently, knowing Hector would come.

Hector and Sidney slowly descended the stair. Hector stood looking down at his angry cousin. Callum, at thirty, was ten years younger than Hector and thought the world owed him everything. Like Mitchell, Callum blamed Hector for stealing his inheritance when it had never been his. It had been his grandfather's lies that caused his presumption.

Hector remembered the volatile-tempered boy with bright red hair and startling blue eyes. His stance of hands-on-hips and eyes flashing anger did not bode well for a peaceful meeting. Hector, however, remained calm and silent. He saw his father about to say something and just put his hand up to stop him.

Sidney shut his mouth, then followed Hector into the library and quietly closed the door behind Callum; the discussion that transpired remained between the three of them. However, no raised voices were heard emanating from the room.

The upshot was that Callum was to travel immediately to the Hawkesbury River area and was being sent to stay with Des and Hetty until he sorted his life out. Hector set out conditions. Callum was to have their apartment above the stables and stay with Des until they returned. Callum needed money to flee the country. He had found himself in big financial trouble, and Hector's arrival was perfectly timed for their plan to work. Callum had visited Mr Featherstone to get an advance on his allowance to flee, only to find no money was available. Callum wondered where to go, and he was thinking of Canada to his brother, Hamish. But New South Wales was equally as good. At least there, he didn't have to start from scratch. He would be out of reach of his angry creditors, particularly Morag's father. She'd been willing enough, but he had no intention of marrying the chit. Thankfully she was not carrying his child.

Hector realised that Callum had no skills or talents except knowing how to drink, whore, and spend money. He would have to learn how to make a living from scratch, and Des was the perfect person to teach him. Hector warned him that he was to keep his hands off every other person there, particularly the girls. Without Hector extracting that promise from him, he would not have allowed Callum to go. Hector wrote to Des, outlaying his ideas for his cousin, and suggested that he be sent to David in Bathurst or to live at *Narrowgate* and taught how to farm. Callum readily accepted that his life in Scotland was at an end no matter what occurred; he packed his anger away. He was thrilled that Hector would settle all his debts if he left immediately. He also gave him a fat wallet of cash for his new life, but there would be no more when it was gone. He would have to make his own way in the world.

Sidney had been ready to restrain Callum as he spoke with such disrespect, but once again, Hector's kind and gentle words had won over the angry young man.

Now realising his error and innocence of his cousin's actions, Callum departed to his room to pack. He needed to leave as soon as possible before Morag's father caught up with him. Hector had promised to settle all his accounts, but that would not save him from an angry father of the tavern wench. Callum needed to leave as fast as he could.

In England, when the topic of Callum had first arisen, Hector had said to his father, "God will prepare the way, so leave it to Him," and he was not to worry. Hector's only concern was that Callum's departure would leave his grandmother alone in the ancient castle. In a conversation with her the evening Callum left, Hector was regretful that his cousin had, in essence, banished himself.

Lady Sheila had a suggestion. "Hector, I told you the family had all gone; they have, but they are not all dead. Some returned to other clan lands. Many live in crofts and bothies around the country, but I could ask them back again if you did not mind. I know some of them are in great need. I admit, Callum was at least company in this great grey Keep. With him not using the funds, we should be fine. I'm sure Mr Featherstone will eke out what remains, and hopefully, things will improve." She gave a resigned sigh. Sidney turned to Henry and nodded.

Henry coughed, smiled and piped up; he had not had a chance to report his find from Mr Featherstone's second set of estate books. "Ma'am, at Hector's request, I studied your Estate accounts and discovered your husband made some long-term investments. One was purchasing a tea plantation in Ceylon. I saw that the first shipment from the plantation arrived in Glasgow last October. I believe the funds from that shipment are awaiting deposit. Mr Featherstone kept them separate from the normal castle account until Hector arrived in case Callum demanded to see the books. So, ma'am, there are sufficient funds for many years, as the sales of this commodity were extremely successful. Mr Featherstone informed me that further shipments are expected in the next few months. Your husband also invested in the Commercial Bank of Scotland when it was formed in 1810. Ma'am, those shares are of immense value now. Let me assure you; you can fill the castle to the brim and barely touch the interest, let alone the capital. Mr Featherstone never told Callum, but your agent knew it was there. He drew my special attention to this money in the second set of books."

Lady Sheila gasped. "Truly, Henry? Can I get the family to return? Oh, that would be wonderful. I have been rattling around this place for years, wishing for company. Now I can have them back. I may even ask some of my poorer friends as well." She turned to Hector. "Hector, would you stay until we get them sorted and repairs are done?"

The upshot was that they stayed for over a month and saw the castle slowly filling and put back to order. Fran didn't mind the influx of new faces as they came a few at a time. All were related to her husband, so they were family. However, one guest came uninvited. This was Riordan's brother, Knox Macdougal. Soon after his arrival, Hector had asked about his daughter, Mary, and the air was so thick with tension that he could have cut it. The reply of "She's dead along with most of her brats" boded no further enquiries. Knox was unpleasant enough as it was, but he stayed for three days upsetting everyone and making himself free with items in the castle. Hector repossessed all of them before he left, upsetting the egotistical man by accusing him of taking items that were not his. Knox was very like his older brother, domineering and extremely rude. He left empty-handed after an explosion of his temper. Fran had remained in their rooms for most of his stay. She emerged after she saw his carriage leave.

Each day brought another relative returning, many were elderly, and most were emaciated. Lady Sheila's ankle had healed, and she was upright again and walking with a stick. She and Juliana had found that they liked each other immensely regardless of their different backgrounds. Both ladies were in their late seventies and were otherwise fit and well.

Sidney, Henry, and Hector travelled to Edinburgh several times to view and sign various documents for Mr Featherstone. Sidney promised he would return with Joey at least twice a year, and Lady Sheila knew she could refer to him when required. Sidney could now manage any complex things from London until Joey was of age in 1847. Hector, Sidney, and Lady Sheila agreed that after Hector and Fran returned, Joey would need to visit Scotland and learn the ropes of running the Estate and Clan from Mr Featherstone and his partners. Joey would grow up with a foot in three countries. He would have many decisions to make and many responsibilities to learn. Henry's wealth may be new money, but any money was useful when running an ancient Estate in Scotland. It would be a backstop if the castle were in need.

Before they returned to England, Lady Sheila and Sidney spent some time each day discussing Sarah. He told her of their short time together in Edinburgh and later in Kent. They were two gaps in her life that her mother knew nothing about. One day Sarah was in Edinburgh, and the next, she had vanished from Fiona's house. Unbeknownst to her, Sidney had arranged Sarah's move through Mr Featherstone as he knew of their marriage. Sarah had said a special goodnight to her mother and left at dawn the following day for her sister's place. From there, she travelled by ship under her married name. Not knowing that detail, Lady Sheila could not find her. She heard that Sarah had died two years after leaving, and Hector vanished from Susanna's estate. Sidney didn't know where Hector was either. Riordan, Fergus, Callum, and the abominable Knox didn't care.

Chapter 23   Return Journeys

*T*he return trip from Scotland was once again made by carriage. Their convoluted route was down the country's western side, travelling via Glasgow, Liverpool, Manchester, and then via Sheffield, where Henry wished to see Marcus Ryan's woollen mill to the south of that town. After a few days in Nottingham to see the lace-making and buy some lengths and panels for the girls at home to try and copy, their trip took them back through Birmingham and then eventually towards Kent via Oxford, Reading, Guildford, and Crawley to visit Amelia, Earl Sam and Annie before turning northward for the final leg. This trip was purely tourism as they were all together. Fran and Hector knew they would never return to this area and wished to see as much as possible in the country's west. Although they had plans to return to see Joey in later years, they would prioritise their time to be with family.

On arrival at Sam Garney's stately home near Crawley, Henry was keen to see the faces of the family as they saw the vast size of the abode. Sidney noticed a not-so-subtle smile settle on Fran's lips when she first glimpsed the facade; then, watching all three faces, he saw that all three jaws dropped open in unison. "Dear ones, this is the house where Amelia is living, so while we are here, we will pay visits to Marcus Ryan's home to the West; and over there is Malvern Hall. However, this is Earl Sam's *Meldon Hall*, and it is nearly as large as Stowe House, which I believe has some two hundred bedrooms. I have heard that Earl Sam has many children, waifs, strays, and families in the suites. New staff are retraining and assisting in the estate's upkeep, and they are educated and being taught how to live a new and better life."

Fran's eyes nearly popped when she heard of the vast number of rooms. "And Earl Sam has turned it into a school?"

Her father-in-law smiled at her words. "He has indeed, my dear."

They stayed a week before continuing their journey.

~

Two months after leaving *Glenview Keep* the carriages turned in through a large stone gate. Sidney, Hector, and Fran were alone in the front carriage. They had chatted for most of the journey, catching up on the hidden years in each other's lives. In every conversation, father and son, and father and daughter, drew closer.

Hector noticed they had turned off the main road into a private road. "Where are we, Father? Are we visiting someone else?" Hector asked as they turned into an oak tree-lined driveway. He enquired softly, "Are we not going to London?" Julia was asleep on his shoulder.

Sidney smiled. "We will later, son, but this is my country home. I thought we could spend some time out of the city where the children could run and play. We are just east of Westerham. It was from here that I used to ride to see your mother. It's about two hours by road, but I travelled cross country. I used to have horses at various stages along the route. Once there, I would often stay at a friend's house nearby. My house here is where I, no, where we, Mother and I call home. My brother, Clayton, has his own estate not far away. He won it in a game of chance." Sidney looked at the faces of his son and daughter-in-law. They had all enjoyed their journey, but now they could all relax. Hopefully, they can unwind and enjoy life in England here. They could learn to fit into their new titles and lives. He knew they would eventually return to the Hawkesbury River, but until then, he hoped both boys would be settled into their school, that is, if the boys stayed. He would spend every moment he could with them.

The mile-long driveway was a stately curving gravel road lined with grey river rocks and overshadowed by the immense arched avenue of the ancient oaks. The house that soon came into view amazed them. The grey stone building stood on a grassy knoll, nestled amongst another stand of mature oak trees. The home overlooked a moat that curved around the front.

Hector appreciated the age and atmosphere of the view before him. "Oh, Father, this is a bit of all right. You must tell me its history while we're here." Hector said while gazing at the ancient home. It was not too big and had obviously stood in its regal spot for some generations. Hector spied a rounded turret similar to his house in Edinburgh and knew the boys would love investigating this place too.

The children received much the same information from Lady Juliana and Henry in the carriage following them. Joey and Alec were whispering about the turret and how much fun exploring every nook and cranny in this house would be.

Joey was amazed to know that one day it would all be his. He was old enough to realise the responsibility before him and knew he had much to learn. His paternal grandfather had already discussed schooling with him, and although fearful, the lad realised that he must learn all he could. He sat spellbound, watching the sprawling property reveal itself. He didn't want to stay here alone. As Alec was only a bit over a year younger, Joey was going to ask if they could go to school together while his parents were still in England. At least then, he would have someone nearby. Joey hoped that maybe Alec could even stay when they went home. He was very nervous but excited as well.

His great-grandmother watched him and saw various expressions wave over his face. Lady Juliana said, "Joey, don't be afraid. We know it's a lot to ask of a young lad, but you will not be alone. You at least will be titled and therefore have a much easier time than your grandfather did." She saw the look of astonishment on his face. "Joey, you are The Master of Glenview, son of the Baron. Alec, you have the lesser title, as do the girls. You are all 'The Honourable,' and as such, doors will open for you that have remained firmly shut for your grandfather. You are also great-grandchildren of an Earl." She always felt sorry for her sons, but they had made their way, and both were successful.

Joey felt Alec dig him in the ribs. "Did you know we got titles?" he asked in a not-so-quiet voice.

His great-grandmother said, "What you should ask is, 'Did you know that we have titles.' One thing you will all have to learn is the correct usage of the English language. You must improve that before heading to school, or the boys there will tease you mercilessly." She let that sink in briefly before adding, "Alec, would you like to accompany Joey to school while you are here? You may even wish to stay with him when your parents return home." She saw a look of fear in his eyes, so she added, "Don't worry about that now; we'll cross that bridge later; enjoy the time you have until then." As they were pulling up to the front door of the manor house, he thankfully he didn't have to answer.

Sidney, Hector, Fran and Julia were waiting in the driveway. As their carriage drove off, the second one took its place. Skye alighted first and stood with her mouth open. "Nice house, Grandpa," she said with admiration. Considering they lived in two rooms above a stable, the size of the houses in this land still took her breath away.

Sidney smiled at his granddaughter. "Wait until you see what your room is like." He didn't elaborate, but he had arranged for her to have the blue room. He designed this room many years ago, especially for Hector, but it wasn't particularly masculine. The light blue velvet was luxurious but still relatively simple in taste. He hoped she would like it. Fran and Hector would be in the royal suite here too, and his mother would be in her old rooms. He had looked forward to this day for a long, long time. His son was finally coming home.

Henry came and went for work in London for over a year before he needed to return home to Australia.

Sidney assured him that he would permanently have a room, either here or in Sidney's London house, whenever he needed it. He was now family; the two older men had become firm friends. Sidney had introduced Henry to many of his business contacts; using these, he arranged various produce shipments to his warehouse in The Rocks in Sydney. Spiritous liquids were always saleable in the colony, so on one of the trips to Scotland, they visited a distillery and set up a new trade contract. Henry then returned to Australia on the *Lord Lyndoch*.

~

For two years, life for the family was an adventure every day. Fran was even beginning to enjoy living in the country, but she had no intention of staying. Her father awaited her at home.

The time drew near for Hector to say his farewells. They had visited his grandmother in Scotland several times, usually by sea. Lady Sheila was back to her active self. Since the cousins had moved back in, she was no longer lonely and had blossomed.

Hector promised to write frequently, and on their final visit, when he went to say farewell, he enfolded her tightly in his arms and, after kissing her on her cheek, whispered, "Thank you so much, *Seanmhair*, for everything." He had hardly seen her show emotion all the time they had been together. However, those few words broke her.

Rather than let Hector go, she grasped him and wept. "I have only just got you back, and now you're leaving again."

Hector was not expecting her reaction and was somewhat stuck for words. Eventually, he said, "We'll come back, *Seanmhair*, and probably in only a few years. Take care of the boys for us, won't you? Can you ensure they aren't told about the priests' hole until they have more sense? I'd hate to see them locked inside like I was."

She looked up at him and saw the mischievous twinkle in his gaze. She said, "I won't promise. This house is such a fabulous adventure for two small boys. You certainly enjoyed climbing those spiral staircases and hiding from your grandfather and great-uncle." She waited until he was seated in the coach before adding, "I have since found a secret passageway." She heard him gasp as the carriage departed. She had said her farewells with more tears, but now she chuckled at his expression. She stood surrounded by her cousins until the carriages were just puffs of dust in the distance. Determined to cry no more, she took a deep breath and turned to face her relations with a false smile on her face. "Right, the Lord of the Castle has gone; who's for a game of croquet?"

There was a murmur of chuckles. All knew how she was feeling and admired her bravery. With Hector gone, she had to begin life anew with her extended family now surrounding her. She would keep her promise to write every month.

~

When the family decided to return to Australia, they planned to leave in September. They presumed they would say farewell while the boys were at school. They knew that seeing the ship go would be too hard for everyone. But a three-month delay in finding a ship had changed everything. It was their turn to weep.

For some time, they had debated as to how they would travel. There were few options for them. *The Kinnear* was a convict ship; therefore, it was a vessel far too similar to what Hector and Fran had both travelled on their first journey to New South Wales, and Sidney refused to permit them to travel on such a vessel. *The Ferguson* was a merchant ship with no convicts, so Sidney eventually chose her. Also, both Sidney and Henry had used *The Ferguson* to ship consignments of cargo before, and Captain Farquharson would make sure the family were kept safe. However, Sidney had sent a letter on the earlier vessel with instructions for Henry to meet them on their return. The one drawback to catching this ship was that it departed on Christmas Day.

Sidney, Lady Juliana, and the boys made arrangements to celebrate this festival a few days early. Both groups felt the pain of their parting.

"However did I let you talk me into allowing both boys to stay here, Hector?" Fran was drawn into her husband's arms as the ship pulled away from the wharf. She had managed to hold her tears, but she knew they would come. Saying goodbye to both her sons was horrible. She knew it could be years before she saw them again and that they would be grown beyond recognition. Her hands fell to her stomach. She wondered if it were too soon to tell Hector of her suspicions. Having this child born at home was her only motivation to leave her sons. She was shattered at the choice she had been forced to make.

Hector felt the same sadness about leaving his sons but knew it was for the best. At that moment, he understood what his father had done for him. His father had put his son's well-being ahead of his own happiness. At least the boys knew that he adored them both. But at home, Henry awaited their return.

Sidney, Lady Juliana, and the boys stood waving until *The Ferguson* turned the bend in the river. Fran could still identify her sons' redheads; she continued to wave until the ship floated from view.

The large ship was quickly going out with the tide, although it would still take them a few days to reach the sea. The river was too narrow to set more than one small sail. The current carried the sturdy vessel for miles until the slack water drew them to a halt; they anchored there for six hours until the flood tide changed. They would stay moored until the ebb tide returned; then, they would slip into the flow along with other ships and travel the next leg of the journey. The chill December winds assisted their passage downstream as they went with the flow.

~

The four months on board eased the hurt of leaving their sons in England. Fran felt as though her heart had torn in two. What was worse was, three weeks into the trip, she had lost the child she carried. She cried into Hector's shoulder for over a week. Sidney put it down to leaving their sons in England; Fran did not contradict him, but she was emotionally exhausted. She had asked Hector not to explain her melancholy.

More cabin class passengers were on board than expected, and there were some other children for the girls to play with. Julia was a handful as, at nearly five, she was a wilful child. Fran and Hector had come prepared, and she wore a leather harness whenever she was awake. Julia had wandered down to a dam in Kent and been knee-deep in the frigid water when found. The child was fearless, and was also very annoying. Thankfully, after Fran lost her baby, the trip had been uneventful as to storms, illnesses, other tragedies and the like. However, only two weeks after the miscarriage, the steerage class passengers were amazed when Hector and Fran made their first sojourn down to their deck. Over the months at sea, these visits became a frequent occurrence. They knew what life was in front of the steerage passengers and decided to ease their worries and assist where able.

Hector realised that helping others would be one way to help Fran. It wasn't long before Fran arranged a class where the female passengers could learn to read and discuss what was before them. She told them how different their lives would be and the opportunities they would have if they were prepared to work.

Skye and Julia needed lessons, and Fran decided to hold them down in the steerage dining room. She started lessons with the only book she had with her, her Bible. The captain allowed her to write on a wall at the end of the room.

Hector managed to garner some interest amongst the men. Soon the lessons were enjoyed by all. Often their efforts were also a source of great mirth. The laughter at the attempts of those prepared to read aloud was soon quashed when Hector told the teasers they were to read next. Soon, they started a competition to see who could read best by the time they docked. The prize was £1.

Not long after their first visit, Fran had found two young girls travelling alone and asked if they had positions lined up. They didn't; their stepfather had purchased tickets soon after their mother died. They had quite literally been set adrift. Something in Fran made her want to reach out to them. As Hector and Fran had no staff, she asked the captain if they could hire them as maids while on board. Maggie and Lynne Woods joined the family as staff. Fran hoped they would come and stay with them in Windsor. She realised their life would not return to what it was.

Before he had left London, Henry had finally extracted a promise that they would move into his house in Windsor. As Callum was now in residence in their rooms above the stables, they realised they had little option.

Maggie and Lynne sat with the children and cleaned up the toys from the day's activities. Lynne was only a couple of years older than Skye, but she had been out working as a laundry maid for some years. Maggie said she was eighteen, but Fran thought she was far too worldly-wise to be as innocent as she should be. It didn't take long for Fran to work out the reason. Some weeks into the trip, Maggie had confided that she was in the family way and that her stepfather was the culprit. It was why he banished them. The abuse had occurred while their mother lay dying; Maggie was distraught until Fran explained her own past. She promised both girls would always have a home with them or even with Hetty. The choice would be theirs, but they would be kept safe. Fran's life had gone full circle. She could now help others as she had once been helped herself.

~

By the end of March, they were approaching Melbourne. With a few days in port to unload cargo, Hector and Fran were escorted around the small town by another couple on board who had once lived there. They now lived near Orchard Hills, west of Parramatta.

Fran clutched Hector's arm and kept a veil over her face. She still wished she was old and wrinkly, but her beauty had grown as she aged. She had taken to wearing a dark net veil when out in public, such was her concern about being ogled. She still hated it and what men did to her.

Hector encouraged Fran out on deck as the ship turned northward from Melbourne. The past evenings were cooling, but as they headed further up the coast, the evenings were warm enough to spend some time outside. Occasionally they saw the sea glowing, but never as vibrantly as that night on the way to London.

Maggie and Lynne now slept in the room next to their girls, as their steerage berth was far too small for Maggie's advancing condition. She was now getting close to six months along. They had turned their spare cabin into the maid's room. As she was now showing, Maggie rarely stepped outside the family's rooms, and if she did so, she wore one of Franny's enveloping cloaks, which all but hid her condition. They had also made some gowns for her to wear as the ones she had with her no longer fitted.

One blessing was that both girls could read. When they were little, their mother had insisted that they attend a Sunday School, and both had realised the benefit of this skill and so studied hard. The minister who taught them even gave them an old, tattered Bible with half of Genesis missing. They had read from this whenever they could. When they saw that Skye had brought some books, the four girls sat reading them together. Moreover, Julia loved story time, so getting her to sit still for this was never hard. Fran soon discovered that Julia adored Lynne.

During the first week of April, the ship was within sight of Sydney's heads. Hector insisted that Fran watch the approach to the harbour. It was a sight neither had seen before, as both had been locked below decks. In the many conversations over the past years, both their fathers had mentioned how awe-inspiring the view was while entering the harbour. It was one of those sparkling autumn days when the sun seemed to sprinkle the sea with diamonds. The sun was warm but not so hot that it burnt. It was glorious weather to welcome them home. As Hector held Fran cradled in his arms, the soft spray of the breaking waves cooled them down. Fran rested against his chest as she said, "Our fathers were not wrong, Hector; look at that magnificent sight." For what would be one of the last times, they heard a call of "tacking" from the crew. Hector held Fran tight as the ship heaved too. Many hands were pulling ropes, and sails were adjusted again.

The ship heeled to the port and turned into the magnificent heads. The towering cliff stood like an impenetrable barrier, then as the vessel drew close to the land, it was like a magical opening door, only it was an optical illusion. The headland divided into three, and opening before them was the most incredible harbour. With the wind blowing onshore, the ship sailed on at nearly full speed. Fran and Hector stayed at the ropes, drinking in the sight before them.

Maggie and Lynne were watching with the girls from the dining room portholes. All had agreed that Julia could not be trusted outdoors. She was so excited to nearly be home, not that she remembered much of it, but she remembered wide open spaces to run and play. No one had told her they would no longer live on the farm. Skye knew but kept the information to herself. At fourteen, she was the image of her beautiful mother. Fran looked more like her sister than her mother. The nineteen-year difference between them only showed on Fran with some tiny smile-wrinkles at the corner of her eyes. Skye was nearly her height. Hector and Fran knew they would have their hands full, keeping men away from her. Even on board, some of the younger sailors were making eyes at her. Skye had elected to stay inside until they arrived at the dock. She didn't like being ogled either. They all now had titles, so their lives would never be the same. Money and titles would ruin the peaceful life they had previously lived. Hector was determined to restore that peace and tranquillity somehow.

Chapter 24 A New Home

s *The Ferguson* docked, Hector and Fran saw Henry, Hetty, and Des on
the wharf waiting for them. *The Kinnear* had arrived only the week before
and had brought news of their imminent arrival on the following ship.

The three had come to Sydney as soon as they received the letter
and waited for them. For Des and Hetty, it was like a honeymoon they had
never had. They stayed in total luxury at The King's Arms hotel in town.
Henry had booked a suite for them and more for the arriving family. Henry
couldn't wait for his daughter and her family to return. He was looking
forward to showing Alec the Bathurst farm.

The worried look on Henry's face slowly changed from a frown,
then to a smile as he saw his daughter in her husband's arms. Skye and Julia
were now beside them, but no Alec. Somewhat crestfallen, Henry gave a
disappointed sigh; he had wondered if the lad would stay at school with his
brother, and obviously, he had done so, for Henry knew his grandson would
not have missed this sight if he had been on board. Although disappointed,
he understood. Alec was young and needed the education he would receive
in England. What was before the lad was ownership of a big business, and
he had to be able to know how to manage it all. More than anything, Henry
was looking forward to seeing his daughter again. After so many years of
not knowing what happened to his child, to have spent the past year
without her had been hard. His family had finally returned, and he felt he
could breathe again. He had been to Bathurst several times and taken
Callum with him on his last trip. He was somewhat amazed that Callum had
seemed exceptionally interested in life on the distant farm. Having seen his
behaviour in Scotland, he knew of his change of attitude. Des had
mentioned that he had used Bathurst as a punishment for the brash lad on

more than one occasion. David had read the riot act to him and used his three months in the area to make him re-fence the boundary with post and rail split logs. Surprisingly, Callum had relished doing something worthwhile.

Soon after they landed, Hector took Fran on the shopping jaunt she had wished to do for some time, as he knew that there would be little opportunity for purchasing special items once they returned to Windsor. The Argyle Stores on the waterfront offered a vast range of products, from hardware to clothing and everything in between. Both Hector and Fran wished to see Piper's shop and Mary Reiby's stores. Hetty's mother's store had long since been sold, and these two filled the space. Since they left for England, a new wing of shops had been finished. They had seen it under construction as they left in 1835. Now completed, Fran wished to have a look. In letters to her, Hetty had waxed lyrical about both places. Henry had also mentioned the new stores in his letters to Fran. She also wished to see through his own warehouse.

On their tour, they met a new employee; he was a young Scotsman named Brodie Stewart. He and his wife Heather had arrived separately as convicts the year before. When he heard their story, Fran found that Henry had compassion for them and gave them an apartment in the loft. When he arrived, he had only one year to serve; his wife could be transferred to him when free. Brodie was now free.

Hector gave a furrowed frown when he saw the young lad. He shook his head and walked away. Fran saw but did not ask him about the incident.

With a few days in town, Fran asked if they could revisit the stores. She didn't say why, but Hector knew her mind had returned to her vine weaving. She had obviously seen something she wanted. She may now have a title, but Fran was still a weaver at heart. She was itching to return to her craft that she knew and loved. She had bought a few new styles in England and returned with a journal filled with unique designs. While travelling the countryside over the past two-plus years, Fran's mind had never been far from her beloved weaving. When she left them, she had made both great-grandmothers' gifts of handmade baskets filled with assorted handmade crafts.

Fran had found various new ideas in Scotland and sketched them. Things that intrigued her were a variety of rib construction designs. She also wished to make some fishing creel baskets, and some of the lidded food basket designs were ones she had not seen before. Some had leather-bound edges, and others were just wicker. On the stop-over on the return trip from Scotland to Yorkshire, she had found some strange baskets that she thought she would try. Instead of making rolags of wool for spinning, these were rolled together and turned into a soft spool that was carefully placed in the *mudag* baskets that fed out the spools of teased wool and kept it clean and easier to store. She decided to make one for Hetty for her spinning. These would be added to the production items if Hetty liked them.

Fran's journal contained ideas for picnic baskets with split-flap lids, shopping baskets, also lidded storage baskets, flower-collecting scooped baskets like an Aboriginal *coolamon*, and even fish traps. Fran drew it if it could be hand-made with vines, cane, or wicker. Her book was full of a variety of rib designs that intrigued her. There were flat timber ribs, cane ribs, vine ribs, and wire ribs. The final design Fran wished to experiment with was not with vines but with handmade string. Laura had taught her how to make this twine, and she had an idea to make rope or string baskets with wire ribs, also the flat plaited grasses used to make hats. Hopefully, she could find some things in the Bond Store to assist her. She also had plans for new designs of bee skeps. They involved various native types of grass and could be woven before thoroughly drying the plant. These were thicker rolls of reeds, but the structure had a lid that flipped back, which other designs did not have. This lid was to check the honey load; her current design meant the entire skep had to be either tilted or cut open, which destroyed the hive. The new structure would allow inspection without disturbing the bees; Fran planned to modify her existing design to suit. Her mind was running twenty to the dozen, and she had barely disembarked from the ship, let alone returned home. Here, she was almost back in familiar surroundings. As Hector, Henry, Fran, and Des followed her through the store, they carried the few things that she chose. However, even with what they had purchased, she mentioned that she wanted to return for a final visit before they returned home.

Over the years, Hector was intrigued by her near obsession with this natural fibre; however, he had never asked her why. Shortly before they left on their final shopping trip, he had asked her why she loved weaving.

Fran smiled at him as though she expected that he should know the reason. "Hector, I think it's something to do with making something useful out of what is, in reality, rubbish. It's what God did to my life. I thought I was rubbish, a thrown-away child, unloved, uncared for, used and abused. I wasn't, but I didn't know that back then. Thanks to you and Hetty, God took me and wove His love into my life, making me something new and useful. Then He gave me you to love and cherish, and you gave me His words. The vines I use are cut off and thrown away. They are like my life; I intertwine them to make them strong and useful. Alone we are weak and useless, thrown away rubbish. Woven, we become strong and with a purpose. Does that make sense?" She tilted her head and looked at him with a slight frown.

Hector's jaw had dropped. He had never thought that her activity was representative of her life. "I had no idea, love. None at all!"

Fran continued, "Hector, when you first mentioned your five points of belief, the details flew across the top of my head, but those five points stuck, and I learned that God loved me. No one had ever wanted me before Hetty. But I still wasn't loved, so your words rocked me. That alone was huge for me. I was loved and accepted as I am. Then you said the next bit that mankind sinned. I knew that too. I knew that I was abused and used by every one of those men on the ship, and I hated myself, but your words told me that it was their sin, not mine. I had done nothing to encourage them, but you told me I had to forgive them just as God did. Oh, that was so hard, Hector. I fought against that. Then on the verandah, when you were talking to Joel and Hetty, the next bit sank in. God sent his Son to us, meaning we only had one decision. I could either accept Him or reject Him. Well, I'd already had enough of being rejected, so that bit was easy. If God and Jesus could wash me clean and help me to change, I would grab it. I had nothing to lose, Hector. Nothing at all!" Fran paused and looked at her husband.

Hector smiled and said, "Go on."

Fran did after she gave him a quick kiss. "The only possession I had that was mine was the key. Therefore, I only had myself to give to God, so it wasn't that hard. It might have been more difficult if I were a rich person, but I had nothing. Then you took my hand and caressed it. My heart flipped. I knew then that I loved you, but more than that, I trusted you but was so scared." She brushed away an errant tear.

Hector reached out and drew her into his arms. "Now it finally makes sense. It's how I feel about you; I was made new from the inside out."

He was about to kiss her passionately when she asked, "Now can we go shopping again?" The impish look she gave him made him chuckle. His plans temporarily dashed, he said, "Yes, woman, we can!" Hector laughed. He knew Hetty had accompanied her through the new store a few times during the week, and they had made a quick trip hours after arriving at the hotel, but this expedition was to be Fran's big trip. Her previous visits were more to see what was available.

Henry's new ketch, *Franny's Joy*, had arrived, and they could load her shopping straight on board. It was docked behind his warehouse. This vessel was new since Henry returned, so Fran had not yet seen it. He knew the shopping area well, as it was not far from his enlarged warehouse.

When Henry arrived on the *Lord Lyndoch* the year before, he had been impressed with one of the convicts who assisted many smallpox patients. The lad gave and gave until he himself dropped from ravages of scurvy. On arrival, he had seen Major Downes to get some new assignees, and this lad was mentioned. Henry was surprised to find that the boy had a letter of recommendation in his file from the arresting commissioner of police in Glasgow.

Major Downes had been wondering whom to assign the lad to when Henry had walked in and asked about him. Brodie Stewart accompanied Henry to The Rocks and settled into the attic apartment above the warehouse. Brodie's wife Heather arrived with their infant son shortly afterwards. She was assigned to their friends in the adjoining pub, *The Whaler's Arms*. Henry liked them both, and they were hard workers. Now, a year later, Brodie's time was up, and Henry was hoping he would stay on.

As Henry had just finished his new house in Windsor, he had not yet mentioned to his family that he had sold his house in town. Knowing that Fran didn't like to be with many people, he decided to sell up and buy the property next to Andrew Thompson's red house just outside Windsor. It was on a small knoll and well out of any flood range as it was over sixty feet above the river, and in summer, it picked up the cool breezes that came over the water. The wide verandahs, stone walls, and high ceilings should be a delight after the small rooms in the stables where Hector and Fran had previously lived. He was nervous, hoping that his family would like their new home. Henry had planted some imported Japanese honeysuckle vines on the verandah pillars. He had not been able to purchase anything suitable in Sydney, so he asked one of his captains to obtain a few plants for him on his next trip to Japan. The man had also returned with one he called star jasmine. The flowers of this vine had the most beautiful scent, so he planted this on the fence. Henry had planted the honeysuckle up each second verandah post, and it had grown very well. Fran could use the off-cut tendrils to weave as they had to be often trimmed.

On their final shopping expedition, Hector bumped into the young store-man again. His puzzled frown made Fran ask her husband if he knew him. Hector shook his head and replied, "No, at least I don't think so, but he looks so familiar, I can't quite place him. He is the younger image of someone I know from home." Hector shook his head as if to shake away the image of his uncle. However hard he tried to concentrate on the shopping, his attention returned to his father-in-law's assignee, wondering why the lad looked familiar.

Brodie noticed the almost impertinent interest and asked, "Sir do I have a fly on my nose?" He spoke with a Glaswegian accent.

Hearing it, it finally came to him only when Brodie challenged him. "No, you remind me of someone from home, and that is my great Uncle Knox." He saw Brodie blanch, stiffen and stagger backwards.

With a look of horror, Brodie's following words were uttered with a strangled tone, "Whom did you say?" It was not a common name for a first name. Brodie's voice was low and had a jitter to it.

Hector wondered about the change of attitude in the easygoing boy. He explained, "My great uncle's name is Knox Macdougal, with only one 'l'. He is my grandfather's younger brother. You are so like him that you could be a young version of him."

By now, Brodie had broken out in a sweat. He opened his lips to speak, but no words came out. This occurred twice.

"Brodie, are you all right?" Hector was now a little concerned.

Brodie's face was white, and dribbles of perspiration slid down his cheeks. He shook his head; eventually, he swallowed and then nodded. "My mother's father was named Knox Macdougal, and they spelled their name with only one 'l'. Hector, my grandfather, disowned Mama when she went against his will and married my Papa. Papa was a sailor, but he loved Mama dearly, and I adored him. I only met my grandfather once and was not too impressed with him. Quite honestly, a more unpleasant character you would not wish to meet. Mama had written to him for assistance when Papa had not returned from his last voyage. Grandfather eventually came, but by then, it was months after she had begged for assistance. When he eventually arrived, he found her quite obviously with child. He instantly realised it was not Papa's child as he had been gone too long, and my grandfather's ire was such that he struck her violently. I hid, but I could still see him, and he hit her again and again, then he called her a whore, then stormed out. I didn't know what that meant back then. I never saw him again, but I'll never forget him or his name or that he refused to assist us. He could have at least given us some money for rent." Brodie's head dropped.

Hector nodded, and bile from his stomach hit his tongue. "Sounds like the same foul-tempered man, Brodie." Hector had indeed had similar run-ins with his uncle in his early years. "I met him again when we were there recently, and the old brute hasn't changed much. My grandfather was of the same ilk. I asked Uncle Knox about his daughter, my cousin, Mary, and he said was 'she had died long ago with most of her brats.'"

Brodie nodded, then explained. "Mama's name was Mary, and she died in childbirth about two years after Papa left on his last trip. As I said, I was only a kid, and after that, I lived on the street with Heather. That was only a couple of months after my grandfather's visit. We had no money at all by then, and Mama did what she could to keep a roof over our heads." He paused, then said, "Hector, the landlord was the only man who ever visited that way." Brodie needed to explain to Hector that his mother was no whore. "Sir, the landlord used her poorly. In hindsight, I realise now he took the rent differently, and she had little choice as he forced himself on her quite violently. The first time he actually knocked her out before he used her." Brodie paused, remembering when he had arrived home to find the landlord on top of his unresponsive mother. He shook his head as if to scare away the memories, then continued his reverie. "When Mama died, I lay her tiny dead child in her arms and fled. I knew I would not get assistance from the landlord or my grandfather. Not that I knew where to contact him. I just left Mama and the dead baby in our room for the landlord to sort out. He owed her that much. I met Heather that night. We were just innocent little kids." Brodie had sunk onto a barrel as they spoke. The memories washed over him anew. A thought hit him, Hector was related? He must be, but that thought hit hard, and his eyes flew to the man before him. "You're my cousin then, Hector? I didn't know I even had one."

Relief swept over Hector's face, and his eyes glinted with joy. "Yes, I suppose I am, and there are others, as Callum is here too. This also means that you are related to Henry in a roundabout way." Compassion swept over Hector.

Brodie gazed at his cousin, absolutely speechless.

Henry had come in as Hector spoke. "Do I hear my name being bandied around, son?"

Hector smiled at his father-in-law. "You do, Henry. You met my grandmother when we were in Scotland. Do you remember meeting her brother-in-law just before we departed?"

Henry shivered. "Do I ever! Franny remained in your rooms at Lady Sheila's suggestion and out of sight during his three-day stay. I have never been so glad to see the back of a person in my life."

Hector agreed. He continued his not-so-subtle probing. "Do you remember me questioning him about his daughter, Mary?"

Henry nodded. "Yes, you could have cut the air with a knife when you asked about her. Why?"

Hector said, "My cousin Mary was Brodie's mother. The term Uncle Knox used for her was unpleasant, to say the least. Henry, my cousin Mary, did what was required to keep them alive when her husband vanished. She was left penniless. Her father came and refused to help them at all, and he beat her. Mary and I were of an age, and I remember she ran away to marry a sailor just before I left for Kent in about 1814. Henry, Brodie is the image of Uncle Knox."

Henry frowned and stood examining his young employee. Although the boy was still emaciated, he had known he was somewhat familiar when they had first met. He had only met Knox once and avoided him as much as possible. However, he realised Hector knew his uncle well. A raft of emotions showed on Henry's face until, finally, a smile settled on his thin lips. With a laugh, the frown vanished, and Henry said, "Then you're family, Brodie. This also makes it easier to let you live here permanently. I've been wondering how to word it without offending you. This accommodation has previously only been for convict lodging, but I can see you are both happy here. As your term is up, you can now stay. However, the promotion comes with a condition. You will now become the official caretaker of the building, and that means you will also get paid a proper wage. If you now called me Uncle Henry, others would realise that there is a relationship between us."

Brodie was both delighted and horrified. "Sir, you don't need to do this. I'm still just Brodie, an ex-convict." He would have said more, but Henry's hand was now raised, and he stopped speaking.

Henry said in an adamant tone, "You are my son-in-law's cousin; therefore, I claim you. I will tolerate no argument from you, young man."

Brodie grinned and shook Mr Gate's hand vigorously. "Thank you so much, sir." Brodie and his wife, Heather, loved their first home, and now they could stay there.

Three days after arriving in Sydney, the extended Hawkesbury family boarded Henry's small ketch and headed out to sea, then northward to the Hawkesbury River. Hector had spent more time talking to Brodie and decided to take the lad under his care. Having family nearby was good. They had yet to meet his wife as she had been at work, and they had not returned to the warehouse.

Maggie and Lynne had stayed in the hotel with Skye and Julia, keeping them both occupied and safe. They were thrilled they had found a safe family to work with and knew the story of Maggie's condition. Fran had already been telling them about her pet project, and both were willing to learn to weave. Both girls could already spin, and each had other cottage industry skills. During the voyage, Maggie mentioned that she knew how to use a ribbon loom. The Argyle Store had a small flat-packed table loom for sale, and Henry overheard Fran as she pointed it out to Hector, wondering if Maggie could use it as the technique was similar.

Henry smiled; Maggie was in for a surprise as he purchased the table loom and sent it to his boat for the trip back home. Hopefully, Maggie can work out how to assemble it when it was unpacked.

~

When Callum arrived, Des was livid with Hector for sending the rude, spoilt, wild young man to them. Hector knew they did not like men coming unexpectedly to the farm. One with the reputation of being a womaniser and profligate was the worst type. However, in the intervening months, Callum had settled down and changed from the angry, undisciplined boy that Henry, Hector, and Fran had met in Scotland to become a good worker.

Des had laid down strict rules for him when Callum met him at the jetty. Des had banished him to Bathurst on more than one occasion, making him cool his heels for three months before being permitted to return. David and Ernie took him in hand in Bathurst and gave him hands-on experience with the hard work of farm life. He had even learned to shear a sheep.

Callum started his re-education soon after he arrived. He had sworn, and a single look from the giant, Nate, and strong words from Des curbed his tongue. With an eyeful of what Des and Hetty were doing on the farm, Callum learned respect for them and their work of assisting girls. However, it had taken a slap in the face from Clara, and then Hetty threatened to permanently banish him to Bathurst before he finally got the message. A chastised and repentant Callum watched, absorbed, and learned before acting again.

After months of working hard with Des, David, and the boys, Callum finally understood what the girls on the property had experienced. He eventually apologised to Clara, and they finally sat down and talked.

After all her years on the farm, she had never opened up to anyone. Hetty had never pressed her; however, she knew that what she had told them was not the truth. Clara had not been ready to tell her story to anyone. She found herself pouring out her life history to the arrogant red-headed Scotsman. "Callum, I wanted to be a nun; I had applied to a teaching order and was accepted. However, I met and fell in love with a very nice young man on the journey to France. One thing led to another, and I succumbed to his charms. We had an incredible eight weeks together; then I mentioned that I might be with child. Not long afterwards, I woke one morning and found that he had packed and gone while I slept. He had fled; there was not even a note, and I had no way to contact him. With no money, food or job, I used my last coins and returned to England; once there, I soon found myself destitute. I was almost thankful when I lost the child." Clara sniffed, then blew her nose. "Soon after this, I was arrested and sent to Sydney." She did not elaborate on how this happened; she had remained silent about that all these years, and she wouldn't tell him now. She had almost spat her story at Callum and explained that he was the sort of man that her boyfriend had been. It had been almost out of spite that she revealed everything. Callum needed to learn what effect his callous actions had on others. Retelling her history brought her some measure of relief but also left her in tears. She was crushed with remorse and guilt. She had bottled her past for so long that the final release melted her iron-clad reserve. Her hacking sobs hit Callum hard.

Now sitting with a weeping woman, Callum reached out to comfort her. He had no recollection of how it occurred, but Clara ended up in his arms, weeping on his shoulder. He had drawn her close, and she didn't pull away. He found he liked being the protective person a woman turned to for comfort, and Clara smelled so lovely, like roses. He liked roses; he liked Clara too.

It had taken six months more before he kissed her. He only intended his endearment to be a peck on the cheek, but she had turned, and Callum kissed her lips. Rather than draw away, Clara's hand had rested on his chest, and she had deepened the kiss.

Callum, although surprised, found the emotions running through him were not lustful but protective. He had learnt to care for this dear lady.

Soon, they walked along the river's edge almost daily, much as Hector and Fran had done so many years before.

Both were now in their thirties and old enough to know the farm's rules. Callum obeyed them willingly, never walking alone, and he ensured the children were always close by.

By the time Fran and Hector returned, Callum was officially courting Clara. No one could be more surprised than Callum himself. He only awaited Hector's return to ask for her hand in marriage. Callum had already broached the subject of matrimony with her but had not yet asked her officially.

The girls in residence had once again changed. Clara, Mary, Jane and Kitty were the only girls still there from before their departure to England. More had come and gone, and the farm had taken on greater productivity. Children's joyous voices were frequently heard. Oliver and Mary were expecting their third child and kept their eyes on the courting couple. Nate and Jane had just had their fourth child, Nicholas Nathaniel, or Nikki as he was known, in February of the year before. He joined an older sister whom Fran and Hector had not met. Henrietta Frances, known as Letty, was born in 1835. Leonie and Liam were now six, and both had chores to do on the farm.

Kitty's daughter Emmy was now eleven. She, too, had set chores. Her skin had darkened as she grew older, and she spent more and more time with Laura and Billy, sometimes even staying at the camp with her special friend, Carrie. Emmy had picked up their language as fast as Laura had learnt English. Emmy had inherited her father's height and was destined to be tall. Kitty had no idea what life there would be for her daughter. She knew she would have a hard time. If she chose a life with Laura and her family, she understood and would give her blessing. Carrie's oldest brother, Benaroi, always watched over the two girls. Emmy had more in common with them than anyone in either Richmond or Windsor. Kitty knew there were boys in the tribe a little older than Emmy. Ben, in particular, had started showing his interest in her. Emmy was already rejecting offers of visits to town with her mother.

A black girl in a pretty gown drew more gazes than she wished. Kitty knew that whatever her decision in years to come, she would support her daughter's choice, but that was some years away. In the meantime, Emmy and Carrie spent much time learning about each other's cultures. Carrie often stayed in the dormitory with the girls, and they shared Emmy's clothes; Kitty presumed that when Emmy visited the tribe, she discarded her apparel to be like her friend. Hetty said Carrie was welcome to visit as often as she wished but must wear clothing when at the house.

At one stage, Carrie stayed for weeks when Laura and Billy went walkabout with the rest of the tribe and their other children. Occasionally

Carrie brought along some of the boys from the tribe with the excuse of carrying things for her. Her brother, Ben, was always one of them. Kitty wondered. Some of the indigenous boys were very interested in what they could learn from Nate, Des, and Oliver in making metal tools. They loved watching Nate and learning how to make assorted implements at his small forge. Each took turns in assisting.

~

The small ketch finally arrived at the jetty in Windsor. The boat came into sight of the town. Hetty and Des were to stay with them for the night as they wished to see Hector and Fran's reaction when they saw the new house.

Des had worked with Henry for nearly a year to prepare the home for the family. He wasn't going to miss the big reveal. Hetty was as excited as Henry and Des, and they found it hard not to say anything.

Two carriages collected them from the wharf, and without waiting for the luggage, the nine of them piled into the first carriage and, under instructions from Henry, took off through town along the road to his old house.

As Fran was chatting to Hetty, she did not realise they had driven past the old house and were headed out of Windsor. Des and Henry watched her face, waiting for her to realise. Henry had worded Hector up, but not the children.

Skye finally said, "Grandpa, didn't we miss your house? Wasn't it back there?"

Only then did Fran look up and see they were on the outskirts of town. "Papa, where are we going?" She was now looking in earnest at where they were heading.

Henry smiled at her innocent question. "I have a surprise for you, Franny. I sold the house in town and purchased another one. We will be living just out of town, as I thought you would prefer this." The loving smile he saw on his daughter's face showed that he had made the right call.

"Papa, you loved that house, though." Fran was overwhelmed by what he had done for her.

"I did, but I love you so much more. It was just a building. I would do anything for you, Franny. Wait until you see this house. I hope you love living in it as much as I do." Henry kept his eyes on her as she gazed at the building as it came into view.

"Oh, Papa, is that it? That's our new home? It's fabulous!" Fran said.

Henry smiled as she obviously liked what she saw.

The pale stone homestead sat proudly on a grassy knoll; a cluster of outbuildings was well hidden towards the rear of the house and only came into view as they drew into the yard. The gravel in the courtyard crunched as the coach wheels pulled up at the back of the house. A woman appeared at the back door and waved a cheery welcome. A young groom-cum-yardman emerged from the stables and took the reins.

Henry hopped down and assisted Fran and Hetty from the carriage, then introduced Mrs Glassop, his housekeeper. Des helped the children, and Hector assisted an uncomfortable Maggie down.

Lynne scrambled out of the other door and quickly claimed Julia's hand. Lynne reached for Maggie and snuggled close to her older sister. "God is still looking after us, Maggs," she whispered as they stared at the beautiful home. Both girls quickly learnt that the family who had adopted them were strong Christians. They had included the two girls in many Bible discussions from the moment they had rescued them from the ship's steerage area.

Maggie turned to her little sister. "Did you ever doubt Him, Lynnie?" Maggie dropped her hand and slipped her arm around her sister. They waited until instructed on where to go. Maggie hoped they wouldn't be long, as she wished to use the facilities. The baby was kicking on her bladder, and she was looking forward to putting her feet up. At least here, they were both safe. Saying good riddance to their stepfather had been a significant relief. His nocturnal visits had been far more than unpleasant.

As the family walked inside, the girls followed without apprehension, knowing that the life in front of them would be good no matter what happened; here, life would be better than what they had left behind or any future they possibly could have had in London.

Julia dropped Lynne's hand and ran to catch up to her grandfather. Thankfully she had dropped the name of 'Papa Hen.' Now, it was just Grandpa. Henry hoisted her up and led the family into their new home.

Fran's eyes took in everything they could. Henry had intentionally brought them in through the back door. This place was to be their home, which would be the entrance they would use regularly. Fran often heard him say, "Start as you mean to go on." Henry had done just that.

"Welcome home, Franny," Henry said as he conducted them to their new bedroom. He threw open the door to the vast room. The walls were whitewashed but undecorated; the room looked light and airy. There was a huge double bed, but it was not overly ornate. It was simple and functional, furnished in matching dark timber. She noted that it even had a mosquito net knotted over the top. The room overlooked the river, and she saw the town in the distance.

Fran turned to her father and hugged him. "Papa, it's perfect. Thank you so much!" She turned to Hector. "Sweetheart, isn't this just amazing?"

Hector knew his wife well enough to know that she was delighted. "It is, my dear heart! I'm sure we will be happy here, Henry. Thank you." He put the bag he carried down and turned to shake Henry's hand. This was a delight comparing it to the gilt bedrooms at his father's houses. Here, he could relax. "This is far more than we hoped, Henry. Now show us what else you have up that tweed sleeve of yours. Lead on!" Hector tucked Fran's hand in his arm as they left the room. Next would be to see where the girls were and get them settled into their new room.

The housekeeper had taken Maggie and Lynne and shown them a room they were to share for the moment. Henry had written the day they arrived in Sydney and sent instructions that the new maids would be housed inside if possible. The large house had many bedrooms. There was a guest room that Des and Hetty regularly used; Henry's large bedroom and two bedrooms were set aside for his grandchildren near Fran's master room. He had been puzzled about where to house the two new girls and remembered there was an unused back room that was smaller and quite dark. They could be in there until he could sort out some new accommodations for them. Henry realised they had only about three months until Maggie's baby was due.

Henry's yardman was a young man whom he had met on one of his travels. George Darcyville had arrived as a free settler, hoping to get work somewhere with horses. He had already noticed Maggie and saw her condition. Knowing this family and their actions, he wondered if she was married. Smiling as he took the carriage to the stables, he unharnessed the horses with the assistance of the coachman, Victor Champion. They soon had the matched dappled grey horses brushed down and put away. The second carriage was hired, and they wanted to be ready to unload the luggage quickly when it came.

"Did you see the two girls, Victor?" George asked apprehensively.

Victor sighed as he rubbed one of the horses down, "Silly question, George. I helped them up into the carriage. Did you see how pretty the young one was? Dibs on her." Vic chuckled. The two men were good friends in their early twenties and knew they had fallen on their feet with Henry Gates. With the two young beauties who had just arrived with the family, their conversations focused solely on these ladies. Both also realised that no funny business would be condoned; however, both had already discussed the possibility of seeking wives.

George secretly was cheering. At least he didn't have to fight for Maggie. "Good, Vic, because I like the older one. Did you see she's in the family way? I bet she's got a back story. Knowing what Mr Bolton and Mrs Walker do, I bet Mr Hector and Mrs Fran found girls needing help." Hopefully, the girls would be receptive to their advances. There was no hurry as they would be living in the same house.

The men smiled as they went to await the luggage. They were sure the girls would come to explain who owned which bags.

With Hector gone and Oliver in charge of Loganberry Farm, they came at least once a week for church services in town. Both had been delighted at the excitement shown by the returning travellers. When settled at the house, Des dropped an interesting snippet of information he had been storing. "Hector, I thought you would be interested to hear that Clara is courting."

Fran chipped in. "Oh, Des, that's wonderful, but with whom?"

Hetty could not resist joining in. "You will not believe it, but it's Callum."

Hector was gobsmacked. "Whaaat? Clara and Callum? Are you serious? Are they really courting?" Hector asked, amazed. Clara had been a closed book to them all.

Des nodded. "Apparently, she opened up to him, and the next thing I know, he's seeking permission to court her. If you had not been coming back, I think they would have hastened their marriage, but he wants permission from you. He wants to show you that he's changed."

"Has he?" Hector questioned dubiously.

Des smiled and gave a chortle. "More than a bit! The cocky know-it-all brat you sent to me has done an about-face. It started when Clara gave his cheek a big slap. She gave him what he needed, a good slap down. Only in this case, it was literal. He pushed her too far. If Oliver, Nate, or I had been close, it would have been a punch and a broken nose, but coming from her was far more effective." Des's eyes were still smiling, thinking back to the incident.

Hetty and Des only stayed overnight before returning to their farm.

Callum came about three days later, and after staying the night and showing he had changed, he received permission from Hector to get married. However, there were conditions attached. Hector suggested that he consider moving to the Bathurst farm once married. Even if they were only to spend a few months there each year, it would be good for them as a young married couple. It would teach them to stand on their own feet. Surprisingly, Henry was the one to suggest the move to Hector, and Callum was delighted. Callum could not get home fast enough. He stopped in Windsor to buy her a ring, then caught the small sloop back to Loganberry Farm. Word arrived on the return ferry that night with Casey. Callum and Clara were now engaged.

Chapter 25 Weaving a New Future

$\mathcal{K}$nowing Fran would still want to be weaving for Hetty, Henry had built a large and quite luxurious workroom onto the stables, and it had a large fireplace and hob stove where they could make tea while they worked.

Within days of their arrival, Maggie had her new table loom set up and could sit and weave as the others made baskets. The principle was similar to a ribbon loom, only larger. Maggie had asked George's assistance assembling the loom as some bits did not slide in as easily as they should. She was intrigued that he was always nearby if she required. In the time they worked on it together, George discovered her story. He was horrified when he heard what her stepfather had done to her.

Maggie was already in awe of the handsome young man and that he was frequently close by to offer any assistance he could. Their eyes met often, and he always offered his arm as they left each afternoon to return to the house.

George regularly popped into the workroom to ensure they didn't need help. She had realised her heart pounded when she knew he was close. Knowing that her child was to be born soon, George asked Henry for permission to court her immediately. He wanted to marry her before the child arrived, and that didn't leave much time as banns would take a month. This child would become his responsibility. She had been badly used, and he was now so protective of her. This was one way he could look after her. So, only two weeks after their arrival, George asked Henry for permission to court her.

Vic was equally attentive to Lynne but was not in the workroom as often as she usually looked after Julia. However, on cold days, Julia and Lynne would join the workers and occupy themselves usefully, or Lynne would read a story to Julia. At nearly five, Julia would bring her slate and get Lynne to teach her to write words as the others worked. Lynne knew that by making it a game, Julia would wish to show her skills.

As it grew colder outdoors, Vic and George often joined the workers as they polished the tack. The neat's-foot oil was a distinctive scent, as were the lanolin and beeswax they used, but knowing it meant they could all work together in the warmth of the workroom, none minded.

George and Maggie were now allowed to walk together, and it was only a matter of time before he proposed. He had not encroached more than was permissible, not even allowing himself to kiss her. He would take her hand while they walked about the back paddock. Any further was too far for her. With only about eight weeks to go until the child was born, Maggie found that her feet were swollen, and although she needed to walk, she would get light-headed. She complained that she now waddled.

Hector was the only one who was at a loose end. When they had left for England, he had previously been doing what George and Vic now did. Working and caring for the animals was something he loved. He had no idea their lives would change so much once they returned. Being bored, he knew he had to find a worthwhile occupation. He would love a place where he could meet people and share his faith. It didn't take long before God opened that door for him that would benefit everyone.

When Callum had come to seek permission to marry, it later led to a conversation that let the cat out of the bag regarding their titles. Maggie had unintentionally explained why Callum needed to ask Hector's permission to be married. "George, if they were in Scotland, Callum would need approval from the head of their Clan to get permission to marry. Also, his bride would have needed to be endorsed by the Laird, and that is Hector."

George was stunned. "Maggs, do you mean he has a title?"

Maggie nodded very nonchalantly and quickly added, "Yes, of course. He's Baron Glenview, Lord Glenview, if you will. Mrs Grey is Lady Frances Glenview, but they refuse to use their titles." Maggie realised what she had done and clapped her hand over her mouth. "Oh, George, I was not supposed to say anything. Please say nothing. They wish to stay anonymous."

George was stunned and said grumpily. "Anonymous! Why? They are toffs!"

Maggie objected to the term. "They aren't George. They are lovely, and they saved us. They could not care about their titles. They care about people." She went on to tell George how Hector and Fran rescued them from steerage in their uncomfortable quarters. "George, from the moment we met them, they have been nothing but caring and loving. I hope I can stay with this family forever. I feel safe, loved, and accepted."

George reached out and took her hand; they walked up a slight hill as he said, "I will keep your secret, Maggie, but their news will get out sooner or later. It will only take a letter or a note from Government House, and the town will be in an uproar. However, now I know I can protect them. Vic should be told too, as he can be trusted, as can Mrs Glassop, but get Mr Gates or Mr Grey to tell them." George was itching to say more as he had a ring with him, but he noticed she was not looking well.

Maggie waddled on a little further before turning to him and saying, "Georgie, I don't feel really good. I'm dizzy and think I need to lie down. Can we go back?" She wobbled and half-collapsed against him.

George looked at her pale face and swept her up into his arms. Even in her advanced condition, she was a featherweight compared to what he customarily hoisted around the stables. The bags of grain weighed twice what she did.

Fran looked up from her work and saw him carrying Maggie back to the house. Throwing aside the basket she was working on, she quickly went to assist.

George saw Fran coming. "Mrs Grey, she's feeling ill. Can I take her inside, please?" George noticed Maggie had now fainted against him. He added, "I was just about to propose, and she said she wasn't feeling too well."

Fran knew the young man cared for Maggie and could see the concern on his face. "I'll open the doors; you follow, then give me five minutes before you return. I'll check if everything is all right with the child. George, we may need a doctor. Use that time to ask Vic to go and find him, please." George nodded and followed Fran with his precious bundle.

Lynne saw her sister in his arms and left Julia with Skye; she joined the procession into their room. "Is she okay, George? What happened?"

After putting Maggie down, he ushered Lynne out of the room while Fran stayed with Maggie. He replied, "Walk with me, and I'll tell you," He hurriedly left the room, explaining to Lynne as he went. George knew where Vic was and went to find him. He would send him to get the doctor. There was nothing Lynne or he could do until Fran called him back.

Lynne returned to Julia as Vic appeared.

George helped him saddle a horse and watched as Vic rode off.

He turned back to the house. Now out of sight, George was sick with anxiety; he had never felt this concerned about anyone. Then it hit him; he was in love. This is what love felt like. He had heard friends at the pub talk about this. He was feeling way beyond a lustful physical need; this was not sexual at all. It tore at his heart. He was surprised; then he realised that he had even teared up. No matter what life had thrown at him, that had never happened before. He rubbed his eyes and then looked down at the moisture on his fingers. Then a slow smile spread across his face. Another thing then happened; he prayed as he walked, realising she was ill and that he could do nothing. The last few times he had spoken to God was to swear at Him. Now he pleaded with God to heal her. He had reached her door and stood with his head resting against the wall, pleading with God to make her well. "God, I'll even go to church if you make her better. Please don't let her die, please!" He didn't realise he'd voiced the words until Hector spoke from across the hallway.

"You can come with us, George." Hector saw his tear-filled eyes. "What happened, George?" Hector put a caring hand on his shoulder.

"We went for a walk, and we were talking about you, and she explained why Callum had to ask your permission to marry Clara. Sorry sir, but I'll keep your secret. I promise. Anyway, I was about to propose when she collapsed in my arms. I think it's the baby as she grasped her stomach."

Hector nodded his understanding of what had occurred.

George sniffed. "Sir, I think I love her. No, that's not right; I know I do. It just hit me like a ton of bricks, though, sir."

Hector chuckled. "It hurts, doesn't it? I've seen this condition level bigger men than us."

George looked stunned. "What happens if she dies?" He blew his nose before looking up at Hector. "I want to be married before the baby is born, so I can call it mine." He gave Hector a half-smile.

Hector walked to the bedroom door. "Let's see how she is then, lad."

He knocked, and Fran opened it. He could see Mrs Glassop bending over Maggie but nothing more. "How is she, Franny? Up to a visitor?"

Fran came out and shut the door. "Yes, she is, but she is to stay in bed for a few days, if not longer. I didn't know that her feet were so swollen. I also didn't realise she had put on so much weight in the last few weeks."

George blanched. His girl was really sick. "Is she going to live, Mrs Grey? Can I see her? I was just about to propose when she collapsed."

Hector said, "You may, but not for long and not alone. I will send Mrs Glassop to the kitchen for something. We will both stay but will try to be out of earshot."

Fran opened the door and asked Mrs Glassop to bring some tea for them all. When she left, George crept in and went to Maggie's bedside.

Fran and Hector stood looking out the window, and they could hear them whispering, but not much of what they initially said. Fran then heard Maggie gasp and say, "I can't, Georgie! It's not your child; I can't expect you to bring up another man's bastard."

George was on his knees beside the bed. "Maggs, I don't care; I want to look after you. I want to be your child's father and be with you both. It's your child, and that's all I care about."

George turned his tear-drenched face to Hector and Fran. "Sir, ma'am, tell her, please, let her know I'm serious." George's expression showed he was distraught. "Maggie, please, don't cut me out now. I want you. I need you, Maggs." With that, he put his forehead on the bed, his shoulders shaking with deep feelings of rejection, thinking she would decline him.

He felt her hand rest on his neck. "Are you sure, Georgie? Really sure?" she whispered.

He lifted his head with a hint of hope. "As sure as eggs are eggs, Maggs. I want you even if you had twins or triplets; I want you all. I also want to marry you before the baby is born so it will have my name. Margaret Woods, will you please accept me before my heart breaks?"

Maggie nodded with a chuckle. "Yes, Georgie, I will." She reached out for him.

Without asking permission from anyone, he drew her into his arms and kissed her. He then dug into his back pocket. "I even bought you a ring, Maggs. It's not a big stone, but it's filled with love." He took her hand and attempted to put the ring on her finger but realised they were swollen too. He slipped it on her little finger instead. "Mine, or very nearly! Maggie, may I see if Mr Grey can get us a Special Licence? I want to call you my own as soon as possible."

Again Maggie nodded. "I'd like that, Georgie. I'd like that a lot." She then burst into tears. She thought her stepfather had ruined her life; instead, it had brought her to a man she adored and who loved her. She reached out to give him a big hug.

As he hugged her, the baby kicked him. George chuckled. "I don't think our child liked me hugging you so tightly."

Maggie murmured, then repeated his words, "Our child!" And she released a sigh. "George, for the first time, I can now look forward to its arrival. I've hated it until now. Thinking it had ruined my life."

George grinned, "No, Maggs, it brought us together." He bent over her again and gave her a quick peck on her smiling lips.

Maggie called for Fran and Hector to join her at the bed. "Mrs Grey, you said this child was innocent of its father's actions. I've not accepted that until now. But with George calling it 'our child', it has become real. Ma'am, I can't do this alone anymore. I only had Lynnie to rely on before, and now I have you all." With that, she reached for George and wept against his chest.

George cradled her to him. Being an orphan himself, he had not experienced the delights of being loved and belonging. He loved being needed and knew she cared for him too.

The doctor came that afternoon and checked her over. He suggested she stay in bed for a few days and, noticing the ring on her little finger, called in George, thinking he was her husband. They didn't correct him, as he soon would be just that.

Hector had already sent a note to Bishop Broughton in Sydney, and reluctantly, using his title, he requested a Special Licence and gave George and Maggie's names and details.

~

Three days later, they received a visit from the minister in Windsor. The Reverend Henry Tarlton Stiles appeared on Henry's front doorstep with a letter in his hand and a large book under his arm. "I believe my services are required." He grinned a cheesy smile. "The Bishop has given me instructions to perform a marriage of an unfortunate lady and a fortunate young man. Am I correct?"

Hector and Henry nodded in unison.

Henry led Reverend Stiles into the sitting room while the bride prepared to get married. George had been mucking out the stables when the reverend arrived, so he needed a bath. Everyone else was told to clean up quickly as they were about to have a wedding. By the time George had bathed, and Maggie had put on the only gown that still fitted and added one of Fran's special shawls and a bonnet from London, she was as ready as a very large eight-month expectant lady could be for an unexpected marriage.

Reverend Stiles married the happy couple in the front sitting room of Henry's house. The room was full, and Lynne stood in as a bridesmaid, Julia as a flower girl, and everyone else crowded into the room.

Vic made his way to Lynne's side after the service was over. She was nearly seventeen and showing some interest in returning his affections.

Fran watched them, and during the festivities, when Mrs Glassop departed to get a tray full of special cakes and cheeses, Fran drew Vic aside and laid down some rules regarding Lynne. For years, Fran had been the recipient of unwanted attention and recognised his admiring stares. Fran warned Vic off in no uncertain terms. When she'd finished, she asked his intentions.

Poor Vic felt he had just gone ten rounds with a champion boxer. "But, Mrs Grey, I want to marry her. I'm not toying with her affections, ma'am; I'm deadly serious." His eyes flittered to Lynne on the far side of the room, then to Fran. "Truly, ma'am, I feel great affection for her. I would rather die myself than hurt her in any way. But she's young, and I'm not going to hurry her. We have time, unlike George and Maggie." He was sweating profusely and was sick with nerves.

Fran huffed, nodding her understanding. "I'll be watching you then, young Victor. But so she knows where she stands, do it officially. Ask Mr Gates now to court her and then become betrothed quickly. You can wait to marry her, but it will give you some reason to be together. I would not want her to marry until she is eighteen, do you understand?"

Victor, still sweating, nodded hard. "May I? Truly? Can I ask him now?" He was excited as that was only next year.

Fran smiled at the relief that now showed on his face. "Yes, Lynne will feel somewhat confused with what has occurred today. Be careful of her, lad. She's been through enough trauma in her short life." Fran motioned for him to go directly to Henry. "Go gently."

Victor nodded enthusiastically and left her side. Fran watched him cross the room to her father's side. Victor waited until Reverend Stiles turned to Hector and then posed his question to Henry. Henry gave Victor his full attention. Fran saw her father nod, glance at her, and then nod again. Victor then shook his hand and moved to Lynne's side. The day brought security to both girls. Far from being left out of the proceedings, Lynne was assured of a place near her sister and a secure life with a man who loved her. Fran was satisfied. Hector had seen her conversation and watched as she smiled at the newest couple.

Vic stayed near Lynne all day. He, too, would remain within the bounds of propriety. He knew he could not even kiss her, but at least they could go for walks, as George did with Maggie. She was still next door to Mrs Glassop and knew that at some stage, she would be in the quarters above the stables with Vic, but that was at least a year off. Maggie and George had moved into Des and Hetty's room.

Maggie and George were now married and shared the larger room, but considering Maggie's condition, George brought in his swag and slept on the floor of their bedroom. He hugged her each night, and they kissed a long goodnight, but that was all. He didn't want her to be alone but didn't wish to encroach either.

~

Two weeks after their wedding, George was awoken at night by Maggie's groaning. He was beside her in an instant. "Maggs, are you all right?"

"No, Georgie, the baby is coming, I think. I'm getting bad pain. Can you get Mrs Grey? She knows what to do." With that, she started groaning again. "Hurry, Georgie, hurry. It's too early, far too early."

George threw on his trousers and shirt and went to their door. He was about to knock when the door opened.

Fran stood there in a dressing gown. "Is the baby coming?" Her gorgeous dark curly hair was down, and the soft black waterfall cascaded in a cloud around her face and fell to her waist.

He had never noticed just how beautiful she was. He nodded in reply to her question. He heard Maggie groaning again and returned to her side as soon as possible.

Fran followed him and checked Maggie. "George, go wake Vic and send him for the doctor and midwife. Tell him to hurry. Tell Vic to let the doctor know the pains are only five minutes apart already."

George froze.

Fran spoke again. "George, hurry! I think it will arrive before the doctor does. Go, now! And be quick."

George took off. It was frigid outside, but he didn't feel the icy gravel. He had forgotten to pull on his boots but barely noticed the cold as he raced barefoot across the frost-covered backyard.

Three hours later, George, Hector, Vic, and Henry sat in the sitting room. At least three were seated; George was pacing the room and sweating like the sun was at full blast inside the frigid room. Henry stoked the fire, but it did little to ease the chill. The doctor had arrived an hour ago, and the midwife soon after. Fran had not left Maggie's side. Eventually, the doctor came into the sitting room. "Congratulations, Mr Darcyville; your wife is fine, and so are your children." He gave a sly grin. "You have two girls; they are identical, as they share an afterbirth. It's no wonder your wife was so uncomfortable. I'm sorry I didn't pick up that she was carrying two. She has already fed them and is nearly asleep." The doctor shook his hand and then pushed him towards the door to go and see Maggie.

George was stunned. He stumbled into the room. "Twins, Maggs, we have twins." George had not yet intimately slept with his wife, but they were already a whole family. It was one he would be proud of until he died. "Maggs, we have twins," he said again. He was reeling. But the grin on his face belied his anxiety. He bent and kissed her weary face. "You did good, sweet girl."

She reached out and took his hand. "I am exhausted, Georgie. Stay with me."

It was now three in the morning. He was tired too, but he realised that their life would be vastly different with two babies. He drew her into his arms for a quick hug. It was the first time they had even been in bed together. Her condition and early pains had precluded any intimacy between them. They had their lives ahead of them, and he would never force himself on her, never! That was the last thought he had before he relaxed beside his wife. As she snuggled to him, her deep, even breathing told him she was already asleep. He knew he had much to learn about babies and also about being a husband. He found that having her so close to him warmed his heart. Not wanting to disturb her, he closed his eyes. For the first time, they fell asleep entwined. Secure in their love and looking forward to a future together.

~

Three months after the twin's birth, Callum and Clara were to be married at St Matthew's, Windsor. Clara was to arrive with Hetty and Des and the entire entourage from Loganberry Farm. Henry had sent carriages to collect them rather than come in the sloop.

Callum had spent the last two days with them and was as nervous as Fran had been before her wedding. He had come down often over the past weeks. Henry had been giving him instructions about the farm in Bathurst.

The wedding went off without a hitch. Callum and Clara were to move to Bathurst for a few months each year. He had to carve his place in society but was prepared to learn and work hard. They would go to the farm for their honeymoon and return for Easter. George and Maggie would accompany them with the twins. Vic and Lynne would stay and help with Julia and the house.

There was little enough to do around the property that the newly hired gardeners couldn't cope with. George would drive the travelling carriage, and Maggie and Clara could coo over the adorable girls as they travelled. Callum would undoubtedly join George in the driver's seat for much of the trip. The red-headed Scottish man regularly wore a beaten-up, wide-brimmed, felt hat, but he was now a married man and had cast off any of the remaining sulks he had on arrival. Life for both men had changed. They had liked each other on first meeting, and now their friendship could develop.

Two days after the wedding, the carriage departed with both couples. Hetty and Des had already returned home with promises from Hector and Fran for them to come for an extended stay now that their old room was empty again. They had visited Loganberry Farm a few times, but with Callum in their old quarters, there were no beds for them. Oliver and Mary's children took the spare room. Molly, at twenty-three, had finally begun courting Captain Greg Rourke. For the moment, she was content to stay at home, but they would marry as soon as he had permission from his commanding officer. He was a close friend of Ned Grace and they had met after a somewhat disturbing incident with one of the girls who had come for refuge.

Soon, Henry's house returned to normal. Life for the family was peaceful. Hector had finally found his niche. He had taken over managing Oliver's shop in town. It had outgrown the tiny cottage, and Henry had an empty shopfront and house in the same street. Henry had asked Hector if he wanted to turn his shop into a significant local craft emporium. He had many of his own products to sell, and Oliver could take over one entire section for the Loganberry Farm goods.

Fran would go down to the shop daily and eat lunch with Hector. Henry had purchased her a pony trap, and Victor could have it ready for her in just a few minutes. Hector adored being busy again. He now had a free hand with the store. He had an idea to support other cottage industries in Windsor; one of the rooms would be for consignment sales. These could be anything from fresh produce to crafts or other small saleable items the townspeople wished to sell. However, he also added a conversation table and installed a hob stove so they could make tea in the shop. Lonely people could come into the shop and have a chat and a cuppa. Hector encouraged this, and soon he willingly shared his faith as the various conversations developed. He would arrive home each night content. One table grew to three, and the venue soon became a full tearoom and conversation hub. Another girl was brought from the gaol to make and serve tea for everyone. There was even a small library bookshelf for people to borrow books, bringing in more visitors.

A second shelf was soon added as more books arrived

Six months after their return home, Hector watched as Fran took her big mug of sweet black tea out onto the front verandah and stood watching the river in the twilight. After a few minutes, he rose to follow her.

The sweet smell of the Japanese honeysuckle assailed her nostrils. She heard the front screen door open and felt Hector's hand on her slightly expanded waist as he then enfolded her in his arms.

They had kept the news of another child quiet until after the wedding. Since they had lost a child on the voyage home, Hector would take no risks with her this time. "Hector, Papa said I could name the house, but I have been stumped as to what we should call it." She fell silent but leaned back against Hector, careful not to drop her now empty new pottery mug.

Hector adored the feeling of her trust as she leaned against him. The silence was broken only by the insects and the river burbling in the distance. Hector pulled her a little closer.

After a while, she continued. Her mind was still on her father's request. "I wanted something that tied in with our basket weaving, yet I have only just realised the answer has quite literally been in front of me the entire time." She bent and placed her empty mug on the ground. Then reached up and plucked a blossom of the sweet-smelling honeysuckle vine growing around the pillars of the verandah.

With His hand still sitting on her waist, she slowly turned towards him. "What about Honeysuckle House? This was not one of the native vines that Laura brought us; Papa brought these for me all the way from Japan. It is a strong vine and sweet-smelling, and well, it is just right." She lifted her smiling face to Hector's, who watched her every tiny move.

Hector watched as she fingered the flower and then inhaled its glorious perfume. His eyes could never drink in her essence enough, but this flower was overshadowing her own scent, "I think it's perfect. Just like you, my darling vine weaver. Everything about you is just perfect." He gently reached out and took the flower from her fingers, tucking it into her hair. "Now, my sweet darling, I have not had a good evening kiss." With her hands now empty, she complied with his wishes quite willingly.

Fran stepped into his waiting arms. They didn't care who saw them. They didn't care about society's rules. They didn't ever wish to be far from each other, and both knew that life was short, so they grabbed each moment as it arrived. They had come a long way in such a short time. They arrived as two convicts, so alone in life and had found each other, peace and contentment, then a family. Yes, they now had money and titles, yet neither had brought them what they had desired. The addition of children, then discovering their fathers, had almost made their lives complete. But Hector's sharing of his faith had been the most crucial piece to the jigsaws of their pasts. Without that, none of the rest would have happened. Without his willingness to share his faith, life would have no meaning. God had woven his true vine of faith deeply into their being, drawing the families tightly together. Hector had once said to Franny, "God doesn't leave loose ends. He knows how the story will end before it even begins. All we have to do is trust Him to weave his magic."

Hector bent and kissed Franny again. Her hands wound themselves around his neck like a quick-growing vine. Hector continued talking before he accepted the invitation offered by her rosy lips. "Sweetheart, we all cried when Joel died, but that brought Des fully into our lives. Without his injury, your father would not have visited and discovered you. Then, my father learned where I was, and he arrived at the same time." He gave her a peck on the lips. He caressed her downy cheek and stared deeply into her lovely blue eyes, saying, "And then there is Laura and Billy. Emmy has found a place where she's comfortable. I think she may eventually find her life partner with Ben. He is certainly attentive to her every move. Laura and Billy have a place to stay when they wish, and it is weaving our two cultures together. They know they are both safe and welcome." He drew Fran tightly to him, lifted her chin and kissed her.

"I think back to Martha, then you, and later the reuniting of the sisters and all the rest of the girls who have been through Hetty's care. Each came scared, scarred, and hurt. Each left with renewed vigour and a new path before them." Again, the offer of her lips distracted him contentedly for some time. "The hardest thing in all this, my love, was saying farewell to our boys in England. However, they have a loving family there who will do everything they can for them. Joey has much to learn and can only do it in England. Alec can come back soon and go to The King's School in Parramatta for a few years, as I heard it's reopening again." Hector felt her relax in his arms. "Sweetheart, I think your Papa will enjoy some company on his next trip. So, we may go and collect him ourselves next year. What do you think? Callum and Des can keep things going here." Hector had a twinkle in his eyes as he spoke. He had already spoken to Henry about when they would leave. He didn't care about titles or wealth, as he knew that faith and family were the only valuable things in life.

Fran stood gazing up at her husband's grin. "I think you are the most wonderful and adorable, considerate husband in the entire world, Hector Macdougal Grey, and I love you so much. You wove your magic around me soon after we met. Your words about God's love, and me needing to forgive those who hurt me, opened me to a new understanding of love. Although I will always be fearful of the lustful gazes of other men, I know I am safe with you. Here, in your arms, I am home and safe." She reached up and pulled his head to meet her waiting lips.

Henry stood in the sitting room, observing their embrace with a massive grin. He had heard the name she had chosen. He spoke softly to himself, "Honeysuckle House; I can live with that." He stood watching them for a while when another thought occurred to him. Fran had also woven him tightly into the fabric of her life. Yes, they were a strong family unit now, woven tightly in faith and love, and Fran had been the key.

Fran and Hector were oblivious to the growing delicious perfume of the honeysuckle blossoms from the vine surrounding them. With the sinking sun, the sweet scent of the vines enveloped them.

Brodie's story is in
"Scotch at The Rocks"

Amazon USA

Feel free to email me at
saragpowter@gmail.com
Thank you for reading **The Vine Weaver.**
If you liked this story, the following are similar.
& please don't forget to leave a review for another reader

Characters

Joel Walker b 1790 d Jan 1826
m 1810 Henrietta (**Hetty**) Logan b 1792
    3 Children
    1 Oliver Walker b 1811
    m Mary (a convict)
        3 Children
        #3 b June 1838
    2 Ernest (**Ernie**) Walker b 1813
    3 **Molly** Logan Walker b 1815
m2 Nov 1826 **Des Bolton** b 1790, UK sister Carly died in gang rape
    b Caroline Henrietta (**Carly**) July 18, 1828
    b **Lewis** Desmond Logan Bolton 28 Aug 1831
David McLean (3 daughters - no sons) (Hetty's half-brother)
M1 Bessie (died)
m2 Matilda - *Wambool Station* 3 daughters
Duncan McLean, *Duncan's Reward* (Hetty's half-brother)

Henry Gates - Des's 'owner' Windsor businessman (*Narrowgate* in Bathurst)
m Jan 1803 Julia Penwick
    #1 Frances (**Franny**) Rea (Gates)
    b Sept 1803, see below
Sidney Grey (mother, Lady Juliana- Daug of Earl of Riverdell) (brother Clayton)
m 1794 **Sarah** Bland Macdougal b 1776 in Skye, Scotland)
Hector Macdougal - b 1795 in Scotland. houseman for Walkers - life sentence
m 1822 Frances (**Franny**) Rea- b 1803
    children 4 +
    1 **Skye** Sarah b 1823
    2 Joel (**Joey**) b Easter 1826
    3 Alistair (**Alec**)Hector Desmond b June 1828
    4 **Julia** Susanna Macdougal Grey Dec 1832
    5 baby b 1839

Riordan Macdougal,
m Sile(**Sheila**),
    1 Fergus, not married
    2 **Sarah** m **Sidney** Grey
    3 Fiona
    m Andrew Fraser
    2 children
                Callum Fraser
                b 1805
                m 1838 **Clara** in Windsor
                2 Hamish (in Canada)
Knox Macdougal
        Daughter **Mary**,
        grandson **Brodie Stewart**

Major **Ned** Grace - a soldier in Parramatta *(reoccurring character in other books)*
Janey Brien - emancipated convict in Parramatta
Casey Stake- boat captain - peg leg
Jane Matthews - b 1799 beefy, female cooper, arrived aged 21 (29 in 1828)
m 1829 Nathaniel (**Nate**) Jamison - burned blacksmith b 1799
    1 & 2 twins Leonie & Liam Nov 1832
    3 Henrietta (Letty) Frances b 1835
    4 Nicholas (Nikki) Nathaniel b 1838

Bess, Manda - Dairy/Insulating cabin. Manda left
Trixi, Agnes, - (with Jane) - woodworking - both gone
Clara, teaching - stayed b 1805
Hannah, Dawn, Faith- Basket weaving with Fran
 and **Hope & Charity** (3 sisters - with **Faith**) in the kitchen
4 new girls in May 1826 **Mary**, weaving (marries Oliver)
Catherine (**Kitty**), tatting, lacework & weaving
 #1 **Emmy** - b Jan 1827 rape by father, **Omara** Kaylim.
Bertha and Mildred (Milly) - new cooks (gone replaced by)
1833 **Abigail, Frederica and Helen,** known as Abby, Fred and Nell - all cooks

John (**Jack**) Turner b 1800 Transported 1820 d 1886
M 1820 **Martha** Turner (née Alexander) (Pa and Maa) Arms of Australia Emu Plains d 1886
 1 Marcus (called Marc) b 1820
 2 Alexander (Alex) b 1821
 3 Jennifer Martha (Jenna) b1823
 4 Victoria (Vicky) b 7/1825
 5 Catherine (Cathy) b June 24 1827
 6 Nicholas (Nicky) John b 1830
 7 Malcolm (Callum) b 1832
Thomas Tibbs- Henry's Sydney Stock Manager
Brodie Stewart - Hector's cousin m **Heather** Anderson (see *Scotch at The Rocks*)
George Paisley -Manager at Narrowgate
Rory Featherstone - Agent in Edinburgh
Laura m **Billy,** an Aboriginal couple
 Children
 Benaroi (**Ben**)
 Carrigal (**Carrie**) plus others.
Margaret (**Maggie**) and **Lynne** Woods - sister maids from on board *The Ferguson*
George Darcyville, Henry's yardman/groom m 1838 Maggie Woods
 Twin girls mid-1839
Victor Champion - Henry's coachman, m Lynne Woods 1840
Mrs Glassop - Henry's housekeeper

Real People
Reverend & Mrs Cross - Rector of Windsor - departed the area in 1828
Reverend Henry Tarlton Stiles
Reverend John Dunmore Lang
Bishop Broughton - 1838- 1853

If you loved this book, these are similar.

A prequel for all my books - and a stand-alone story.

Gentle Annie Soames is a First Fleet story with the descriptions taken directly from the Journal of Doctor Author Bowes Smith, who was on board the Lady Penrhyn.

Gentle Annie Soames

A 1788 First Fleet Convict Story

Her dreams lead to unexpected outcomes. An Australian First Fleet story.

Annie Soames is shattered by the cancellation of her debut into society, so when she hears of a position as a carer for the nearby Marchioness, she grabs it.

Oliver Quilpie, the recently married Marquess, discovers his arranged union is not to his taste; he is drawn to his wife's companion. Unfortunately, he is unable to keep his hands off her. For revenge, Annie mimics his every move while riding but is dressed as a highwayman. However, she had now fallen in love with him. This action finally leads to her arrest and transportation to a faraway land.

After some years, Oliver's wife dies, and his thoughts turn to Annie. He seeks to find her, but she has vanished. He is horrified to discover she was transported to New South Wales as a convict on the *Lady Penrhyn*. He follows with a shipload of supplies on the *Kitty*. Will Annie want to see him?

ISBN 9780645441574 ISBN ebook 9781923097063

Coming July 2024 preorder from May

Hunter to Macquarie Trilogy

When Upon Life's Billows

Sydney 1795-1821 - Governor John Hunter

Captain John Hunter was born to a life at sea. The wind blows where no man knows, and John is caught up in the tempest. Although wrecking his ship, the *HMS Sirius*, in 1790, he became the second Governor of the rough and filthy penal settlement of New South Wales. He always seems to be in the wrong place at the wrong time, trusting the wrong people.

Helena Rosedale is not a typical female convict. She fights tooth and nail to stop the men from abusing her. She gains the name of Helena the Hellcat.

Crispin Milroy is alone in the world and one of the new Governor's security detail. Can he win the fair lady's heart? Life in 1795 in Sydney Cove is raw at best. Food is scarce, and disease often ravages the settlement. Life throws everything except death at these three, yet somehow, they survive. Why does John trust this young couple when others betray him? What trials must Helena and Crispin endure to make their new lives in this raw town bearable? How can John ease their path?

ISBN: 9780645783339   ebook ISBN: 9780645783346

Coming 2025

Saddler's Song

London 1790s to Parramatta 1840s

George Ellis is a tanner's son living on the outskirts of London. When disease takes his family. Alone and hurting, he seeks to find a new life for himself. Hearing from a friend about the possibility of setting up a business in New South Wales, he sells up and leaves all he knows. His beloved violin is his most valuable item, and his talent for making beautiful music is hidden from all but a few.

Ben Parker is a saddler, like George; he is also alone in the world. Ben also sells up to move to the new colony. The two young men meet and combine their skills to start afresh in a new world. During the journey out, George's skill as a violinist is revealed. On arrival, they find accommodation with a family with many lovely daughters. Two of these girls steal their hearts, but how will the business survive in an animal-starved land where access to leather is limited? What is the saddler's song?

ISBN : 9780645783353   eISBN: 9780645783360

Coming 2025

Tuppence to Pass

London 1800s to Parramatta 1820s - Governor Lachlan Macquarie

Josh Callan is a London lad who makes the best of the life that has been dealt to him. Stealing from the man who killed his father gives the family a change of direction. Josh is arrested, but the judge belittles him, saying he's not worth tuppence. He is transported to the penal colony of Sydney as a convict just as **Governor Macquarie's** term starts. He proves his worth and falls on his feet, becoming the Governor's groom and confidante.

Life in the Colonial town opens opportunities they could never have dreamed about in England, but can Josh find his niche in life?

Where will this strange friendship take Josh and his family?

ISBN : 9781923097070 eISBN: 9781923097087

Coming 2025

Unlikely Convict Ladies - Trilogy
Dancing to her Own Tune
Co-authored by Sheila Hunter and Sara Powter
Sydney 1790s to England 1830s

Annie White is released after serving seven years as a convict in Sydney. She gets a visitor who, with his help, she can start a baking business. She is then asked to assist another sick man, **Sam** Corbett. Annie nurses him back to health, and a relationship develops. They settle into a life together, barely making ends meet; she realises she's expecting a child. Sam has his past laid bare and must adjust to the revelations. They both must face their accusers and find that the answers to their questions are not what they thought. Their life experiences seem to cling to them, and unable to shake them off, they end up back in England. They must face their ghosts and discover they are not who they think they are. How can they turn their anger and spite into love and forgiveness? The Dance of Life goes on.

ISBN 9780645110715   ISBN9780645110722

Long-listed in the Historical Fiction Company Competition 2022
https://amazon.com/dp/064511071X   https://amazon.com/dp/B09JC378YV

Amelia's Tears
Parramatta 1828 – England 1840s

Amelia Westaweller awaits her assignment in the Parramatta Female Prison. Forced to leave the relative safety of gaol, she is assigned and now faces her worst nightmare. A foul man claims her and makes her life a living hell. Then, her world goes black. A glimmer of hope arises when she hears from her brother, Jim, who has enlisted a friend to help her. She writes to Jim, pouring out her heart and telling him of the horrors of her new life. He encourages her to stay firm in her faith. All she can do is pray. When Major **Ned** Grace, her brother's friend, enters her life in Parramatta, he starts to ease her path. Things have changed, as now she has a child in tow. How can Amelia forge a new life for herself? What man could want her with her background and a child at her side? Who is the gentleman who turns her tears of sadness into tears of great joy?

ISBN: 9780645110739   eISBN: 978-0-6451107-4-6 Hard Cover ISBN 979-842061-7953
https://amazon.com/dp/0645110736   https://amazon.com/dp/B09SS855BR

A Lady in Irons
England 1800s - Parramatta 1808+

Katy Harrington is mourning the death of her husband after he died in a shooting accident. Barely coping, she awaits the birth of their child. If it's a girl, she must hand the family home to her husband's brother. The day after giving birth to a daughter, she and her daughter are left on the side of a road. She collapses and is found by someone she thought had died in a fire ten years before. **Perry White**, badly scarred himself, nurses her back to health. They marry and move in with her widowed friend, Mary.
After some years, she discovers her husband and friend in each other's arms. Now living in a love triangle, she flees. Grasping the only straw available, she intentionally gets arrested and is sent to a colony far away. By doing this, her marriage can be annulled.
What happens in the Colony is different from what she expects. Governor Macquarie comes to her rescue. But what of Perry and her children?

ISBN: 9780645110784   eISBN:9780645441505
https://amazon.com/dp/0645110787   https://amazon.com/dp/B0BCWSXB9Z

The Convict Stain Collection
(Stand-alone stories)
NO MORE, MY Love
Hunter Valley, NSW 1820s

Jess Elkin is distraught when tragedy ravages her family. She becomes the victim of a carriage accident and is nursed back to health by the driver, **Marcus Ryan**. Marcus was not expecting to fall in love. Yet, when Jess's fortunes suddenly turn for the worse, Marcus must decide how far he will go to pursue her. As time passes in Newcastle, Australia, Marcus must take a business trip and is taken by pirates. Jess is left wondering if her will keep his promise to return to her... Will she ever see him alive again?

ISBN: 9780645441536   eISBN 9780645441581
April 2023
https://amazon.com/dp/0645441538   https://amazon.com/dp/B0BSBH143Q

The Vine Weaver
Hawkesbury River area 1820s+
New Beginnings and Old Threats

In the 1820s, Australia, **Joel and Hetty Walker** live on a secluded farm on the Hawkesbury River, which becomes a healing haven for the protection of young convict women. A series of events brings **Fran Rea** to Hetty's attention, and she is taken to the farm. Fran and Hetty develop a cottage industry under the compassionate eye of farmhand **Hector Macdougal;** Hector's loving words change lives. It is to him that Fran turns when threatened.
The vines now must draw them close to survive the future revelations, and of those, there are many.

ISBN: 9780645441512   eISBN: 9780645441529
June 2023
https://amazon.com/dp/0645441511   https://amazon.com/dp/B0C6Z552Y2
The story continues in Scotch at The Rocks…

Scotch at The Rocks
Glasgow, Scotland, early 1800s to The Rocks, Sydney 1830s

Orphaned children Brodie Stewart and Heather Anderson live on Glasgow's streets. Although hungry, somehow they survive and keep out of trouble. Heather finds a job and looks to be settled; things go pear-shaped for them both. Eventually, they marry by declaration, yet even that gets messed up, and they are both arrested soon after they make their vow. In 1838, they were transported to Sydney as convicts. Heather arrives within weeks of Brodie, and they are assigned close to each other. They are now living on the docklands in Sydney, called The Rocks. They now have to forge a new life halfway across the world from their homeland.
Adventures abound, and Brodie gets press-ganged. While he's away, Heather's life changes and soon, she's officially selling Scotch Whisky at a shop in The Rocks.
You can take a Scot out of Scotland, but where did the Scotch come from?

ISBN 9780645441550   ISBN ebook 9781923097001
November 2023

Waiting at the Sliprails
The Bathurst Road 1830s
A Convict's Tale

Bea Dawes's term of conviction nears an end, and she has few options other than marriage to a stranger or going on the street.
Jack Barnes, the hired drover, wants a wife. Bea accepts his offer; then, she discovers that he could be gone for months, leaving her alone with **Billy and Netty**, part of the tribe of Aboriginal tribe who live on his secluded farm. Bea learns to love her husband and also this wonderful aboriginal couple.
Drought ravages the farm, and Jack must hit the long paddock with the flock. In his absence, a visitor arrives, threatening to destroy everything she has worked so hard for. Can Bea touch her heart? Can she cope? Will the drought ever end? And when will Jack return?

ISBN: 9780645441543   eISBN: 9781923097032
August 2023

Convict Shadows of the Past
Two Jennifers, two hundred years apart

When aged eight, **Jenny** Kellow learns of her convict family history and discovers that she was named after a convict from nearly two hundred years ago. Her grandfather's stories inspire her to dig deeper into her ancestors' convict past. From her grandfather, she hears stories of bushrangers, convicts, and life in the infant colony of Parramatta. She sets about retracing the footsteps of her convict great-great-great-grandmother to honour her. Jenny's search starts with microfiche back in the 60s, and she learns about the small tin mining town in Cornwall and the production of a cheese that sets London afire. She discovers her ancestor, **Jennifer Kellow,** has brought these cheese-making skills to Parramatta, where she taught others her craft. Echoes of the past can still be heard if you know where to listen.
Who was the first Jennifer, and what does she have to do with cheese? Why is she so elusive? Did Jenny's ancestor, Jennifer, ever see those two small crosses carved into the bricks of the Female Factory? Would Jenny ever find out her ancestor's story?

ISBN: 9780645783315   ISBN ebook 9780645783322
A NaNoWriMo 2022 book winner
January 2024

In Defence of Her Honour
London 1800s to Parramatta 1819

Bill Miller had been raised and educated with the sons of the family. The youngest, Bert, had been his best friend. However, jealousy intervenes when Bill's excellent schoolwork curtails their friendship. He wins a scholarship and enters Oxford University. When Bill's father, the old butler, dies unexpectedly, Bert insists that Bill take over the position, but it's more to oppress him. Bert's jealousy grows and festers. Now looking for a way to rid themselves of their new butler, a ruckus ensues, and Bill is arrested for assaulting Bert. The housekeeper and her daughter, **Molly Ross**, vouch for him, but it's too late; Bill has been arrested and sentenced to be transported. With Bill gone, Molly now needs to defend herself from Bert. After hitting him with a pan, she is arrested and sent to Sydney. Bill and Molly arrive with letters of introduction and compensation from Bert's father. Soon, they will be running the best inn in Parramatta with an endorsement from the governor.

ISBN 9780645441567　　　ISBN ebook 9781923097049

April 2024

I can't stop Tomorrow
Irish Famine 1840s to Avoca Beach, Australia

Escaping bigotry and prejudice in Ireland, the **O'Shane** family lives on a secluded farm on the west coast of Ireland. The potato blight soon decimates their farm. It's always darkest before dawn, and the two remaining girls cling to the hope of a new life. With the kindness of strangers, the eldest girls, **Clare** and **Kerry O'Shane**, head to their cousin, Sal Lockley, in Parramatta, Australia. A new, wonderful life awaits them both. **Shéamus Connor** is the annoying teenage boy who reluctantly draws Clare's affection. However, living in a convict town means ruffians abound.
John Moore is an angry and troubled Irishman, content to live alone on another secluded farm until he discovers Clare and two other lads need rescuing.
Can John protect her from the pain inflicted by an evil world?
Can Shéamus find his lost love who had fled?

ISBN: 9780645441598　　　ISBN ebook 9781923097056

October 2024

Madeline's Boy
England 1830s to New South Wales 1840

All is not straightforward when money and a title are involved.

Madeline Brougham is asked to care for her best friend's orphaned son when his life is in danger. **Christopher Downes** is the pawn between a greedy, unscrupulous uncle and his inheritance. Maddie must do everything she can to keep him safe, including moving halfway around the globe to take Chip to his guardian, Major Humphrey Downes, in the Australian Corps in Sydney. Humphrey's best friend, another soldier, **Major Tim Hinds**, meets Maddie, and with the support of these two men, a chase around the colony ensues. Will Maddie and Tim be able to find happiness together?
Can the three adults keep Chip safe until he's old enough to claim his inheritance?

ISBN: 9780645783308　　　ISBN ebook 9781923097094

Dec 2024

Jam or Marmalade for Tea
England 1820s to New South Wales 1825

Martha Hamilton is the eldest of four orphans struggling to survive on their own. She is caught stealing, tried, convicted and transported to Australia.
Guy Manning is a frustrated and injured redcoat soldier travelling to Sydney to take up a new assignment. He notices Martha trying to jump overboard and rescues her.
A convict ship is no place for romance, and she's far too young anyway, isn't she?
Can Guy save her and forge a life together for them? What connections does he have to save her siblings? And how does jam figure in their future?

A NaNoWriMo 2023 book winner

Coming October 2025

The Vine Weaver

A 100-year, six-part Australian Colonial series

The Lockleys of Parramatta

Hands upon the Anvil

A blacksmith's life and love are more than work

Parramatta 1830s

Eddie Lockley's parents were transported for their crimes. Can a steadfast lad rise above his origins and guide others to succeed in a land of opportunity?
Ten-year-old Eddie longs to help his mum and dad. Living in a convict town with his family, the keen youngster has been working with the local blacksmith since his sixth birthday. But when a lieutenant doesn't stop abusing his older brother, the young boy yearns for the day when he can stand up and end the torment. Though he's thrilled when his mentor offers to send him off to learn his letters, Eddie fears he won't be around to watch his sibling's back. But as he takes on the biggest adventure of his life, the brave believer soon discovers God is looking out for everyone he loves. Does this young man in the making have what it takes to change everything for the better?

ISBN 9780994578235 Ebook ISBN 978-0-9945782-5-9 Hardcover 9798496177368

Released 2021

https://amazon.com/dp/0994578237 https://amazon.com/dp/B08TB51L19

Out Where The Brolgas Dance

Gold is found, and so is love

Parramatta 1840s

How can a question change so many people?

It's the 1840s, and discoveries across the Blue Mountains continue. Major Mitchell's new road is complete, and towns are planned and being built. Abundant land is available for those who want it.
William "Wills" Lockley, 18, has laid a solid foundation for a respectable career as a blacksmith, but the Lockley lust for adventure flows deeply within his veins. He dreads the monotony of work at the blacksmith's forge and yearns for adventure in a new frontier. Wills meets six Englishmen (*Coping with what is now known as PTSD*) who have the means to make his dreams come true. What they discover changes the Colony and their lives forever. Gold fever ensues. In the West, Wills has to deal with an uncertain romance. Does she even want him?

ISBN 9780994578242 Ebook ISBN 978-0-9945782-6-6 Hardcover ISBN 9798755445504
LP ISBN 9781923097155

Released 2021

https://amazon.com/dp/0994578245 https://amazon.com/dp/B08T6NS3XX

Diamonds in the Dirt

Diamonds, love and money… but there is much more to life.

Parramatta 1850s

Luke Lockley, the youngest Lockley son, has completed University, and his life has no direction. No job, no money, and no love. Desperately alone, he prays for guidance. How can Luke trust that God has a plan for him if he can't even find a job? He does the only thing he can … he prays. Within a week, life has changed … oh, how it has changed as his brother Wills turns up with a suggestion. Would Luke be interested in joining the expedition with John Evans? **Reverend William Clarke** needs assistance on a Government Mineral Survey. The challenge, adventure and finds are life-changing for many. However, it gives Luke meaning, purpose and direction. The condition of his heart problems also takes a turn. Can he walk away?

ISBN:9780994578273 Ebook ISBN: 978-0-9945782-8-0 Hard cover ISBN 979-8788011141

Released 2022

https://amazon.com/dp/099457827X https://amazon.com/dp/B09NH1MLXZ

The Earl's Shadow
Who or what is the 'shadow'? How does it affect so many?
<u>Parramatta 1860s</u>

Charles Lockley is the Earl of Coxheath and spends his youth as a convict in Parramatta; he had no idea he was an Earl. He had minimal education and few social skills. His eldest son, **Charlie**, is no different.

Now faced with his own mortality, Charles has to work out how to live the remainder of his life after a near-death experience. He is called to step way out of his comfort zone in London. His action will change the world for many. The echoes from the past still haunt Charlie. London is calling the family, and they can't postpone the trip. How does the Cobb and Co. coach driver **Jim Leslie** fit in? And precisely what is *'The Earl's Shadow'* that he speaks about? What happens if the 'Shadow' is gone?

<u>ISBN</u>: 9780645110708 Ebook <u>ISBN</u> 978-0-9945782-9-7
Released June 2022
https://amazon.com/dp/0645110701   https://amazon.com/dp/B0B158SKSK

Once a Jolly Swagman
An old black Billy Can contain the secrets of an incredible life
An Australian Historical Novel
Set in 1870s Parramatta and Kent, UK

Rick Lockley, battling his family's expectations, runs away to find himself. **Jack**, a jolly swagman, takes him under his care. Even after years together, Rick knows little about the old man.

On his death, Jack leaves Rick his precious billy can; the contents reveal Jack's identity. Stunned, Rick must travel to England to finalise Jack's wishes. There, he uncovers Jack's life of love, betrayal and a link to his own family. Rick also discovers there is much more to learn about this enigmatic man.

ISBN 9780645110753   Ebook ISBN 978-0-6451107-6-0
Released Sept 2022
https://amazon.com/dp/0645110752   https://amazon.com/dp/B0B5JN1WCV

Jonty's Journey
Gems, Love, Artists and a Golden Lion
<u>Australia and South Africa 1880-1902</u>

Sydney Jeweller, **Jonty** Evans' passion for gems takes him to Africa at a volatile time. He finds the diamonds he wants and gets given a lion cub. Jonty gets all but kidnapped. His experiences in the Transvaal plunge him into questioning everything he knows of life. Soon, nightmares haunt him. (N*ow known as PTSD*).

On return home, he nearly messes up his love life with **Lottie** before it even starts, and he struggles to settle. Lottie's father, **Luke** Lockley from Parramatta, takes him in hand and points him to someone who can help.

Jonty is then recalled to Africa as a liaison and reconnects with his lion, Chimbu, when he saves the life of his security detail. His life journey introduces him to the most amazing Heidelberg artists, politicians, poets, rebels, and the scapegoat soldier Harry Breaker Morant. Can Jonty bury the past and regain the peace he's lost?

ISBN 9780645110777   HC ISBN 9781923097124   Ebook ISBN: 978-0-6451107-9-1
Released Feb 2023
https://amazon.com/dp/0645110779   https://amazon.com/dp/B0BLJ7ND1Q

The Vine Weaver

Australian Colonial Trilogy
By Sheila Hunter
Co-Winner of 1999 NSW Senior Citizen of the Year, In the Year of the Senior Citizen

Mattie
Coming of Age in Convict Australia
Twelve-year-old London street urchin **Mattie Paul** is convicted of petty theft and sentenced to seven years of transportation to the penal colony of Port Jackson, NSW. Peg, another female convict, takes Mattie under her wing and gives her a chance to make something of her life by teaching her to read. Mattie seizes every opportunity that comes her way. Though life is not particularly kind to her, she battles through earning her freedom, marrying and becoming a mother in her homeland. On this journey, she encounters bushrangers, is widowed, and becomes an entrepreneur in the Bathurst goldfields. She mixes with escaped convicts, but her spirit is indomitable, and she becomes a pillar and much-loved treasure of her adopted community. Mattie may be a fictional character, but her experiences are only too real and invest us in immersing ourselves in the lives of those remarkable women who helped to make Australia what it is today. *(Mattie's story continues in The Lockleys of Parramatta - bk 2+)*

ISBN 9781503252370 & ebook AISN BOOTTEDBTO
(The Story continues in The Earl's Shadow)
Released 2015
https://amazon.com/dp/150325237X   https://amazon.com/dp/B00TTEDBT0

Ricky
A boy in Colonial Australia
Ricky English and his mother immigrated from England to join his father in the new Colony of Sydney. Upon arrival, there was no sign of his father. Ricky's mum uses the tiny amount of money they brought to get lodgings in a run-down building. Things go from bad to worse when his mother dies; he is thrown out of the rooms, and the caretakers confiscate all their possessions.
Ricky lives on the streets of Sydney Town as a street waif. Ricky finds safe places to sleep and befriends freed convicts who can help him survive. One day, he encounters a lost child and helps reunite her with her family. These people try to help him, but he insists on doing things his way because of his stubbornness. However, he has found a mentor and confidante. The story follows him through his life. He survives and turns his life around, helping others along the way.   **(The Story continues in Jonty's Journey)**

Paperback ISBN 9780994578211   Kindle ASIN: B00MLYN6IG
Released 2014
https://amazon.com/dp/1500770574   https://amazon.com/dp/B00MLYN6IG

The Heather to The Hawkesbury
Four Scottish families brave a new life in a strange land.
Mary Macdonald and husband **Murd** and family; her brother **Fergus** MacKenzie; sister-in-law **Caro** MacLeod; cousin **Alex** Fraser and all their families who have had to emigrate from the Isle of Skye during the "Clearances."
The story follows the four families from Scotland on the ship out to the NSW colony in the 1850s. Mary does not cope with the changes and losses that occur in the first months in the colony. The other women in the family rely on her, and she nearly crumbles. The families struggle together through accidents, losses, trials, floods, and hard work and forge a strong bond with their new country. Trials, tribulations and triumphs see the four families make a firm mark in their new homeland. The immigrants from Scotland helped make Australia what it is today.

ISBN 978994578228   ebook AISN B01A21JYWQ   Large Print ISBN1533473641
Available on Amazon/Kindle & Large Print
Released 2016
https://amazon.com/dp/1503251438   https://amazon.com/dp/B01A21JYWQ

Bibliography

John Dunmore Lang
https://www.britannica.com/biography/John-Dunmore-Lang

Reverend John Scott, Book of Sermons - printed in 1839.
I have my G. Grandfather, Donald Hugh McLean's copy, which he used to read for home services, just as Hector did, but Donald lived on the Northern Rivers of NSW. Donald Hugh was born on Dunmore Lang's property at Largs near Newcastle and inspired Hector's character.

Hawkesbury Flood years.
https://ehq-production-australia.s3.ap-southeast-2.amazonaws.com/
1395fd8e9cd10c0f64b111d9b6257ce391926fff/documents/attachments/000/102/207/
original/Flood_Height_Historic_records_Hawkesbury_River.pdf?X-Amz-Algorithm=AWS4-HMAC-SHA256&X-Amz-Credential=AKIAIBJCUKKD4ZO4WUUA%2F20220208%2Fap-southeast-2%2Fs3%2Faws4_request&X-Amz-Date=20220208T100413Z&X-Amz-Expires=300&X-Amz-SignedHeaders=host&X-Amz-Signature=82f7b0d5d10fa2e5bdc893904f1b2ff59fe3799b67dafef923497f78c68e208d

Hawkesbury flood years.
1799 Mar 10.5 ;1806 Mar 12.9 ;1809 Aug 14.7 ;1816 Jun 14.1 ;1817 Feb 14.4 ;1819 Mar 12.9 ; 1857 Aug 11.9 ;1860 Apr 11.8 ;1860 Jul 11.1 ;1860 Nov 11.4 ;1864 Jun 15.1 ;1864 Jul 11.4 ; 1867 Jun 19.7

Bathurst Rebellion
https://aguidetoaustralianbushranging.com/2020/10/30/a-concise-guide-to-the-bathurst-rebellion/
https://en.wikipedia.org/wiki/Bathurst_rebellion

Chap 18 miniatures are painted by
ROBERT WILLIAM SATCHWELL (BRITISH, FL. 1793-1818)
https://www.christies.com/lot/lot-two-english-portrait-miniatures-one-by-5322289/?
pos=3&intObjectID=5322289&sid=&page=13
&
STEPHEN THORN BY GEORGE AUGUSTUS BAKER Sr. (1760–after 1830) Date: 1818
https://www.metmuseum.org/art/collection/search?
q=George+Augustus+Baker+Sr.&sortBy=Relevance&pageSize=0

Sydney Bishops
https://en.wikipedia.org/wiki/Anglican_Archbishop_of_Sydney

Author Bio

Sheila Hunter and Sara Powter were a passionate mother-and-daughter team of amateur genealogists. While working together on their family tree, Sheila and Sara made many captivating discoveries. The greatest of these was finding four convicts, and these four had very different perspectives. They were sent to Australia from 1792 to 1814 during the height of Convict transportation.

Before her *passing* in 2002, Sheila adapted some of these histories into enchanting stories, her Australian Colonial Trilogy. Sara later had these published. A fourth she left unfinished, and this inspired her to finish it. However, before she did, **The Lockleys of Parramatta** were created. The first two in the series were completed before she completed 'Dancing to Her Own Tune' for her mother.

Vividly living through the Colonial Era, these books delve further into the theme of overcoming adversity in Colonial Australia and how it developed, the demise of the Convict system and the discovery of mineral wealth.

Sara intricately weaves accurate, archival data and a charming narrative to create a series of tales of faith, love, loss, and redemption.

And so, two hundred years after her family arrived in Australia, Sara continues the Australian Colonial stories started in *Lockleys of Parramatta,* followed by the **Unlikely Convict Ladies** Trilogy.

No More, My Love, The Vine Weaver, Scotch at The Rocks, Waiting at the Sliprails and Convict Shadows of the Past are stand-alone novels, and all are part of my *"Convict Stain Collection."*

More Historical Fiction books are to follow… as more are already in the editors' queue.

Amazon Aus QR

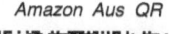

See her web page to keep up to date with more stories.
With an online store available for a signed copy of Sara's books.
www.sarapowter.com.au
(Australian Postage only)

Feel free to email me at
saragpowter@gmail.com

BOOK BUB https://partners.bookbub.com/authors/6273615/edit

FACEBOOK https://www.facebook.com/profile.php?id=100063887262514

FREE Newsletter signup
https://preview.mailerlite.io/preview/41388/sites/77987646202184961/wCAAcK

241